BLIND PANIC

Misquamacus is back

The President of the United States is suddenly struck blind. Thousands more people mysteriously lose their sight, and America descends into chaos. Self-styled mystic Harry Erskine is telling fortunes in Miami when his friend Amelia Crusoe calls on him for help. Algonquin medicine man Misquamacus has come back to life to seek a final revenge for the massacre of his people. But, this time, the odds of beating Misquamacus are suicidal indeed...

BLIND PANIC

Graham Masterton

Severn House Large Print
London & New York

This first large print edition published 2011
in Great Britain and the USA by
SEVERN HOUSE PUBLISHERS LTD of
9-15 High Street, Sutton, Surrey, SM1 1DF.
First world regular print edition published 2009 by
Severn House Publishers Ltd., London and New York.

British Library Cataloguing in Publication Data

Masterton, Graham.
  Blind panic.
  1. Shamans--Fiction. 2. Blessing and cursing--United
States--Fiction. 3. Women psychics--Fiction. 4. Horror
tales. 5. Large type books.
  I. Title
  823.9'2-dc22

ISBN-13: 978-0-7278-7980-6

Severn House Publishers support The Forest Stewardship Council
[FSC], the leading international forest certification organisation. All
our titles that are printed on Greenpeace-approved FSC-certified paper
carry the FSC logo.

MIX
Paper from
responsible sources
FSC® C018575

Printed and bound in Great Britain by the
MPG Books Group, Bodmin, Cornwall.

ONE

Washington, DC

He was little more than halfway across the White House lawn when the President of the United States went blind.

He swayed, and his arm swung out to catch the First Lady's hand.

'David?' she said. 'What's wrong?'

'Christ, Marian, I can't see.'

Marine One's rotors were already turning and she could hardly hear him.

'What?'

'I can't see, Marian. Hold on to my hand, steady me. Guide me up to the steps. I don't want anybody to know that anything's wrong.'

'David, we have to take you to the hospital, now!'

'Dr. Cronin's on board, he can take a look at me first.'

'David—'

'Marian, please! Think what could happen, even if I get my sight back!'

'I don't care what could happen! I care about *you*, that's all!'

But the President gripped the First Lady's hand even tighter, and continued to walk with jerky determination toward the helicopter, and all she could do was make sure that he didn't veer off in the wrong direction.

5

'*Steps*,' she warned him. He reached out with his right hand felt for the guard rail. Then he turned back and waved to the assembled press corps, smiling broadly as if nothing were wrong.

'Help me climb up. Count the steps for me.'

The two of them mounted the steps, both of them still smiling, while the First Lady said, through her teeth, 'One – two – three – Doug Latterby's standing at the top, to your right. Don't bump into him.'

'Hi, Doug!' said the President, trying to sound cheery. 'How's it going? Got those security reports in yet?'

'Just came through, Mr. President. You can look through them right now.'

'Great stuff.'

'Top step,' the First Lady cautioned him.

The President turned around again and gave another wave for the cameras. Then the First Lady steered him through the door of Marine One and along to his private cabin.

'Mrs. Perry?' said Doug Latterby, trying to follow her.

'Go fetch Dr. Cronin, right now! And get this thing off the ground as fast as you like. Head for George Washington Hospital.'

'I'm sorry, Mrs. Perry – is the President sick?'

The President stopped and looked over Doug Latterby's right shoulder. 'I can't see, Doug. I've suddenly gone blind.'

'Jesus Christ. When did this happen?'

'Only a couple of minutes ago. Maybe it's only temporary. But get me Dr. Cronin, will you, and get us into the air.'

6

TWO

Tyler was dreaming that he was playing poker in a smoky upstairs room in Ho Chi Minh City, but he didn't recognize the symbols on any of the cards. Instead of diamonds and clubs and hearts and spades, they were decorated with orchids and stars and fish hooks and teacups, and the court cards all had grinning green monkeys on them.

'I'll raise you two thousand and disturb you,' said the elderly Vietnamese sitting on his right, and shook his shoulder.

'What?' he frowned. He didn't understand this game at all, and he was terrified that he was going to lose all of his money. How would he get back to the States if he lost all of his money?

'Sir?' the Vietnamese repeated, and shook him again.

Tyler opened his eyes. A red-headed flight attendant was standing over him, looking worried. 'I'm sorry to disturb you, sir, but we have kind of a situation.'

Tyler coughed, and sniffed, and awkwardly unfolded his legs. He was six foot two inches, and very broad-shouldered, and he always found

7

it impossible to get comfortable in coach class, especially since he had an artificial left kneecap. 'Situation?'

'Maybe you could come up to the flight deck.'

Tyler looked around him. 'Shit – this isn't a hijack, is it?'

The flight attendant touched her finger to her lips. 'No, sir. Nothing like that. But I do need you to come up to the flight deck.'

'OK.' Tyler unfastened his seat belt and followed her, limping slightly, along the aisle. Most of the other passengers were either asleep or lolling back listening to iPods. Only one or two of them had their blinds raised and were staring out into the night. The Sangre de Cristo Mountains were crawling slowly below them, ghostly and blanketed in snow, and the sky was glittering with late-summer stars.

The flight attendant punched out the security number outside the flight-deck door and Tyler followed her inside. The pilot and co-pilot and navigator were all sitting in their seats, as he would have expected, but three flight attendants were crowded in there, too – two male and one female, and now him and the red-headed flight attendant. The female attendant was blowing her nose and had obviously been crying.

'Thank you for your cooperation, sir,' said the oldest of the male flight attendants.

'Hey, whatever I can do,' said Tyler. He wasn't used to this kind of respect. Even though he was thirty-one, he looked five years younger, with straggly blond hair and pebble-gray eyes and a squarish jaw that he had inherited from his

8

Swedish mother. His last girlfriend Nadine had said that even when he was wearing a business suit, he looked as if he ought to have a surfboard tucked under his arm.

'I won't beat around the bush, sir,' said the flight attendant. 'About twenty-five minutes ago, Captain Sherman lost his sight, followed about ten minutes later by the rest of the crew.'

Tyler stared at him, and then looked down at the navigator, who was sitting in front of his instruments with his hand over his eyes.

'They've lost their sight? All three of them? They're *blind*?'

The flight attendant nodded. 'We don't know why. *They* don't have any ideas, either. Maybe there's an airborne virus in the flight-deck ventilation system. There's no way of telling for sure.'

'So, what you're telling me is – we're flying at thirty-five thousand feet with a flight crew that can't see?'

'It's not as serious as it sounds,' said Captain Sherman, turning around in his seat. He was silvery-haired and deeply tanned, with a large head that reminded Tyler of the TV actor Gene Barry, but his eyes were completely unfocused, as if he were staring at a spot about twenty feet behind Tyler's back. 'We have automatic pilot, of course, and ALS.'

'Well, that's reassuring, not. Do your people on the ground know what's happened? The flight controllers?'

'We've advised LAX that we have an emergency. In fact they combed through the passen-

9

ger manifest to see if there was anybody on board who might conceivably have some flying experience. One of the flight directors recognized your name and that was why I called for you to come forward.'

Tyler said, 'Holy shit, I'm a stunt person. The biggest airplane I've ever flown is a Cessna 172, and that was mostly loop-de-loops. I couldn't fly a thing like this. I mean, there are all these *people* on board. Supposing I kill them all? Supposing I kill *me*?'

'You don't have anything to worry about, Mr. Jones. I can guide you through all of the landing procedures. With any luck you won't have to touch anything at all, except a couple of switches. Your granny could do this, but as an extra precaution I want somebody sitting up front who knows how to fly.'

'I don't even know if my insurance covers anything like this.'

'Mr. Jones – your insurance is the least of your problems. Nobody on this flight is going to sue you for saving their lives, and if you *don't* save their lives it isn't really going to matter, is it?'

The co-pilot turned around, too. He was Chinese-American, with shiny black hair and a wispy moustache. He was staring sightlessly up at the ceiling.

'You can do this for all of your fellow-passengers, sir. If you bring us down safely, you will be a great hero. Look–' and here he reached into the breast pocket of his shirt and produced a photograph of a young girl in a red checkered dress sitting on a swing – 'if you don't do it for your

10

fellow-passengers, or even for yourself, do it for this little girl who will otherwise lose her father.'

Tyler looked from one flight attendant to the other. He had always loved to take risks – jumping over five parked cars on his Kawasaki dirt bike, free-falling out of hot-air balloons, setting himself on fire and throwing himself off buildings. But when he was performing stunts like that, he wasn't responsible for other people's safety, only his own. Being responsible for other people's safety was about the only thing that ever scared him. That, and spiders. He seriously didn't like spiders.

'We'll be here to guide you every step of the way,' said Captain Sherman. 'I promise you, Mr. Jones – this will be a walk in the park.'

'You could have put *that* better,' Tyler told him. 'The last time I took a walk in the park, somebody's Doberman bit me in the rear end.'

THREE

Los Angeles
A cattle truck had broken down on Interstate 101 about a mile and a half east of Encino. The freeway had come to a standstill for nearly an hour while professional wranglers had been called in to calm down the panicking livestock and transfer them to another truck, and now Jasmine was running over forty-five minutes late.

11

She hated running late. She had worked too hard to build herself a reputation for always making her deliveries on time, or ahead of schedule. Her call-sign was 'Early Bird', and on the door of her tractor there was a picture of a cartoon crow pulling a stretched-out worm out of the ground.

She put her foot down flat on the floor of her big red Mack CH truck until it was bellowing along at nearly 60mph. The radio was playing *Bat Out Of Hell* at top volume. She didn't usually like white music but Meat Loaf was different, and she sang along with him as she sped underneath Sunset and Santa Monica Boulevards. *'The sirens are screaming and the fires are howling ... way down in the valley tonight.'*

On the back of her flatbed she was carrying three bright yellow 120kw diesel generators, weighing nearly a ton each, and she was supposed to deliver them to a construction site on Mateo Street before nine a.m.

Jasmine had always regarded life as a serious challenge, and felt that she had to prove herself better at anything she chose to do than anybody else, especially men. When she was sixteen years old she had taken lessons in Korean unarmed combat at school, for the express purpose of throwing her father across the room. She had broken his nose and his left wrist, and after that her father had never beaten up on her mother, ever again.

Her *taekgyon* training had stood her in good stead ever since. She was strikingly exotic, almost Ethiopian-looking, with short upswept hair and gold hoop earrings and sulky-looking lips. She also had a cleavage that made men walk into lamp posts. Any man who tried to hit on her, however, was taking a serious risk of physical injury.

'Like a bat out of hell,' she screamed, in a high falsetto. *'I'll be gone, gone, gone!'*

Even though it was right in the middle of the morning rush, and the traffic was heavy, she was able to switch lanes to keep her speed up. As she approached the East Los Angeles Interchange, she overtook an Amoco gasoline truck, and then a coachload of seniors. She was driving at well over 45mph as she steered onto the off-ramp which crossed over the Los Angeles River.

'...and I never see the sudden curve until it's way too late...'

Without warning, right in front of her, a green Hummer swerved sideways and struck the concrete divider. She saw bits flying off it, and it slewed around a hundred and eighty degrees so that it was facing her. She stood on her brakes but there was no way of avoiding it. The front of her truck hit the Hummer head-on and smashed it backward into the retaining wall.

She heard nothing at all, not even the shrieking of tires, and all she could see was a jumble of sky – bridge – trees – and traffic. She wrestled with the wheel as her truck careered toward the edge of the off-ramp, dragging the smashed remains of the Hummer with it like a huge monster making off with its mortally injured prey.

Oh God, she thought. *This is where I'm going*

13

to die.

Her truck slammed against the right-hand wall, and then against the left-hand wall, and then it rammed the mangled remains of the Hummer right through the right-hand wall and over the edge of the off-ramp. The Hummer dropped forty feet and landed on its nose on the dry concrete river bed below, toppling over and over with its doors flapping open.

Jasmine thought that her truck was going to go thundering after it, but right on the brink of the off-ramp the CH came to a wrenching halt. Jasmine's forehead hit the steering wheel and her sunglasses snapped in half and she was almost knocked out. Dazed, she sat up straight again. *I'm OK*, she thought. *I'm not going to go over.* But then she felt a hefty jolt in the small of her back, and then another, and another, and another, and her cab was forced further and further forward, until its front wheels went over the edge, and it lurched right down onto its bodywork.

Her hearing returned, as if somebody had switched a radio back on. Checking her rear-view mirror, she could see that some of the steel cables holding the generators onto her flatbed had snapped, and that two of the generators had fallen sideways onto the roadway. They had acted as 2,000lb anchors, preventing her truck from careening through the gap in the off-ramp's retaining wall.

But the repeated jolting was being caused by scores of vehicles crashing into the back of her truck – cars and SUVs and buses and trucks. The entire off-ramp was a tangled clutter of wrecked metal, with smoke rising from it. Some drivers were climbing out, but many of them were trapped in their seats, their doors wedged against the vehicles next to them, or up against the retaining walls.

'God Almighty,' said Jasmine, and she didn't say it as a profanity. 'God Almighty, I seriously got to get out of here.'

The cab of her truck was tilted forward at an angle of twenty degrees, and through the windshield she could see the concrete river bed and the Hummer lying on its roof. There was no sign that anybody had managed to crawl out of it. Cautiously, she opened her door and looked downward. She would have to climb out of her cab and try to make her way back onto the off-ramp, and hope that the remaining cables holding the generators didn't suddenly snap.

With the door open, she could hear people shouting and screaming, and the ceaseless banging of even more vehicles adding to the pile-up.

Come on, Jazz, she told herself. *You can do this.*

She eased herself out of her seat and climbed down onto the top step of her cab. Vehicles continued to crash into each other, all the way back along the interstate, and two helicopters started to circle overhead, one from the Highway Patrol and another from KNBC news.

Now that she was outside her cab, Jasmine could see that there were more than two hundred vehicles caught up in the accident. The off-ramp looked like the road to Basra at the end of Desert

15

Storm. What alarmed her most was that a Ford Explorer right in the middle of the pile-up was pouring out thick black smoke, and that it was only three or four vehicles away from the Amoco truck.

She edged her way up the sharply tilting step until she reached the back of her cab. Then she swung herself downward and sideways, until her boot reached the concrete lip of the roadway. With an awkward hop and a skip, she jumped down onto the off-ramp and caught hold of one of the generator handles to steady herself.

The piled-up cars and SUVs were jammed so close together that she had no choice but to clamber across their hoods. Drivers and passengers were sitting helplessly in their seats, some of them blowing their horns, which added to the pandemonium, and others beating on their windshields with their fists. Several managed to open their side windows and climb out, but Jasmine saw one overweight driver who had managed to squeeze out of the rear window of his Shogun SUV, only to tumble down the narrow gap between it and the FedEx panel-van behind him, and become inextricably wedged. He was beating on the panel-van's radiator with his fists, red-faced and sobbing like a baby, while there was nothing that the FedEx driver could do, nothing but stare back at him.

Jasmine still had more than a hundred yards from the interstate, climbing over one vehicle after another, when the smoke from the burning Explorer suddenly began to blow more thickly. She turned around just as the Explorer blew up, and a huge orange fireball rolled up into the air. The explosion was deep and deafening, but even worse were the muffled screams of the hundreds of people caught in their cars. They sounded like mice.

Within seconds, a station wagon next to the Explorer was blazing, and then a van directly in front of it. Dense brown smoke poured across the pile-up, making it look even more like a battlefield. Jasmine clambered over the sloping silver hood of a Cadillac STS, and managed to reach the retaining wall on the opposite side of the off-ramp. Now she was able to balance her way along the top of the wall, occasionally grabbing onto the vehicles next to her to stop herself from falling.

Over the *flack-flack-flack* of the helicopters, she heard a sharp series of pops and crackles, and then the Amoco truck exploded. Even though she was making her way up the opposite side of the ramp, shielded from the full force of the blast by a Jeep, she felt a wave of superheated air on the back of her neck, and she was blown so violently to the right that she almost lost her footing.

Another car's gas tank blew up, and then another, and another. The screaming began to rise in a crescendo, an opera from hell. Within less than a minute, more than fifty vehicles were blazing, and the smoke was so thick that it blotted out the sun.

Jasmine saw six or seven people staggering and stumbling across the wreckage, some of them smoking and blackened, some of them still

17

ablaze. Only two vehicles away from her, she saw a father and a mother and four young children, all of them frantically knocking on the windows of their burning Voyager. They were all sandy-haired. She didn't know why that made such an impression on her, but it was like seeing a whole family album thrown into a fire.

She had almost reached the top of the off-ramp when she heard a woman screaming, *'Save my baby! For God's sake! Save my baby!'*

Jasmine lifted her hand to shield her face from the heat. The smoke was so thick now that she could hardly breathe. Right in the center of the pile-up, a young blonde-haired woman had managed to open the passenger-side window of her SUV and was holding up a baby boy in both hands. Next to her, in the driver's seat, a man in a white T-shirt was slumped over the steering wheel, his hair matted with blood. He was either unconscious or dead.

The baby was red-faced and kicking its legs and crying, but the woman managed to keep him aloft, and continue to scream out, *'Save my baby! Somebody save my baby!'*

Jasmine climbed onto the hood of a taxi that had been crushed between the retaining wall and the side of a lowboy trailer. The taxi driver was slumped sideways in his seat, unconscious or dead, but the woman passenger in the back was shouting hysterically and trying to break the window with a gilt high-heeled sandal.

Jasmine crawled across the hood on her hands and knees and then walked across the trailer. Less than a hundred yards away, five or six more vehicles exploded, and one old Chevy pickup was flung right into the air, landing on its roof with a thunderous crash.

Once she had crossed the lowboy, Jasmine was able to climb onto the roof of the dark-blue newspaper-delivery van which was crushed up alongside the woman's SUV. The woman held up her baby as high as she could, and begged her, 'Save my little boy, please.'

Jasmine leaned over the edge of the van's roof and tried to take hold of the baby's hands, but he kept waving his arms and she couldn't reach him. 'Ma'am – can you lift him just a little higher?' she asked.

'I can't, both of my legs are trapped.'

'OK, then, I'll see if I can climb down further.'

There was another explosion, much closer this time. The woman said, 'Oh my God, listen to all of those poor people!'

Jasmine managed to get a grip on the van's side mirror with her left hand, and lean over a few inches further. She touched the baby's fingertips with her fingertips, and suddenly the baby stopped crying and blinked up at her in bewilderment. He lifted up one hand toward her, and in that instant Jasmine thrust herself over the edge of the van's roof as far as she dared, and snatched the sleeve of his pale blue romper suit.

For one instant she thought that she had reached out too far, and that she was going to drop the baby and fall on top of him. But with something between a grunt and a scream, she heaved herself back upward, inch by inch, even though the mirror that she was holding onto was

19

gradually bending.

'Please take care of him,' said the baby's mother.

'Of course,' Jasmine told her. 'You'll be OK. The rescue services will be here any minute, they'll get you out.'

The young woman gave her a panicky, wide-eyed stare, as if she didn't believe her for an instant.

Jasmine climbed back toward the edge of the off-ramp, holding the struggling baby close to her chest. As she reached the retaining wall, she heard another explosion, right behind her, and then another. She turned around and saw that the young mother's SUV was blazing fiercely, and that she was sitting in her seat, shaking her head from side to side in agony. The young man beside her was still leaning against the steering wheel, not moving at all.

'Oh dear God,' said Jasmine. 'How could You let this happen?'

But more and more vehicles exploded, with a complicated series of bangs that made Jasmine's ears ring. By the time she reached the main highway, the smoke was so thick that she could hardly see where she was going. She could hear fire trucks whooping and warbling and blasting their horns, but there was no way that they could force their way through a half-mile tangle of wrecked vehicles to reach the off-ramp.

Jasmine kept on walking along the side of the freeway, with the wailing, wriggling baby held tight against her shoulder. 'There,' she kept saying, patting his back. 'Everything's going to be fine, l'il feller. You just wait and see. Everything's going to come up roses.'

At last they were clear of the smoke. Jasmine kept on walking in the hot morning sunshine and didn't once look back, even when she heard more explosions, and more echoes of explosions. Just before she reached the off-ramp that would take her down to Alameda Street, the baby fell asleep, snuffling and bubbling against her neck. She couldn't even guess what he was dreaming about.

FOUR

Miami, Florida

'I dreamed that my driver took me to the Classic Grille. I just *had* to have one of their lobster- and crab-burgers. My driver opened the door of the car for me, and I high-stepped it into the restaurant as if I was a fashion model. Everybody turned to look at me but I stuck up my nose and swung my pearl necklace around like I really didn't care.

'It was only then that the maître d' said, "Hasn't madame forgotten something?" I said, "I don't think so, Luigi. What?" He leaned forward and whispered in my ear, "Madame is wearing no clothes."

'I looked down and he was right. Except for

21

my pearls and my black patent Prada pumps, I was absolutely butt-naked. Brazilian and all, for pity's sake.'

I almost choked on my rainbow-colored cocktail, and if you had ever seen Mrs. Zlotorynski you would have known why. She was seventy-one, and skeletally thin, with huge Chanel sunglasses and a nose like a buzzard on the lookout for a baby prairie-dog to swoop on.

'You know what that means, don't you, Mrs. Zee?' I told her.

'It means that I'm insecure?'

I shook my head.

'It means that I'm frightened of people finding out that I was born in the South Bronx, and that my father sewed linings for a living?' (She leaned closer when she said this, and spoke in a very hoarse whisper, even though the nearest sunbather was over twenty feet away, and he was snoring.)

I shook my head again.

'It means that I'm worried about losing my money and ending up with nothing?'

'No, Mrs. Zlotorynski, your dream has nothing to do with your social status or your lack of self-esteem or God forbid your late husband's investments in Pfizer pharmaceuticals. Men will always need Viagra! It simply means that you have an inner glow that you very rarely share. In your daily life, as you go about your business, you hardly ever display your natural warm-heartedness.'

'My natural warm-heartedness?'

'That's right. You *understand* people, Mrs.

22

Zee, you feel what they feel. You have so much spiritual radiance. But most of the time you keep it tightly locked up in your inner jewelry box, so that nobody can appreciate how caring you are.'

Mrs. Zlotorynski swung her scrawny legs around and sat up straight. It was impossible to see her eyes behind those sunglasses, but I would have bet you ten portraits of Benjamin Franklin that they were piggy with self-approval. Well, piggier than they usually were. You know what too much blepharoplasty can do to a girl.

She prodded my shoulder with one orange-polished fingernail – once, twice, three times. It was like being bitten by a particularly annoying mosquito.

'You – are – *so* – right!' she agreed. 'I *do* have spiritual radiance. I *do* have warmth. I *am* beautiful. Inside of myself, I *shine*. Yet – do you know – you're one of the very few people who has ever recognized it. Apart from Morry, of course, *alev ha sholem*, but then Morry was hardly ever home, what did he know?'

I sat up, too, trying to shift myself out of fingernail range. 'I've seen your driver. What's his name? Emigdlio. The way he scowls at you behind your back, it's a disgrace, don't you think? Just because you asked him to drive your friends home to Key West, at two-thirty in the morning! It's only three hundred twenty-eight miles, there and back! And Rosita! She's supposed to be your maid. Yet when you told her to worm little Q-Tip for you, what did she do? She said that she wasn't an animal doctor, and she

23

stamped her foot and turned all sulky on you.

'Don't these people understand how much you *feel* for them? I guess they don't. But that's what makes them "little people." That's what you call them, isn't it? And don't they deserve it!'

'You're *so* right,' Mrs. Zlotorynski repeated. She opened her orange suede purse and took out her mirror, so that she could adjust her Marilyn Hikida straw hat with the orange feather trim, and reapply her matching orange lipgloss. 'They *are* little people, God help them. Well, God *has* to help them, doesn't He, because they don't know how to help themselves!'

I lifted my cocktail in salute. My friends, I was having the time of my life. My old poker-playing buddy Marco Hernandez had gone on a three-month tour of Europe with the Joe Morales Mariachi Orchestra, and he had asked me to take care of his house in Coral Gables. Well, wouldn't you? The humidity had been ninety-three percent on the day I left New York. The streets had smelled like a salami-slicer's armpit and when I climbed out of the cab at La Guardia the handle had broken off my suitcase. But here I was, sitting on the beach outside of the five-star Delano Hotel, with the sun broiling the soles of my yellow plastic Crocs, and the blue Atlantic reassuring me with every languid splash that life had taken a turn for the very contented.

Marco had been a true friend. Before he left for Berlin, he had taken me to meet Eduardo, who was the concierge at the Casa Espléndido, and the smoothest-looking Cuban in Miami. Eduardo wore a professionally plucked pencil moustache and walked with a shimmer. For a modest percentage he had agreed to pass my cards around to every luxury hotel on South Beach. Harry Erskine, Foreteller of the Future and Diviner of Dreams – especially the dreams of wealthy widows who were starved of flattery and suggestive conversation.

You can be as cynical as you like, but those seventy-plus babes with their vulture's talons for fingernails and their withered necks and their wind-tunnel eyes, they just *melted* when I told them how gorgeous they were. And when I promised each of them that there was a hunky young stud in their reasonably near future, with gym-sculptured muscles and overcrowded Calvin Kleins, they almost lost consciousness with gratitude.

OK – maybe I was less of a bona fide clairvoyant than a supplier of fruity fantasies, but I told those old aardvarks exactly what they wanted to hear, and my fee was not to be sniffed at, one-seventy-five an hour – and even more if I thought that I could get away with it. And since I *called* on my lady clients, rather than having them come to visit me, I got to visit almost every swanky hotel on Collins Avenue, and have lunch and cocktails bought for me, too. Today, Mrs. Zlotorynski had taken me into the Blue Door Brasserie and treated me to their signature dish of slow-roasted duck and bananas. I had ordered it mostly as an ironical comment on the two of us. In her dark-brown Zara bathing-costume, Mrs. Zlotorynski looked just like a slow-roasted duck, and I was bananas for not having left New

25

York and come down to Miami twenty years ago.

'What can I *do*, then?' Mrs. Zlotorynski begged me. 'How can I make people appreciate how warm I am?'

I checked my watch. I had to be at the Biltmore by three thirty, to give a Tarot reading to Mrs. Kaplan-Capaldi's Burmese cat. That's right, Mrs. *Benjamin* Kaplan-Capaldi, whose third husband owned half of Hialeah.

I took hold of Mrs. Zlotorynski's paperyskinned, sun-withered hands, and admired my double reflection in her sunglasses. I looked so much younger with a suntan and blond highlights. In New York, I always looked baggy-eyed and asbestos-gray, as if I subsisted on a diet of hotdogs and Guinness and never left my apartment, which was not too far from the truth.

'Emigdlio and Rosita, they're little people, sure. So what are you going to give them?'

'I don't know, Harry. What do little people want?'

'No! That's exactly it! *They* may be little people, but *you* – you're *big* people, so give them *more* than they want! They won't believe your generosity! They won't believe how caring you are! You *are* caring, aren't you?'

'What do you mean? Of course I'm caring. I'm *beyond* caring.'

'So what do you do to show how caring you are? You give Emigdlio some time off, to spend with his family. Not just a single night. Not even *two* nights. You give him a long weekend, and you pay him a bonus, too, so that he can take his

26

kids to Parrot World, or Chuck E. Cheese's, or wherever little people go to amuse themselves.

'And Rosita, give *her* a bonus, too, and the pick of your wardrobe. I mean – why not? That will give you an excuse to go out and buy yourself a whole lot of new clothes.' As if you needed an excuse.

For a second, I felt the tendons in Mrs. Zlotorynski's wrists tighten up like piano wires. Generosity was so much against her nature that the very thought of it brought on a muscular spasm.

But I gave her my oiliest, most Liberace smile, and said, 'Think how it's going to get around. Emigdlio will tell all the other drivers how understanding you are; and Rosita will tell all of the other maids how happy she is to work for you; and before you know it, you'll have such a reputation for warmth and humanity that – who knows – you may even win a civic award for it.'

Mrs. Zlotorynski slowly started to nod, and then nodded even more emphatically, like a dipping bird. 'You're right, Harry! *That* was what my dream was all about! You've seen me as I really am – it's about time the rest of the world did, too!'

But for God's sake spare them the Brazilian, I thought.

I kissed her hand. She was wearing so many emerald rings I almost broke my front teeth. Then I noisily sucked up the dregs of my Nagayama Sunset, although I really could have used another, especially since they were $18 a hit and she was paying. 'I really have to go now, Mrs.

27

Zee. As always, it's been a delight.'

I waited, and waited, and then I repeated, 'As *always*, it's been a delight.'

'Oh! What a muddle-head I am!' she exclaimed, and picked up her purse. She took out a Delano Hotel envelope, reassuringly fat and squishy. 'I don't know how I coped, Harry, before you came into my life.'

The envelope vanished into the top pocket of my blue-and-yellow Hawaiian shirt as if it had never existed. A stage conjuror called something like the Great Nintendo had taught me that, when I was doing bar-work in the Village. 'It works both ways, Mrs. Zee. What would I do without *you*?'

I stood up and I was just about to leave when she clung to the leg of my flappy linen pants. 'You don't have a *date* yet, do you?'

'A date?' Jesus – don't tell me she was going to ask me out for the evening.

'I don't mean to be pushy, but you did say that it would come to you very soon, and I'm just dying to enter it into my diary. The date – you know – when my new young beau will be coming into my life.'

I let out a scream of laughter. 'Of course! Haha! Your new young beau! Well – I checked your Tarot cards late last night, and they're still saying March-ish, without being specifically specific as to which specific day.'

'I can hardly wait.'

'Well ... don't get yourself too excited.' Especially since I'm making this all up and I shall be long gone by March, back to New York.

28

I was trudging back across the soft, hot sand when Mrs. Zlotorynski shrilled out, *'Harry! Didn't you forget something?'*

I patted the front of my shirt. Forget something? I don't think so. My cellphone, my sunglasses, my Mega Money lottery ticket, my $525 in large-denomination bills – all there.

'My mystic *motto*! You forgot my mystic *motto*!'

'Oh, your mystic motto! How could I? And I looked it up specially, after I'd read your Tarot cards!'

'Yes?'

I walked back to her. 'It's a very mystical mystic motto, Mrs. Zee. More mystical than most. "Freedom is the greatest luxury of all. No matter how much caviar you heap onto a baked potato, it can never fly like a seagull."'

'Oh, Harry! That's so *deep*! And so true, too!'

'You won't forget it, will you, when you're being naturally warm-hearted?'

'Of course not. How could I? "No matter how much caviar you heap on a seagull, it can never be a baked potato."'

'Nearly right. It'll do, anyhow.'

FIVE

I was fighting my way through the billowing white sheers which hang in the Delano's lobby when my cellphone rang.

'Harry?'

'Hold on here, I've just gotten myself tangled up in forty yards of muslin.'

'Harry, it's Amelia.'

'Amelia?' My heart stopped in mid-beat, as if I had been bouncing a tennis ball against a school-yard wall and somebody had unexpectedly caught it. 'How did you know where I was?'

'I don't know where you are. I've been ringing your home number but you never pick up.'

'I'm in Miami. You remember Marco Morales? Marco the Taco, we always used to call him. I'm house-sitting for him, while he's off on tour, tootling his ocarina or some such.'

Amelia, I couldn't believe it. Amelia Carlsson, née Crusoe. She could have been the love of my life if our lives had turned out differently. She was thin, elegant, curly-haired, and highly bewitching, if you're attracted to women with high cheekbones and prominent shoulder blades and out-of-focus eyes. We had always attracted each other, but the problem was that we hadn't always attracted each other at the same time. When she broke up with that bearded grump MacArthur, I was happily married to Karen, with Lucy just born; and when I broke up with Karen, she was happily married to Bertil, this literal-minded Swede who thought that *Friends* was a reality-TV show.

I hadn't seen Amelia for over two years now, after a nightmarish experience that both of us preferred to forget. But it wasn't just the nightmarish experience that kept us from seeing each other. Bertil seriously didn't like me, mainly because he had as much sense of humor as a pickled herring, but also because he was jealous of our past, mine and Amelia's, and he wasn't so literal-minded and pickled-herring-like that he couldn't sense our mutual attraction. Those glances, those smiles, those brushings-together in the kitchen doorway.

'Harry, something terrible's happened and I couldn't think who else to turn to.' She sounded very close to tears.

'Something terrible? What is it?' I managed to unwind myself from the sheers, and find myself a pea-green leather armchair where I could sit and talk to her.

'It's my sister Lizzie,' she said. 'She's gone blind. Her whole family's gone blind.'

'*What?* Did you say *blind*?'

'Totally. Lizzie and Kevin and the kids, too.'

'Amelia, that's just awful. How the hell did that happen?'

'Lizzie doesn't know. They were on a biking weekend, at the Hell's Canyon Recreation Area,

31

in Oregon. Apparently they were halfway up a hill when little David started to wobble and just fell off his bike. Then Shauna. Both of them were screaming that they couldn't see. Lizzie and Kevin went to help them, but before they could reach them, *they* went blind, too.

'They didn't dare to move, because they were so close to the edge of the canyon, and it was over five hundred feet down. They were lucky that a ranger came driving past, or they might have had to stay there for hours, or even *days*.'

'They all went blind? Just like that? And Lizzie doesn't have any idea why?'

'None at all. And so far the doctors don't have any idea, either. But something so strange has happened, which is why I've been trying to get in touch with you.'

'Something strange? How strange? I'm not too sure I like the sound of this.'

'Harry – I really need you to come with me. Please.'

'Where exactly are you thinking of going?'

'The Casey Eye Institute in Portland. We need to get there as soon as we can.'

'Did you say *Portland*? Portland, *Oregon*? That's so far west it's practically Japan.'

'United have a flight to Portland from Miami and Continental have one from Newark and they both connect in Denver, within about an hour of each other. We could meet up there.' She paused, and then she added, 'I can pay for your tickets.'

'What about Bertie? Can't Bertie go with you?'

'Bertil's in Geneva, for a really important

conference. He can't get back here for another four days.'

'All the same, he won't be very happy if *I* come with you, will he? What about that gay friend of yours, what's his name, Blake Thingy III? Or that woman you met when you were teaching, the one with the teeth? You must have a million friends you can call on.'

'Harry, it has to be *you*.'

A very pretty young waitress in a white uniform with gilt buttons appeared through the sheers and asked me if I would like anything from the bar.

'I'll have another Nagayama Sunset, thanks. But go easy on the Nagayamas. Oh – and bill it to Mrs. Zlotorynski, would you, in seven-fifteen?'

Amelia said, 'I hate to ask you, Harry. But nobody else will understand.'

'Understand *what*, exactly?'

'I've been talking to Lizzie on the phone. She's so confused. She keeps saying things that don't make any sense. I asked her if she was feeling any pain, but all she says is, "We spread the disease, didn't we?" but when I ask her *what* disease, she doesn't answer.'

'Go on,' I coaxed her.

'This morning, she said, "We deserve this, don't we?" I said of course they didn't. The doctors would soon find out what was wrong with them, and give them their sight back. But she said, "*No* – we deserve it, and it's not just me and Kevin and the kids, it's all of us. We're *all* going to go blind and we're all going to die, every single one of us.'"

'She's in shock,' I suggested. 'People say the weirdest things when they're in shock. I was hit by a bus once, on Broadway, and for hours afterward I kept asking the way to Sarge's Deli. Why would I want to go to Sarge's Deli? Their blintzes are never hot enough and they have the rudest staff in the world.'

Amelia said, '*I* thought it was shock, to begin with. I told her to relax. I told her I'd make sure that she and her family got the best treatment possible. But she said, "Doctors can't treat this blindness, Amelia. It's not a medical condition. It's medicine."'

'*Medicine?* What did she mean by that?' This was definitely starting to disturb me, big time. Unlike me, Amelia was a genuine clairvoyant and medium and she could discuss pasta recipes with dead people. She could tell you what kind of person you were going to marry and what stinky old bag-lady you were going to bump into when you crossed Lexington Avenue tomorrow. She knew all about plants and herbs and mirrors and crystal balls, and she could look at the worn-down pattern on the soles of your shoes and tell you that you were going to die by choking on a fish bone. She could even tell you what kind of fish.

'I asked her that, too,' said Amelia. 'She didn't answer me directly. She said, "We saw them, before we went blind. They were standing by the side of the road." I said, "*Who* was standing by the side of the road?" She hesitated for a moment, and then she said, "The One Who Went

34

And Came Back. He had two mirrors with him."'

I felt my scalp tingle, as if my hair were infested with lice. *'The One Who Went And Came Back?* Are you sure?'

'She said it twice, Harry.'

'So what did you do?'

'What do you think? I asked her if she could tell me what he looked like. I asked her how she knew who he was.'

'And?'

'She said a word I didn't understand. She kept repeating it. Something like "fatality," but not quite that.'

'And that was all? *"Fatality"*?'

'She put the phone down, and when I called back the nurse told me that she was too tired to talk to me any more. So I did a bead reading.'

'A *bead* reading? I never saw you do a bead reading before.'

'A smoke reading would have been better but I was at work and there was no smoking. The beads are Navajo misfortune beads. They're like Tibetan *tala* beads, only they're not so concerned about how your rice is going to grow at twenty thousand feet above sea level. They're more concerned with who your enemies are, and what's going to come jumping out at you when you least expect it.'

The waitress brought my cocktail and I signed the check, including a two-fifty tip. I took a sip of frosty *cachaca* and then I said, 'OK ... so what did they say, these beads?'

'They said that a great darkness was coming.

35

They said that a black cloak was sweeping across the sky. They said that men who cannot see can no longer be the masters of the world.'

'Go on,' I told her.

'They said that a great wonder-worker had turned air and water and fire into flesh, and was walking the land of his ancestors, just as *they* had, in times long ago.'

I didn't say anything, not right away.

Amelia said, 'Harry? Are you still there?'

'I'm still here. How good are these beads, as a general rule? Misguided, fairly misguided, pretty accurate, or smack on the nose?'

'They've never been wrong in all the years that I've been using them. They predicted nine-eleven, almost to the minute.'

'OK. You'd better book me a ticket, then.'

I hung up the phone. *The One Who Went And Came Back*. I hadn't heard that in a long time and I had hoped that I would never hear it again. It was one of the many names for the most fearsome Wampanaug medicine man of all time, Misquamacus. The prospect of a newly resurrected Misquamacus was seriously unfunny.

Misquamacus was born nearly four hundred years ago. Native American legends say that when he was a very young adept, under the guidance of the notorious shaman Machitehew, he discovered a way to make spiritual contact with the Great Old Ones. These were the gods who had ruled the North American continent in the so-called Empty Time – in the days before days even existed – but had eventually been

36

banished by Gitche Manitou to the furthest reaches of time and space.

From the Great Old Ones, Misquamacus was said to have acquired the power to bring on a thunderstorm, just by shouting at the sky. He could fell hundreds of pine trees in a single day, or bring down whole herds of deer with nothing more than an incantation and a tapping of medicine sticks. It was also said that he could appear in several different places simultaneously – sometimes thousands of miles apart.

In the seventeenth century, he had fought more ferociously against the English colonists than any other Native American, but in the end the Wampanaug had been cheated of their land and sold into slavery and even He Who Brings The Terror of Eternal Darkness had been forced to throw in the towel. In the spring of 1655, he had made a solemn oath that he would drive out every last colonist, if not then, some time in the future, and he had taken 'the way of the oil' – swallowing blazing oil to burn himself alive.

When he did that, he was able to be reborn in the body of any unsuspecting woman who happened to be in the locality of his self-immolation – either in the past, or in the future, whichever he chose. And the reason why *I* had gotten involved with him was because he had started to grow inside the body of a young woman in Manhattan called Karen Tandy, and Karen Tandy had started to have terrifying nightmares. Because of that, her mother had brought her to the only clairvoyant she knew – which was me – desperately asking for help. In turn, I had called on

Amelia. I knew all of the patter and I could shuffle the Tarot cards faster than Wild Bill Hickok could shuffle a poker deck but Amelia was the genuine article.

With the reluctant help of a Sioux medicine man called Singing Rock, we had managed to use cutting-edge technology to send Misquamacus back to the spirit-world. We had discovered that *everything* has a spirit – a manitou. Not just a tree, or a rock, or a turkey-vulture, but a laptop, or a Blackberry, or even a Wii. And the modern manitous were far more powerful than the ancient manitous.

But Misquamacus had constantly struggled to return, and every time he did so he caused destruction and death on a greater and greater scale. He took his revenge on Singing Rock, and killed him. And if you lived in Manhattan at the time, you'll remember the so-called 'seismic event' that brought down so many buildings. You'll also remember the 'blood disorder' that affected so many New Yorkers in the summer of 2002. Both euphemisms for the destructive rage of Misquamacus.

About five years ago, I came across a picture of Misquamacus on the Internet, on some obscure website devoted to Keiller Webb, a nineteenth-century frontier photographer. There he was, Misquamacus, standing in the background of a daguerreotype taken at Pyramid Lake in Nevada on August eighteenth, 1865. He was wearing a black stovepipe hat and was glaring at me furiously, as if he had *known* when this picture was taken that I would be looking at it one day.

He was stony-faced, his cheeks scarred with magical stigmata, and his deep-set eyes were glittering.

Then – less than eighteen months later – I came across another picture that had been taken only the previous day – August seventeenth, 1865 – at the Hassanamisco Indian Reservation near Grafton, Massachusetts. A group of Nipmuc Indians were posing in their finest clothes to celebrate the meeting of their tribal council. And right at the back of the group, on the left-hand side, was Misquamacus. It was unmistakably him, even though the distance between Pyramid Lake and Grafton is more than two thousand four hundred miles.

His face was slightly blurred, because he must have moved during the exposure, but he wore the same black stovepipe hat, and around his neck he wore a large silver medallion, like intertwining snakes. However, I had learned from Singing Rock that they weren't snakes at all. They were the tentacles that grew from the face of the greatest of the Great Old Ones.

It was the symbol that Misquamacus carried of his mystical connection to a time when there was no time, and to inconceivable distances that made your head ring to think about them, and to beings that could turn the entire universe upside down, and walk around underneath the earth, in infinite darkness.

SIX

Modoc County National Forest,
North California

Lightning flashed behind the clouds as their battered old Winnebago Vista jostled and creaked down the rocky path that led to the edge of the river; and as they turned into the recreation area and parked, there was an ear-splitting burst of thunder that shook the windows and rattled every plate and mug in the galley.

'Sounds like the Great Trout God isn't too happy to see us,' said Charlie, as the first fat drops of rain pattered onto the windshield.

'Totally the opposite, dude,' said Mickey, swinging around in the front passenger's seat and rubbing his hands with enthusiasm. 'Weather like this, it's perfect for brown trout. It damps down the flies, and that brings up the fish.'

More lightning flashed, like a cheap theatrical effect. 'You're going fishing in *this*?' Remo asked him.

'Oh, sure. I'm going to stand up to my knees in water in the middle of an electrical storm, holding a carbon-fiber extension rod up in the air. You think I got some kind of death wish? I'm going to tie a few poxybacks and wait for it to

40

roll over.'

'Well, I think I'll treat myself to another beer and watch you. How about you, Charlie?'

'Absolutely. You can't beat treating yourself to a beer and watching somebody tie a few poxy-backs. World-class entertainment.'

Cayley came struggling out of the tiny bathroom. 'I *hate* nature. I mean it majorly sucks. I don't know why I came.'

'You came to keep an eye on me,' Remo reminded her. 'You imagined that me and the guys were going to spend the entire weekend with half a dozen naked hotties, having an orgy.'

'Actually, we were,' said Charlie. 'But when we found out that you were coming along, we had to call Naked Hotties R Us and cancel.'

Cayley was one of those girls who had a permanently surprised expression on her face, as if everything that happened in her life was like, *what*? She had spiked up her blonde pixie-cut hair, thickened her eyelashes with mascara, and slicked her lips with sparkly pink gloss, as well as misting herself liberally with J-Lo perfume. She was wearing a white sleeveless bolero and very short safari shorts, and wedge-shaped sandals which made her totter when she walked. She peered out at the rainswept scenery as if it were a personal insult.

'You *did* bring a poncho?' asked Mickey, although he could guess what the answer was. Mickey was the thin, pale, serious one, and he blinked a lot. He wore heavy-rimmed eyeglasses on his large, bean-shaped nose, and he always looked as if he cut his own hair in the bathroom

41

mirror. Mickey had always wanted to be a zoologist, but his father's pet store had gone bankrupt in 2001, and he had never been able to raise enough money to go through college.

Charlie was chubby, with a wild mess of chestnut-brown curls, and cheeks that flamed crimson whenever he drank too much beer. Charlie was always joking and playing the fool, but Charlie had lost both of his parents when he was six years old, in a horrific auto crash on I-580. His grandparents had brought him up in a house that was airless with inconsolable grief, and so he had a whole childhood of silence to make up for. Charlie suffered from chronic asthma, and he always wore swirly psychedelic shirts, size XXL, but his friends tolerated his constant wheezing and his lurid wardrobe because he was always the first to pitch in whenever they got themselves into a fight, which was frequently.

Remo was half-Italian, with blue eyes and black stubble and very hairy wrists. He came from a noisy family of five brothers and two sisters and countless aunts and uncles, and every time they met for birthdays or family reunions it was like the Battle of Anzio. Remo liked to think that he was a younger and more handsome version of Nicolas Cage, and that he could have made a career in movies. Just like Mickey and Charlie, however, he had ended up as a telesalesman for Tiger Electronics in Palo Alto, marketing software and laptops and replacement ink cartridges.

The Emperors of IT, they called themselves. They had all joined Tiger on the same day, after a company recruitment drive two summers ago, and they had become inseparable – drinking too much beer together, going to ball games together, playing stupid practical jokes together.

They would all meet the same fate together, too. From the moment they arrived at the Pit River recreation area, the Emperors of IT had less than seven hours before they were struck by tragedy.

Just after three in the afternoon, the clouds began to fragment and the sun started to shine. They climbed out of the Winnebago and walked to the river's edge. Remo picked up pebbles and skipped them across the water. Charlie tried to copy him, but all of his pebbles dropped into the river with a single plop.

Only a half-mile to the west, the ground rose into a high volcanic precipice dotted with conifers, and the Pit River was forced to rush through a narrow ravine. Here by the recreation area, however, it was shallow and quiet, with sparkling rock pools, and riffles, and swampy banks, where bulrushes nodded.

The air was clean and sharp and aromatic with pine, and the marsh wrens were rattling and buzzing and trilling to celebrate the passing of the storm. Even Cayley, as she came balancing across the boulders like a tightrope-walker, said, 'This is so *beautiful*, I can't believe it. It's better even than *Bambi*.'

Charlie plopped another pebble into the water. 'I thought you hated nature. I thought it majorly sucked.'

'Not *all* the time. I don't mind it when it's like this. You know, when it's behaving itself.'

'That's the whole point about nature,' said Mickey. He was hunkered down beside his fishing bag, sorting through his reels and his lures. 'Nature *never* behaves itself. That's why it's called, like, "nature."'

Charlie leaned over his shoulder and picked up a fly. 'What do you reckon for this stretch of the river? Stonefly nymphs? Or coppertails?'

'I guess either. Or black midge pupae, maybe. You have to be careful which pools you choose, that's all, or you wind up with nothing but squawfish. Did you know that a squawfish can digest another fish as fast as it can swallow it?'

'Sounds like Charlie and submarine sandwiches,' said Remo, and twisted open another bottle of Michelob Amber.

'Hey, Remo! You no fish?'

'Nope. I'm going to treat myself to another brew, and enhance my tan. There's plenty of time for fishing tomorrow.'

Mickey pulled on his green felt-top waders and sloshed out into the middle of the river, while Remo and Charlie and Cayley sat on the rocks and watched him. As the sun sank closer to the edge of the rimrock, the surface of the water glittered like broken glass, and all they could see was Mickey's silhouette, as he cast his line across the riffles. There was no sound except for the gurgling of the river and the zizz of Mickey's reel as he paid out more line.

After a while, Cayley said, 'It's beautiful and everything. But it's so darn *quiet*. At least when you watch these nature programs, they have music.'

Charlie shook his head in amazement. 'She's on a fishing trip, out in the wilderness, hundreds of miles from anyplace at all, and she wants a *soundtrack*.'

'So?' Cayley retorted. 'A soundtrack helps you to understand what's going on.'

'Oh, you mean like tinkly harp music, so you know that it's a river, and loud trumpety music, so you know that it's a real high rock?'

'You're such a scream,' said Cayley. She teetered across to the Winnebago and came back a few minutes later with her portable stereo and a flowery foam cushion. She put on a trance track by Duke of Motion, and lay back on one of the boulders, with her pink sunglasses on top of her head, basking in the last warmth of the afternoon sun. So now they had the river gurgling, and Mickey's reel zizzing, and the endless *tikka-ti-tikka-ti-tikka* of Cayley's music.

Mickey screamed out, 'Take a look at this, guys! Moby Fricking Dick!' He was holding up a thrashing brown trout, at least eighteen inches long.

Remo held up his beer bottle in salute. 'You the man, Mickey! Lord of the Flies!' Mickey carefully unhooked the fish and let it slide back into the river.

The sun burned its way into the top of the rimrock. The sky turned a lurid orange, and the temperature began to drop. Mickey came splashing in from the river and pulled off his waders. 'You just have to be careful, man. The bottom is so darned slippery, it's like trying to walk on bowling balls covered in snot.'

Charlie collected armfuls of dry brush and built a circular hearth out of small boulders. He flicked his Zippo, and the brush crackled into life immediately, so that sparks whirled across the river like fireflies.

'Anyone for wieners?' he asked, once the fire was burning up hot.

'Absolutely,' said Remo. 'And bring out those chicken legs, too, will you? And lots more beer. It's like we're suffering some kind of a Michelob drought out here.'

'Is that all, O master?'

'No. Bring out those cheesy Doritos, and those giant pretzels, and those knobbly jalapeño things.'

'Of course, O master. A balanced diet is so important, don't you think?'

As Charlie climbed the steps into the Winnebago, they heard a deep, hollow roar, like half a ton of coal being emptied down a coal-chute.

'What was that?' asked Cayley, sitting up straight.

'Mountain lion, probably,' said Remo. 'They usually start prowling around this time in the evening.'

'Oh my *God*, are they dangerous?'

'Well, sure they're dangerous. But they don't usually attack humans. Not unless they're provoked, anyhow.'

'Don't you think we'd better go inside?'

'No, it's OK. Mountain lions don't like fire, and I'll bet you fifty dollars they have a serious aversion to trance music, too, *and* psychedelic shirts. The only time they'll jump on you is if you act chickenshit and try to run away from them.'

'Maybe you ought to go get your gun.'

'Cayley, for Christ's sake, we'll be *fine*. I know it sounded close, but that lion is probably more than a mile away.'

'All the same.'

'OK,' Remo relented. He went back to the Winnebago, and returned with the Remington 700 hunting rifle that he had borrowed from his uncle. He slid back the bolt to check that there was a round in the chamber and it was ready to fire, and then he propped it against the boulder next to Cayley. 'You happy now?'

'You didn't tell me there were going to be mountain lions.'

'We're in the mountains, babe. The mountains. What did you expect, sharks?'

'You still didn't tell me. I wouldn't have come, if you'd told me.'

'If I'd told you there were going to be mosquitoes, you wouldn't have come, either.'

'No, I wouldn't. I hate mosquitoes. And I don't like sharks, either.'

Remo put his arm around her and held her tight. 'You don't have to worry. We're safe, we're going to be fine. When you hear a helicopter fly over your apartment building, you're never worried that it's going to crash on top of you, are you?'

'Yes.'

Remo looked over Cayley's shoulder at

47

Mickey and Charlie and made a face which meant 'girls – what can you do?' Mickey shook his head and stifled a laugh, and Charlie waved a wiener at him.

'Come on, sweet cheeks,' said Remo. 'Sit down and help yourself to something to eat. There's nothing to be scared of.'

They sat around the fire. Charlie had heaped even more brushwood on it now, and it was burning up fiercely, so fiercely that it scorched their faces. He had impaled a dozen wieners on sticks, and they were sizzling and popping, and he had arranged eight chicken drumsticks on a wire rack from the Winnebago's galley.

They passed around bags of taco chips and pretzels, and swigged Michelob Amber out of the bottle, and Remo said, 'The Emperors of IT! This is the life, dudes and dude-ess! As Teddy Roosevelt once said, give me the sunset and give me the sausages, and you can keep your palaces and your peacock pies!'

'Teddy Roosevelt said that?'

'Well, he would have done if he'd been here.'

'Yeah, but he's not, is he?' Charlie retorted. 'For starters, you forgot to invite him.'

The sky grew intensely black and thousands of stars came out, Andromeda and Cassiopeia. They traded jokes and campfire stories, and Remo passed a large untidy joint around.

Charlie was telling a horror story. 'So it's pitch dark, right, and the guy stumbles back into bed. But after a couple of minutes he feels something tickling him. He tells the woman to stop it, but the tickling goes on. He feels a tickle on his back

48

and a tickle on his neck. He even feels a tickle right inside his ear. He *hates* being tickled, and in the end he loses his temper and he reaches across and switches on the bedside lamp. And there she is, lying close beside him, but she's a heaving mass of white maggots. Wrong bedroom. Wrong sister. He's climbed into bed with the dead one instead.'

'That is *so* gross,' Cayley protested.

'I know. But it gets even grosser than that. He screams, and he jumps out of bed. He knocks the lamp over, so that he can't see where he's going. He's groping around in a panic, but after a while he finds a door, and a doorknob.'

He stopped, abruptly, and frowned, and then he raised his left hand to shield his eyes from the glare of the fire.

'He finds a door and a doorknob,' Cayley prompted him. 'What then?'

But Charlie kept on frowning into the darkness.

'What is it, man?' Remo asked him.

Mickey turned around. 'Something out there?'

Charlie pointed toward the edge of the river. 'There's somebody there. No, just *there*, see him? Just left of those tules.'

It was hard to see anything, because the smoke from the fire was blowing in front of them. But they could just make out the figure of a man, in a black wide-brimmed hat. He was standing not more than seventy feet away, not moving, but obviously watching them.

Remo picked up his rifle and stood up. 'Hey, man! What you doing there? You're not spying

49

on us or nothing?'

The man didn't reply, and he didn't move. Sometimes they could see him quite clearly, but then the smoke would billow in front of him and he would disappear.

'You going to tell us what you want?' Remo shouted. 'Otherwise, vamoose, OK?'

Still the man said nothing, but now he began to walk toward them, appearing through the smoke like a stage magician. The crown of his hat was cone-shaped, with a braided leather band around it, and he wore a long black coat and a high-buttoned black vest. He had a flat, leathery face, with a mouth that was almost lipless. As he came nearer, they saw that his eyes appeared to be totally silver, with no pupils, as if he had steel ball-bearings in his eye sockets.

'What do you want, man?' Remo repeated. 'Is there something wrong? You *blind* or something?'

'*Gituwutabudeu?*' the man shouted back at him, so harshly that all four of them jumped. '*Gi besa! Poohaguma! Soongapumaka!*'

'What the hell is he talking about?' said Remo. 'What kind of language is that?'

'Vulcan, most like,' said Charlie. 'Whatever it is, he seems to be pretty pissed about something.'

The man came closer, until he was standing less than twenty feet away from them. Remo kept his rifle pointed at him, but he wasn't sure if the man could see him or not. The firelight danced and sparkled in his silver eyes.

'*Teyabe?*' he asked, turning to Mickey and

50

Charlie. Then he spoke in English, although his tone was still aggressive. 'Why is your friend so frightened? In my language we say *tsegwab-betuma* for such a man – he who aims his gun but never pulls the trigger.'

'Listen, is there something we can help you with?' said Remo. 'We're just having a cookout here, that's all.'

'I told you,' the man replied. 'I am *pooha-guma*, medicine man. But I am more than that, I am *soongapumaka* – medicine man making breath. My name is Wodziwob, but you – if you prefer – you can call me Infernal John.'

'Phew! Good to know he's not called anything remotely scary,' said Charlie, out of the side of his mouth.

Mickey said, 'Sir – we're not, like, trespassing, are we? The signs all say that this is a camping zone. And we haven't done any damage. I caught a trout but I think it was well over the regulation size and anyhow I put it back in the river.'

'What?' demanded Wodziwob. 'You think you have done no damage? You have done more damage than you can possibly know.'

'Oh, come on, bro,' said Charlie. 'We're only here to drink beer and cook a few wieners and catch a couple of trout, and when we've gone, you won't even know we've been here.'

'We will *always* know that you have been here, even when you are gone forever.'

'We'll pick everything up, I promise you. Every last bottle.'

'You think I care about your paper and your

51

bottles and your rubbish? All those will vanish, in time. But you have polluted the land in a different way. You have stained its spirit, and a stain like that has *gi tokedu*, no end.'

'I'm sorry, man,' said Remo. 'I really have no idea what you're talking about.'

'It does not matter if you know or if you do not know. You will suffer the same consequences.'

Mickey said, 'Look, if we've upset you or anything, we apologize. But we've been real careful not to make a mess and our RV has its own chemical toilet facility so we won't be leaving any kind of stain whatsoever.'

But at that moment, two figures materialized. They seemed to rise right out of the ground, one on Wodziwob's left and one on his right. They were both impossibly tall, nearly twice Wodziwob's height, and wide-shouldered, and they were both dressed in black box-like coats. Their faces were covered with expressionless wooden masks, painted chalky white. On top of their heads they wore antlers, decorated with beads and small bones and birds' skulls.

They stood beside Wodziwob, swaying slightly, while the smoke from the campfire whirled around their legs. They looked more like living totem poles than men.

'Where the hell did *they* come from?' said Charlie, with a wheeze.

'Remo,' said Cayley, clutching at his arm. 'Remo, I think we'd better just get out of here, don't you?'

Remo raised his rifle higher, swinging it from one of the figures to the other, but all the same he took two or three steps backward, toward the Winnebago.

'They came out of *nowhere*, man,' said Charlie, and he was wheezing more painfully now. 'They came right out of the fricking *ground*.'

Mickey said, 'Maybe we're hallucinating. Where did you get that shit we've been smoking, Remo?'

Remo continued to keep the figures covered, but he continued to back away, too. 'That was good shit, man. I got that from Louie.'

'Then maybe it's the campfire. Maybe there was jimson weed in some of that brush.'

'So what do *you* see?' Remo asked him. 'Do you see a guy in a pointy black hat and two tall guys who look like they're wearing coffins?'

Mickey glanced at him quickly. They all knew that everybody has different hallucinations, when they're high.

'I think Cayley's right,' said Charlie. 'Like, let's say that the better part of valor is getting the hell out of here, *prontissimo*.'

They began to stumble back to the Winnebago, but the man who called himself Infernal John came after them, stalking across the boulders with a terrible sure-footedness. The two totem-like figures followed close behind him, with long articulated legs like stilts. As they walked, they made a complicated clicking noise, and a loud rattling whirr.

'Shit, man!' said Remo, and there was panic in his voice.

'Why are you running away from me?' Wodziwob demanded. 'Are you afraid of *ggwo tseka'a*

53

– that I will scalp you?'

'Just get away from us, man!' Remo shouted. 'We haven't done nothing but if you want us to leave, we'll leave!'

He lifted his rifle and fired one deafening shot into the air. It echoed and re-echoed from the rimrock, and all the surrounding mountains. The last echo was followed almost immediately by the roar of a mountain lion.

'You have disturbed *kaggwe toohoo'oo*,' said Wodziwob. 'Just as you have crushed every blade of grass that you have trodden on; and poisoned every insect; and shot down every bird that flies through the air. You have despoiled everything, and now you must pay the price for it.'

Remo pointed the rifle directly at Wodziwob's chest. 'You take one step nearer, Mr. Infernal What's-your-name, and the next one's for you. I mean it. Me and my friends, we're going to leave now, and you're going to stay right here and let us go. *Capisca?*'

But it was then that Wodziwob lifted both of his hands, palm outward, and started to sing in a high, strangulated warble.

'Jesus,' said Charlie. 'Sounds like my mom's tomcat, when it's on heat.'

'I sing to each of you as *gi tuwutabuedu!*' Wodziwob called out, and his voice was no longer mocking, but hard with anger. 'This means blind person. I bring to your eyes *toohoo-ggweddaddu nabo'o*, which means black paint. *Pooga'hoo* – I blow out your candle.'

The totem-like figures stalked closer, until

they were towering over them. Behind the expressionless slits in their marks, the Emperors of
IT could see faint blue-white lights flickering.

'Come on, man,' said Charlie. 'We really need
to go.'

'Look at them,' Remo protested. 'They're not
even human. They're just, like, *robots* or something.'

He leaned forward and peered at them more
intently. The two totem-like figures made a
creaking noise, and swayed slightly. Then, without warning, the blue-white lights suddenly
flared up, crackling and spitting as fiercely as
welding torches. They were so bright that the
Emperors of IT had to raise their hands in front
of their faces to stop themselves from being
dazzled.

'Holy crap,' said Mickey – yet almost as
quickly as the lights had flared up, they died
down again, and he found himself in total darkness. He lowered his hand, but he was still in
total darkness. He blinked furiously, and rubbed
his eyes, but it made no difference. He couldn't
see anything except seamless black.

It was Cayley who screamed out first. 'I'm
blind! Remo, I can't see! Remo, I'm blind! *Help
me!*'

But Remo was blundering around in circles,
with his arms flailing, and he was shouting out,
'Aah! Aah! Shit! What have you done to me, you
bastard? What have you done?'

Charlie had sunk to his knees on the ground,
rotating his head around and around and tilting it
from side to side as if his eyes had simply come

loose and he could somehow shake them back into place, and bring his sight back.

'What have you done to me?' Remo screamed. 'Where the fuck are you, and what have you done to me?' He fired off another shot, and Cayley screamed and stumbled against Mickey's side. Mickey took hold of her arm and steadied her and said, 'I'm here, it's Mickey. I can't see anything either. Don't move. Charlie, where are you?'

'I can't see nothing,' moaned Charlie. 'What's happened to me, Mickey? I can't see nothing!'

Mickey reached out with his other hand and found Charlie's shoulder. 'Don't move, Charlie. He's blinded us. Those lights that came out of their eyes.'

'Are you still here?' Remo yelled out. 'Are you still here, Mr. Infernal Fricking John?'

There was a long pause. Apart from Cayley's persistent whimpering, the only sounds they could hear were the wind, fluffing against their ears, and the river gurgling, and the lurching of the logs on their campfire. But then they heard the cicada-whirring noise of the totem-like figures, and wooden footsteps clattering around in back of them.

'Don't come any closer!' Remo shouted. 'I'm warning you! Maybe I can't see you but I'm going to go on shooting till I blow your fricking head off!'

Wodziwob said, 'You are helpless, like nursing babies. You can do nothing to save yourselves. You are the same now as we once were. When you first appeared in our land, we too were

56

blind. We were blind to your greed and blind to your cruelty and we were deaf, too – deaf to your lies, which buzzed like a thousand blow-flies on the corpse of our happiness.'

Mickey said, 'We really don't know what you're talking about, sir. We're sorry if we've done anything to upset you, but if we did we sure didn't do it on purpose, and if there's any-thing we can do to put it right? And this blind-ness. It's only temporary, right? Like looking at the sun, right?'

Wodziwob must have come right up close to him, because Mickey could actually *smell* him, some herbal smell like cilantro, and a dry spice, a little like nutmeg. He could smell buttery grease, too, and an underlying reek of tobacco.

'What you did to our people, *that* was not temporary, was it?'

'We don't understand you!' Mickey screamed at him – and this was Mickey, who hardly ever lost his temper. *'We don't know what you mean! I can't stay blind for ever! I can't be a blind person!'*

'You should not be fearful,' said Wodziwob. 'You will not be blind for very long.'

'What?' said Mickey, and now he was shaking. 'What do you mean?'

Wodziwob didn't answer, but Mickey heard him step away, and call out, 'Tudatzewunu! Tubbohwa'e! Let us show our friends the way to join their forefathers!'

Remo said, wildly, 'You're going to *kill* us? You think you can fucking *kill* us, and nobody's going to come after you? Everybody knows where we are, Mr. Infernal John. Our parents know we're here. Our friends know we're here. The park rangers know we're here. We have GPS, too.'

He heard one of the totem-like figures creaking up behind him, and he wheeled around and lost his balance and fell heavily onto the rocks, dropping his rifle with a loud clatter. Mickey took two groping steps forward and tripped over one of the logs on which they had been sitting to roast their wieners. He pitched forward into the fire, hands first, in a huge shower of hot sparks. He shouted, and rolled over, his hands scorched and his hair alight. He sat up and banged at his head with both hands, and then furiously rubbed his scalp to make sure that his hair wasn't still burning.

Charlie said, 'OK, OK. We won't tell anybody what you did to us. We promise. But please don't hurt us, OK?'

'I don't want to be blind!' Cayley suddenly screamed. 'I'd rather be dead than blind!'

Wodziwob said, 'We will do to you, child, only what your ancestors did to us.' With that, he knelt down next to Remo and beckoned to the totem-figure he had called Tubbohwa'e. The totem-figure bent down with a complicated series of jerks and clicks, and seized hold of Remo with jointed fingers that were so realistically carved out of oak that they looked almost human.

'Let go of me, you bastard!' Remo swore at it. 'Let go of me, you're breaking my fucking wrists!' He struggled and kicked and twisted, but the totem-figure was far too strong for him, and he remained pinned to the ground, grunting with pain and frustration.

Wodziwob unbuttoned his coat. Wound around his waist was a long thin rope, which he loosened, and dragged free, yard after yard of it, and dallied around his right elbow. There were more than ten yards of it, in all, with a loop in one end, like a lariat. While the totem-figure held Remo's wrists tightly together, Wodziwob tied a double knot around them, and yanked it tight.

'Shit, man!' Remo protested. 'You're cutting off my goddamned circulation!'

Wodziwob said nothing, but stood up and walked over to Charlie, his open coat flapping in the smoky wind. He beckoned to the totem-figure he had called Tudatzewunu, and this figure came looming up behind Charlie and gripped both of his forearms. In the meantime, Tubbohwa'e heaved Remo up from the ground, and dragged him closer, so that he and Charlie were standing less than three feet apart.

'They're going to come looking for us, man,' said Remo, although now he was beginning to sound seriously frightened. 'The park rangers, the cops. The FBI. If we don't come back they're going to come looking for us, and you guys are going to be toast.'

Wodziwob tied Charlie's wrists, and then Cayley's, and Mickey's last of all. The four of them now stood together like a chain gang. Cayley was quietly weeping, but the other three were silent, their heads lowered, as if they had already accepted what was going to happen to them. Mickey had not been too seriously burned, although the front of his hair was short and prickly, and his forehead and his nose were reddened; but he was shivering with shock, and his teeth were chattering.

'Now you must climb to the place where our people were forced to climb, and your people climbed after them, and murdered them all.'

Cayley sobbed, 'Why are you doing this? What did we ever do to you? I've never been here before! I don't even know who your people are!'

'Exactly,' said Wodziwob. 'You do not know who our people are because our people's bones are lying buried in the dirt and their names have all been carried away by the wind. Now, we will start to climb.'

The totem-figure called Tubbohwa'e took hold of the rope, and started to pull them past their Winnebago and up the slope toward the rimrock, which rose in front of them like a great dark wall. They kept staggering and stumbling and bumping into each other, but whenever they lost their footing, the totem-figure called Tudatzewunu would forcibly wrench them upright again, with those jointed wooden hands that gripped them as tight as a vise.

'I can't do this,' sobbed Cayley, as the gradient grew steeper and steeper, and the rough scrub prickled and tore at their legs. 'I just can't do this. Please don't make me do this.'

Charlie said nothing, but after the first fifty feet of climbing he was already wheezing for breath.

'Listen to him, man!' Remo panted. 'He has asthma!'

But Wodziwob said, 'Many of my people were sick, too, when they came to hide on this mountain. Many were women, and many were defenseless children, and many were old. But they all had to climb, regardless.'

From the sound of his breathing, he was obviously finding the climb as laborious as they were, but he doggedly plodded upward, and Tubbohwa'e kept on pulling the rest of them after him, scaling the loose volcanic rubble like some monstrous black spider, with a deathly white face, and Tudatzewunu followed behind, to heave them up on their feet again, if they fell.

It took them over two hours to reach the top of the promontory, and although the ground was still rocky and uneven, and covered with loose volcanic shale, it began to level off beneath their feet. They could see nothing at all, only blackness, but they could feel the night wind blowing more strongly in their faces, and all around them they could hear the soft roaring of thousands of pine trees, which surrounded the rimrock like the ocean.

Wodziwob stopped, and Tubbohwa'e pulled sharply at the rope, to stop the four of them from climbing any further. Charlie dropped to his knees, whining with asthma.

Wodziwob said, 'It was September, one hundred fifty years ago, and three tribes had gathered here – Paiute, Modoc, and Pit River. Usually, they were enemies. But this was a Big Time, which happened once a year, when enemies would forget their hostility, and come together for feasting, and games, and trading, and for marriages to be arranged between the tribes.'

'And what the fuck does that have to do with us?' Remo demanded, although he was still out of breath.

'It has everything to do with you,' Wodziwob told him. 'Your white soldiers did not understand about Big Times, even though they used to be common in California before the Europeans came. Because three enemy tribes had gathered together, your soldiers assumed that they intended to attack them, and so they decided to wipe them out.

'But, tell me, if the tribes had been here to plot war, why did they have their women and children and their old people with them? If they had not had their women and children and their old people with them, they would not have been forced to stay here at Infernal Caverns and fight. They would have melted away, like shadows, so that they could fight another day.

'Any soldier with any intelligence would have realized that. And any man with any humanity would have let these people go. But they murdered more than twenty of them, including women and children and old people, and that is a crime that still cries out for justice.'

'But it wasn't *us*,' wheezed Charlie, in desperation. 'It wasn't even our grandfathers' grandfathers.'

But Wodziwob took no notice. 'Let me tell you what they did, these white soldiers. They took five prisoners, including Chief Si-e-ta. Their Indian scouts took thorn branches and pulled their eyes out onto their cheeks. Then they bound them together, and told them to walk to the edge of the rimrock and keep on walking.

'It is six hundred feet to the valley floor below.'

Mickey said, in a haunted voice, 'You're not expecting *us* to do the same?'

Wodziwob circled around them, prodding each of them with his finger. 'If I did, would you not call that justice? What does it say in your holy book? "Life for life, eye for eye"?'

Cayley started to cry again, inconsolably, like a miserable child.

Wodziwob said, 'Don't you think that we cried, too, when *our* children were killed?'

SEVEN

Washington, DC

After twenty minutes, Dr. Schaumberg and Dr. Henry came into the room, followed by Dr. Cronin.

'David, the doctors are back,' said the First Lady, taking hold of the President's hand.

Dr. Schaumberg approached the bed, holding up an ophthalmic scan, even though the President was unable to see it. He was lean and stringy, with a thinning gray comb-over and

63

half-glasses and a withered neck like an iguana. He cleared his throat and said, gravely, 'We have the results of your tests, Mr. President.'

'Well?' demanded the President. 'What's the verdict?'

'Mr. President – you have one hundred percent corneal opacification.'

'What? I have *what*?'

'Your corneas have become clouded,' said Dr. Henry. He was black and bulky, like a retired wrestler, with a bald, well-dented head that was polished to a high gleam. 'In other words, the transparent lens covering your iris is no longer transparent.'

'Is it permanent?'

Dr. Henry shook his head. 'We don't yet know, Mr. President. First of all we have to run a whole series of tests to find out what might have caused it, so we may send you over to the Washington National Eye Center. It's highly unusual for corneal clouding to happen so quicly and so completely, and without any warning.'

Dr. Schaumberg nodded in agreement. 'In almost every case of corneal opacification, patients show very obvious symptoms before they lose their sight. For example – with any form of conjunctivitis, the eyes will be pink and sore and weeping for at least five to twelve days before the patient's sight starts to be affected.'

'I had nothing like that, no soreness. I just blinked, and the lights went out.'

'Don't you have *any* idea why it happened?' asked the First Lady.

'Corneal clouding can be caused by a whole

variety of different conditions,' Dr. Schaumberg told her. 'Conjunctivitis is one of them – but as we know, the President had no "pink-eye" or other ocular irritation before his blindness occurred. A drastic lack of vitamin A can sometimes be responsible, but I doubt very much if the President is subsisting on a Third World diet. There's Sjögren's syndrome, which is associated with rheumatoid arthritis, but that's very rare, and usually found amongst middle-aged women.'

'There's trachoma,' said Dr. Henry.

'Trachoma?' said the President. 'You mean that disease that African children get?'

'That's the one, sir. *Chlamydia trachomatis.* But trachoma usually affects the cornea in several stages, and causes blindness only through a gradual process of repeated scarring and repeated healing. What happens is that—'

'All right,' interrupted the President, impatiently. 'How long are these tests going to take?'

'At least three days. Maybe longer, depending on what we find.'

'OK, then. I'll have Doug Latterby clear my diary, and I'll be back here first thing tomorrow morning.'

'You're not thinking of *leaving*, Mr. President?'

'Of course I am. I have a meeting in two and a half hours' time with the President of the Russian Federation.'

'David,' the First Lady protested. 'You can't meet Gyorgy Petrovsky if you're *blind*. Kenneth will have to do it.'

'Oh, yes? And how are we going to explain my failure to show up at one of the most critical political meetings since the break-up of the Soviet Union? Are we going to tell the media that I've had a heart attack? Or a stroke maybe? That's just as bad as going blind – worse. Or maybe we can announce that I simply forgot that Petrovsky was coming and went fishing instead.'

'Mr. President, I really have to advise you to stay here,' said Dr. Schaumberg. 'Your condition came on very suddenly – if we delay treatment it could get very much worse. Not only that, most conditions that cause corneal problems are extremely infectious.'

Dr. Cronin said, 'That's true, sir. They can be spread by hand contact, saliva, or sinus secretions. I don't think it would help our relations with the Russian Federation if you sneezed on President Petrovsky and *he* went blind, too.'

The President laid his hand on Dr. Cronin's shoulder and eased himself down from the bed. 'It's a risk I'll have to take. This meeting is a showdown about Russian criminal activities in the United States. We've been preparing our intelligence for three years at a cost of millions of dollars and the only person who can face down Petrovsky is me.'

'How are you going to face him down if you can't even see him?'

'I can wing it. If Doug Latterby stays close by, he can act as my guide dog.'

The First Lady said, 'David – darling – I'm begging you. Supposing you go to this meeting

66

and you lose your sight for ever?'

'I ask young men to go to foreign countries on behalf of the United States of America, and to risk a whole lot more than their eyesight. This time, Marian, my country has to come first. And I can do it. You just watch me. I was elected as the Can-Do Man. "If anyone can, the Can-Do Man can."'

'If you don't mind my saying so, Mr. President,' said Dr. Cronin, 'you're not only blind, you're nuts.'

The President turned and stared over Dr. Cronin's right shoulder. 'Just this once, Andrew, I'll pretend that I'm deaf, too.'

The President was waiting on the steps of the South Portico when President Petrovsky's motorcade arrived. It was a warm afternoon, but the sky was gray and overcast, and it had just stopped raining, so the air was steamy and the limousine's tires made a fat, wet sound on the asphalt.

President David Perry was well over six feet tall, barrel-chested, with a large rough-hewn head and dense iron-gray hair. His gray, deep-set eyes always seemed to be narrowed, as if he were trying to focus on something that was just a little too far away for him to see. This morning, of course, he could see nothing at all. He was heavily built, but he worked out with a Marine trainer every day, so that his waist was taut and he swung his arms when he walked, as if he were wearing a corset, even though he didn't.

His wife Marian, standing close beside him on

his left, was a petite woman with blonde high-lighted hair and a flat, pretty face that photographed well. This afternoon she was wearing a pink-and-white floral-patterned jacket and a pink skirt by her favorite designer, Peggy Jennings.

Doug Latterby hovered only inches behind President Perry on his right. His long, big-nosed face was usually relaxed and genial, but as President Petrovsky climbed out of his limousine, his mouth was tightly puckered and his shoulders were hunched with tension.

'He's walking up the steps now. He's smiling at you. He's holding out his hand. Raise your hand, extend it. More to the left. More to the left. That's it.'

President Perry grinned and said, 'Welcome to the White House, Mr. President. Trust you had a comfortable journey. Sorry about the uninspiring weather. Not like the last time Marian and I visited Moscow, and you put on that spectacular blizzard for us.'

This was hurriedly and rather flatly translated, while President Petrovsky continued to smile and nod. He was a small man, with protuberant eyes. Marian Perry always called him Gollum.

'I prefer warm,' he replied, through his interpreter. 'And don't they say that a little rain has to fall in everybody's life?'

After all of the formal introductions in the Diplomatic Reception Room, with President Perry's dog Sergeant circling around and furiously slapping his tail against everybody's legs, the President ushered Gyorgy Petrovsky along the corridor to the Oval Office. Marian Perry glanced at Doug Latterby as he gently nudged President Perry away from the wall, and Doug Latterby raised his eyebrows to show her that he was beginning to believe they could actually pull this off. After all, halfway through his second term, David Perry had been President long enough to be familiar with every turn along the way to the West Wing.

They sat in the Oval Office with President Perry flanked on one side by the Vice-President Kenneth Moran, and by Doug Latterby on the other. Secretary of State George Smirniotakis was also there, tugging out his large white handkerchief every now and then to blow his nose, and Warren Truby, Director of the FBI, who Marian Perry had once described as 'Herbert Hoover's less cheerful brother.'

As the butler brought coffee and cakes and toll-house cookies, Doug Latterby leaned close to the President's left shoulder and murmured, 'Petrovsky is slightly more to your right. That's it. And keep your eyeline a little lower.'

Eventually the doors of the Oval Office were closed, and President Perry said, 'Gyorgy, I think we can cut to the chase. You've had all the briefing papers, but just for the record, the reason I've asked you here today is to ask for your active assistance. At least three highly organized gangs of Russian criminals are bringing fear and corruption and a great deal of human misery to every major city throughout the United States.

'Once it was the Sicilians, and the Mafia. Now it's Russians and Ukrainians, and they're into everything ... drugs, prostitution, gambling, fraud – and theft on a scale such as we've never encountered before.'

Gyorgy Petrovsky listened to the translation. Then he said, 'America has always advertised itself as the land of opportunity, where anybody can make good, no matter what their place of birth.'

'Oh, for sure,' said President Perry. 'But there's a heck of a lot of difference between making good and making off with somebody else's goods. There's a heck of a lot of difference between opportunity and extortion.'

Gyorgy Petrovsky shrugged. 'Every orchard produces one or two bad plums. I cannot see how you can hold me personally responsible for the misdemeanors of a few people who happen to have been born in Russia. You admitted them to your country, after all. It is up to your own law-enforcement agencies to curtail their activities, and your courts to punish them. All I can say is that if you wish to impose on these people the severest of penalties, I will give you nothing but my blessing.'

'I'm afraid I need more than your good wishes, Gyorgy.' President Perry was finding it difficult to judge whether Gyorgy Petrovsky was being deadly serious or mildly sarcastic. 'I need your active cooperation.'

Normally, at this point, he would have stood up and walked behind Gyorgy Petrovsky's chair, so that the Russian would have had to turn his head awkwardly around in order to reply to him. But now that he was blind, it was out of the question. He couldn't afford to stumble, or to lose his sense of direction.

'In particular,' he said, 'we need to nail down a character called Lev Khlebnikov, who runs a highly sophisticated drugs-and-prostitution racket in New York City. So far we haven't been able to bring any charges against him, because nobody will give evidence against him. The most humane way that he deals with anybody who crosses him is to tie them over a mailbox, douse them with gasoline, and set fire to them.'

'I know of this man,' nodded Gyorgy Petrovsky.

'Then there's Viktor Zamyatin, who operates out of Cincinnati. He's not as powerful as Khlebnikov, but his activities are spreading all across the Midwest – labor rackets, protection, arson, prostitution, drugs. You name it, Zamyatin's got his finger in it.'

'I know also of this man,' said President Petrovsky. 'He is what you call "a piece of work," yes?'

'That just about sums him up.'

'So what do you expect me to do? You want my security people maybe to kidnap these two men and spirit them back to Russia? I don't want them any more than you do.'

'Of course not,' said President Perry. 'But almost all of the money that Khlebnikov and Zamyatin make out of their illegal operations is being laundered through banks in Moscow and St Petersburg. We're talking billions of dollars

71

every year. I need you to clamp down on those banks and freeze any and all of their assets. Also, I need you to confiscate all of their property in Russia – houses, yachts, you name it. I want those two guys to be left with nothing but their undershorts.'

'This is easy to say but not so easy to do. There are laws of confidentiality, even in Russian banking. Also, I would be seen as acting at the behest of a foreign power, which would not exactly enhance my Presidential authority, would it?'

'Maybe not,' the President began.

'Little more to the left, sir,' Doug Latterby told him, in an urgent murmur.

'Maybe not,' the President continued, adjusting his position in his chair. 'But the damage that these two men are inflicting on the social and financial fabric of America is such that if you are disinclined to cooperate voluntarily, I'll have to consider persuasion.'

'Persuasion? You mean you are going to "lean" on me?'

'You can put it any which way you like. But if you continue to allow Khlebnikov and Zamyatin to launder their money through Russian banks, I intend to begin a systematic reduction of financial assistance to the Russian Federation. For every one billion dollars that Khlebnikov and Zamyatin spirit out of the United States, based on FBI estimates, I will order the withholding of ten billion dollars of aid, loans, and investment.'

There was a very long silence, interrupted only by coughing and embarrassed shuffling. The

President could only imagine what kind of expression Gyorgy Petrovsky had on his face.

'Gollum angry,' said Doug Latterby, under his breath. 'Gollum very, *very* angry.'

When at last he replied, Gyorgy Petrovsky sounded preternaturally calm, but even before his words were translated, the President could tell how furious he was. 'I think we should adjourn this meeting. I require time to consider what you have suggested, and talk to my deputies. After all, this has radically altered our relationship, don't you think? I came into this room thinking we were political allies, equals.'

'We still are,' the President insisted. 'Nothing has changed that.'

'You don't think so? Allies don't threaten one another.'

'Allies don't allow the scum of the earth to rob the people who matter to them, and refuse to do anything to help.'

Gyorgy Petrovsky stood up. Doug Latterby cupped the President's elbow in his hand to indicate that he should stand up, too.

'I will consider very seriously what you have said, David,' said Gyorgy Petrovsky. 'I will give you my response as soon as I can.'

'Listen,' said the President, 'I want you to know that whatever we're discussing here, it doesn't affect our personal friendship.'

'Of course not. I understand what pressure you are under. But you also have to see the situation from my point of view. Oh – before I forget, let me show you the latest picture of *our* two villains.'

He took a color photograph out of his inside pocket and passed it over. Doug Latterby intercepted it and placed it in President Perry's hand.

'It's OK,' said President Perry, handing it back. 'I already know what these two bastards look like.'

Gyorgy Petrovsky stiffened, and stared at President Perry in bewilderment. Then, without another word, he turned and stalked out of the Oval Office, followed hurriedly by his aides and deputies.

'What's wrong, Doug?' asked President Perry, turning around.

'The photograph, Mr. President. I think you kind of missed the emphasis on *our*. That wasn't Khlebnikov and Zamyatin. That was President Petrovsky's children.'

EIGHT

AMA Flight 2849, Atlanta–Los Angeles
'Cabin crew – fifteen minutes to landing,' said Tyler, over the intercom. He was sitting in the co-pilot's seat now, with headphones on. 'Holy shit,' he added. 'I never thought in a million years that I'd ever get to say that.'

Captain Sherman cleared his throat. 'Maybe you should have switched off your intercom before you shared that little nugget with two hundred and nine unsuspecting passengers.'

'*Shit*, sorry! Beginner's jitters, I guess.'

'Well, I'm sure glad they didn't hear *that*.'

The 747-400 dipped and swayed in the cross-winds. Up ahead of them, in the darkness, Tyler could see the sparkling lights of the southern California coast scattered all the way across the horizon.

'EO system set?' asked Captain Sherman.

'Check,' said Tyler.

'Pressurization set? Humidifier off. Set the airfield altitude so that the plane is depressurized on landing. One hundred twenty-eight feet above sea level, in this case.'

'Erm ... check.'

'Set the HSIs to radio navigation mode.'

'Check.'

'Set auto brakes. Wouldn't want to touch down safely but find we can't stop, would we? Don't think the residents of Inglewood would appreciate it too much.'

Tyler pulled a pretend-scared face, but Captain Sherman couldn't see him, and in any case he wasn't really pretending.

'Cabin signs and exit lights on. Ignition on. Fuel system set for landing. Fuel heat off. QNH set. Check hydraulics. Landing flaps set at twenty-five degrees.'

Tyler had to blink the perspiration out of his eyes, and every muscle in his shoulders and upper arms was locked with tension, like an anatomical drawing. He was seriously beginning to believe that he couldn't do this, even if his own life and the lives of more than two hundred other people depended on it. All the movie stunts he performed were meticulously calculated, worked out to the very last millimeter by people who knew exactly what they were doing, and if he suspected that the risks were unacceptable, he simply wouldn't do them. But with this stunt, he didn't have any choice. He had to do it. And he had no opportunity to rehearse it, either.

'Now I want you to locate the flight management system,' said Captain Sherman. 'There are two buttons on the glareshield marked LNAV and VNAV. Then take out the Jepp map for LAX. Set it on a hundred-mile scale using the EFIS control panel. When it's time to land, you'll get a yellow FM message on the middle screen.'

Tyler fumbled over setting the Jeppesen map, and the lights of Los Angeles seemed to be frighteningly close already.

'There's a knob on the control display unit between our seats. You got it? Twist it until the little numbers go down to one hundred feet above field elevation – two hundred twenty-eight feet.'

'OK ... done it.'

'Now announce, "Cabins secured for landing."'

Tyler could see LAX now, its runway lights tilting as they made their final approach.

'Press the LOC and G/S buttons on the glareshield,' said Captain Sherman. 'All three CMD lights should go on.'

'Yeah, right, roger, they have.'

The engines screamed as the 747 descended at two hundred fifty knots toward Runway 7L.

'Flaps thirty,' said Captain Sherman. 'Turn on the auto brakes.'

'Fifty,' said the radar altimeter, in a flat, mechanical voice. *'Thirty.'*

For a long moment Tyler was sure that the four-hundred-ton aircraft was flying too fast and too high and they were going to miss the runway altogether. He had prayed only a few times in his life before – prayed and really meant it – but as the 747 sped above the runway at a height of less than ten feet, and still hadn't touched its wheels to the ground, he whispered, *'Save me, God.'*

There was a jarring jolt, and the plane bounced off to the left. Then there was another jolt, and then another, and then the 747's eighteen tires started squealing like a chorus of slaughtered pigs. The plane's throttles reversed with a thunderous roar, but Tyler could see that it was veering toward the left-hand side of the runway.

It was still seventy-five feet away from the threshold, however, when it finally came to a halt. Captain Sherman turned blindly toward him and said, 'That's it, Mr. Jones. You've done it. Cake.'

'Hey, come on,' said Tyler. He was trembling with relief, as if he had been holding up a hundred-pound barbell for an hour, and had just been allowed to put it down. 'I don't think I could have managed it without this automatic-landing gizmo.'

'You're right,' said Captain Sherman. 'I certainly wouldn't like to belittle what you just did, but without ALS you would have probably killed the lot of us.'

'Oh,' said Tyler. 'Thanks for the vote of confidence.'

'No offense intended, Mr. Jones. Just being realistic.'

Outside on the runway, on both sides of the aircraft, they had been joined by fire trucks and ambulances with flashing red lights. The cabin crew had opened the doors and deployed the emergency chutes, and the first of the passengers were sliding down to the runway.

A sandy-haired man in white shirtsleeves appeared in the cabin doorway, accompanied by the senior flight attendant. He smelled strongly of D&G aftershave. 'Captain Sherman? My name's George O'Donnell, assistant operations manager. The tower informed us about your vision difficulty.'

Captain Sherman didn't turn around. 'It is not a "vision difficulty," Mr. O'Donnell. I've been struck blind, somehow, and so has my crew. This gentleman very bravely assisted us to bring the bird down.'

George O'Donnell reached across and shook Tyler's hand. 'It's deeply appreciated, sir. Believe me, AMA will be showing you their gratitude.'

'Don't worry about that,' said Tyler. 'All I want to do is get out of here.'

'Well, we'd prefer it if you didn't just yet. Not until all of the passengers have been deplaned. We don't really want them to see the flight crew being assisted off the aircraft because they've gone blind. Who knows what kind of legal mess we'd have on our hands if *that* happened.'

'With all respect, Mr. O'Donnell, *I'm* not blind, and I just want to get the hell off of this plane.'

'I realize that, sir. But there are media people around, and we wouldn't want you talking to them before we've had a full debriefing.'

'You mean before you'd had the chance to make absolutely sure that this wasn't AMA's fault? Or it *was* AMA's fault, how you're going to explain it away?'

'There's no need to take that attitude, sir. Like I say, we're deeply grateful for what you've done. You're a hero. But it's my job to think about the airline's reputation and to make sure that passengers continue to choose AMA with complete confidence.'

He laid his hand on Captain Sherman's epaulet, and said, 'We have a paramedic team waiting for you and your crew outside, Captain. Just as soon as the passengers are clear, they'll be taking you to the Doheny Eye Institute out at Lincoln Heights for a thorough check-up.'

Tyler took off his headphones, unbuckled his seat belt, and stood up. 'You can tell the captain and his crew to wait for the all-clear, Mr. O'Donnell, but I don't work for you and I'm leaving now and going home.'

He was at least four inches taller than George O'Donnell, and probably twenty-eight pounds heavier. George O'Donnell lifted both hands and said, 'OK ... have it your way. But I would still ask you please not to talk to the media. We don't want to create any kind of hysteria, do we?'

'Hysteria?' Tyler retorted. He was still shak-

ing. 'You weren't on this plane when they told me that the pilot and his crew had gone blind. You don't even know the meaning of the word hysteria.'

George O'Donnell said, 'OK, let's not have any trouble here,' and stepped out of his way. Tyler turned back to Captain Sherman and said, 'I really hope you guys get your sight back, Captain. I'll call the eye clinic tomorrow, find out how you're doing.'

'Thanks,' said Captain Sherman. 'And thanks again for saving all of these people.'

'That's OK,' Tyler told him. 'I wasn't in a hurry to die, either.'

He was just about to go back to coach class and retrieve his bag when a distorted voice came over the radio.

'Tower to AMA 2849! Tower to AMA 2849! Evacuate that heavy fast as you can! We have incoming, out of control!'

Captain Sherman picked up his headset. 'Say again?'

'Get everybody out of that aircraft as quickly as possible! We have a private jet coming in from the southwest, approximately two hundred seventy knots. It's locked on Runway 7L and it's losing altitude fast but we can't raise the pilot.'

Without hesitation, Tyler took hold of the navigator's arm and heaved him bodily out of his seat. He pushed him out of the flight-cabin door, and then he grabbed the copilot. George O'Donnell and the senior flight attendant were helping Captain Sherman to unbuckle his harness.

80

The upper-class and first-class lounges were almost empty, except for one or two passengers who were gathering the last of their hand luggage together, but along the aisle from coach class there was still a line of thirty or forty passengers who were being shepherded by the flight attendants toward the emergency chute. None of them were panicking, or pushing. Now that they felt they were safely on the ground, everybody was chattering and joking. 'Haven't been down a slide since I was eight years old!'

A warm wind was blowing into the cabin from outside, tainted with the smell of aviation fuel and diesel, and the red fire-truck lights were still flashing.

Tyler shouted out, *'Listen up, everybody! Listen! You need to get out of this plane real fast! There's another plane landing on the same runway!'*

The senior flight attendant shouted out, too. *'Forget about taking your shoes off! Just get out of here as quick as you can!'*

There were screams and shouts of alarm, and the passengers started to jostle each other. Tyler pulled the navigator and the co-pilot toward the exit.

The navigator said, 'God, don't push me, I can't see!' But Tyler pushed him all the same, and he somersaulted down the emergency chute, followed by a fat woman in a bright pink jumpsuit and a businessman still clutching his briefcase. Two elderly Japanese tourists tumbled down after them.

Tyler looked back to see if Captain Sherman

was close behind. The pilot was feeling his way unsteadily down the spiral staircase from upper class, clinging to the handrail to prevent himself from falling. George O'Donnell was close behind him.

Tyler was about to go to the foot of the stairs to help him when he heard a piercing whistle noise, and then a deafening explosion, which echoed from one side of the airport to the other. Somebody out on the runway was screaming, and somebody else was shouting, *'Oh my God! Oh my God!'*

Tyler pushed his way back to the exit, where the last four or five coach-class passengers were being hurried down the emergency chute. The red-haired flight attendant who had first woken him up was there, along with a young black flight attendant, with cornrow hair.

'What was that?' asked the red-haired attendant, and she was white-faced with fright. 'Was that a *plane*?'

Tyler leaned outside, shielding his eyes with his hand. Less than a hundred yards away, he saw the fiery framework of a twin-engined private jet, rolling toward them on blazing tires. It had exploded on touchdown, but it was still trundling along the tarmac at sixty or seventy knots like a burning funeral wagon.

Tyler grasped both flight attendants tightly by the hand, and pitched himself out of the doorway. In a tangle of arms and legs they slithered down to the bottom of the emergency chute, and firefighters helped them onto their feet.

'Run!' the firefighters shouted at them, and

Tyler and the girls all ran across the runway, away from the 747, as fast and as hard as they could. Even the firefighters turned and ran now.

Captain Sherman and George O'Donnell were still standing in the 747's open doorway when the private jet crashed into its inboard port engine. There was another thunderous bang as the first of the 747's fuel tanks exploded, and a huge dragon's tongue of orange fire licked up into the night.

Tyler stopped running and turned around. By now he and the two flight attendants were nearly three hundred yards away from the 747, but they could still feel a wave of heat against their faces. The plane's fuel tanks blew up, and fiery chunks of aluminum spun up into the night like Catherine wheels.

Exhausted, sweating, gasping for breath, Tyler slid himself down against a taxiway sign, and the two flight attendants sat down beside him. Together they watched as fire engulfed the 747 from nose to tail. They were too winded to speak, and in any case the noise from the burning aircraft was overwhelming. There was a series of smaller bangs, as oxygen tanks exploded and the tires burst, followed by the crackling and popping of windows. Five fire trucks jetted thousands of gallons of white foam all over the aircraft's carcass, and foam tumbled across the runways in the early morning wind, like frolicsome ghosts.

Up above them, helicopters from the police and fire departments circled the 747, their floodlights criss-crossing through the thick black smoke. Shortly after five thirty a.m., with a terrible groan, the aircraft sagged in the middle and collapsed onto the runway.

A Latino woman paramedic came bustling over to check that Tyler and the two girls were unhurt. She had very wide hips, but Tyler thought that she had a comfortingly beautiful face, like a Madonna. Then a tired-looking Federal Aviation official approached Tyler for his home address, so that he could question him later for the FAA's official inquiry. He was followed by another manager from AMA Airlines, with a gray buzz cut and rimless eyeglasses.

'Did Captain Sherman get out?' Tyler asked him.

The manager's eyeglasses caught the first light of the morning sun. 'Sorry,' he said. 'So far we believe there were eleven fatalities altogether. Captain Sherman I regret to tell you was one of them.'

Tyler said, 'Shit. There wouldn't have been any casualties at all, if that second plane hadn't come in.'

'Well, we have no idea what caused that yet. But, yes, it's a tragedy.'

Tyler stood up and was ready to leave when a square-jawed blonde woman in a red polo-neck sweater approached him. 'Mr. Jones? Tina Freely, *LA Times*. I understand you're the man of the hour.'

'I don't know about that. In any case, I don't think I'm supposed to talk about it just yet.'

'Oh come on, now, Mr. Jones. You don't mind

if I call you Tyler? AMA couldn't keep a lid on it for very long. I've been talking to some of the air-traffic controllers, and they all know what happened.'

'I'm sorry,' said Tyler. 'I'm totally busharoonied, and I really need to get home.'

Tina Freely walked beside him as he limped toward the airport terminal. 'The whole flight crew went blind and you had to land the plane by yourself?'

'It was totally automatic. All I had to do was press a couple of buttons, flick a couple of switches, and tell the passengers not to smoke in the toilets.'

'That was still pretty brave of you.'

'The crew was blind. I didn't really have much choice, did I?'

'Do you know *why* they went blind?'

'Not a clue. The captain thought it might have been a virus in the a/c. You know, like Legionnaire's disease. But if *that* was true, how come nobody else went blind? How come *I* didn't go blind?'

They had almost reached the terminal. Planes were still landing and taxiing and taking off on other runways, and Tyler could hardly hear what Tina Freely said next, except that she finished up by saying '—called up to report that *he* had gone blind, too.'

'Somebody else went blind? Sorry. I didn't catch that.'

'The private plane that crashed into the 747, that was a Learjet 45 owned and flown by Norman Rossabi, one of the partners in Kerwin,

85

Rossabi, and Prink. Big showbiz lawyers.'

'Sure. I've heard of them. Who hasn't?'

'Well, Rossabi was flying himself and one of his clients back from a weekend in Albuquerque, New Mexico. He called from someplace over the Tonto National Forest in Arizona and said that he had suddenly lost his sight. That was the last they heard of him. At least until they picked up his plane on their radar, winging its way back home. Non-stop.'

Tyler said, 'Maybe it's just a coincidence.'

'You think so?'

'I don't know. Maybe it's some kind of disease that pilots get – you know, people who fly at high altitude. Maybe it's the pressure; or the effect of UV rays, from the sun. The atmosphere's thinner up there, isn't it? Doesn't give you so much protection.'

'Well, maybe,' said Tina Freely. 'You don't mind if I take your picture, do you? Try to look – you know – *heroic*.'

NINE

Ladera Park, Los Angeles

'What time did that Children's Services person say she was going to be here?' asked Jasmine's aunt, for the seventh time. 'He *is* a sweet little fella, I have to admit that, but I never did no baby rearin', not myself, apart from mindin' you when you was teeny and your momma had to go to work at Ralph's, and I swear I hardly know one end of a baby from the other.'

'It's easy,' said Jasmine, without turning around. 'All you have to do is sniff.'

Jasmine's aunt stepped out onto the balcony, holding the baby in her arms. She was small and skinny and stooped, with a dried-up-looking face that had always reminded Jasmine of a dark-brown leather mask, rather than a face. On her head she was wearing a red silk scarf that she had knotted up into an extraordinary floral shape, like a giant rose; and her dress was red silk, too, reaching almost to her ankles, with wide sleeves and yellow embroidery around the hem and the cuffs.

She wore dangly gold earrings and more gold-and-silver bangles than Jasmine could count, and her two front teeth were gold, too. She called herself Auntie Ammy, here in Ladera Park, but her real name was Amadi, which meant 'great rejoicing', because she seemed destined to die at birth.

She lifted up the baby and inhaled. 'Seems OK for now. But if I catch even one whiff of doo-doo, I am passing him directly over to you, you hear?'

'I hear.'

Jasmine was watching the high gray veils of smoke that were still rising from the airport. They were leaning to the left now because the wind had changed around to the northwest. It reminded her of the line from the Bible which her grandmother used to quote: *'And I will show wonders in the heavens and in the earth, blood and fire and pillars of smoke.'*

Three helicopters were still droning and clattering around the end of the runway. She and Auntie Ammy had heard the explosion when the AMA 747 had blown up at three twenty-five this morning, and they had rushed out onto the balcony in time to see the fireball rolling up into the darkness.

A TV news bulletin had told them less than ten minutes after the explosion that two aircraft had collided on the runway at LAX, with an unknown number of fatalities. An hour later, Chief of Police William J. Bratton had announced at a hastily arranged media conference that although the LAPD had not ruled out a terrorist attack completely, they had information which led them to believe that what had happened was nothing more than 'a tragic and catastrophic accident – but an accident all the same.'

Auntie Ammy rocked the baby boy in her arms. He wasn't asleep, but he seemed to be mesmerized by her rocking.

'This was not no accident,' she said, emphatically. 'Just like what happened to you yesterday, that crash you had on the freeway, that was not no accident neither.'

'How do you know?' Jasmine asked her. She turned around and stroked the baby's forehead, and then his hand. He clung to her finger and stared at her seriously, as if he didn't want to lose sight of her.

'I know it because I know it, that's all. I feels it in the air.'

'Now you're getting all psychic on me again. You been throwing them bones?'

'I don't need to throw bones to know when there's trouble brewin'. I *feels* it. It's like the air all around us is startin' to thicken up, like soup.'

Auntie Ammy jiggled the baby a few more times. Then she said, 'Maybe you should give Children's Services another call. Maybe they forgot.'

'Don't be so impatient. They'll be here. I need to speak to my insurance company, that's a whole lot more urgent. I've tried them four times and still there's nobody answering.'

'I told you. Didn't I told you? There's trouble brewin'.'

After another hour, Jasmine called Children's Services again, but all she heard was a recorded message, asking her to leave her name and number.

89

'Maybe I should take him down there myself.'

'Happen you should. You can't take him home with you, can you, and *I* can't take care of him, poor little fella.'

Jasmine tried her insurance company one more time. She had the same response as Children's Services, a recorded voice telling her that 'no associates are available to speak to you right now ... please leave a short message and we'll get right back to you.'

'You can lend a borrow of my car,' said Auntie Ammy. 'Take the poor little fella downtown and then drive yourself home. You can ask Hubie to fetch it back for me tomorrow.'

'OK, thanks,' said Jasmine. She held out her hands for the baby, and Auntie Ammy started to pass him over, but he clung tightly to Auntie Ammy's red silk dress and started to cry.

'Hey, shush,' said Auntie Ammy. 'Jazz is going to take you to meet some real nice folks who is going to take real good care of you.'

Jasmine took hold of him, but he wailed even louder and wouldn't release his grip on Auntie Ammy's dress.

'I think he wants you to be his new momma,' said Jasmine.

'Well, I'm sorry, little fella, but being nobody's momma just ain't my for-tay. Even a little fella as cute as you.'

At that moment, however, the baby abruptly stopped crying, and looked up at the ceiling, his blue eyes still sparkling with tears. He looked as if he had heard something, or was waiting for something. He frowned, and then he lifted one hand and pointed directly upward.

'What is it, little fella?' Auntie Ammy asked him. But the baby continued to point and look upward.

'*A gah,*' he said.

'A gah?'

'*A gah,*' he repeated.

'I'm sorry, honey,' said Jasmine. 'I don't speak baby. I used to, once upon a time, but I'm afraid I clean forgot it all.'

'*A gah,*' said the baby, and as he did so they heard a rumbling sound, and the windows in Auntie Ammy's apartment began to rattle and buzz, and a brown pottery vase dropped off the shelf and smashed on the polished-wood floor. The rumbling grew louder and louder, until the whole apartment was shaking, and a picture of some Santería saint fell off the wall.

'Earthquake,' said Jasmine, but it was more of a question than a statement, because she had never heard an earthquake like this before. The rumbling became a roaring, and then the roaring turned into an ear-splitting scream, and a dark shadow passed over the apartment block as if a huge dragon had flown overhead. Pink clay tiles flew from the roof in a blizzard and leaves exploded from the trees in Ladera Park.

Jasmine and Auntie Ammy rushed back out onto the balcony, Auntie Ammy holding the baby tightly against her chest. They were just in time to see the eighty-foot-high tail of an Airbus 380 disappearing behind the apartment buildings opposite. It was dazzlingly white, and so enormous that the buildings looked completely out of scale, like models.

'*Santa Theresa*,' said Auntie Ammy, but Jasmine knew that she was not praying to any Christian saint – rather to Oyá, the Santería goddess of storms and lightning and cemeteries.

As well she might, because the giant airliner came down on the intersection of West Centinela and La Tijera Boulevard with a bang as loud as every thunderclap that there had ever been, its nose tearing into the teeming mid-morning traffic, crushing automobiles and overturning trucks, its two-hundred-sixty-feet wingspan ripping up palm trees and street lights and overhead gantries.

It slid along La Tijera and buried itself underneath the concrete pillars of the San Diego Freeway before it blew up, throwing chunks of roadway into the air. A speeding bus plunged at fifty miles an hour into the gap that it had created, and buried itself at a sixty-degree angle in the fiery fuselage. It was rapidly followed by one automobile after another, like metal lemmings throwing themselves off a cliff.

Jasmine and Auntie Ammy saw debris scattered high up into the sky, including several tumbling fragments that looked like people. The noise was horrendous: the screeching of steel and aluminum, the thumping of automobile gas tanks blowing up, and the seemingly endless clattering of falling wreckage. A brown mushroom cloud of smoke rolled up over the treetops, and even through the trees. Jasmine and Auntie Ammy could see the lurid orange flames as a shallow rip tide of blazing aviation fuel spread across the streets.

'My God,' said Jasmine, and crossed herself. She didn't know what else to say. She went back into the living room and sat down on the red brocade couch, shaking with shock. 'My God, that almost landed right on top of us.'

Auntie Ammy came in, too, and sat down next to her. The baby was sitting up now, not crying, but staring at Jasmine with great solemnity.

'He knew what was going to happen,' said Jasmine. She took hold of the baby's hands and said, 'You *knew*, didn't you? You could feel it coming, even before either of *us* could.'

Auntie Ammy touched the baby's cheek. 'Maybe he got the power. Maybe he got the vision, he can see things before they arrivin'.'

'My God, all those poor people,' said Jasmine. 'Nobody could have lived through that. And it must have come down right on La Tijera. God knows how many people got killed on the ground.'

The baby leaned his head against Auntie Ammy's shoulder. His eyes were drooping as if he were tired. Through the open balcony window they could hear more explosions, and the honking and scribbling of fire-truck sirens.

'Turn on the news,' Auntie Ammy suggested.

'I'm not so sure that I want to. This is just as bad as nine-eleven.'

'Maybe – exceptin' nine-eleven was Ayrab terrorists and this is somethin' altogether different. I know it, girl. I *feels* it. It's like the air's grown thicker, like soup, and the floor is crawlin' underneath the soles of my feet. Some-

body's out to get us, you mark my words. Somebody who hates us with a *pashun.*'

Reluctantly, Jasmine switched on KCAL 9
News. It was too soon for them to have pictures
of the Airbus crash, but Kent Shocknek was
already announcing with a grave expression that
there had been a devastating air disaster in South
Central Los Angeles.

'The Airbus 380 is the world's largest airliner
and is capable of carrying over eight hundred
passengers. Since its first commercial flight in
two thousand six it has had an unblemished
safety record, but we are already receiving
reports that there are substantial numbers of
casualties, and emergency crews who are attending the scene of the crash are warning us that the
figure may eventually run into hundreds.'

'*Santa Theresa,*' Auntie Ammy repeated, and
she began to intone an invocation to the goddess
Oyá. '*Oyá yegbe iya mesa oyo orun afefe iku
lelebe oke ayaba—*'

She was interrupted, however, by the baby,
who wriggled around on her lap and pointed to
the opposite wall, where a looking-glass hung,
with an elaborate border of seashells around it.

'A *gah,*' he said, and twisted around to make
sure that Jasmine was looking at him, too.

'What now, baby boy?' asked Jasmine.

'A *gah.*' Now he was pointing with both hands,
and nodding, too, like a little dipping-duck.

Jasmine said, 'Please, God ... don't tell me
another airplane's coming down.'

She and Auntie Ammy sat quite still and
listened. They could hear the frantic screaming

94

of fire trucks and ambulances that were speeding toward the Airbus crash from all over South Los Angeles, and the flackering of police and media helicopters. Then there was a salvo of twenty or thirty explosions as more and more automobiles and trucks blew up. But they couldn't hear any jet engines approaching.

'What is it, honey cheeks?' Auntie Ammy asked the baby. 'What can you see?'

'A *gah*. A *mm-mm*.'

'I don't know,' said Auntie Ammy. 'He must be seeing somethin', but I'm darned if I can guess what it is.'

The baby kept on pointing his fingers and nodding his head and bouncing up and down in Auntie Ammy's lap, and eventually Jasmine said, 'Do you think he's pointing at the mirror?'

'The lookin'-mirror? Why should he be doing that?'

'That's your special mirror, isn't it? That's what you always told me.'

'Yes, but.'

'You always said that was your special mirror on account of the shells.'

'Well, it is. The shells, they're cowrie shells, and they are stuck around the mirror in a special pattern. Up above, they say *eyiolo osa*, which means revolutions, and trouble, and fire. Down below, they say *irosun oche*, which means that the dead are circling around to see who they can grab. My grandfather, he gave me this mirror. He was a santéro, a Santería priest. He said it would protect my family, because it would always show us what was wrong.'

95

'A *gah*,' said the baby, still pointing with both hands toward the mirror, and nodding his head even more.

'What is it, little fella? If only I could understand what you is tryin' to tell me. Or better yet, if you could suddenly start to talk.'

Auntie Ammy stood up and carried the baby over to the mirror. He stared at his reflection with great seriousness, as if he half-expected it to say something. He moved his head slowly to the left, and then to the right. 'A *gah*,' he repeated. 'A *mm-mm*.'

'Well, we know what a *gah* means,' Jasmine pointed out. 'But I have no notion at all what a *mm-mm* is.'

As the baby continued to stare at himself, however, the mirror gradually appeared to be growing darker.

'Look at this,' said Auntie Ammy. 'It looks almost like it's night-time in there.'

Jasmine came and stood beside her. She was right: the room inside the mirror was so gloomy that all she could see was their silhouettes – Auntie Ammy with her huge petal-folded headscarf and Jasmine herself with her short, brushed-up hair and her big hoop earrings.

'What's happening, Auntie Ammy?' Jasmine asked her, frowning into the darkness.

Auntie Ammy slowly shook her head from side to side. 'I don't know, Jazz, for sure. I seen things in this lookin'-mirror from time to time, shinin' bright images that are gone in a flash, like as if somebody was passin' a window. But I ain't not never seen nothin' like this here *dark* before.'

The baby pointed to the mirror again, and turned his head to look up at Jasmine. 'A *mm-mm*,' he said.

'That's a *mm-mm*?'

'A *mm-mm*. A *mm-mm*.'

Jasmine peered into the mirror again. Their silhouettes were still there, but it looked as if there were somebody else in the living room, standing between them and the balcony window.

She cried out, 'Ah!' and turned around, but the living room remained brightly sunlit and there was nobody there.

She turned back. In the mirror, she could clearly see somebody standing about ten feet behind them. A very tall man, wrapped in a dark maroon blanket, with a strange kind of headdress on his head, like the skull of a bull complete with its horns. The headdress was hung with beads and feathers, and also with what looked like birds' skulls, although the living room in the mirror was so gloomy now that it was impossible for her to tell for sure.

'Do you see him, Auntie Ammy?' she whispered.

Auntie Ammy nodded, and shifted the baby over to her left arm so that she could cross herself. 'I sees him. The baby's showin' us a vision. Whoever is making the floor tingle and the air as thick as soup, that's what he looks like.'

The figure remained unmoving, although the warm breeze that was blowing in through the balcony window made his beads and feathers stir. As Jasmine's eyes grew accustomed to the darkness, she began to make out a stern face with an aquiline nose and henna-like whorls of decoration on his cheeks. His eyes gleamed silver. In his hands he was carrying a stick tied with clumps of fur and black birds' feathers. The shaft of the stick had rows of teeth hammered into it, at least a hundred, possibly more. They looked like a mixture of human and animals' teeth.

Jasmine turned quickly around for a second time, but there was still nobody standing behind them in the *real* living room. In the mirror, however, the figure remained where he was, watching them.

'Who is that?' she whispered to Auntie Ammy. 'How come we can see him in the mirror but he's not actually here?'

'A *gah*!' said the baby, and began to jump up and down in Auntie Ammy's arms. 'A *mm-mm*!'

'Hush up, little fella,' said Auntie Ammy. 'Whoever that is, I don't think it's wise to rile him none.'

Jasmine could now see the figure quite clearly, although he seemed to be transparent, because she could see the brocade couch that was standing behind him, and the bookshelf with Auntie Ammy's books and figurines.

'Is it a *ghost*?' she asked Auntie Ammy.

'I don't think so. It's more like a *divination*, if you understand my meanin'. What we're seein' here in this lookin'-mirror is what this little fella can see inside his head, and since he can't explain it to us, or draw it, he has to show us in the glass.'

'But who is it? *What* is it?'

'It's a *mm-mm*, that's all I can tell you as of right now.'

Jasmine went right up to the mirror and cupped her hands on each side of her face to mask the bright sunlight from the real living room. The figure appeared to be looking in their direction, but she couldn't be sure. Even if he was, his eyes seemed to be focused on something very much farther away. His lips were moving, as though he were reciting some incantation to himself, repetitive and obscure, like Auntie Ammy's prayer to Oyá.

She felt spooked, in much the same way that victims of vicious crimes feel spooked when they have to identify their assailants through two-way mirrors. But she didn't feel for a moment that the figure was any kind of a threat. As Auntie Ammy had said, he was only a vision. The question was: who was he, and why had he appeared in Auntie Ammy's mirror?

As she peered at the figure more intently, she saw that small black specks were dropping from its headdress and its horns, and onto the floor. When she looked down at them she realized with horrified fascination that they were scuttling in all directions. They were beetles of some kind, like cockroaches, and as the figure continued to recite his incantation, more and more of them showered down from his headdress, and from his blanket, and scurried across the living-room floor. Within a few minutes, there were hundreds of them.

She backed away from the mirror and said to

Auntie Ammy, 'Just look! Look at those *bugs*! Aren't they *disgusting*?'

Auntie Ammy crossed herself again; but the baby pointed at the beetles in the mirror and said, *'Wah-wahs.'*

'So that's what they are,' said Auntie Ammy. 'Wah-wahs.'

'Wah-wahs,' the baby repeated.

Auntie Ammy said, 'Jazz, honey, why don't you turn the lookin'-mirror around, so that it's facin' the wall? I don't like this divination one little bit, I can tell you.'

'OK,' said Jasmine. 'Whatever you want.'

She stepped back toward the mirror, but as she did so, her shoes crunched on something on the floor. She looked down, and saw that she had trodden on a huge cockroach, which was lying on its back half-crushed with its antennae waving. Three or four more cockroaches were running across the floor close by, and within seconds more and more appeared. They were pouring out of a narrow crack between the baseboard and the floor, dark brown and shiny, and as they poured out they made a rustling, rattling noise.

'This ain't possible!' Auntie Ammy exclaimed, in horror. She lifted the baby higher in her arms and retreated across the living room, toward the balcony. 'What's in that lookin'-mirror, that may be a sign of somethin' real that's really goin' to occur, but that's not really real! That's no more real than what you might see in a crystal ball!'

Jasmine was performing a frenzied flamenco, stamping on as many cockroaches as she could.

But the insects kept gushing out of the crack beneath the baseboard, and soon they had covered almost half the living-room floor, and were swarming all over Jasmine's shoes, and up her calves.

'The lookin'-mirror!' Auntie Ammy cried out. 'Turn the lookin'-mirror to the wall!'

Crunching her way back across the room, Jasmine took hold of the mirror and tried to lift it away from the wall so that she could turn it around. It was unbelievably heavy, and she could only manage to lift it three or four inches. And inside it, she saw the figure suddenly begin to flicker, like a character in a speeded-up movie. As it flickered it began to move toward her, in quick, threatening jerks.

She was more than spooked now: she was terrified. She let go of the mirror and it banged back flat against the wall. The nail that was holding it gave way, and it dropped to the floor and smashed. Cowrie shells and triangles of broken glass were scattered all around Jasmine's feet.

'My lookin'-mirror!' wailed Auntie Ammy. 'My precious, precious lookin'-mirror!'

But Jasmine was too busy scanning the floor. The swarm of cockroaches had vanished, as if they had never existed. Even the dead ones that she had squashed beneath her feet had disappeared.

'They're gone,' she said. 'I can't believe it. They're all gone.'

'Wah-wahs,' said the baby, wriggling his fingers at her as if he were trying to imitate a cockroach.

Jasmine came over and took him out of Auntie Ammy's arms. 'No, sweet thing. No more wah-wahs. The wah-wahs have taken a powder, thank God.'

Auntie Ammy placed a cushion on the floor and knelt down on it, so that she could pick up the remains of her mirror.

'I don't know what my grandfather would say if he could see his lookin'-mirror now. He always made me promise to keep it safe, because it would keep *me* safe, that's what he said. He said it would help him to rest easy in heaven, knowin' that this lookin'-mirror was always here to protect me.'

'I'm sorry, Auntie Ammy, I truly am.'

'No, Jazz. It wasn't not your fault. Whoever it was, that divination we saw, he was copiously powerful, I can tell you, and maybe the lookin'-mirror protected me in the only way it could, which was to fall, and to break, so that there was no way for that divination to come through to us.'

'You think it really could of?'

Auntie Ammy gripped the side of the couch and eased herself back onto her feet. 'I've heard of that happenin' before, but only once or twice. Once was a woman in Mexico whose husband had been lost at sea and one night before she went to bed she saw him in her lookin'-mirror just crossin' past her bedroom door. When she woke up the next morning his wedding band was restin' on the nightstand beside her and there was wet footprints all the way across her carpet.'

Jasmine said nothing, but gently swayed the baby in her arms. The baby said, 'Wah-wahs. A mm-mm.'

'No, little fella, all the wah-wahs have gone now, and so has the mm-mm.'

'I should take him over to Children's Services,' said Jasmine. 'It doesn't look like they're going to send anybody to collect him, does it?'

'Well, I just hope he stays safe, with that gift of his. I wouldn't like to think of nothing unspeakable comin' through no lookin'-mirror and inflictin' no harm on him.'

'Auntie Ammy, we can't possibly keep him.'

'I don't know. Would he be such a burden? And maybe I could learn to tell his ass from his other end.'

'I don't believe you sometimes. I really don't. Only twenty minutes ago you couldn't wait to get rid of him.'

'Twenty minutes ago I still had a mirror to protect me. Now all I got is this child.'

The baby lifted up his arm again, and pointed to the ceiling.

'A gah.'

'You see what I mean?' Auntie Ammy demanded. 'The whole world is goin' to fall apart and this child is the only one who can save us.'

She had barely finished speaking when they heard a thunderous rumble from the northeast. It sounded like an airliner approaching, decelerating wildly as it came toward them. The rumble was interspersed with high-pitched engine-screams as the pilot tried to reduce his speed, and to bring his airplane in line with the runways at LAX.

'Oh, Jesus,' said Jasmine. 'We need to get out of here.'

But it was too late. They heard the airliner descending less than a mile to the south of them, over Rogers Park, and then there was a devastating explosion, followed by a complicated series of crackles, like a firework display. Only a few seconds later, another airliner came down over the Hollywood Park Race Track, and then another, over Culver City. It sounded as if Satan were banging all the doors of hell, one after the other.

'Oh, my God,' said Auntie Ammy. 'It's the end of the world.'

They went back out onto the balcony, and saw three black plumes of smoke rising up high into the sky. The baby pointed to each of them, and looked up into Jasmine's eyes, and said, 'A *gah*! A *mm-mm*!'

'Yes, sweetheart,' said Jasmine. 'You're absolutely right. A gah. A mm-mm.'

TEN

Portland, Oregon

I knew nothing about those airliners dropping out of the sky until we were making our approach to Portland International and I looked out of the window and saw that the afternoon sun was intermittently blotted out by clouds of brown smoke.

'Looks like they're having some serious cookouts here,' I said to Amelia, who was engrossed in her book, *Shengong Soul Projection*.

'What?' she said, taking off her half-glasses. I loved her in those glasses. She looked academic and sensual, both at the same time. She had short Titian hair and a sharp, sculptured face, like a Pre-Raphaelite princess. But she had a really great figure and I would have bet money that underneath that gray woolen skirt she was wearing only a tiny black-lace thong. Actually that was only my fevered imagination working over-time, but we fortune tellers have a license to use our fevered imaginations not only for fun and profit, but for our own amusement, too.

She leaned forward and peered out of the window. 'My *God*, Harry. It looks like half the airport's on fire.'

I craned my neck so that I could see around her

shoulder. She was right. The northeastern side of PDX was crawling with flames, and thick gray smoke was pouring across the Columbia River, almost blotting out Lemon Island and Government Island and the Glenn Jackson Bridge, which carries Route 205 over to Washington State.

As we circled slowly around the airport, I could see that the flames were forming the cruciform outline of a burning airliner. Its tail fin was still intact, with its US Airways stars-and-stripes still emblazoned on it, but the fuselage had been gutted, and I could even see the ash-gray rows of incinerated seats.

'Holy Veronica,' I said. But everyone else in the business-class cabin was remarkably hushed, except for one man who began to warble a prayer in Yiddish. *'Y'hi ratzon milfanekha A-donai E-loheinu velohei avoteinu...'*

Amelia leaned close to me and said, 'You hear that? He's praying for a safe journey.'

'How do you know that?'

'I was engaged to a Jewish guy once. That was before MacArthur. Well, the guy before the guy before MacArthur.'

'You never told me.'

'We broke up after three months. His mother hated me. She called me a *mechascheife*. A witch. I predicted his father would have a heart attack, and he did.'

It was then that the captain came on the PA. 'Ladies and gentlemen, you can see for yourselves that there has been a serious incident here at Portland International Airport. I ask you all to

106

assist me and my crew by remaining calm.

'I have been in contact with the tower and requested an alternative landing destination, but they have informed me that there have been similar incidents at a number of other cities, and there are no suitable airfields within our range that can take us. Because of this our safest course of action is to make an immediate landing here, on runway 28R.

'I have not been given any further details about the reported incidents at other airfields, but I will pass on any further information that I receive from the tower just as soon as I get it.

'I realize that you will be very anxious for news but I must ask you not to switch on your cellphones until we have safely landed and come to a complete stop at the terminal building.'

Now, suddenly, there was a bustle and a flurry as everybody switched on their cellphones and started to make calls.

'Joanne!' gabbled the old guy just across the aisle from me. 'I have to make this quick ... but there's been a crash at Portland Airport and the pilot's telling us there's been more crashes at other airports, too.

He paused, and nodded, and then he looked across the aisle at me and said, 'It's my daughter. She says that it's been on the news for the past half-hour. Over twenty planes have come down, all across the country. Miami, Boston, Kansas City, Missouri. Hundreds of people killed. Maybe *thousands*!'

Amelia took hold of my hand and squeezed it tight. She didn't say anything but I could guess

107

what she was thinking.

The man in front of me stood up. He was wearing a red plaid coat and he had a greasy black comb-over and two protuberant front teeth like a beaver. 'Ay-rabs!' he announced. 'Those rag-heads did it again! What happened to all that tightened-up security they were supposed to give us?'

A flight attendant came down the aisle, asking people to switch off their cellphones. A middle-aged woman caught hold of her sleeve and begged her, 'Please ... do you have any news of other flights? My daughter and her family are flying to Cincinnati today.'

'I'm sorry,' said the flight attendant. 'All they told us was "similar incidents." Now, please, *sir*! The captain requires that everybody turns off their cells.'

'Do they know *how* the planes came down?' asked Beaver Teeth. 'Was it hijackers?'

'I'm sorry. I don't have any more details. Now will you please sit down and buckle up. We'll be making our approach in a very few minutes.'

'Ay-rabs!' Beaver Teeth repeated. 'Al-Qa-fricking-eda! We should've kicked the whole goddamn lot of them out of the country right after nine-eleven!'

Now the aircraft was making a tight turn over the river and reflected sunlight revolved across the cabin ceiling. The engines were giving out a loud descending scream and the air-conditioning was hissing. Amelia kept on tightly holding my hand but I wasn't entirely certain which one of us was reassuring the other.

'We're going to be OK, Harry,' she told me. 'I promise you.'

Since she was a genuine clairvoyant, as opposed to a lucky blusterer like me, I was almost inclined to take her word for it. All the same, I really disliked the feeling that I might die within the next five minutes. *Horribly*, too, like being disemboweled by a jagged segment of torn-open fuselage, or mushed into human salsa against the seat in front of me, or cremated alive by blazing aviation fuel, grinning and screaming with agonized laughter like the Crypt Keeper.

Not only that, there wasn't enough time remaining to have even the most perfunctory sex with Amelia, or a last shot of Jack Daniel's, or to order a hand-held electric fan out of the in-flight catalog.

We came down so fast that we almost burst out of our seat belts, and hit the runway with a bounce that jolted the breath out of us. Then the engines roared into reverse, and the pilot jammed the brakes on so hard that the airplane dipped and bucked like a giant canoe plunging down the rapids. Almost immediately, he swerved off the runway to the right, and sped us away from the burning carnage of the US Airways flight, but we still passed through dense curtains of drifting smoke, and a strong smell of burning rubber blew in through the air vents.

The other passengers clapped and whooped and whistled, and some of them stamped their feet, but Amelia and I did nothing but look into each other's eyes and our eyes said *phew*. I think we both realized then that we were not yet ready for the spirit world. There was still too much for us to do in solid real-people world. Maybe there was even a chance that she and I might consummate a love that both of us had always acknowledged, but never openly admitted. Or maybe I was just being slushy. I admit that I can be, especially when I watch repeats of *The Way We Were*.

As we taxied toward the terminal buildings, the Jewish guy was giving thanks to God for his safe arrival, as well he might, and Beaver Teeth was already talking on his cell to his brother in Cedar Rapids. 'How many? Thirty-four? Christ Almighty, I don't believe it! And what? Auto wrecks? *How* many? I don't believe what I'm hearing, Malcolm. It's Armageddon. That's what it is. Arma-fricking-geddon.'

Inside the terminal it was chaos, with crowds of weeping relatives and TV crews and firefighters and police. There must have been over a hundred paramedics there, too, but all they were doing was standing around the baggage carousels looking glum, because there was nobody left alive for them to tend to. I overheard one of the TV reporters saying that flight 4/90 from Chicago had nosedived straight into the end of the runway and exploded on impact. There had been one hundred seven passengers and crew on board, and no survivors.

There was no hope of collecting our bags, so Amelia and I went straight through the terminal and managed to hail ourselves a cab. The cab driver was a gloomy type with a big nose and a gray buzz cut who relentlessly chewed gum all the way. As we left the airport and headed south toward the city, I turned around and looked back at the smoke rising from the end of the runway.

'You know what I think?' said the cab driver. 'I think we should retaliate, right now, because this ain't going to stop.'

'Retaliate?' I asked him. 'Against who, exactly?'

The cab driver flapped one hand. 'The what's-their-goddamn-names. The terrorists. All of them. We should nuke the Middle East and show them they can't get away with it.'

'OK. Any particular part of the Middle East, or all of it?'

'Wipe 'em out, that's what I say. They've never been nothing but trouble, have they? Palestinians, Eye-ranians. Goddamned Eye-raqis.' He sniffed, and added, 'Greeks.'

As we drove through the center of Portland, he turned up his radio so that we could listen to the continuing news bulletins from all over the country. It was just past five in the afternoon, and since one o'clock in the morning, thirty-seven airliners had crashed, most of them at airports, but some of them into suburbs or forests or mountains. Early estimates suggested that nearly four thousand five hundred people had been killed, and thousands more seriously injured.

All commercial and private flights had now been grounded, and John Rostoff, the Secretary for Homeland Security, had warned that they would not be resumed until his department understood how so many airliners could have been being brought down, and who was responsible for it.

At the same time, there had been thousands of serious traffic pile-ups all across the country. Drivers had collided with oncoming traffic, or driven straight across busy intersections without stopping, or simply run off the road.

There had been countless other accidents, too, such as people stepping off the sidewalk in front of speeding cars, or falling down stairs or escalators, or walking into swimming pools or lakes.

The cab driver turned the radio down. 'You know what I think?'

'No, we don't,' said Amelia. 'But I'm sure you're going to tell us.'

'They've put something in the water, that's what I think. Like maybe LSD or something like that.'

'Who have?'

'The terrorists. The goddamned Eye-ranians.'

'Well, you could be right,' Amelia told him. 'But it could be somebody who hates us even more than the goddamned Eye-ranians.'

'You mean like the Canucks?'

We turned at last into the aspen-lined campus of the Oregon Health and Science University, and stopped outside the Casey Eye Institute: a dazzling white building, six stories high, with hundreds of shining windows: more like a luxury cruise-liner than a clinic. As I paid him, the cab driver said, 'You know what I think? I think this is the end of America as we know it. You mark my words.'

Amelia and I took the elevator up to level four, where her sister Lizzie and her family were being treated. The floor of the reception area was made entirely of toughened glass, and it glowed phosphorescent blue in the early afternoon sunlight, so that it looked as if we were walking across the set of a science-fiction movie.

On a normal day this would have been a cool haven of clinical calm. But today, half a dozen doctors and nurses were gathered around the nurses' station, grimly watching the TV news. The volume was muted, but a streamer across the bottom of the screen was telling the whole apocalyptic story. Thirty-nine airliners were now confirmed as having crashed. What was even more alarming, two Super Hornets had collided over the ocean off San Diego, with the loss of all four crew. If our military planes were falling out of the sky, too, then it was pretty obvious that we were in deep and serious doo-doo.

Amelia and I joined the doctors and nurses, and we watched as the news grew more apocalyptic by the minute. Remember that terrible pit-of-the-stomach feeling we all had, as we watched the World Trade Centre towers coming down? We had that same feeling right then, only worse.

John Rostoff, the Secretary for Homeland Security, appeared on the screen, and a tall crimson-faced doctor standing next to me told the nurse, 'Turn up the sound, will you, Janet?'

Rostoff was saying '—everything we possibly can to identify the cause of all these tragic accidents.'

He squinted at the teleprompter in front of him, and then he said. 'From the flight recordings that we have so far managed to retrieve, it seems highly likely that the pilots of the ill-fated airliners were affected by sudden and totally unexpected attacks of one hundred percent blindness. And eyewitness accounts of some of the worst vehicular accidents across the country seem to suggest that drivers, too, have suffered sudden loss of sight, with disastrous consequences.

'We have no idea yet whether this blindness was caused by some naturally-occurring phenomenon, such as trachoma, or whether it could be the result of terrorist activity. But both victims and survivors are being examined by experts from the Center for Disease Control as a matter of extreme urgency.'

'It's an epidemic, in my opinion,' said the crimson-faced doctor, turning around and talking to me as if I was some kind of well-known expert on eye diseases. 'It could be a virulent form of CMV. That's spread by nothing more than human contact.'

'Could be some contaminated food product,' suggested a Korean doctor. 'A particular brand of soda, maybe, tainted with methanol. That happened in Louisiana a few years ago. Thirty, maybe forty people went blind before they found out what the cause was.'

A coppery-headed nurse came over to greet us. In a hushed voice, she said, 'Mrs. Carlsson?'

'That's me.'

'Your sister has been *so* excited about your coming, Mrs. Carlsson. She's been talking about nothing else all morning.'

'Does she know about any of *this*?' I asked her, nodding toward the TV.

The nurse said, 'Lord, no. We haven't told any of our acute-cure patients yet. We think they have enough stress to deal with, coping with their blindness.' She paused, and then she said, 'It's just terrible, isn't it? A dear friend of mine was supposed to be flying to Miami today and I still haven't heard from her.'

She led us along the corridor, her white sneakers squeaking on the shiny polished floor.

Lizzie was sitting up in bed with a pale green mask over her eyes. She was three or four years younger than Amelia, and a little plumper, with freckles across the bridge of her nose, but just as pretty. When Amelia came into the room and said, 'Lizzie?' she lifted both arms and let out a painful sob. Amelia embraced her, and shushed her, and then she sat down on the side of her bed, and held her hands.

'How's Kevin? And Shauna? And David?'

'They're just the same as me. Totally blind, and the doctors don't know why.'

'How are they coping?'

'Kevin and David seem to have accepted it, but poor Shauna can't stop crying.'

'I brought Harry with me,' said Amelia.

'*Harry*? Harry Erskine? My God, I haven't seen Harry for years.' She tried to smile, and said, wryly, 'Not that I can see him now.'

'Hi, Lizzie,' I told her. 'I'm real sorry about

115

what's happened to you guys.'

Lizzie held out one of her hands in my direction. 'It's so good of you to come, Harry. It's been like a nightmare.'

I took hold of her hand and kissed her on both cheeks. 'Let's hope this is only temporary, huh? What have the doctors told you?'

'Nothing, so far, except that the lenses in our eyes have all misted over, and they don't know why.'

'They don't have any idea at all?'

Lizzie shook her head. 'At first they thought it might have been caused by some rare kind of infection that we caught in the woods. But they've done dozens of tests and there's nothing else wrong with us, except that we're blind.'

'Maybe it's traumatic,' Amelia suggested. 'You know, like people who have a terrible shock and find that they can't speak for a while.'

'We didn't suffer any trauma,' said Lizzie. 'We were just cycling up the side of the canyon and there he was, standing by the side of the road.'

She hesitated, as if she had forgotten what she was going to say. Amelia and I frowned at each other, and Amelia had just started to say, 'What did he look like?' when Lizzie interrupted her. Her voice sounded oddly flat and expressionless, as if another woman were reading her words from a cue-card. 'Of course, we deserved it.'

'You told me that before, on the phone,' said Amelia. 'What do you mean, you *deserved* it?'

Underneath her mask, Lizzie frowned. 'I don't understand you,' she said, and this time she

116

sounded like her normal self.

'You just said "we deserved it" and I wanted to know *what* you deserved.'

'I didn't say that.'

'Lizzie, you said it quite clearly. Harry heard you, didn't you, Harry?'

'He was standing by the side of the road,' said Lizzie. 'He was standing by the side of the road and there were two reflections, one on each side.'

I hunkered down close beside the bed. '"Reflections"?' I asked her. 'What do you mean by "reflections"?'

She made a slow up-and-down motion with her hand, as if she were cleaning a pane of glass. 'They were like two long mirrors, standing beside him. They were like men but they were like reflections of men.' Again, that subtle change in tone. 'We deserved it, though. We deserved to go blind. We spread the disease, after all.'

'Lizzie, what did he look like?'

'He looked like The One Who Went And Came Back. He looked like Hin-mut-too-yah-lat-kekht. Tall, very tall, with a face like a stone.'

'He looked like *who*?'

'Hin-mut-too-yah-lat-kekht. Thunder Rolling In The Mountains.'

'I see,' I said, although I didn't have the faintest idea what she was talking about. 'And this Hin-mut-too-whatever, he spoke to you?'

'He said that we deserved to go blind and die. He said that we spread the disease and the bones of his fathers were singing to him to show us no mercy.'

117

'Listen to me, Lizzie,' said Amelia. 'Can you remember what happened then? After he spoke to you, what did he do?'

Lizzie began to move her head from side to side, very emphatically. 'We are all going to go blind and die. All of us. We deserve it. We *deserve* to be punished.'

'Lizzie,' I said, 'Did he tell you his name?'

'He looked like Hin-mut-too-yah-lat-kekht. But he was not really Hin-mut-too-yah-lat-kekht. He was The One Who Went And Came Back.'

I glanced meaningfully at Amelia and Amelia glanced meaningfully at me. We both knew the various names of The One Who Went And Came Back. But who had told Lizzie about him? And who the two-toned tonkert was Hin-mut-too-yah-lat-kekht?

Lizzie suddenly turned toward me and announced, 'He knows who you are. He knows that you have come to see me. He says that – this time – you will be ground into dust. And he says that the wind will carry your dust far away from this land so that you will never be remembered here and there will be no trace of you to taint the ground in which the bones of his fathers are buried.'

'Lizzie,' I urged her, 'listen to me, Lizzie. I need you to tell me his name. It's important.'

'I cannot speak his name. He was driven out of this world, but he has returned. This time, he has many faces and many names.'

I grasped her hand and held it tight. She was very cold – so cold that she was shaking. 'Was

118

his name Misquamacus?' I asked her.

'Harry, *no* – !' said Amelia.

But it was too late. Lizzie's back stiffened. Her fingers splayed out and her entire body went into spasm. She thumped her head back onto the pillows and started to scream. It was like no scream that I had ever heard before. It was half scream and half roar, terrifying, and it went on and on without her taking a breath.

The door burst open and two nurses came hurrying in, followed closely by a Chinese intern.

'What happened?' one of the nurses asked us, while the other one bent over Lizzie and pressed her hand over her forehead, trying to calm her down.

'I don't know,' I told her. 'She just suddenly lost it. I really don't know.'

What else could I say? That I had spoken the name of the most powerful Indian wonder-worker who had ever walked the North American continent? He Whose Face Appeared In The Sky? He Who Brings The Terror Of Eternal Darkness? Misquamacus? The One Who Went And Came Back?

Lizzie kept screaming. Her voice was so piercing and harsh that we could hardly hear each other. Without any further hesitation the intern unlocked the drugs cabinet on the wall, took out a small bottle, and quickly filled a hypodermic needle. Then he walked around the bed, lifted up Lizzie's left arm, and injected her.

'Just a little sedative,' he told us. 'Something to settle her down.'

We waited, but over half a minute went by and Lizzie continued to scream, her mouth stretched wide open and every muscle in her body locked tight.

The intern kept his hands cupped over his ears. 'I don't understand ... she should have calmed down by now.' He paused. 'To be totally frank with you, she should be unconscious. That dose would have dropped a horse.'

One of the nurses looked up and said, 'She's hyperventilating, but I don't know how. She's screaming but she's not breathing in.'

The intern took another bottle of tranquilizer out of the medicine cabinet. Amelia said, 'My God, how much are you going to give her?'

'Only a very small dose,' the intern assured her. He filled up his hypodermic again, but before he could approach the bed, Lizzie abruptly stopped screaming, and lay panting as if she had just run a marathon.

'That's better, Lizzie,' said one of the nurses, soothingly, stroking her arm. 'Try to relax. Try to think warm, peaceful thoughts. Think about walking along the seashore, in summer. Think about lying in the long grass, watching the clouds roll by.'

Lizzie stiffened again, opening and closing her mouth as if she wanted to say something but had lost the power of speech, as well as her sight.

'Come on, Lizzie, relax. Think of that lovely windy day.'

Lizzie made a guttural sound, deep in her throat.

'She's not choking, is she?' asked Amelia.

But Lizzie said, '*Misquamacus*.'

'What?' asked the nurse, in bewilderment.

'*Misquamacus*,' Lizzie repeated.

The nurse turned to Amelia and said, 'Do you have any idea what she's saying? It sounds like "missed the markers."'

Lizzie said, 'We deserved it. We *all* deserve it.'

She opened her mouth wide and I thought that she was going to start screaming again, but then she closed it again and gradually she began to relax. She shuddered and jerked a few times, but then she lay still, and even though I couldn't see her eyes she seemed to be sleeping. The nurses checked her pulse and her blood pressure and took her temperature.

'How is she?' asked Amelia.

The nurse gave her a reassuring smile. 'Her heart rate's nearly a hundred, and her BP's a little high, but that's no more than you'd expect after a paroxysm like that.'

The intern was still shaking his head. 'I never saw a patient fail to react to ethchlorvynol before. *Never.* Normally, that dose is enough to put a patient to sleep on the count of three.'

I didn't say anything, and neither did Amelia. But now we knew for certain who we were up against, and we knew what we had to do next, and both of us were dreading it.

Amelia bent over and kissed Lizzie. 'God protect you, my darling.'

The nurse said, 'Don't worry. Fits like this always *look* scary, but they're usually harmless. It was probably nothing more than delayed shock. It can come out anything up to five or six days later. Sometimes it doesn't come out for weeks.'

We left the room, closing the door behind us, and walked along the corridor to see Kevin.

'So whose voice was that she was speaking in?' I asked Amelia. 'It certainly wasn't *hers*. What would Lizzie know about Hin-mut-who-ever? Or even Misquamacus for that matter? You've never told her about Misquamacus, have you?'

'Of course not,' said Amelia. 'I think it was a message. You know, like post-hypnotic sugges-tion. As soon as she started to talk about what happened to her, out it came.'

'OK, but who was the message for?'

'*Us*, Harry. You and me. Why do you think Misquamacus chose Lizzie to strike blind, of all people? She's my sister. She was *bait*.'

ELEVEN

'We're all going to get our sight back,' said Kevin. 'I'm convinced of it. I don't know what happened to us out there, but nobody goes blind for no reason at all, do they? Not *permanently* blind. Not for ever.'

He was a big, overweight man, with wide shoulders and no neck, more like a college foot-ball coach than the manager of a sportswear store, which he actually was, but because his eyes were covered with a pale green mask, like Lizzie's, he looked childlike and vulnerable. He was sitting in a high-backed hospital armchair, with a can of Diet Coke and a half-eaten cheese sandwich beside him. On the wall behind him hung an oil painting of an empty room, by somebody called Vilhelm Hammershøi. I thought it was a pretty appropriate picture for a clinic in which nobody could see anybody.

'Kevin – can you describe what happened?' I asked him. 'Lizzie says you met some guy with two long mirrors beside him. We didn't exactly understand what she meant.'

Kevin bent forward in his chair, and wedged his stubby fingers together. 'I couldn't tell you for sure. It all happened so fast. We were cycling up the west side of the canyon. It was pretty steep, and Lizzie was maybe twenty or thirty yards ahead of me because she's always been the stronger cyclist, and I was riding drag to keep the kids company. Then suddenly this guy stepped out from the side of the track. I don't exactly know where he came from. He just kind of *materialized*.'

'What did he look like?'

'He was tall – taller than me. Maybe six-one, six-two. He had on this black hat, with a wide brim, so that his face was in shadow. He was wearing a black suit and a big silver medallion and he was carrying some kind of a walking cane. It had dangly things hanging off of it, maybe feathers or fur, I didn't really see exactly what they were.'

'And how about the mirrors? Did you see

those?'

'Well, they didn't exactly look like mirrors to me. They were more like a mirage, I guess. I was sure I could see two other guys, one standing on either side of him, but when I looked directly at them, there was nobody there. You know you get that thing sometimes when you're tired, and you think you see a black cat out of the corner of your eye, but you turn around, and it's not there at all? They were just like that.'

'What did they look like to you?'

Kevin thought for a while, his head slightly raised and cocked to the right, as if he were trying to visualize the shadows in his mind.

'They both had these very white faces. Chalk-white, I can remember that. But sometimes they looked tall and sometimes they looked quite small, as if they were quite a distance away from us. I know this sounds crazy, but I can remember thinking that they looked like *puppets*, rather than real men.'

'What happened then, Kevin?' asked Amelia.

'Lizzie cycled up to this guy in the black hat and the black suit and stopped and I could see that she was talking to him, although me and the kids were still a little ways from catching up, and what with the wind blowing I couldn't clearly hear what she was saying to him at first. I thought that maybe he was out walking and he'd gotten himself lost and he was asking her the best way to go.

'Then I got closer and he started to jab his walking cane at her, and shout. It was like, "I blame all of you! Your forefathers and you and

124

your children and your children's children!"
Naturally I didn't like the sound of this at all, so
I cycled up beside Lizzie and said, like, "What
the hell's going on here, man? Why are you
yelling at my wife?"

'But he didn't answer me. Didn't say a word.
He just stared at me and lifted up both of his
arms as if he was going to try flying. He said
something which I didn't understand and then I
saw this dazzling blue light. I mean it was like
staring directly into a halogen headlamp from
about two feet away. I kind of staggered back,
because I couldn't see nothing at all, and I stumbled over Shauna who was standing right next to
me and we both fell over. I could hear Lizzie and
David fall over, too.

'That was it. I didn't hear the guy walk away.
Lizzie was sobbing and the kids were both crying and I feel like crying myself. But I wanted to
make sure that we stayed where we were
because there was a five-hundred-foot drop on
the right-hand side of us.'

'*Puppets*,' Amelia repeated.

Kevin shrugged. 'Like I say, I couldn't see
them straight-on. Only, like, *sideways*. But there
was something about the way they walked, like
a funny little dance, and the way they tilted their
heads. Don't ask me. They just put me in mind
of puppets, that's all.'

I stood up and gripped his shoulder. 'Thanks,
Kevin. Take care of yourself. OK if we talk to
the kids? We'll try not to upset them.'

'Sure, but be gentle with Shauna, won't you?'

Amelia gave Kevin a kiss and then we walked

along the corridor to the children's rooms. David was asleep, lying on his back with his mouth open, breathing in that clogged-up way that kids do, so we left him.

Shauna was awake, but she was bundled up in bed clutching a brown stuffed rabbit and looking sorry for herself.

'Shauna?' said Amelia. 'How are you feeling, darling?'

'*Sad*,' said Shauna, and she started to cry. Amelia took her in her arms and hugged her. Even with her green mask on, I could see that she was a cute little girl, with a snubby little nose and Titian hair like Amelia's, but curly. We couldn't see her eyes, of course, but tears kept sliding out from underneath her mask, and she spoke almost entirely in painful sobs.

'Mommy and Daddy are going to buy me a *puppy* for my birthday,' Shauna wept. 'Now I'll never be able to see what it looks like.'

'Don't you give up hope, darling,' said Amelia. 'Harry and me, we know some pretty clever tricks, don't we, Harry?'

'Tricks?' I said, trying to sound cheerful. 'We know more tricks than a five-legged pony.'

'*Harry*,' said Amelia. I loved it when she scolded me.

I went across and tugged a couple of Kleenex out of the box on Shauna's nightstand, and I carefully dabbed the tears away from her cheeks.

'A very bad thing has happened to you, sweetheart,' I told her. 'It was horrible and it wasn't fair. But your Aunt Amelia and me, we think we're beginning to understand what it was. I just

126

need to ask you if you can remember anything at all about the man in the black hat, or the two people who were with him. Anything. It doesn't matter if you think it's not important, because it might be, and it might help us to bring your sight back.'

Shauna shivered, as if a goose had walked over her grave. 'I didn't really see him. He was shouting at Mommy about something.'

'Did you see his face?'

'Unh-huh. Not really. But he was wearing this kind of medal thing. I noticed it because the sun was shining on it. It was silver, and it was like all snakes, knotted up together.'

I glanced at Amelia again. The sunlight was illuminating her face and her hair, making her look even more Pre-Raphaelite than usual: fey and pale, with plum-colored circles under her eyes. Both of us were pretty much bushed.

I turned back to Shauna. 'How about the two people on either side of him? Your mommy said they looked like mirrors. Your daddy thought they looked like puppets.'

Shauna lowered her head and twisted her fingers together, the way kids do when they're trying to explain something they don't really understand.

'I know there was *somebody* there because I kind of saw them. But when I looked at them they were gone.'

'OK, that's OK. But when you kind of saw them, what did they kind of look like?'

'They looked like boxes.'

'They looked like *boxes*?'

Shauna nodded. 'They looked like boxes with arms and legs and white faces on top.'

'I see. What color were they? Do you remember?'

'I don't know. Black or maybe they were dark red.'

'Black or dark red boxes with white faces on top?'

Shauna nodded again. 'I had a bad dream about them last night,' she said, and the tears started to flow again. 'They were looking in my window and I was frightened.'

'Hey, come on – I get bad dreams, too, about all kinds of things, like losing my shorts when I'm swimming in the ocean, or finding great big hairy tarantulas swimming in my soup. Mostly I have bad dreams about the IRS. But dreams are only dreams, sweetheart. They're not real and you shouldn't let them scare you.'

'OK.'

'If you dream about those boxes looking into your window again, clap your hands and shout out, "Scrammo boxerooni!" You got it? It works every time.'

We left Shauna and went back to say goodbye to Kevin, and also to check on Lizzie.

Amelia said, '"*Scrammo boxerooni*"?'

'That's right. If you're having nightmares about boxes, it never fails.'

'What about the IRS?'

'Pretty much the same thing. Clap your hands and shout out, "Scrammo taxerooni!"'

Amelia had booked us a junior suite at the Inn at

Northrup Station on NW 23rd, the so-called 'Trendy-third' district of Portland. She had booked it mainly because it had two separate queen-sized beds (for the sake of propriety, her being married to Bertie and all) and because it wasn't too pricey. But she had also booked it because a wacky friend of hers in the West Village had told her that the interior decor was 'totally mind-bending.'

She wasn't kidding. It was like stepping into a Bugs Bunny cartoon from the mid-1960s. The walls and the drapes were a jazzy melange of reds, oranges, purples, yellows, and pinks, and the furniture was what they used to call 'contemporary' when women wore beehives and Cadillacs still had residual fins. The front of the reception desk was quilted in purple and there were dangly free-form mobiles hanging from the ceiling.

Zany as it was, the welcome they gave us at the Inn was distinctly snooty. A supercilious young man who looked like an Art Garfunkel impersonator told us that Amelia's credit card would be charged extra if our suite smelled even faintly of smoke after we had left.

'Damn,' I told Amelia. 'That puts paid to the human sacrifice.'

To be fair, our room was vast and airy and it had a cast-iron balcony overlooking Northrup Avenue. If we had been so minded, we could have sat outside and smoked Havana cigars and watched the trolley cars go by and thrown pimento-stuffed olives at the passing pedestrians.

But Amelia and I didn't have time for relaxing. I went into the kitchen and opened up a bottle of Geyser Peak Shiraz, but that was only to give us some alcoholic bravado.

'You're sure you want to do this?' Amelia asked me.

I handed her a large glassful of pungent red wine. 'The way I see it, we don't have a choice, do we? If we try to tell their doctors the *real* reason why Kevin and Lizzie lost their sight, they just won't believe us. You can just imagine it, can't you? "It's not actually a medical problem, you guys. They've been blinded by a Native American medicine man. Not only that – a Native American medicine man who kicked the bucket in sixteen-fifty-something and should have stayed dead, but refused to."'

Amelia thought for a while, and then she said, 'The more I think of it, the more I'm convinced that Misquamacus *chose* Kevin and Lizzie.' She took off her short black linen coat and hung it over the back of the chair. 'I'm sure he chose them on purpose, to bring *us* here. Like I say, they were bait.'

'But why? You and me, we never caused him nothing but the utmost grief.'

'No, think about it, Harry. He brought us here because he knows exactly what we're going to do next.'

'You mean he knows we're planning to hold a seance? He knows we're going to put a call through to the Happy Hunting Ground, and try to get in touch with Singing Rock?'

Amelia nodded. 'I think he not only knows, he

wants us to.'

'But why? Singing Rock gave him even more grief than we did. Without Singing Rock, you and me would have been toast the first time he reappeared. And a few thousand other palefaces would have been, too. Maybe *millions*.'

'Exactly,' said Amelia. 'I think he wants to punish Singing Rock for saving us. He also wants to make sure that we don't get any help from Singing Rock to thwart him again.'

'*Thwart*. That's a great word, isn't it? I thwart I thwar a puddy-tat.'

Amelia didn't rise to that. When she was being serious, she was *deeply* serious, and believe me, she was never so serious as when she was talking about the spirit world.

'Think about it,' she said. 'Any spirits who want to make a physical reappearance in the world of the living have to be able to produce some kind of ectoplasm.'

'You mean that white stuff that mediums used to pull out of their sleeves, and pretend it was the ghost of Uncle Casper?'

'Well, that was fake. A few yards of chiffon, usually. There was one famous medium who used to hide it up inside her, and drag it out from under her dress whenever she wanted to produce a ghost. But real spirits have to generate *some* material substance, no matter how filmy and transparent it is, otherwise they simply wouldn't be visible. They wouldn't reflect the light, the way that phantoms do, and they wouldn't be able to move things around, like poltergeists.'

I went back into the kitchen to find a mammoth-sized bag of Combos Cheese Pretzels. 'OK,' I agreed, tearing the bag open and spilling pretzels all over the kitchen counter. 'But when you and me chased Misquamacus off the last time, we took away his ectoplasm, didn't we? I guess we de-ectoplasmacized him, if there is such a word.'

'Yes, we did. All that was left of him was his spirit – his memories, and his emotions, and whatever it is that makes one person different from every other. There was no *him* left, no possibility of self-reincarnation. No substance. Only the idea of Misquamacus.'

'So how come he's managed to show up now? And how did he make Lizzie and Kevin and the kids go blind?'

'I don't know, and that's why we have to call on Singing Rock.'

'But if that's precisely what Misquamacus *wants* us to do...?'

'I'm guessing, of course, but he can't touch Singing Rock in the spirit world. The spirit world is ruled by different natural laws than the real world – especially the world of Native American spirits. After death no Native American spirit can ever harm another, even if they were the bitterest of enemies when they were alive.'

'You mean that after I've snuffed it, I won't be able to sit on Jimmy Shapiro's head for stealing my Jim Bibby card?'

'If you want to put it like that, yes.'

Slowly, I began to understand what Amelia was trying to explain to me. '*I* get it. If he's found a way of materializing himself – and it looks like he has – and we call on Singing Rock, and Singing Rock materializes, too – then it's a whole different kettle of scrod. They'll both have some kind of physical substance – so Misquamacus *can* get his revenge on Singing Rock. Again.'

'Not only on Singing Rock. You and me, too, if we don't have Singing Rock to protect us any longer.'

'So,' I asked her. 'Are we going to do this, or not?'

On the opposite side of the room, the huge plasma television was showing news footage of a massive traffic accident on the LI Expressway. It looked as if hundreds of vehicles were involved – buses, trucks, automobiles, SUVs, even ambulances – and several of them were burning.

'It's a war, isn't it?' said Amelia. 'What choice do we have?'

TWELVE

We closed and locked the balcony windows and drew the drapes, so that the room was bathed in gloomy greenish light, like the inside of a tropical aquarium. I took off the bracelet that Singing Rock had given me. It was made up of twenty-one polished black stones from the bed of the Okabojo River in South Dakota, and he had told me that when he died his spirit would be divided up between each of the twenty-one stones, and that I would be carrying him around my wrist for the rest of my life.

I don't really know why a Native American medicine man should have chosen a white fortune teller of dubious repute to safeguard his spirit, but I guess in our battles against Misqua-macus we had formed one of those inexplicable brotherhoods that don't have anything to do with race, or heritage, or even affection. I never thought that Singing Rock liked me very much, particularly when I was bee-essing elderly ladies with titillating predictions about their up-and-coming love lives. Singing Rock believed in absolute truth. He used to say that absolute truth was the most powerful weapon he possessed against the demons of the spirit world. 'One lie always leads to another lie, and spins a web, and up this web runs Inktomi the spider-demon, who brings darkness and confusion and paralyzes the soul of anyone he bites.'

He also bitterly resented us palefaces for every gratuitous act of slaughter that we had com-mitted – especially the massacre at Whitestone Hill, in South Dakota, in the summer of 1863, in which his great-great-grandmother had been killed, along with two hundred other men, women, and children. Not our noblest moment, among a whole lot of other not-so-noble mo-ments, like Conestoga and Gnadenhutten and Sand Creek and Wounded Knee. You should Google those places, check out what we did there, and weep.

Apart from being scrupulously truthful, however, Singing Rock was a realist. He knew that the days of magic and buffalo were gone for ever, and that it was futile to try to bring them back. He didn't believe in revenge, either. He was confident that Gitche Manitou the Great Spirit would punish those who had killed out of greed, or prejudice, or cruelty, and their punishment would be far more terrible than anything that a vengeful human could ever think of, like seeing their children strangled in front of their eyes – not just for two or three horrifying minutes, but for ever.

Amelia placed a thick red candle in the center of the dining table, and arranged my bracelet around it. Then she pointed to the ceiling and said, 'The smoke alarm.'

'What?'

'You should take out the battery. It's going to get very smoky in here and we don't want the management calling the fire department, do we?'

'Got you,' I said. I pulled out a chair and climbed up onto the table. While I unscrewed the cover of the smoke alarm and pried out the battery, Amelia lit the candle. By the time I climbed down, the room was already filling up with the overwhelming aroma of cinnamon and cloves and assorted wild berries.

I knew what the candle was for: I used to have a line in magic herbs and spices myself, which I sold to my elderly ladies at spectacularly-inflated prices, although most of mine had come from the out-of-date grocery bin at Gristede's.

The cinnamon and cloves were supposed to exorcize any disturbing memories that might still be lingering in the room from previous guests – any wife-beating or sadistic sex acts or suicide attempts – and the wild berries were meant to purify the air and protect us from any malevolent and mischievous spirits which might try to sneak through the portal without us noticing them.

'Smells like Christmas,' I remarked, as she and I sat down facing each other.

'This doesn't have much to do with Christianity,' said Amelia. The candle flame made her eyes glitter. 'This is a portal ritual I learned from a witch who lived in the Dakota Building.'

'They really have witches living in the Dakota Building? Like in *Rosemary's Baby*?'

'You wouldn't think this one was a witch if you met her. Her husband is a theatrical producer on Broadway and she lunches at Le Cirque most days.'

'Sounds like just my type. Wealthy, elderly, a sucker for the supernatural. You'll have to give me her number.'

'Oh, she's not elderly, even though her husband is. She's thirty-two, and used to wait table. But she's a very good witch. How do you think she persuaded a seventy-seven-year-old multi-millionaire to marry her, and make her the sole beneficiary of his will?'

The candle started to burn up brighter, and to pour out smoke, and the smoke twisted upward and around, in a spiral. Amelia laid her hands flat on the table and began to call out for

Singing Rock.

Whenever she recited incantations to the spirits, her voice always rose higher and higher, and she started to warble, until it sounded as if she were singing an aria from *Norma*. God knows what the people in the next-door suite thought we were doing. Operatic asphyxiation, probably.

'I am calling for the spirit of the medicine worker Singing Rock,' she sang. 'I am calling any spirit who can take his hand, and touch his heart, and lead him here. I have only affection and good wishes for him, but I need to speak to him about matters of the world beyond.'

She waited a moment, with her eyes closed, and then she trilled, 'I am calling for the spirit of the medicine worker Singing Rock. Whoever can guide him to me will be rewarded. Singing Rock? Can you hear me, Singing Rock?'

Smoke poured out of the candle thicker and thicker, until the room was filled with it. I thought I could hear a noise, too – apart from the trolley cars sliding along Northrup Avenue outside, and the faint caterwauling of Nina Simone on somebody's TV, and a woman laughing as if she had drunk too many Sex on the Beaches, or Sexes on the Beach, or whatever.

What I could hear was a repetitive rasping noise like one of those fish-shaped guires they play with a scraper in Mexican bands, only much softer, and much more complicated. It sounded as if it was very close, but at the same time it sounded very far away.

'I hear some kind of percussion instrument,' I

told Amelia.

She nodded, without opening her eyes. 'That means that they have found Singing Rock. He's holding a prayer-meeting.'

'He's holding a *what*? A prayer-meeting? What's he doing that for? He's *dead*. He's a spirit.'

'Harry – the dead pray for the living just as much as the living pray for the dead. They might have passed over, but they still care about us.'

She pressed the palms of her hands together, and then she sang, 'All spirits, listen to one who can speak the language of the dead! Bring Singing Rock to me, clothe him with light! Bring Singing Rock to me, dress him in dust! Bring Singing Rock to me, so that he can talk with me, and help all those that he has left behind!'

With that, she gave a sharp clap, then paused, and called out, *'Abbona!'*

She clapped again, and this time she called, *'Yoaw!'* Then, *'Nis!'* (clap) and *'Nees!'* (clap) and *'Aquit!'* (clap).

She held up both hands, with the palms facing me, and then she opened her eyes. 'So what was that all about?' I asked her.

'I was counting backward, in Wampanaug. It was my way of telling Singing Rock that Misquamacus is approaching.'

I couldn't help shaking my head. 'I'll tell you something, Amelia. You never cease to amaze me. I can't even count *forward* in Wampanaug.'

'Shh!' she admonished me. 'Don't say anything. Just wait.'

The smoke was so dense now that Amelia

138

looked as if she were sitting behind a thick net curtain, like a fake medium in one of those old-time seances, although I knew that Amelia was the real deal, and didn't have seven yards of butter-muslin rolled up inside her muff.

'What are we waiting for, exactly?' I asked her.

'Shh,' she repeated. 'It's starting. He's very close.'

Very softly at first, Singing Rock's shiny black bracelet began to rattle, but it wasn't long before it started to shake even more violently, and then it jumped two or three inches into the air, and clattered back down again. It did this five or six times, and each time it jumped up higher.

At the same time, I heard that guire sound even louder. *Shikka-trikka, shikka-trikka*, with all kinds of tricksy little *chikkety* noises in between.

Amelia closed her eyes again. 'The way is open!' she sang. 'I need all of you to guide Singing Rock back to the world of touching flesh! Two-legged spirits, I call on you! Four-legged spirits, I call on you! Spirits of the trees and the mineral kingdom, guide Singing Rock through to me! Spirits of the wind, blow against his back! Show him the path! Show him the portal!'

Now – still shivering and rattling – the bracelet rose up around the shaft of the candle, until it was floating about six inches above the flame. Neither Amelia nor I were anywhere near it, and I can swear that on any telephone directory you care to bring me, even the yellow pages from Wasilla, Alaska. As we watched it, the bracelet slowly twisted itself into a tight, complicated

139

knot, and rotated in the heat of the flame. Its black polished stones sparkled as brightly as Amelia's eyes, and each stone reflected a brilliant point of white light into the smoke, like fireflies. At first the fireflies seemed to be whirling aimlessly around the room, darting over the ceiling and across the walls. I almost felt like swatting them. But gradually they swarmed closer and closer together, in the densest part of the candle smoke, and they began to weave themselves into a recognizable pattern. It was the outline of a man, drawn in endlessly circling pinpricks of light, like a whirling model of the solar system.

'Singing Rock!' sang Amelia. 'Singing Rock, come through!'

Inside the sparkling outline, the smoke began to thicken, and even more smoke was drawn into it from the rest of the room – only slowly, to begin with, in shuddering eddies, but then faster and faster, as if somebody had switched an extractor on to full suck. The outline was filled by a dark, blurry figure, which rapidly became denser, and darker. Right in front of my eyes, it developed shadows, and depth, and shoulders, and a head, and a face. A man made out of solidifying smoke.

At the same time, the whole room was shaking and vibrating, as if we were having the longest continuous earth tremblor ever known. A vase of artificial poppies crept across a side table and dropped onto the floor. A silk-screen print of scarlet tomatoes and yellow summer squash fell off the wall, and its glass cracked. In the kitchen

140

drawers, I could hear the cutlery jingling together, and mugs rattling in the cupboards, and behind the living-room drapes, I could hear the windows buzzing in their metal frames.

After three or four minutes, however, the vibration died away, and the room was miraculously clear of smoke. Standing beside the table, less than five feet away from me, was Singing Rock – looking as he had always looked, more like a small-town realtor than a powerful Native American shaman – but formed this time out of constantly swirling smoke. It made him appear as if he were standing in front of a home-movie projector, with a black-and-white film of long-dead children playing across his face.

His eyes were open, but they were focused on the wall by the window, off to the left. He didn't move.

'Amelia?' I said. Amelia remained utterly motionless, her head tilted back, her arms hanging by her sides, her eyes still closed. Her cheeks were drained of all their color and I couldn't even tell if she was breathing. 'Amelia, he's here. You did it. You brought him through.'

There was a long silence, punctuated only by the sound of trolley cars, and the barely audible *shikka-tikka-tikka* of the guire, or whatever it was, but then that faded, too.

I stood up and circled around the table and laid my hands on Amelia's shoulders. The flickering figure of Singing Rock seemed to be staring directly at me, but he gave me no indication that he recognized me.

'Amelia,' I said, gently, close to her ear.

'Amelia, sweetheart, you've done it! He's here.'

She opened her eyes. She looked up at me first, and I nodded toward Singing Rock.

'Singing Rock!' she said. 'You came back to us. Thank you.'

Still Singing Rock said nothing, nor showed any sign that he knew who we were. He was dead, and he was formed out of nothing more than coagulated smoke, but he was still Singing Rock, and I surprised myself by feeling so emotional about seeing him again. I just hoped that dying hadn't given him some kind of astral Alzheimer's, and he had forgotten who we were.

I stepped right up to him. The candle smoke had formed a rough outline for his reappearance, like a charcoal sketch, but I could see that he was gradually producing his own ectoplasm, and with every passing second he was becoming more and more solid, and more detailed. His black greased-back hair had now restored itself, and even the fine wrinkles around his eyes were beginning to crinkle back into existence.

He looked at me short-sightedly. Maybe ectoplasm wasn't capable of recreating eyeglasses, or maybe they had gotten broken when he was killed. But he was wearing the same dark suit in which he had died, with its wide flappy lapels and its Elks badge.

'Singing Rock?' I said. I reached out my hand and cautiously took hold of his shoulder, and I could actually *feel* it, underneath his coat. It was kind of bony, and the coat itself was thick with dust, as if he had found it in a closet in some long-demolished building, but he was solid

142

enough. 'Singing Rock? It's me. Don't you recognize me?'

Singing Rock closed and reopened his eyes, as slowly as a lizard on a hot rock.

'I know who you are, Harry Erskine,' he replied, hoarsely. 'Why have you called me back here? I thought that I was done with you for ever. I gave you my bracelet, didn't I? I gave you custody of my spirit, in the world of touching flesh. Was that not enough?'

'Didn't you hear Amelia counting backward, in Wampanaug?'

'Yes. I heard her.'

'She was trying to tell you that Misquamacus has found a way of coming back to life.'

'I knew that. That was one of the reasons I was praying for you. But you called me, and I am a spirit, and no spirit can resist a summons from the world of touching flesh, no matter how reluctant he may be to answer it.'

'Well, I'm sorry if we interrupted your devotions, but if you knew that Misquamacus had found a way to come back, why the hell didn't you warn us? Amelia's sister and her family, they've all been struck blind. And it looks like he's been doing the same thing all across the country. Airliners have been falling out of the sky like flies. Cars have been crashing. People have been falling off of balconies.'

'I am aware of that. The spirits keep a vigilant watch on the world of touching flesh. But it is not the responsibility of the dead to interfere in the destiny of the living, no matter how catastrophic it may be.'

143

'Christ on rubber crutches, Singing Rock! You could at least have given us the heads-up! Do you know how many innocent people have been killed? Thousands, and more every day!'

Singing Rock remained impassive. Native Americans are good at impassive. In fact it's the only expression they do. Did you ever see a photograph of a Native American grinning and giving you the finger?

'Like I told you, Harry. It is not the duty of the dead to save the living from their manifest destiny.'

Manifest destiny. I liked the sarcasm of that. 'Manifest destiny' was the excuse the whites had given in the nineteenth century for killing the Indians and grabbing all of their land for themselves. It wasn't our fault, guys. God said we should do it.

I turned to Amelia. Calling Singing Rock had obviously taken a whole lot out of her, and she was trembling. I bent over her and felt her forehead, to make sure that she wasn't running a temperature. 'Are you OK?' I asked her.

She nodded. 'I'm OK. But don't take too long. It won't take Misquamacus more than a few minutes to realize that Singing Rock has come through. You need to ask him how Misquamacus has managed to come back, and how he's making so many people go blind. And *why*.'

Singing Rock circled slowly around the table. Although he appeared almost solid now, I could dimly see one of the table lamps shining right through him, and his voice came and went like somebody trying to call out to me from a boat in

144

the harbor, on a windy day.

'You need to understand something about Misquamacus, Harry. His magical powers were not conferred on him by Gitche Manitou, or by the spirits of the wind, and the lakes, and the land around him. They came from the Great Old Ones, and because of that, nobody from *this* world can ever take them away.'

He came up close to me, and said, 'The Great Old Ones were banished to the very rim of existence, but they are eternal, and deathless. Even Gitche Manitou cannot diminish their influence on those like Misquamacus who know the secret of contacting them, and speaking to them in Yyharuti – the tongue that was spoken before men learned to speak.'

'OK, I get that,' I acknowledged. 'You can't totally erase anybody's spirit. But I thought we made it impossible for him to come back *physically*. Like, he can't produce ectoplasm any more. And if he can't produce ectoplasm, he can't take on any kind of solid shape, like you just did. Am I right? And he can't pull that blazing-oil stunt, either, and get himself reborn in some other poor unsuspecting woman, the way he did with Karen.'

Singing Rock went across to the window. He lifted his left hand, and the drapes shuddered apart, although I wasn't entirely sure that he was actually touching them. The living room filled up with sunlight, which made Singing Rock look even dustier than he had before; and even though he threw a shadow across the polished-wood floor, it was fainter than the shadow of a

145

living man would have been. More like the *memory* of a shadow, when you think about it years later.

Outside, Northrup Avenue was bustling. Bright red trolley cars rolled past the window, the sidewalks were crowded with shoppers. The sky was a clear ceramic blue, with ragged white clouds.

'Misquamacus swore that he would destroy all those who had killed his people and plundered his country,' said Singing Rock. 'He swore that to the Great Old Ones, so that they could return out of exile; and the Great Old Ones will hold him to that pledge for all eternity. He will never be able to escape his commitment, even if he wants to.'

He turned around. 'He is unable to reappear in his original form, as I am. But what he has done is to possess the spirits of some of the most powerful shamans who ever lived, such as Machitehew, the Wampanaug wonder-worker who first taught him how to make magic. Machitehew, in the Wampanaug language, means "he who has an evil heart."

'He has also possessed the spirits of Wodziwob, who was known to the white settlers in Oregon as Infernal John; and Loco, who was a Chiracahua chief from Warm Springs; and Chief Jump Off, whose real name was Nantan Dole Tasso; and Chief Low Dog, Xunka Kuciyedano; and Nakaidoklini, a great medicine man who could bring dead warriors back to life.

'Even though they are all long dead, these wonder-workers still inhabit the spirit world, and they can visit the world of touching flesh, just as I have. That is how Misquamacus has managed to come back.'

'So he's a spirit who has possessed other spirits? Borrowed their clothes, as it were, because he doesn't have any clothes of his own?'

Singing Rock said, 'Borrowed their smoke, yes. Borrowed their dust. Borrowed their faces and their voices and their magic, too. And you can judge for yourself how powerful he still is by the fact that he has possessed so many spirits, all at once. When he was alive he could appear in many different places at the same time. In the same way, even though he has no substance of his own, he can occupy twenty or thirty different spirits, and bring them back to life, even though they are scattered all across the country, many hundreds of miles apart.'

'What about "Thunder Rolling In The Mountains"?' asked Amelia.

'Where did you hear that name?'

'He was the one who blinded my sister, when she and her husband and her kids were cycle-riding up the side of Hell's Canyon. I need to know how he did it, and if they can ever get their sight back.'

'That was Hin-mut-too-yah-lat-kekht, also known as Chief Joseph of the Nez Percé. A wise leader and a noble warrior, but also a very powerful medicine man. In life, he never wanted to fight the white man, but in death it seems as if he has been persuaded by Misquamacus to change his mind, and to take his revenge.'

'Jesus,' I said. 'All this revenge crap. Why

147

can't people accept that the past is the past, and it's over?'

'Easy to say if you are on the winning side,' said Singing Rock, sourly. 'Easy to say if it was *your* culture that prevailed; and if your entire way of life was not washed away for ever, as if by some terrible storm.'

'OK,' I told him. 'I'm sorry. But Hin-mut-thingy was definitely responsible for blinding Amelia's sister. She and her husband and her two kids all told us that he had two figures with him.'

'What kind of figures? Men, or ghosts, or demons?'

'They looked like a couple of mirrors, apparently; or boxes, maybe; or puppets. Their faces were dead white, but their bodies were black, or red.'

Singing Rock was about to speak when there was a sharp, aggressive rapping at the door. It sounded like somebody knocking with a stick, rather than their knuckles. Amelia looked across at me, anxiously, and I looked across at Singing Rock.

'Who is it?' I called out. Singing Rock raised his hand, as if he were warning me to be cautious.

There was no answer, but the rapping was repeated, louder this time.

'Should I open it?' I asked.

'No, Harry, don't,' said Amelia. But Singing Rock said, 'Whoever is standing outside, you will have to face them sometime.'

'Maybe it's the maid, come to put a chocolate

mint on our pillows,' I suggested.

There was another burst of rapping. I walked across to the door and called out 'Who is it?' again, and 'What do you want?'

Amelia said, 'Harry, for God's sake.' But I knew that Singing Rock was right. Whoever it was, I would have to face them sooner or later.

I grasped the handle, took a deep breath, and then I opened the door.

THIRTEEN

Modoc County National Forest,
North California
They shuffled cautiously over the loose volcanic shale, sometimes tugging at each other, sometimes bumping into each other. Thorn bushes snagged their jeans, and scratched their legs. Somewhere in the vast empty darkness beyond their blindfolds a buzzard screeched, as if it already knew what was going to happen to them, and couldn't wait for them to be lying broken on the rocks, six hundred feet below them.

Cayley couldn't stop sobbing, and Remo couldn't stop cursing, and Charlie kept wheezing and gasping for breath.

Only Mickey remained silent, because he was trying to remember what his parents looked like, and his house, and his younger sister. They say your whole life flashes in front of your eyes before you die, but he had discovered that it wasn't true. He couldn't picture anything coherent – only flashes, like walking into the kitchen and his mother had her back turned to him, or running across the baseball diamond across the street, kicking a bright red ball. It was like his mind's eye was a jerky hand-held camera. His mother turned around from her baking and said, 'Hi, honey,' but her face was nothing but a blur.

'Keep walking!' called Wodziwob. 'You have not reached your destiny yet!'

Remo stopped and twisted around and shouted. 'Fuck you, man, and fuck my destiny! You think we're just going to walk off this cliff like a whole lot of fucking sheep?'

But Tudatzewunu jabbed him in the side of his hip with a spear, and he screamed out 'Fuck!' and then 'Fuck!' and staggered forward three or four paces, before dropping to his knees and pulling Cayley and Charlie down with him. Mickey knelt down beside them.

'You must keep walking!' Wodziwob ordered them. 'This is the day when you start to pay my people back for what you have taken from them!'

'We didn't take nothing!' Remo screamed. 'We didn't take nothing! So we took a fish, OK? We'll put it back in the river, how's that? We'll put it back in the river and then we'll get back in our RV and we'll drive off and we'll never come back!'

'Stand up, like a man!' Wodziwob shouted. 'Stand up, and walk!'

Tudatzewunu and Tubbohwa'e jabbed them again and again, and they managed to climb back onto their feet. Cayley's sobbing had turned into a thin, puppy-like whimper; while Charlie was whining in the back of his throat. Mickey was praying – a prayer that his mother had taught him, when he was little.

'I am placing my soul and my body in Thy safe keeping this night, O God, in Thy safe keeping, O Jesus Christ, in Thy safe keeping, O Spirit of perfect truth. The Three who would defend my cause by keeping me this night from harm.'

'Will you shut up!' Remo ranted at him, as they stumbled forward. 'Will you just shut the fuck up?'

'I don't want to fall!' wailed Cayley. 'Please don't let me fall!'

Charlie said, 'God, oh God. Oh God.'

All four of them suddenly stopped. Although they were totally blind, they could sense from the wind and the sound of the river far below them that they had reached the edge of the precipice. Only a few steps in front of them was emptiness.

'Walk on!' Wodziwob demanded. 'Follow in the footsteps of Chief Si-e-ta! You will meet him soon enough!'

'We're not doing it, man!' Remo shouted. 'This is murder! This is plain out-and-out murder!'

But Tudatzewunu and Tubbohwa'e came forward and stabbed them again and again with their spears – in the shoulders, in their buttocks, in the back of their thighs. The boys yelled

151

hoarsely, while Cayley screamed.

'Walk on!' Wodziwob ordered them. 'This was always your destiny, from the day you were born! Are you afraid of it?'

Mickey could feel warm blood running down his legs, inside his jeans. He took a deep breath, and then he said, 'Let's do it!'

'What?' said Remo.

'Let's do it! Let's jump! They're going to kill us anyhow! Let's show them that we're not afraid!'

'Are you fucking crazy?'

But Cayley suddenly said, 'Yes! Let's jump! Let's all go together!'

'You're out of your minds!' said Remo.

'No,' said Charlie. 'We can fly, I promise you.'

Remo said, 'This is going to *hurt*, man.'

'No it's not,' said Mickey. 'Not if you think of the very best thing that ever happened to you. Not if you think that your life was really worth it.'

'Walk!' roared Wodziwob. 'This is no time for talking!'

The two box-like figures prodded them again. This time, Tudatzewunu prodded Remo just behind his ear, so that the point of his spear penetrated right through the gristle.

'Aaah! Fuck!' Remo cried out. Then, in an hysterical scream, *'Yes!* Let's jump! Let's just do it!'

The four of them jostled themselves closer together. They shuffled a few more cautious paces forward, and now the rock began to slope down sharply, and their feet sent loose shale sliding

152

into the void ahead of them. They could hear the shale clatter for a few seconds. Then there was silence, as it dropped into empty space, followed after a lengthy pause by a distant knocking sound, far below.

'Ready?' said Mickey.

'Ready,' said Remo. Then, 'I love you guys, all of you. The Emperors of IT!'

'*Geronimo!*' shouted Charlie, in his thin, asthmatic voice.

They stumbled forward, until they felt the rock drop away from under them, and then they jumped into nothingness. They twisted and tumbled and turned, and the ropes that bound them together kept yanking at their wrists, so that they collided together in mid-air, knocking their heads and their knees together.

They fell and they fell and Mickey thought: *I can't believe it. I'm actually going to die now. This is the end of my life.* But then Charlie's sneaker caught the side of his forehead and jolted his head back, and all four of them were brought to a sudden and devastating halt, banging into each other so hard that they were almost knocked unconscious, and then hitting the rock face.

'Christ Almighty,' said Remo.

They were so bruised and winded that it took them a few seconds to realize what had happened. Being blind, they couldn't tell how far down they had fallen, but it didn't feel as if it had been more than thirty or forty feet. All the same, Mickey hurt as if he had been beaten all over with a baseball bat, and his wrists felt as if

153

they were on fire. One of his knees was wedged between two sharp rocks, but almost all of his body weight was hanging by the rope that bound them together.

He tried to grab hold of the rope, so that he could raise himself up a little, and ease the burning in his wrists. As he did so, he began to understand where they were.

'Remo?' he gasped. 'Charlie?'

'Are you OK?' Remo asked him. 'I think I'm OK. Charlie?'

'I'm OK,' said Charlie. 'Twisted my ankle, maybe. Hurts like hell.'

'Cayley?'

'What happened to us?' asked Cayley. Her voice was slurred, like someone in deep shock. 'Are we dead?'

Mickey said, 'No, we're not dead. We didn't fall too far. We got caught by a tree.'

'What?' said Remo.

'I can't be sure, but it feels like you and Charlie are on one side of it and me and Cayley are on the other. If they hadn't roped us all together we would have been dead by now.'

Remo was silent for a moment. The tree creaked, and a few loose stones rattled down the precipice. Below them, they could hear the Pit River as it rushed through its narrow canyon, and it sounded as if it was still a very long way down.

'My wrists hurt,' said Cayley. 'My shoulder hurts.'

'We need to get ourselves free,' said Mickey.

'You think?' Remo retorted. 'We're blind,

man, all of us, and we're halfway down a mountain, and we're wrapped around a fucking tree. What exactly did you have in mind?'

'Come on, there must be a way. If only one of us could work his hands loose.'

'Well, I don't know about your hands, but mine are trussed up so tight I can't even feel them.'

'Maybe we could rub the rope against the rocks.'

'Dude, I can't even move. I have Charlie hanging off the end of my rope, all half a ton of him.'

'This is worse than us hitting the ground,' said Charlie, and went into a coughing fit. 'We're going to die of exposure up here, hanging off this tree, and it's going to take us days.'

'Let's wait for sun-up. Maybe Wodz-his-face will see us, and put us out of our misery with a couple of well-aimed spears.'

'Listen,' said Mickey. 'We're not dead yet. I said a prayer for God to keep us safe, and so far He has.'

'Oh, great, I knew we could rely on good old God.'

'Are you dead?'

'No, I'm not. Do I sound dead? But I think I've broken a couple of fingers.'

'We're going to get out of here. There has to be a way.'

Cayley started to sob again. 'My shoulder hurts. It hurts so much, Mickey. Please get us down from here. I can't bear it.'

'We're going to get out of this,' Mickey insisted. 'We got saved for a reason.'

Without warning, Remo started to sob, too. It was a desperate, lonely, childhood sobbing, like a small boy who has lost his mother in a supermarket. It frightened all of them more than Wodziwob could ever have done, because it meant that the brash, arrogant, confident Remo had lost all hope that they were going to survive.

'For Christ's sake, Remo,' said Charlie, gasping for breath.

But Remo said, 'You're right. We're just going to hang here, until we die of exposure, or thirst, or the buzzards peck our eyes out. If we'd have hit the ground, man, at least it would've been over. *Blam*, oblivion. But not this, man. I can't take this.'

They hung suspended like four dead polecats tied to a fence, while the tree creaked and the river splashed and the wind blew around them, and for almost twenty minutes they suffered in silence. Remo tried to bend his head sideways and bite through the rope that held them together, but he could only manage to touch it with his left cheek.

Mickey said, 'Maybe we can bounce up and down. Tear the tree out of the ground. Like, it's halfway up a rock face, right? It can't be rooted very deep.'

'Oh, I see,' Remo retorted. 'And then we all fall the rest of the way down to the ground, and get smashed to smithereens?'

'You said you couldn't take it, hanging here like this.'

'I can't. But that still doesn't mean that I want to die.'

'You jumped, didn't you, just like the rest of us?'

'Sure, yes, but that was different. When I did that, I still thought that something might save us. Like angels, or a freak updraft. Some kind of miracle. I don't know.'

'A tree saved us, man. A tree. That was a miracle. Now all we have to do is work out how to disentangle ourselves. This didn't happen by accident. God saved us, and we're going to live. I promise you.'

'Keep your damn whining down,' said a twangy voice, very close to them.

They listened, although they were still grunting in pain.

Charlie panted, 'Who said that? Was that you, Remo?'

'Unh-hunh. That wasn't me, man.'

'Mickey? Did you hear that?'

'I don't know. Is anybody there? Hallo? Is anybody there?'

'I said keep your damn noise down,' the voice snapped at them. 'Clem, you throw me that rope, boy. Jethro, you climb across there. That's right. And stay out of sight. Those Pay-oots could still be up on that rimrock.'

Mickey said. 'Who's there?'

'Who d'you think's here, feller? Thirty-Ninth Mounted Infantry.'

'We can't see you,' Charlie told him. 'These Indians struck us blind.'

'Those no-good sonsa bitches. You just hang on there, feller, and we'll get you off of that tree. But stay real quiet. Those Pay-oots, they can

157

hear a beaver breakin' wind, five miles off.'

Dangling in agony from their tree, they heard the scraping of boots on the rock face, and the clatter of metal implements. The next thing they knew, they were being grasped by strong, callused hands, and lifted bodily upward. Mickey could feel rough serge coats, and buttons, and smell whiskey and very strong body odor.

Being blind, it was impossible for them to work out exactly what was happening, but Mickey and Cayley were heaved up the side of the tree trunk, and then rolled over the top of it to the other side, where Remo and Charlie had been hanging. The four of them staggered and collided with each other, their feet sliding on the steep and slippery slope, but their rescuers held onto them, and prevented them from falling further down the precipice.

With great care, they were guided down a narrow, scrub-choked gully. Mickey had the impression that they had been rescued by at least six or seven men, because every time he lost his footing there were two or three hands that were quick to hold on to him, and keep him upright.

When they were deep in the bushes, their bindings were cut, and they were separated. Mickey rubbed his wrists and he could feel the deep indentations that the ropes had scored in his flesh.

'They sneak up on you, those Pay-oots? They got themselves a habit of doing that. Those Modocs, too. Come out of no place, like ghosts.'

'We weren't doing anything,' said Mickey. 'We were just fishing, that's all.'

'Fishing? That was kind of foolhardy, considering.'

'We didn't know that the Native Americans would take it so bad.'

'The who?'

'The Indians,' said Remo. 'They said that we were messing up their land. They said that white men had blinded their chief and forced him to walk off the top of this rock. That's why they made *us* do it, too.'

'Well, you're safe enough now,' said the twangy voice. 'A few of them sonsa bitches stood their ground, but most of them scurried off like rabbits and hid in the caverns. Maybe a dozen or so managed to get off the rock but we chased them into the tules and caught almost all of them. Let's put it this way: they won't be making no war on us no more. Not those Payoots, anyhow. Nor those Modocs. Nor those Pit River Indians, neither.'

'I don't get it,' said Mickey. 'When did all this happen?'

'Careful now, it gets kinda precipitatious right here,' the twangy voice warned them. 'That's right, take it real slow.'

They were helped to slide down a steep, smooth rock face, and then to clamber over a heap of loose stones and small volcanic boulders. After that, the ground began to level out, and they could hear that the river was much closer.

'We didn't hear any fighting,' Mickey persisted.

Another voice said, 'Mebbe them Injuns made

you deaf as well as blind.'

'Just surprised we didn't hear it, that's all.'

Now they had reached the foot of the palisade, and their rescuers held their hands as they waded knee-deep across the ice-cold river.

'So where you folks from?' asked the twangy voice.

'Palo Alto. We only came here for the fishing.'

'Palo Alto? Never heard of it.'

'You never heard of it? It's about thirty-five miles south of San Francisco. IT capital of California.'

'Eye tea?'

'Information technology,' said Remo, patiently. He slipped on a rock under the water, but one of their rescuers caught his arm before he fell over.

'Sorry, son,' said the twangy voice. 'Don't know what in the blue heck you're talking about.'

They reached the far side of the river and now they could hear more voices and horses whinnying. They could also smell woodsmoke, and a strong aroma of frying bacon.

'Where did you tie up your horses?' the twangy voice asked them. 'Kind of an academical question, I know. The Indians will have stole them as soon as look at them.'

'We drove here,' said Remo.

'You *drove*?'

'That's right. We left our RV by the recreation area.'

'Ah vee?' There was a long, bewildered pause. 'You folks Chinese or some such?'

160

They were led close to a smoky, crackling fire. From the sounds all around them – the talking, and the coughing, and the jingling of metal – it was obvious that they were right in the middle of some kind of encampment. Mickey guessed that there were twenty or thirty people here at least, all men if their voices were anything to go by. He hadn't yet heard any women or children.

'You hungry?' asked a hoarse, reedy voice.

'No, no thanks,' said Charlie.

'Do you have a Coke or something?' asked Cayley.

'A what?'

'Anything. So long as it's not root beer.'

'You want a drink? I got coffee, or water.'

'Water's fine, thanks.'

The four of them were helped to sit close to the fire. Mickey said, 'OK if we borrow a cell? We need to get back home as soon as we can, and have our eyes seen to.'

'You want to lend a borrow of a what?'

'A cell. That's if we can get a signal out here. If we can't, maybe one of you could drive us. We don't mind paying for the gas.'

Another long pause. Then the twangy voice said, 'I'm real sorry, son. I can't make heads nor tails of what you're talking of.'

'A cell. A cellphone. One of you must have one.'

'I'm sorry. You got us stumped.'

'Who are you, exactly?' asked Charlie.

'Who *are* we?'

'Don't get me wrong,' said Charlie, hastily. 'We're really grateful that you saved our lives

161

and everything. But we didn't see you here when we first arrived, and you say that you've been fighting the Indians, and we didn't hear you doing any of that. And you don't seem to understand anything we say. Well, not much, anyhow.'

'I told you,' said the twangy voice. 'We're the Thirty-Ninth Mounted Infantry, under General George Crook. The general hisself is further up the river.'

'But what are you fighting the Indians for?' asked Mickey.

'What are we fighting them for?'

'Yes. Like, what have they done?'

'What have they *done*?' There was another of those mystified pauses. Then the twangy voice called out, 'Jethro! Hey, Jethro! What are we fighting these here Indians for?'

'On account of they're no damn good.'

'That's it,' said the twangy voice, apparently satisfied. 'They're no damn good, that's why we're fighting them. They don't never normally get together, the Pay-oots and the Modocs and the Pit River Indians. Some Shoshone, too. Normally, they're beating five shades of shit out of each other, begging your sensibility, miss. So the only reason they were gathered together was to mount an attack on *us*.'

He gave a loud sniff, and then he added, 'Just as well we pre-emptified them, wouldn't you say?'

'We didn't see any Indians,' said Cayley.

'You didn't? Was that before or after they put your lights out?'

'Before. We were camping, right by the river.

162

We didn't see anybody.'

'Well, you amaze me, miss, you surely do. There was more than seventy-five Pay-oots and there was thirty Pit River Indians and more than a handful of Modocs and Shoshone. And there's more than a hundert of us, including a cavalry company and fifteen Indian scouts. And there was all hell let loose – shooting and hollering and running around.'

Somebody called out, 'Caleb! Sergeant Briggs wants to see you! On the double!'

'Coming right over,' the twangy voice answered him. Then he turned back and said, 'I'll have to leave you young folks for a while. Just settle yourselves down and relax, OK? If you need anything to eat, just call out for Chowder. He's the cook, or at any rate that's what he likes to style himself.'

Mickey heard him get up and walk away. Remo said, 'Who the hell *are* these guys?'

'Soldiers, obviously,' said Charlie. 'But not *real* soldiers. Maybe they're one of those historical societies that go around recreating old battles.'

'You could be right,' Mickey agreed. 'Like, they keep saying that they've been fighting the Indians, but we never saw any Indians, did we – apart from that Infernal John guy, and those two characters with him, whoever they were. Or *whatever* they were.'

'I have to see a doctor,' Cayley whimpered. 'I can't move my arm at all.'

'Sounds like maybe you dislocated your shoulder,' said Mickey.

Charlie said, 'I really need my inhaler. And I have to have my ankle strapped up, too.'

'All I want to do is get out of here,' said Remo. 'We just need to persuade these guys to step out of character for five minutes and stop making out that they can't understand what we're talking about.'

Caleb came back and hunkered down close to them. 'The sergeant says that we can borrow you a coupla horses that you can double up on and ride back to Goose Lake, and an Indian scout to guide you. We got a camp at Goose Lake, and a doctor.'

'Horses?' Remo protested. 'Are you kidding me? Apart from the fact that I'm totally blind, I never rode a horse in my life.'

'You never rode a horse?' The twangy voice sounded incredulous. 'You mean, *never*?'

'Never. And I don't intend to start now. Like, thanks for the offer and everything, but absolutely not.'

There was a thoughtful pause. Then the twangy voice said, 'I guess we could rig up a travois for you.'

'A what?'

'A travois. That's if we can spare the mules. But I won't pretend that it's going to be comfortable.'

'Listen,' said Remo. 'All we want you to do is to lend us your cell. You got it?'

'I'm sorry, son. I still don't understand you.'

'You must have some kind of radio transmitter.'

Silence, this time. The twangy voice had

apparently decided that their tumble down the precipice had unhinged them.

Mickey said, 'What if somebody drives our Winnebago for us? How would that be?'

'Son, I have to tell you straight, I don't have the slightest notion what you're trying to say to me. The best thing you can do is settle down for the rest of the night and get yourselves some sleep. Private Johnson here will lead you to the mess tent and find some blankets for you. We can decide what to do with you in the morning.'

Remo said, 'For Christ's sake, dude! All I'm asking you for is to borrow your cell!'

'I know,' said the twangy voice. 'But we don't have a cell here, of any description. When we catch an Indian, we shoot him. General Crook's specific orders, we don't take no prisoners.'

'Jesus,' said Remo. 'Forget it, man. Just forget it.'

'I'm sorry,' said the twangy voice, yet again; and he sounded as if he sincerely meant it.

They were led to a musty-smelling tent, where four rough woolen blankets were laid on the ground for them, and they were helped to lie down and wrap themselves up.

Charlie said, 'Maybe these guys have gotten themselves so involved in this role-playing thing that they genuinely don't understand what we're talking about. I've heard about that. Regression, that's what they call it. My aunt Mimi used to believe that she was the reincarnation of Betsy Ross. She even took to sewing Old Glories and mailing them off to the White House.'

'But they can see that all of us need to see a doctor,' Cayley protested. 'Like, a joke's a joke, right? But this is ridiculous.'

'Maybe this isn't really happening at all,' said Remo. 'Maybe that shit I got from Louie was stronger than I thought.'

'Oh, you think we're still high?' Mickey retorted. 'You want me to squeeze your broken fingers, just to check?'

'Listen,' said Charlie, 'we survived, didn't we? And let's hope we're not going to be blind for ever. Maybe it's just like a detached retina. That makes you go blind, but they can fix it. My uncle Stanley had a detached retina, and after he had an operation he didn't even need glasses.'

'Who was he a reincarnation of? Hawkeye and the Last of the Mohicans?'

Mickey said, 'There's nothing more we can do tonight. Even if these guys *do* have a radio, we're not going to be able to find it, are we? The best thing we can do is try to get some sleep.'

'How do you expect me to sleep?' asked Cayley. 'My shoulder hurts too much.'

'Just lie there and think of that boyfriend of yours,' said Remo. 'That should send you to sleep.'

'He's not my boyfriend.'

'Oh, you know who I mean, then? That dummy who flips burgers at Taxi's?'

They talked on and off for almost an hour, sometimes bantering, sometimes complaining, sometimes almost sobbing in desperation. But eventually the shock of going blind and falling down the precipice began to take its effect, and

166

one by one they dropped off to sleep, although they twitched and muttered as they slept, and Cayley even began to cry, a strange muted mewling like a cat that wants to come indoors out of the rain.

Mickey dreamed of Wodziwob, but in his dream Wodziwob kept his back to him and refused to turn around. Mickey walked up to him and laid a hand on his shoulder, and it was only then that his head swiveled around, with a harsh scraping sound. Wodziwob's face was a mask – deathly white, with dazzling blue lights instead of eyes. Mickey tried to cry out, but there was something in his throat, something fat and dry and foul-tasting, as if he'd swallowed a toad, and all he could manage to do was retch.

Remo argued in his sleep. He kept saying, 'You can't leave me here, man. There's no going back. What? I can't touch it.'

Charlie hardly moved beneath his blanket, but his breathing was high-pitched and labored, and several times he stopped breathing altogether. Almost a minute would pass, and then he would let out a squeaking noise, and continue. Although his friends were unaware of it, he came closer to dying that night than any of them.

'I can't touch it,' begged Remo. 'Please don't make me touch it.'

Mickey was woken in the morning by the rattling cry of a jay, which was perched in a pine tree nearby. He grunted and turned over, and tried to drag up his blanket to cover him better, but his blanket seemed to have been taken away.

He sat up. He was still totally blind, but he could hear the Pit River rushing over the rocks, and a breeze blowing softly through the tules. He must have alarmed the jay, because it let out a guttural *'Wah! Wah!'* and flew away.

'Remo?' he said, groping all around him. 'Remo? You awake?'

There was a pause, and then a groan. 'Jesus, my fingers. Jesus.'

'Are you OK?' Mickey asked him. 'Charlie? Cayley? How about you?'

Charlie wheezed and coughed and Cayley said, 'Oww, my shoulder.'

'Where's my blanket?' said Remo. 'Hey, dude! Did you steal my blanket?'

'I don't have your blanket. I can't find my blanket, either.'

'Mine's gone, too,' said Cayley. 'I can't believe it. I'm just lying on the dirt.'

Remo stood up and shuffled around, with both arms extended in front of him. 'Hey!' he called out. 'Hey! We're awake now! Can anybody help us?'

There was no reply; only the endless rushing of the river.

'Hey!' shouted Mickey. 'Thirty-Ninth Infantry guys! We could really use some help here!'

Still no reply. Remo circled around cautiously, still with his arms stretched out. 'Is anybody there? I said, is anybody there? Come on, man, this really isn't funny!'

He flapped his right arm from side to side. Then he said, 'The tent's gone.'

'What?'

'The tent's gone. They took it away. I don't believe it. They left us lying here, with no tent and no blankets. Nothing.'

Mickey and Charlie stood up, too. 'Hey!' they yelled. 'Caleb! Are you still here? Caleb! Anybody!'

Cayley said, 'They've gone, haven't they? They've left us.'

They listened, and listened, and Cayley was right. There were no voices, no jingling of spurs and bridles, no whuffling of horses, no sound of any human presence. Only the water, and the wind, and the restless rustling of the trees.

'I can't get my head around this,' said Remo. 'We're all blind. We all need medical attention – like, *urgently*. And they just fricking left us. Right in the middle of no place at all with no way of finding our way out of here.'

Charlie started another of his wheezing fits. 'I have to find my inhaler, man. I'm going to die if I don't.'

'In that case, we need to get back to the RV,' said Mickey. 'Come on, we know roughly where we are, don't we? We're close to the canyon, so the parking area must be upstream from here. If we follow the river, we're bound to find it.'

'Unless those bastards have taken our RV, too.'

'Well, if they have, they have, and there's not a damn thing we can do about it. But at least we'll know where the road is.'

'Oh, like you're suggesting we *walk* back? Do you know how far it is, even to Route Three-fifty-nine? Eight miles at least, and that's if we don't get lost, which we probably will.'

'There's no future in being pessimistic,' said Mickey. 'What are you going to do? Sit here and starve to death? Come on, Stevie Wonder made himself rich and famous and he's just as blind as we are.'

'Stevie Wonder didn't get himself abandoned in the middle of Modoc County with nobody to show him how to find his way back to civilization.'

All the same, they groped their way to the edge of the river, and waded across it, balancing and slipping on the rocks that Mickey had described as 'bowling balls covered with snot.' When they reached the far side, they began to make their way upstream, toward the recreation area where they had parked their Winnebago. They walked Indian file, with Mickey in the lead and the others keeping a hand on the shoulder of the one in front of them.

'I could murder an Egg McMuffin,' said Charlie.

'That's so typical of you,' Remo told him. 'Out of all the food in the entire world which you can't have, you choose an Egg McMuffin.'

Mickey said, 'Do you smell smoke?'

Remo stopped, and sniffed, and said, 'Yes. I can. And I think I can hear a fire burning.'

'Maybe we've caught up with them,' said Cayley.

Remo sniffed again. 'That's no campfire. That's more like oil, and rubber.'

Charlie said, 'You don't think—'

'Oh, shit,' said Mickey. 'I'll bet it is. I bet they've set fire to it.'

They negotiated the rocks by the side of the river as quickly as they could, although Charlie and Cayley both lost their balance, and had to be helped back onto their feet. But the ground gradually began to level out, and from the echoes of their voices and their footsteps they could tell that they had reached a much wider space. Mickey said, 'Listen? Hear those riffles? I'm sure this is where I was fishing.'

The Winnebago must have been very close now, because the stench of burning rubber was even more toxic, and they all began to cough. They crossed the parking lot, and then they stopped, because the heat was scorching their faces. They could hear metal clicking and pinging as it expanded, and windows cracking, and the soft flaring noise of foam-rubber seat cushions.

'The *bastards*,' said Remo.

Mickey said, 'We'd better stand way back. This smoke is totally poisonous, and the gas tank's probably going to blow.'

'I don't understand,' put in Cayley. 'Why did they go to all that trouble to rescue us, when all they were going to do was burn our RV?'

''Less those Indians set fire to it.'

'I don't care who the hell set fire to it. It's all burned out now.' Mickey paused. 'Not that we could have driven it.'

'So what do we do now?' asked Remo.

Mickey was just about to answer when the Winnebago blew up, with a bang like a huge door slamming. They felt a wave of heat, and pieces of aluminum clattered onto the rocks all around them.

'Everybody OK?' asked Mickey.

'Fricking-A,' said Remo.

'I'm terrific,' said Charlie. 'I can't breathe and I can't hardly walk, but otherwise – terrific.'

Cayley said, 'I'm so darn tired. And my whole arm feels like it's burning.'

'I could use my belt and make you a sling,' Mickey told her. 'That would take some of the weight off of it.'

'And then what?' asked Remo. 'Then we start walking?'

'Do you have any other ideas? So long as we follow the road, we should be OK.'

He felt his way across to Cayley, and then he took off his wide canvas belt and looped it around her wrist. All the time he was buckling it up and tying a knot in it she said, 'Ow!' and 'Ow!' and 'Ow*wahh*!'

He was still fixing the knot when they heard a deep beating noise in the distance.

Remo said, 'That isn't *drums*, is it? Not more Indians, please!'

But the beating quickly grew louder and louder, and then they heard a high-pitched whistling sound, too.

'*Helicopter!*' gasped Charlie.

Remo let out a whoop. Cayley took hold of Mickey's hand and gripped it tight; and then Mickey found Remo's hand; and Remo reached out for Charlie. Together, they lifted their arms upward, and shouted out, '*Here! We're here! Don't go away! We can't see! Don't leave us here! We're blind!*'

But as they linked hands together, Mickey saw

a flash of white light in front of his eyes. For a split second he glimpsed bright blue sky, with dazzling white clouds floating in it. He even saw the brown blur of a jay flying past. Immediately, he let go of Cayley's and Remo's hands, and put his fingers up to his eyes, but the instant he did so, he went blind again.

Cayley yelped, 'I *saw* something! I saw the sky!'

'Me too, man!' said Remo. 'It's gone again, but I saw it for sure!'

Charlie started coughing, but between wheezes he managed to splutter out, 'I saw it! I saw it too! Maybe we're getting our sight back!'

The beating of the helicopter was much louder now, and it sounded as if it were hovering directly overhead. Mickey said, 'Hold hands again!'

'What?' said Remo.

'Hold hands again! Now!'

They groped around until they found each other's hands. Then they lifted their arms up, as they had before. Again, each of them saw a flash of light, and their eyes were suddenly flooded with the brilliance of the sky, and the dark green pine trees, and the sparkling Pit River. Only thirty yards away, they saw the black smoking skeleton of their Winnebago. But right above their heads a white LongRanger helicopter was slowly circling, its nose dipped, its rotor-blades shining in the sunlight like two scimitars. For a few seconds it blew gusts of smoke all around them, and ruffled the surface of the river. Then it tilted sideways and landed on the far side of the parking area.

Mickey dropped to his knees, exhausted and relieved, but he made sure that he didn't lose his grip on Cayley's hand. Cayley knelt down beside him, and then Remo and Charlie, too.

'You know what this means?' said Remo, hoarsely. 'We'll have to hold hands for the rest of our lives!'

'Hey,' said Charlie. 'That's better than being blind.'

'Oh, yeah?' Remo retorted. 'Think about it, man. We'll even have to go to the bathroom together.'

'You *would* think of that,' said Cayley.

The helicopter's doors slid open, and two khaki-uniformed park rangers climbed out, a man and a woman. 'You folks OK?' the woman called out, over the whistle of the rotors. She was handsome and bespectacled, her hair tied back like Sarah Palin. 'Need any urgent medical attention?'

Mickey gave Cayley's hand a squeeze. 'There,' he said. 'Didn't I promise you that God would take care of us?'

The four of them awkwardly stood up, and started to walk toward the helicopter, still holding hands. The woman park ranger turned to her colleague and pulled a quizzical face, but all he could do was shrug. Who could tell why four young people would walk around holding hands, as if they were on a peace march?

As they approached him, the male park ranger looked them up and down. He had red-tinted Ray-Bans and a bristly brown moustache. 'My name's State Park Ranger Edison and this is

State Park Ranger Butowski,' he announced. Then he nodded toward the burned-out Winnebago. 'What in hell's name went down here? How did you all get yourselves so messed up? How's that arm, miss? Is it broke?'

'I think I dislocated my shoulder,' said Cayley, miserably.

Ranger Butowski came around behind Cayley and gently felt her shoulder. Cayley winced, but Ranger Butowski gave her a sympathetic smile. 'I'd say you've pulled it pretty bad, honey, but it's still in its socket. Believe me, I dislocated my shoulder once, when I was skiing, and I never stopped screaming.'

'We – uh – we were kind of *attacked*,' said Mickey. He wasn't sure how they were going to explain what had happened to them – or what they *imagined* had happened to them. He was beginning to wonder himself if their experience had been nothing more than a spectacularly bad trip.

'Well, we can fly you down to Alturas,' said Ranger Edison. 'You can have yourselves checked over at the Modoc Medical Center, and then you can talk to the Highway Patrol – tell them who did this to you. Who was it? Bikers? We get a whole lot of trouble from bikers. Neo-Nazis, too.'

Mickey and Remo looked at each other but neither of them could think what to say. *We were attacked by a Native American in a black suit who called himself Infernal John, and two white-faced creatures who looked like packing cases on stilts? They struck us all blind and then made*

175

us jump off the top of the rimrock?

'Let's get you aboard,' said Ranger Butowski. She climbed up into the helicopter and shifted a rucksack and a medical bag off the seats, to make room for them. While she was sorting out their seat harnesses, Mickey looked around him. They wouldn't be able to hold hands in the helicopter, and if his sight never came back to him, he wanted to make the most of these final few seconds.

He frowned. On the far side of the river, standing amongst the tules, he thought he could see twenty or thirty men, staring back at him. They were strangely colorless and almost transparent, so it was difficult for him to make out who they were. It was like looking at a black-and-white photograph that had been faded by the sun.

'Remo,' said Mickey. 'Charlie. Look over there. No, that way. Do you see those guys?'

Remo narrowed his eyes, 'Yes. Yes, I do. They are *soldiers*, aren't they? Like old-style cavalry.'

He was right. The men were wearing wide-brimmed hats and they were all dressed in military uniforms, with epaulets, and some of them had swords hanging from their belts.

'Maybe those were the guys who rescued us,' Charlie suggested.

'Oh, you mean the guys who rescued us and then took away our blankets while we were sleeping and left us to die of hypo-what's-it's name?'

'Ready?' asked Ranger Butowski. 'Let's get this young lady in first, shall we? What's your

176

name, honey?'

'Please – wait just a second!' said Mickey. But when he looked back across the river, the soldiers had vanished, as completely as if they were ghosts.

FOURTEEN

Washington, DC

'All commercial and private flights have been grounded, Mr. President,' said Doug Latterby, snapping his cellphone shut. 'All incoming foreign flights have been instructed to turn back to their points of departure, or the nearest non-US airport, except if they have insufficient fuel.

'Military and rescue flights are now restricted to essential and emergency operations only, and all flight personnel are subject to stringent eye tests before take-off.'

President Perry was sitting up in bed at the Washington National Eye Center where he had been taken for further tests. He was wrapped in a green silk robe with white spots, and Doug Latterby thought that he was suddenly looking much older than his fifty-six years, and deeply tired. His eyes were puffy and although he was blind, his pupils kept darting from side to side, like two trapped blowflies.

The entire fourth floor of the WNEC had been commandeered for the President's stay, with

Secret Service agents guarding every stairwell and elevator, and a temporary command center had been set up in the rooms immediately adjoining his treatment suite.

Outside, on Irving Street NW, it was a bright, windy afternoon, with huge white cumulus clouds rolling past like a heavily laden fleet of galleons, and the trees waving at them madly, but of course the President couldn't see them.

So far – despite five intensive examinations – his team of five leading ophthalmologists had still been unable to determine how and why he had lost his sight. As far as a cure was concerned, they had discussed both corneal transplants and laser treatment; but without knowing the exact cause of his blindness they were reluctant to subject him to radical surgery. They were worried that they might blind him permanently, without any hope of recovery.

'How many planes have come down so far?' the President asked.

'Forty-seven altogether, with a total fatality figure of seven thousand, four hundred six.'

'Holy Mother of God. How about the road-traffic situation?'

'Impossible to say, as yet. But somewhere in excess of eleven thousand serious accidents, with two thousand reported victims.'

'We've imposed restrictions on highway use?'

'Pretty much the same as air traffic. No civilians are allowed to drive on major roads – only military, police, and emergency services, and in every case they have to carry a backup driver with them. Civilians can drive on minor roads, but no faster than ten miles an hour. We may cut that down to five, if necessary.

'Similar picture on the railroads. Freight trains only, with two extra engineers on every run. And shipping, too, especially oil tankers and ships carrying toxic chemicals. None of this is going to be easy to enforce, but we're appealing to people to be sensible, and not to panic.'

'What's the public reaction so far?'

'What do you think? They're as scared and as mystified as we are. There's been looting in some of the major cities. Baltimore, parts of Chicago, Detroit. But the National Guard seem to be containing the worst of it. It's not like people are angry, like they were in Watts. They just want to make sure they don't run short of supplies.'

'Any further developments from the FBI?'

Doug Latterby shook his head, but then remembered that the President couldn't see him. 'No, nothing. I talked to Warren Truby only a half-hour ago. There's been no chatter on terrorist networks. No overt threats. No Al-Qa'eda-type videos. And up until now no faction has claimed responsibility, nor made any demands. Except for the usual loony-tunes on the Internet, and almost all of those have checked out negative.'

He prodded at his Blackberry. 'There's one worrying development. We've had six outbreaks of blindness on army bases – Fort Lewis, Washington; Fort Ord, California; Fort Carson, Colorado; Fort Sill, Oklahoma; Fort Sam Houston, Texas; and Fort Meade, Maryland. So far the numbers of military personnel going blind isn't anywhere like as many as civilians – only two or three hundred at most. But each of the outbreaks on army bases seems to have spread very rapidly.'

'How's it being done, Doug? What do you think? Lasers, maybe?'

'I don't have any idea, Mr. President. But I think *why* is more important than *how*. This isn't some collection of nut-jobs, blinding people for the hell of it. They want something. If only we could work out *what*.'

'What time is my broadcast?'

Doug Latterby checked his watch. 'Six-oh-five, Eastern time. We put it back five minutes so that we could run the latest news headlines first. Henry and Leland have almost finished recording your announcement, so you'll have plenty of time to listen to it and make any changes.'

'OK. But I prefer to ad lib. "My fellow Americans, I think we're all in the shit. However I can't be one hundred percent sure. I can feel that it's soft and I can feel that it's warm but for the hell of me I can't see what color it is."'

At that moment, the President's personal secretary, Jean Fallon, came knocking at the door. 'Mr. President? You have a phone call.'

'The President isn't taking any calls,' said Doug Latterby. 'He's tied up in a meeting with the Joint Chiefs of Staff.'

'I'm sorry, Doug, it's President Petrovsky and he knows where the President is, and why.'

'Fuck. You're kidding me.'

The President held out his hand and said, 'Give me the phone, Jean. I'll take it. Right now, I don't think there's any future in pretending that everything's hunky-dory.'

Doug Latterby said, 'Mr. President, you need to be real careful here. This is the President of Russia we're talking about. The same Russia which has six thousand six hundred eighty-one nuclear missiles aimed at us, at a time when we have never been so vulnerable in our entire history.'

'I know which Russia, Doug. And I also know how many warheads they have.'

'Come on, Mr. President. Let me tell him you're otherwise engaged, and you'll call him right back. Let's you and me talk this through first – decide exactly what we're going to admit to, and what we're not.'

'Doug, forty-seven airliners have crashed. Thousands of Americans have been killed and injured in serious traffic accidents. Our soldiers are going blind.'

Jean Fallon said, 'There's also been an accident on that giant roller coaster on King's Island in Cincinnati – the Mother Of All Monsters. It was just on the news. More than fifty people dead, thirty-six in one of the trains and more than a dozen on the ground. They're saying that one of the operatives went blind, and pressed the wrong switch by mistake.'

'Hand me the phone,' said the President.

'Whatever you do, do *not* admit to Petrovsky that you've lost your sight,' Doug Latterby hissed at him. 'Or if he's found out already, tell

181

him that you're going for an operation this evening, and that your doctors are predicting a complete cure.'

'Mr. President!' said Gyorgy Petrovsky. The phone line was so clear that he sounded as if he were calling from only a few blocks down the street, instead of the Kremlin.

'Gyorgy,' the President greeted him. 'Good to hear your voice, my friend. And right now, I need all the friends I can get.' He waited while President Petrovsky's translator told him what he had said.

'You have my sincerest condolences for all of your countrymen who have perished,' President Petrovsky replied. 'What a terrible scourge, this blindness. Do you know yet what is causing it?'

'Our security services and our disease-control people are working on it flat out, as you can imagine. They have a number of leads; but so far nothing definite.'

'So ... you don't know how *you* became blind, and if you will ever get your sight back?'

The President didn't answer that, but covered the receiver with his hand and mouthed to Doug Latterby: *'He knows.'*

'You are maybe wondering how I found out,' said President Petrovsky. 'But of course I started to have my suspicions when we last met, and my people have been keeping a very close eye on you, if you will forgive me for such a phrase.'

'Well, Gyorgy, I guess there's no point in my trying to deny it.'

'You have my sympathy, believe me. My own mother went blind when she was eighty-one

182

years old, and it was a tragedy. She could no longer read, or sew, which she loved. She used to make such embroidery! Flowers, cats, dragons!' He paused, and then he asked, 'What is your doctors' prognosis?'

'Pretty good, as a matter of fact. They're planning to operate tonight.'

'Really? So soon? What has led them to change their minds?'

'What do you mean? We're talking about corneal transplants, that's all.'

'That is not what I heard. But of course I must be mistaken.'

'So what did you hear?'

'I heard that your doctors could not yet come to a decision. They were afraid that if they chose the wrong procedure, you would stay blind for the rest of your life. And, of course, they cannot be certain that they will choose the right procedure – not until they know exactly what has happened to your eyes.'

'Well, let me put it this way, Gyorgy. An operation has been scheduled, but I'm not entirely sure if it's going to go ahead.'

'Mr. President! Whatever happens, operation or no operation, I wish for you a very speedy recovery. I want you to know that we Russians will assist you in every way possible. If you need them, we can send doctors, or transportation, or manpower. In the face of such a crisis, let us set aside all of our differences of opinion.'

President Perry pulled one of his famous scowling faces, which early in his political career had earned him the nickname of 'Pug

183

Dog'. He may have been blind, but he wasn't stupid, and he knew when he was being flim-flammed. All the same, the inescapable fact was that most of the air force was grounded, most of the navy was confined to various harbors around the world, and if the blindness spread to any more military personnel, the United States would be dangerously incapable of defending itself.

To President Perry's politically attuned ear, *'let us set aside all of our differences of opinion'* sounded like an exact paraphrase of *'we will not take advantage of your present vulnerability if you decide not to deploy a missile shield in Poland.'*

'That's a very generous offer, Gyorgy,' said the President. 'And I thank you for your consideration and your good wishes. Maybe I can get back to you if I need to call on you for any logistical support.'

'Of course, my friend. Please give my affectionate best wishes to your beautiful wife. Oh – and one thing. One small favor.'

'Oh, yes? And what would that be?'

'I understand that the district attorney's office in New York is about to file charges against Mr. Lev Khlebnikov for certain financial dealings.'

'And?'

'And ... Mr. Khlebnikov has influential friends here in the oil industry who would be very un-happy to see him face such charges.'

'And?'

'I think you understand me, Mr. President. There is a saying, is there not, about boots and

184

other feet?'

President Perry took a deep breath. Then he said, 'Very well, Gyorgy. I'll see what I can do. But I can't make any promises.'

'I understand, Mr. President. Promises never buttered any bread.'

With that, Gyorgy Petrovsky hung up. President Perry slowly lowered the receiver, and then he dipped his head from side to side, frowning, trying to sense where Doug Latterby was standing.

Doug Latterby said, 'What? What did he say?'

'Douglas? I want Kenneth and George and Dick here, ASAP. I also want the Joint Chiefs. Gyorgy Petrovsky has already started asking me for favors.'

'What does he want?'

'Not much this time. Lev Khlebnikov to be let off the hook for racketeering. But if I know Gyorgy Petrovsky this is only the beginning. We need to formulate a totally new national defense plan, and we need to do it right now.'

'You think the Russians are causing this blindness?'

'I don't know, Doug. I really don't. But we're bleeding and Gyorgy Petrovsky has a very keen nose for blood.'

The First Lady came in to see him once his emergency defense conference had finished. She was looking as pale and strained as the President, but she had made a point of dressing up in a pink silk blouse and spraying herself with L'Air Du Temps, which was the President's favorite perfume. Even if he couldn't see her, she wanted him to feel that she had made the effort to look attractive for him.

'How did it go?' she asked, sitting on the side of the bed and taking hold of his hand.

'It's going to be pretty damn complex,' the President told her. 'All three forces have to arrange contingency procedures in case a pilot or a ship's captain or an army commander suddenly goes blind. But I'm not going to leave this country with its ass hanging out.'

'Do you want something to eat?' Marian Perry asked him. 'How about some chowder?'

'That sounds good. I don't think I could manage much more than that.'

Once a smiling Korean waitress had brought his supper, Marian Perry fed him.

'I feel so goddamn helpless,' he said, as she crumbled up crackers for him and dropped them into his chowder.

'You're still the President.'

'A President who can't even find his own mouth with a soup spoon?'

'You'll soon learn to cope. What about Eugene Salsy? And Thomas Pryor Gore? He was elected Senator for Oklahoma three times. And Kristin Cox? They were all blind.'

'I know that. But I don't *want* to be blind, Marian, for Christ's sake. I want to read books. I want to look at the sky. Most of all, I want to see you again.'

The First Lady carefully wiped her husband's mouth with a napkin. 'I talked to the doctors again, after you had that retinal scan. They're thinking of trying a lens implant in just one eye, to see if that works.'

'I'll try anything, believe me. One eye is better than no eyes at all.'

'Maybe I shouldn't have told you. They didn't want me to get your hopes up. But I think they've pretty much run out of ideas. They've been looking at dozens of other people who have gone blind in exactly the same way that you did, and they can't understand how it happened to *them*, either.'

'I'll bet you anything you like that Petrovsky's involved in this, somehow. And a few other countries that want to see us brought to our knees.'

Marian Perry put aside the President's chowder bowl, and said, 'You really look like you could use some sleep, darling. You should let Kenneth do more of the worrying. Concentrate on resting, and getting yourself better.'

'Maybe you're right,' he told her. 'The trouble is, every time I sleep, I have nightmares. And when I wake up, I can't even tell if it's day or night. It's so damned *dark* in here.'

All the same, Dr. Cronin gave him a shot of Zolpidem, and by one thirty a.m. he was sleeping. He scarcely seemed to be breathing, and his hair and his face were so white that he looked like his own death-mask, cast out of alabaster. His bedside lamps were kept on, and the connecting door to the nurse's station was left ajar, so that the nurse and the two Secret Service agents sitting outside could keep a constant eye

187

on him, throughout the night.

They talked to each other in low voices – about the nationwide cancellation of all major sporting events, and about the news that five prominent Hollywood actors had all been struck blind after the premiere of *Enchanted Hunters*, the new Rachel Keston picture, at Mann's Chinese Theater on Hollywood Boulevard.

Public hysteria was growing, with countless families barricading themselves in their homes. Random shootings were rife: many by blind people who feared they were being attacked or robbed, firing wildly at imaginary assailants they couldn't even see. Thousands more were trying to escape from city centers into the wilds, ignoring the blanket ban on all freeway driving to create glaciers of traffic. But – proportionately – there were just as many incidents of sudden blindness in the remoter regions as there were in metropolitan areas. In northern Minnesota, seven hunters were killed or seriously injured by black bears as they stumbled blindly through the woods. In the most catastrophic single incident, in Salt Lake City, the entire Mormon Tabernacle Choir was struck blind during a concert, all three hundred and sixty of them. The *Salt Lake Tribune* reported that 'in their white robes, arms extended, they tumbled screaming from the stage like angels falling out of heaven.'

As the nation descended into chaos and darkness, the President continued to sleep. Now and then one of the Secret Service agents looked in at him, but for three hours he remained utterly motionless.

'He's not dead, is he?' asked one of the agents.

The nurse checked his monitor. 'No, no. But he's probably dreaming.'

At three forty-five a.m., however, the President was disturbed by a sharp tapping noise, like a faucet dripping. He lifted his head off the pillow and listened.

'Is anybody there?' he called out, but there was no reply.

The tapping grew louder and more complicated by the minute, and soon it was accompanied by a low humming, and a rustling sound.

'Who's there?' he repeated. There was still no reply, but then the President felt something run lightly across his hand, like a spider or a cockroach, and then he felt more insects scuttling over his neck and his face and into his pajamas. He was about to shout out for help, but as he opened his mouth, five or six hard-shelled beetles tried to penetrate his lips, and he ended up spitting and spluttering.

'Jackson! Kaminsky!' he managed to call out. 'Jackson! Kaminsky! Get in here!'

But there was still no response from the Secret Service agents outside, nor from the nurse.

'Who's there?' he demanded. 'Where are Jackson and Kaminsky? Who the hell's there?'

Frantically, he brushed more beetles away from his lips. They seemed determined to wriggle their way into his mouth, and they tasted foul, like dark brown cough linctus. Some of them were scurrying down his arms, and he repeatedly clutched at the sleeves of his pajamas in an attempt to crush them. Others ran down his back.

'Get these bugs off me!' he shouted. 'Whoever you are, you're in a whole heap of trouble, I can promise you that! *Get these goddamned bugs off me!*'

It was then that he realized that he could see a man standing in the far corner of the room. Actually *see* him, even though he still couldn't see the surrounding room, which remained seamlessly dark. The man looked like a photographic negative, white on black. He was very tall, and he was wearing an elaborate headdress of bull's horns, with strings of beads and feathers hanging from it, which made him appear even taller. He was carrying a stick with a bird's skull on the end of it.

At first the President thought that the man might be only some kind of after-image, imprinted on his retinas. He blinked, and blinked again, to see if he would disappear. But the man not only remained there, right in front of him, he took three or four steps nearer, and raised his right hand, palm outward.

Because his face appeared as a negative, it was difficult for the President to make out exactly what he looked like. His eye sockets were two white smudges, and his teeth were black. But he appeared to have a strong, impassive face, with high cheekbones and a curved hawklike nose.

As he stood there, the bugs began to scuttle off the President's bed, and drop with a soft rattling sound onto the floor. The President could see

190

them as a living torrent of white specks as they rushed over the man's feet and up his legs and into his robes. Soon they had all disappeared from sight.

'I can *see* you,' the President said, hoarsely.

'Of course you can see me,' the man replied, in a harsh, strangely accented whisper. 'I am the one who painted your days black. What you see and what you cannot see, that is for me to decide.'

'Who the hell are you? Are you an actual person, or am I having a dream here?'

'You are asking a dream if he is a dream?' The man paused, and slowly raised his hand to touch his forehead, as if he were trying to visualize something that had happened very long ago.

He said, 'We thought that *you* were a dream once, when you first appeared in your ships.'

'What?'

'We thought that you were gods, sent by Gitche Manitou to bring us prosperity and divine guidance and years of plenty. But you drove us off our hunting grounds and desecrated our sacred places. You slaughtered our women and children as if they were animals. Then we thought that you were a nightmare.

'In the end, though, we made the worst discovery of all. We discovered that you were real.'

'Jackson! Kaminsky!'

The man came closer still, and now the President could actually *smell* him, as well as see him. A smell of uncured hides, and smoky wood fires, and frosty mornings in the woods. A smell of America as it used to be, before the colonists came.

'They cannot hear you,' the man told him. 'I can bring deafness, as well as blindness. I can open and close time, like one of your holy books.'

'Who are you?' the President repeated. 'What the hell do you want?'

'I have many names,' the man replied. 'To some tribes, I am He Whose Face Appeared In The Sky. To you, I am He Who Brings The Terror of Eternal Darkness. But when I was first born, I was given the name of Misquamacus.'

'*Misquamacus?* Is that supposed to mean something to me? I don't speak any Native American.'

'It means what it means. It means He Who Went And Came Back. It means that I was the only one who refused *ever* to accept what your people did to us. So long as you walk over this land as if it belongs to you, I will not allow my bones to lie in it, and I will not allow my memory to blow in its winds. I will take back every forest and every river and every mountain, and they will be ours again, and everything that you have built will be buried in absolute darkness forever.'

'You don't exist,' said the President. 'Either you're a bad dream, or else you're some kind of optical illusion.'

'You will soon find out how real I am,' Misquamacus replied. 'When my ancestors rise up from the earth in their thousands, and overwhelm you. When you see your great monuments collapse, and your bridges fall. When your dams burst open and your cities are drowned. When the sky shakes with such devastating thunder that every window shatters from Ogunquit in the east to Tsurai in the west. Then you will know that I exist.'

'And you're telling me this why?'

'Because I am Wampanaug, and because the Wampanaug have always been a people of great honor, unlike you. When you scattered us, and slew us, you showed us no mercy, even though you knew that we could not withstand you. Now it is *you* who cannot withstand us, yet I am prepared to spare the lives of many millions.'

The President narrowed his eyes, but the white figure remained blurry and out of focus.

The President said, 'That's very magnanimous of you. Pity about the thousands you've killed already.'

'I have killed many of your people, yes,' said Misquamacus. 'But what did you do? You killed not only our people but our whole culture. You killed our traditions, and our religion, and stole out of our children's minds the sacred stories that made us what we were, as if they had never been spoken.'

'But you say you're prepared to be merciful? What's the catch?'

Misquamacus came even closer. The President was sure that he could see beetles dropping off his headdress, and his robes moving as if they were alive.

'You are the chief of your people, are you not?'

'I am the elected President of these United
193

States. That's correct.'

'Then tell all of your people to tear down their houses, and dig up their roads, and learn to live the way that *we* used to live. Tell them that they can fly in the sky no more, nor travel by any means except for walking, or riding on horses. Tell them that they must learn respect for the land, and its seasons, and that they must listen to the spirits of the trees, and of the grass, and of the winds that blow in winter.'

The President said, 'You're serious, aren't you? Whoever you are – *whatever* you are – even if you're nothing but a dream. You really mean it, don't you?'

'You have experienced my power for yourself, my friend. You know what I can do. But I am giving you the chance to be the savior of your people. This soil on which we stand has soaked up too much blood already.'

The President shook his head. 'What you're asking for, fellow – it's insanity! You can't expect us to turn the clock back two hundred years. How would we feed ourselves?'

'In the same way that we did, off the land.'

'Are you out of your mind? You can't sustain three hundred and five million people on buffalo and berries! Besides, the whole world has changed beyond any understanding. It's high-tech, and it's overcrowded, and it's hostile. How would we defend ourselves? With bows and arrows?'

'If you had to do that, perhaps you would then understand what it was like to be us.'

'This has got to be a nightmare. I'm going to

wake up in a minute, and you're going to be gone.'

'No, my friend. I won't. Not until you promise me that you will give our land back to us, and that you will treat it with care and humility, as we once did.'

'Listen,' the President protested, 'there's no way we can go back to living like that, and I doubt if many of your people could do it, either. We're still the most technologically advanced nation on earth. You think we could simply *forget* all of that? You think we'd forget that we ever had airplanes, or automobiles, or computers?'

'You tried it with our people,' said Misquamacus dryly. 'Mostly, you succeeded. You took thousands of Indian children away from their families, didn't you? *Thousands* – and you forced them to forget their tribal stories and their ancient customs, and you brought them all up to be white. What did your great educator say? "Kill the Indian and save the man!"'

The President said, 'I'm sorry, OK? I'm very sorry for what happened to your people. But it's far too late. Time marches on, my friend, and there's no going back, no matter what.'

Misquamacus was silent for nearly a quarter of a minute. As far as the President could make out, his face remained impassive. He had been waiting for centuries to take his revenge, and a few more hours would make no difference. As he had said, the Wampanaug were people of honor and dignity, and of infinite patience, too.

'I will allow you one day and one night,' he

said. 'I will return at this time tomorrow, and then you can tell me what you have decided.'

'I don't need any more time. The answer is no. You're crazy even to ask me.'

'Perhaps. But your own God will know that at least I gave you the chance.'

With that, his image started to tremble, and collapse, and he shrank smaller and smaller until he was nothing more than a faint dot of light, like a switched-off television.

'Jackson!' shouted the President. *'Kaminsky! Get in here!'*

His two Secret Service agents burst in. 'Mr. President?'

'Did you see him?' the President demanded.

'Uh – *who*, exactly?' asked Kaminsky.

'There was somebody in here. An Indian.'

An embarrassed pause. Then, 'An Indian, sir? What kind of an Indian?'

'A Native American kind of an Indian. He had some kind of cockamamie headdress made out of bull's horns, and he was all over bugs.'

'Excuse me?'

'How in hell's name did he get in here, that's what I want to know!'

Jackson crossed the room and looked behind the drapes. He tested the window catches but they were all firmly locked. He opened the closet, but there was nothing inside except for the President's dark gray suit. Kaminsky ducked down and checked under the bed, but came up and said, *'De nada.'*

Now the nurse came in. 'Is everything all right, Mr. President?'

196

'No – everything is most assuredly not all right. There was some raving Red Indian in here, and there were bugs swarming all over my bed.'

The nurse lifted his blankets. 'No sign of any bugs now, sir.'

'You think I'm making this up? He was here – he was right here, standing where you're standing now. I saw him!'

There was a long pause. Then Jackson ventured, 'You *saw* him?'

'He was right in front of me, I'm telling you. He was so close that I could smell the bastard. He said that he was responsible for blinding me, and everybody else, too.'

'Well, that's exactly it, Mr. President. You're blind.'

'Do you think I don't know that?' the President raged.

'Of course you do, sir. But since you're blind, how did you see this character? And how did he get in and out of here without us seeing him?'

The nurse plumped up the President's pillows. 'I just need to check your blood pressure, sir, and your temperature. You could be running a little fever.'

'Goddammit!' the President retorted. 'I *saw* him! He said his name was Marcus something. He said that he was going to strike everybody blind, so that the Indians could take their lands back.'

Jackson cleared his throat. 'I'm real sorry, Mr. President, but I think you must have been having some kind of a night terror. All those drugs they've given you – some of them can have

197

pretty weird side effects.'

'The only weird side effect around here is *you*, Jackson. Now search the whole damn clinic and ask if anybody else saw this joker. For all you know, he could still be here.'

'Yes, sir, Mr. President.'

When the Secret Service agents had gone, the nurse took the President's blood pressure and temperature and checked his heart rate.

'You seem fine,' she said. 'Your heart's beating a little fast, but you can expect that, after a nightmare.'

The President groped around the top of his bedcover until he found the nurse's hand. He squeezed it tight, and said, huskily, 'It wasn't a nightmare. I swear to God.'

'Why don't you try to get some sleep, sir? Maybe I could bring you some hot milk.'

'I don't need hot milk, sweetheart. I need somebody to tell me what in Hades is going on. Do you know what he told me, this Marcus character? He told me that millions of Americans are going to die, unless I give in to him. And do you know what?'

'No, Mr. President, I don't.'

'Well, I'll *tell* you what. I believe him.'

FIFTEEN

Hollywood, California
Tyler unlocked the front door of his apartment
and said, 'Welcome to the Casa del Jones. Come
on in. Make yourself at home.'

Tina stepped into the living room and looked
around, with Tyler limping right behind her.
'Nice place,' she said. 'Very Mexican. They
didn't film *Bring Me the Head of Alfredo Garcia*
in here, did they?'

'Hey, don't blame me,' said Tyler. 'It was
decorated like this when I first moved in, and
I've never had the time to remodel. Personally, I
prefer the Scandinavian look. Like chrome, you
know. And white leather. And glass-topped
tables.'

His apartment was on the second floor of a
cream-colored Spanish-style house on Franklin
Avenue. The living room was paneled in dark
burnished oak, and the floor was dark oak, too,
with a red-and-purple Mexican rug in the center.
The two massive couches were upholstered in
crushed red velvet, with gold tassels, and the
coffee table was dark and squat, with elaborately
carved legs, and strewn with dog-eared copies of
Hot Bike and *American Iron*.

Over the carved-oak fireplace hung a huge,

gloomy oil painting of a bullfight, with a mata-
dor delivering the *estocado* to a black and
bloodied bull.

Tina lifted off her pink Prada shoulder bag and
collapsed onto one of the couches. 'I'm *bushed*,'
she said. 'Two and a half hours from the airport.
That was insane.'

'What can I get you?' asked Tyler. 'Pome-
granate juice? Pepsi? How about a strawberry
smoothie?'

'What's the time?' Tina asked him. She peered
short-sightedly at her watch. 'Jesus, it's not even
eleven yet. Oh, to hell with it. Scotch, please.
Rocks.'

Tyler went through the archway to the kitchen
and came back with a cut-crystal tumbler of
whisky for Tina and a bottle of Heineken for
himself.

'Here's to the hero,' said Tina, clinking her
tumbler against his bottle.

Tyler said, 'Here's to staying alive in the face
of impossible odds.'

He went across to the wide-screen plasma TV
and switched on the TV news. Homeland Security secretary John Rostoff was in the middle of
announcing his coast-to-coast restrictions on
private traffic. In spite of the studio make-up, his
face was pale and his eyes were puffed up.

'He wants us to drive at ten miles an hour?'
said Tina. 'We should be so lucky!'

Their journey from the airport had been almost
unbearable. Both the San Diego Freeway and the
Harbor Freeway had been jammed solid with
wrecked and abandoned vehicles, and the traffic

along every other street had been inching along so slowly that by the time their taxi had reached Olympic Boulevard they had been tempted to get out and walk the rest of the way.

Ragged curtains of brown smoke hung over Los Angeles so that it looked like Baghdad after an air strike, and the smell of burning had even permeated the interior of their air-conditioned taxi, making their eyes water and their noses run.

They had shared a ride because Tina lived only five minutes away from Tyler, on La Presa Drive. But by the time they had reached Franklin Avenue, he had suggested that she come up to his place for a drink and maybe a pizza. She had opened up her laptop as they crawled along La Cienega Boulevard, and written up her report on the AMA disaster before they had reached Rodeo Drive, emailing it directly to the *LA Times* office.

'Do you have to go back to the office today?' Tyler asked her.

'I'm supposed to check in around five. I've been up for twenty-two hours straight, so my editor said that I can take a break. He won't expect me to go back to my desk, though, not now. If he has any assignments for me, he'll text.'

They stepped out onto the balcony that overlooked the gardens. Even here they could smell oily smoke, and hear the distant yipping of police sirens and the honking of fire trucks. In spite of that, a warm breeze was rustling through the orange trees, and four or five plume-topped

201

quail were contentedly warbling on the rooftop, 'chi-cah-go', 'chi-cah-go', which made Tyler feel as if the whole morning was completely unreal.

'Apocalypse Now,' said Tina. 'This is what it must have felt like in New York, on nine-eleven. Like the whole world is falling apart.'

'"*And the fourth angel poured out his vial upon the sun*,"' Tyler quoted. '"*And power was given to him to scorch men with fire. And men were scorched with great heat. And he gathered them together in a place called Armageddon. And there were voices, and thunders, and lightnings, and the cities of the nation fell.*"'

'Hey,' said Tina. 'I'm deeply impressed.'

'My dad's a preacher,' said Tyler. 'A lay preacher, anyhow. He always wanted me to recite the psalms. You know, *"The Lord is my shepherd,"* all that. But when I was a kid I always liked Revelation the best. All those avenging angels. All those earthquakes, and plagues. All those fountains, spouting out blood.'

'Well, well. You have hidden depths, Mr. Jones. What made you decide to become a stuntman? Your father can't have been too pleased about *that*.'

'He didn't mind at all. In fact I think he was pretty proud of me. He always said that young people should follow their hearts. You can worship the Lord by doing what you do best, that's what he used to tell me.'

'You know what my father wanted me to be?' said Tina. 'A florist, just like him. Can you imagine me arranging lilies for a living?'

'Sure, why not?'

Tina gave him a playful shove on the shoulder. 'Hey, I'm a tough nut, me. I broke that Culver City vice-ring story last month – prostitutes-for-planning-permission. Me. All on my own. Even after some hoodlum came up to me in the parking garage at the office and threatened to break both of my arms.'

'OK. I take it back. I *can't* imagine you arranging lilies for a living.' He paused, and grinned at her. 'But I can imagine you pulling the wings off flies.'

'Get me another drink, stunt boy, before you put your other foot in your mouth.'

Tyler was on his way back to the kitchen when his phone started ringing. He picked it up and said, 'Yes?'

'Tyler? Thank God I caught you.' The voice on the other end of the phone was faraway and crackly, as if Admiral Peary were calling him from the North Pole, from 1909.

'I can hardly hear you,' said Tyler. 'Who is this?'

'This is Dan Greeley. I live across the street from your parents.'

'Yes, Mr. Greeley. I think we met the last time I came home. Is everything OK?'

'I'm afraid not. Well, I don't have to tell *you* what's been happening – I saw you on the news. Very courageous thing you did there, Tyler.'

'What's wrong, Mr. Greeley?'

'It's happened here. Over a hundred people in Memory Valley have gone blind. I'm sorry to have to tell you that your parents and your sister Maggie were among them.'

'Oh, God. When did this happen?'

'Yesterday afternoon, around three. They were holding a craft fair in the community center. The photographer from the local paper was taking some pictures and suddenly people started to scream out that they couldn't see. It was pandemonium, I can tell you.'

'Where are my parents now?'

'We took them back to their home, like most of the others. We didn't have any choice. Marin General and Kentfield hospitals were both turning people away.'

'Are they OK? I mean, they're not hurt, are they?'

'They're as well as you could expect them to be, considering. Not injured or anything. My wife Julia's with them, at the moment. All our phones have been on the fritz, so if you want to call them, I guess that now would be a good time. I'm just relieved that I've been able to get in touch with you.'

Tina was standing in the doorway, with the sunlight behind her. 'What's wrong?' she asked him.

'It's my mom and dad, and my sister. Their neighbor just told me they've all gone blind.'

'Oh, no. I'm so sorry.'

'Mr. Greeley?' said Tyler. 'Mr. Greeley?' But the line had gone dead, apart from a soft, persistent crackling noise.

Tyler called his parents' home number. After a long wait, Julia Greeley answered. Her voice, too, was tiny and faint. 'Tyler? Oh, Tyler. Dan said that you would call. Here – your father's right here.'

There was another long wait, and then Tyler's father came onto the line. 'Tyler. Thank God. I tried to get in contact with you yesterday but I couldn't get through.'

'How are you, Dad?'

'Not too good, to tell you the truth. We haven't been able to get any medical attention. We're doing our best here, but your mom's in shock. Maggie's doing her best, but jeez.'

'Listen, Dad,' said Tyler. 'I'll come up now to take care of you. Stay indoors, keep your doors locked. I'll be with you as soon as I can.'

The phone went dead. Tyler redialed, but all he heard was a monotonous busy signal.

'That's it,' said Tyler. 'I'll have to go see them.'

'Do they live far from here?'

'That's the snag. They live in Memory Valley, about fifteen miles north of San Francisco. Question is: how do I get there, if all flights are grounded and there's a total ban on driving?'

'I guess you could try the back-roads.'

'Get real. It's over four hundred miles. How long do you think that's going to take me, even if I ignore the speed limit?'

'Maybe you could rent a powerboat.'

'Now that's a good bit of lateral thinking. You're not just a pretty face, are you?'

'Watch yourself, stunt boy.'

Tyler leafed through his address book until he found Jim Lacuna's number, in Santa Monica.

Jim owned a small fleet of seven powerboats which he rented out for movie productions, and Tyler had worked with him on at least five different movies, including *Jaws 5: Blood in the Water*.

'Jim? It's Tyler Jones.'

This phone line was crackly, too, and there was a surging noise in the background, like a river that had burst its banks.

'Tyler, you crazy son of a bitch! I saw you on the news this morning! When they said that a stunt guy had landed a seven-forty-seven when the pilot went blind, who was the first person I thought of? You, you crazy son of a bitch! And it *was* you! They should give you a medal!'

'Thanks, Jim, but I don't need a medal right now. I need a boat.'

'A boat?' Jim Lacuna paused, and coughed. 'What the hell do you need a boat for?'

Tyler told him about his parents going blind. Jim listened, and then he said, 'Real sorry to hear that, Tyler. That's rough. Believe me, I'd let you have a boat like a shot. I wouldn't even charge you for rental. But you wouldn't get more'n a couple of hundred yards. There's at least two Coast Guard cutters patrolling offshore and they're not letting nobody sail nowhere. They say they can't risk no one going blind way out on the ocean someplace, with no way of giving them a bearing.'

'No way of getting past them?'

'Not even the way that *you* can steer a boat, *muchacho*.'

'OK, Jim. Guess I'll have to find another way.

206

Everything OK with you?'

'I'm keeping my fingers crossed, like everybody else. I'm still waiting to hear from my best mechanic. Dan Bradley, you met him when you were working on that Samuel L. Jackson picture? His wife called me late last night and said he hadn't made it home. I have a bad, bad feeling that this blindness thing is going to get a hell of a lot worse.'

He started to say something else, but suddenly the crackling grew louder and surging background noise swelled up so much that Tyler couldn't hear him at all. 'Jim?' he repeated. 'Jim?' But then the phone went completely dead. Tyler banged the receiver in the palm of his hand and tried listening to it again, but it was still silent.

'What's happening?' asked Tina.

'We can forget boats. So Jim says, anyhow. The Coast Guard aren't allowing anybody out on the ocean. They've running some kind of blockade.'

'I don't know what else to suggest,' said Tina. 'Looks like there's nothing much else you can do but sit tight and wait for news.'

Tyler shook his head. 'The way things are, I'm not going to get any news. The phones are all out.'

'Let me try calling the office,' Tina suggested. She took her cellphone out of her purse and pressed the speed-button for the *LA Times*. She listened, and waited, and then she tried dialing again, but eventually she shook her head and said, 'There's no signal. I'll try texting them.'

She quickly typed out a message, her long pink fingernails tapping on the keys. She peered intently at the screen, but after only a few moments, she said, 'It didn't get through. The whole network's down.'

Almost as soon as she said it, the television blacked out. Tyler switched to another channel, and then another, and another, but the screen remained blank.

He gave up, and tossed the remote-control onto the couch. 'Maybe the phone and the TV people have gone blind, too.'

'It could be much more serious than that,' said Tina. 'It could be a terrorist attack. Or maybe an invasion, even. I mean, what's the first thing you do when you invade another country? You cut off all of their communications.'

'Oh, come on,' said Tyler. 'Who's going to invade us? The Russians? The Chinese? The Mexicans?'

'I don't know, Tyler. But my editor says that I should always think "worst-case scenario." Apart from anything else, "worst-case scenario" always sells papers – a whole lot more than "not-so-bad-case scenario."'

Tyler said, 'I have to get up to Memory Valley somehow. The cops are stopping cars on the highway, but I could try my hog.'

'I made an intelligent guess that you owned a motorcycle,' said Tina.

'Oh. Yeah. Very observant. The biking magazines.'

'Don't tell me,' she said, squeezing her eyes tight shut. 'A Harley Softail.'

'Almost right. Ultra Classic Electra Glide.'

'Hey, top of the range,' said Tina. 'I guess it wouldn't hurt to give it a shot. But you need to rest up first.'

'No way. I need to leave now.'

'You're out of your mind. You're going to ride a motorcycle all the way to San Francisco when you haven't slept for twelve hours straight and the only nutrition you've had in all that time is one bottle of Heineken?'

'Tina – I'm OK. I'm one hundred and ten percent fit. I can always take a couple of breaks along the way.'

Tina pulled a face. 'It's your funeral. Don't blame me if you fall asleep and ride slap-bang into a telephone pole.'

Tyler went through to his bedroom to change into jeans and a white promotional T-shirt for *Hammer of God*, the last movie that he had worked in, and a faded blue denim jacket. While he did so, Tina tried to contact her city desk again, but she was still unable to get through to them, either by landline or cellphone or email or text.

'I'll just have to go down to West First Street and see what's happening,' she said, as Tyler came out of the bedroom. 'How about giving me a ride home on that motorcycle of yours, so that I can pick up my car?'

They left the apartment and went down to the garage at the side of the house. Tyler unlocked the up-and-over door and pushed it open with a creak of unoiled springs. Inside the garage stood a metallic-green Mercury Marquis sedan, circa 1971, covered in a fine film of sandy-colored dust, a Kawasaki dirt bike, still speckled in mud, and a motorcycle shrouded in a black custom-made cover. Tyler lifted the cover and revealed a glossy black Harley Davidson Electra Glide. It smelled of polish and leather and fresh oil.

'I've always thought that there's something very erotic about motorcycles,' said Tina, as Tyler climbed astride the saddle.

'Well, the price was sexy enough,' said Tyler. 'Not so much change out of twenty thousand dollars.'

'Yes, *but*,' said Tina, as he started up the 1500cc engine, with a deep, masculine burble.

Tyler steered the motorcycle onto the driveway. He climbed off to pull down the garage door, and then he climbed back on again and said, 'You coming? Or what?'

Tina lifted herself onto the pillion seat, and wrapped her arms around Tyler's waist. They burbled slowly down the driveway, but as soon as they turned into the street, Tyler opened up the throttle.

'Orgasmic!' said Tina. 'I love it!'

As they sped westward, however, they could see that the sky up ahead of them was growing darker and darker, almost charcoal-gray, even though it was not yet noon. Tina leaned forward and shouted, *'Armageddon!'*

Up in the hills and canyons, even more fires were burning. Behind the smoke, orange flames were leaping over a hundred feet into the air, and shoals of sparks were whirling everywhere. The

210

dry leaves of the yucca trees that lined Franklin Avenue were spontaneously starting to burst into flame. *And power was given to him to scorch men with fire.*

When they reached the intersection with North Highland, Tyler tilted the motorcycle north, and then he tilted left onto Camrose. But as they approached La Presa, they saw thick gray smoke billowing across the road. Tyler slowed down, and as they came around the last curve, they saw that the street ahead of them was blocked with blazing cars, and strewn with bricks and torn-down fencing. They could see people running everywhere, and struggling with each other.

Tyler brought his bike to a halt, with the front suspension dipping. 'It's a riot,' he said. 'For Christ's sake, look at them. They're looting.'

At least thirty young men were smashing their way into one house after another, breaking windows and kicking down doors. The house owners were trying to stop them, but it was obvious from the way that they were waving their arms and shouting and milling helplessly around in circles that they were blind.

One white-haired man in a maroon tracksuit came lurching across his driveway brandishing a shotgun. 'Get the hell out of here!' he screamed. 'Get the hell off of my property!' One of the looters struck him across the back with a piece of fencing post, and he fired his shotgun wildly into the air. Another looter dodged up behind him and pushed him, and he fired again. His second shot hit the door of his own Ford Explorer. He was immediately knocked to the ground and kicked by three or four jeering young men.

'Holy Christ,' said Tyler. 'Can we reach your home any other way?'

'We could try Outpost Drive,' Tina suggested. 'Go back down North Highland, and hang a right.'

But as Tyler began to maneuver his motorcycle around, so that they could go back the way they had come, they saw a pattern of bright flashing lights inside the smoke, as if a crowd of hidden photographers were taking pictures.

Tyler said, 'What the hell is *that*?'

The lights flashed again and again, almost *dancing*, and each time they flashed even more intensely. One of the looters suddenly fell to his knees, with his hands clamped over his face, and started screaming.

'I can't see, man! *I can't fucking see!*'

Another looter abruptly dropped the television he was carrying, so that it fell on its edge onto the sidewalk, and smashed. He whirled around and around, waving his arms, before he lost his balance and pitched over onto his side.

'I've gone blind! Martinez! Help me! I'm blind! *Martinez!*'

A few of the looters started to stumble away, but it was obvious that most of them were confused about what was happening, and reluctant to leave their plunder behind. They had loaded themselves up with computers and hi-fi equipment and plastic refuse bags crammed with anything they could lay their hands on – silverware, clocks, food-blenders, bottles of spirits. One of them was even toting a full bag of Callaway golf

212

clubs. But as they hesitated, the lights flashed again, and the smoke was pierced by dazzling shafts of brilliance. Six or seven of the looters were blinded instantaneously. They toppled sideways onto the ground as if they had been hit hard with baseball bats, and then they began to twitch around on their backs, like dying cockroaches, or crawl across the roadway on their hands and knees, shouting for help in a hoarse and desperate chorus.

'Man! Help me, man! I can't see nothing! Help me!'

Tina said, 'My God, Tyler. What's happening?'

'I don't think we ought to stay here to find out.'

'But this is the *story*, Tyler! These lights! These lights must be the reason why everybody is losing their sight!'

'Maybe they are, but I don't fancy losing *my* sight, do you?'

He revved the Electra Glide's engine, but just as he was about to release the brakes, a heavily built man appeared out of the smoke, like a stage magician. He was wearing a black suit with a black vest, and a wide-brimmed hat with a conical crown. He was at least seventy yards away, so Tyler was unable to see his face clearly, but he was sallow-skinned, with high cheekbones and deep-set eyes – either Hispanic or Native American.

The man stood in the middle of La Presa Drive, looking around at the blinded looters as they moaned and shouted and begged and screamed, but making no attempt to help them. The rest of the looters were scattering now, most of them running down Glencoe Way. They left behind them a trail of discarded ornaments and DVDs, as well as a coffee-maker and a brown leather jacket.

'Give me your cell,' said Tina.

Tyler took out his phone and listened to it. 'It's still not working. Come on, hold tight, we're getting out of here.'

'I don't want to make a call, *stupido*. I want to take a picture.'

'What?'

She snatched the phone from him and held it up to focus on the man in black. She had only taken two photographs, however, before the man in black turned his head and saw her. He frowned, and then he started to walk toward them, with a steady, unhurried, but distinctly menacing stride.

'That's it,' said Tyler, and he twisted the throttle so that the motorcycle surged forward.

But Tina slapped him on the back and screamed out, 'Stop! *Stop!* Just for a second! *Stop!*'

Tyler jerked to a halt and twisted around in the saddle. The man in black was no longer walking toward them, since he could clearly see that he had no chance of catching them up. But behind him, out of the smoke, at least eight figures had emerged, all of them dressed in bizarre costumes. Their faces were as flat and as white as dinner plates, with slitted eyes, and their bodies looked like makeshift coffins, painted black, with dark red designs on them, and double-jointed arms and legs.

'Now what in God's name are *they*?' said Tina.

Tyler shielded his eyes with his hand. He couldn't work out if the figures were human or if they were some kind of mechanical automata. They certainly looked more like giant puppets than real people, but how could they be? He couldn't even work out how many there were. Maybe it was the smoke, drifting across the road and briefly obscuring them, but sometimes he thought there were nearly a dozen of them, and then he thought that he could only count five, or maybe six. He also found it difficult to decide how near they were, or how far away. Sometimes they appeared to be standing in front of the man in black, and standing only five or six feet high; but then they appeared to be standing well behind him, which would have meant they were almost twice that height.

'They're an optical illusion,' said Tina. 'Maybe some kind of laser projection.' She took three more photographs, but then the man in black and his white-faced figures started to walk toward them again.

'Hold on to me!' Tyler shouted, and they roared back down Camrose Drive, swerving right on North Highland Avenue, and then right again on Franklin, cutting in front of a speeding SUV, whose driver blared his horn at them and gave them a furious finger.

'Do prdele!' Tina screamed back at him.

'What did you say?' Tyler shouted.

'Sorry. My dad is Czech. My family name is Fiala, not Freely. *Do prdele* is Czech for "up

215

yours"!'

They tried Outpost Drive, but they had only ridden uphill for quarter of a mile before they splashed into water that was running across the roadway in a crisscross pattern. A few hundred yards further on they reached a fire-department barricade. Through the trees, they could see that six or seven houses were burning and three fire trucks were parked at an angle across the road.

Tyler brought his motorcycle to a halt. A fire captain with a heavy moustache waddled up to the barricade in his rubbers and said, 'Road's closed, sir.'

'But this is Tina Freely, from the *LA Times*. She urgently needs to reach her car. It's only up on La Presa Drive.'

'Wouldn't matter if she was Tina Turner, sir. Road's closed.'

'Maybe one of your guys could get her car for her?' Tyler suggested.

'We're firefighters, sir, with all due respect. Not parking valets.'

Tyler turned around to Tina and said, 'Maybe I can take you down to your office myself.'

'*LA Times* office?' asked the fire captain. 'Wouldn't bother, if I was you. Last I heard, a media helicopter crashed on the rooftop, Bell Jet Ranger, fully loaded with fuel. They had to evacuate the whole building.'

'Oh, God,' said Tina. 'Was anybody hurt?'

'Haven't had an update. All of our communications are out.'

Another firefighter called out to him, 'Captain! We're losing pressure fast!' and without

216

another word, the fire captain left them by the barricade.

'So what do you want to do now?' Tyler asked Tina.

'I'm not sure. I think we should tell somebody about those flashes of light, don't you? And those things we saw, whatever they were. I mean, supposing they're aliens, and this is a real genuine alien invasion? Like *The War of the Worlds*? We should warn people.'

'So who do we tell? And more to the point, *how*?'

'Let's flag down the first police car we see.'

'And say what, exactly? We know why everybody's going blind? There's all these flashes of light, and men dressed up in boxes? Only they're not really men at all, they're optical illusions? Or maybe they're not optical illusions – maybe they're men from Mars?'

'Tyler, we saw those boys lose their eyesight. That wasn't any kind of optical illusion. And what else could have caused it, except for those lights?'

Tyler checked his watch. It was still only twelve twenty-five, but he wanted to make a start for Memory Valley as soon as he could.

'Look,' he said, 'why don't you come with me? Over a hundred people up in Memory Valley, they've gone blind, too. If we can find out why, maybe we can link the two together, and then we'll have some *real* proof to take to the cops.'

Tina brushed her hair back, and thought for a moment. Then she looked around, and nodded.

'OK ... maybe you're right. It doesn't look like there's much I can do here, does it? What with all the phones out and the office evacuated.'

She laid her hand on his shoulder and attempted a smile. 'In any case, this should make a really great story in itself, shouldn't it? Us riding to San Francisco, trying to prove that America has been taken over by aliens?'

'Let's go, then,' said Tyler. He steered the motorcycle back down Outpost Drive, and then he headed back along Franklin Avenue toward the Hollywood Freeway.

All around them, Hollywood was burning, and the sun was only a pale white disk suspended behind the smoke. There was hardly any traffic on the streets, although somewhere to the southwest they could still hear ambulance sirens scribbling, and the chesty honk of fire trucks. As Tyler reached the ramp that led up to the freeway, a police squad car approached them, on the opposite side of the street. It slowed down, and they were coldly scrutinized by two pairs of mirror sunglasses. But after a few slow-motion seconds of suspense, the cops seemed to decide that they didn't look like looters, or vandals, or arsonists, and that stopping them would be too much trouble. They sped away, and Tyler and Tina turned north.

SIXTEEN

Portland, Oregon

'Yes?' I asked.

A man in a black three-piece suit was standing right outside the door. He was tall, at least three inches taller than me, and stockily built, with a big moonlike face pitted with acne scars, and tiny glittery eyes. His hair was gray and greasy and very long, tied at the back in a ponytail. Underneath his suit he wore a white collarless shirt and several heavy silver chains around his neck, although if they had pendants fastened to them they were all tucked well out of sight. In both hands, like a respectful mourner attending a funeral, he was holding a black wide-brimmed hat, its crown and edges shiny with wear.

I looked down at his shoes. I always check out people's shoes, almost the first thing I do, because shoes speak volumes about people's character, and their aspirations, and most important of all, how much of the old folderooni they have stuffed in their wallets. All of which is vital information for a fake teller of fortunes: fair fortunes or foul.

This fellow's shoes were black and dusty, with chisel toes that were slightly turned up. Well made, but oddly out of style, and they could have done with a touch of the famous Lincoln Stain Wax.

'Help you?' I said.

He gave me the ghostliest ghost of a smile. 'It has been far too long,' he said, in a whispery-rattly voice, like dry leaves blowing across a driveway.

'Erm, are you sure you have the correct room here? This is room two-one-three.'

He leaned slightly to one side, as if he were trying to look past me. I leaned the same way, to block his view.

'Harry?' called Amelia. 'Who is it?'

'Wrong room,' I called back. I gave the man one of my toothiest, insincerest grins, and repeated, 'Wrong room. Sorry. Ask at the desk why don't you?'

'He is here,' the man in black whispered. 'I have waited with great patience for this moment, and now it has arrived.'

'Look,' I told him, 'I have absolutely no idea who you are, or why you've come knocking on my door, but you've made a mistake here, pal. This is room two-one-three, OK? Go back downstairs and check.'

The man in black showed absolutely no indication that he was going to go away. 'I have come for the one who betrayed us,' he said. 'This is the time of reckoning, at last.'

'Well, whatever time it is, too bad,' I replied, and shut the door in his face. But then I turned around, and shouted out, *'Ha!'* in shock. The man was standing *inside* the room, right in front of the balcony door, still with his hat held in both hands.

I think Singing Rock was as shocked as I was. *'Tácu eniciyapi hwo?'* he demanded.

'Háu kola,' smiled the man in black. *'Khoyá-kiphela he?'*

'Tácu eniciyapi hwo?' Singing Rock shouted at him. I don't think I had ever heard him sound so angry and so frightened – even in the Sisters of Jerusalem Hospital, back in New York, when Misquamacus had called on the Great Old Ones to wipe us all out, and the ceilings had been collapsing all around us.

'Tácu eniciyapi hwo? What is your name?'

The man in black stepped toward him. 'You can call me Wovoka, if you like, my little brother from the plains.' He pressed one hand across his heart. 'This, after all, is Wovoka's body. This is Wovoka's face.'

'What is your real name?' asked Singing Rock. 'Wovoka was a Paiute. You speak to me in Sioux.'

The man in black continued to come closer. *'Whoa,'* I said, holding out one hand. 'Why don't you just keep your distance, feller?'

The man in black ignored me. 'I am all men, from all tribes. I speak all tongues, although the tongue of the Sioux always leaves a bitter taste in my mouth. The taste of snake venom.'

He turned to me, still with that ghostliest ghost of a smile on his face. 'Do you know how the Sioux got their name? It is what the French invaders called the Nadewisou people, when they first encountered them, and Nadewisou means "treacherous snakes."'

He turned back to Singing Rock. 'And *here*, of all the snakes – here is the most treacherous. The one who betrayed his own people not just once, when he was living in the world of touching flesh, but in the afterlife, too, when he was a spirit. And again, now, by helping you.'

Singing Rock raised both arms, his fists clenched and his wrists crossed. 'You are not Wovoka, even if you stand here in Wovoka's body. I know who you are! You must leave Wovoka, let him sleep in peace! Leave all of the spirits that you have disturbed!'

'I have not disturbed them, but raised them,' said the man in black. 'Life and death are one circle, and all of those wonder-workers left so much unfinished when they died. Divided, and alone, they were defeated. But together, they will bring us back our sacred lands, and our languages, and most of all they will bring us back our pride. We will breathe the wind again, and it will no longer be tainted by the white man's smoke.'

Now he was towering over Singing Rock, although Singing Rock kept his arms up and his wrists crossed.

'You must leave Wovoka's spirit!' Singing Rock shouted. 'In the name of Something That Moves, Takushkansjkan the Sun! In the name of Wi the Moon, and Wohpe his daughter, the Falling Star! In the name of Ite, the Face!

He hesitated, and then he almost screamed out, *'In the name of White Buffalo Calf Woman!'*

One night, after too many shots of Jack Daniel's had rendered both of us almost unintelligible, Singing Rock had told me all about the gods who were worshipped by the Lakota Sioux, and I knew that White Buffalo Calf Woman was the goddess they revered the most. White Buffalo Calf Woman was the business, apparently, and no Sioux shaman would dare to invoke the name of White Buffalo Calf Woman unless he was desperate.

But the man in black didn't seem to be at all fazed by these invocations, even the great and holy WBCW. He placed his hat carefully on his head, and then he grasped Singing Rock's upraised wrists.

Amelia snapped out, *'Misquamacus!'*

The man in black hesitated, and lowered his head a little, as if he were waiting for her to say something else.

Singing Rock glanced across the room at her, and then turned back to the man in black. His face was taut with dread, his eyes bulging and the veins standing out on his forehead. He was already dead. He was nothing but a mirage of a human being who had once been John Singing Rock, a memory made visible only by smoke and light and spiritual energy. In reality, he had little more substance than a hologram, but I could see that he was terrified by what he knew the man in black could do to him.

'Misquamacus!' Amelia repeated. 'Let him go!'

'You are white, and you are a woman,' said the man in black, without looking at her. 'Who are you to command me?'

'I may be a woman,' Amelia replied, defiantly,

223

although her voice was trembling with strain. 'But at least I'm a *real* woman, who lives in the world of touching flesh. What are you, Misquamacus? You're nothing but an echo, in empty space. You're nothing but a shout in the forest which nobody can hear. You can't exist except in the spirits of others – like Wovoka, or those other wonder-workers whose souls you've been dressing yourself up in.'

'You have no idea of my strength,' said the man in black. As he did so, he gradually forced Singing Rock's arms downward, and at the same time he pried his wrists apart. Singing Rock may be have been made of nothing more than ectoplasm, but he grimaced in pain and effort. Even though, technically, he was a ghost, he was substantial enough for the man in black to hurt him.

'OK, that's enough!' I said. I came away from the door, crossed the room, and took hold of the man in black's sleeve. He turned his head and spat at me.

He didn't punch me, or give me a head-butt. He didn't even take his hands off Singing Rock. But I had never been hit so hard, ever. I was flung back across the room so violently that I hit one of the armchairs and two of its legs collapsed. I rolled sideways onto the floor, twisting my shoulder.

'Right, that's it!' I told the man in black. I climbed back onto my feet and approached him again, my knees slightly bent and my hands raised in what I hoped was a convincing kung fu posture. Maybe I had never taken lessons, but I had seen *Enter the Dragon* four times.

But Amelia caught at my arm and warned, 'Harry – don't even think about it. He could easily kill you! It's your bracelet! Get your bracelet!'

'What?'

'Your *bracelet*, Harry! Blow out the candle and get your bracelet back! Singing Rock's trapped here until you do!'

I didn't really understand what she was trying to say to me, but I stepped away from Singing Rock and the man in black, my hands still raised, and backed over to the dining table, where the cinnamon-smelling candle was still burning, with my black-pebble bracelet shining around its base.

When I reached out for it, however, the man in black spat at me again – and I was given a hefty shove on the shoulder that sent me sprawling onto the rug.

'You will stay where you are, white fool!' he cautioned me. 'It is not your place to interfere.'

'Oh, you think? I'm calling the desk. Let's see how a three-hundred-year-old echo deals with hotel security.'

The man in black stared at me balefully, and even though he looked like the Paiute wonder-worker Wovoka I could see in his eyes who he really was. Misquamacus, The One Who Went And Came Back.

'Bring it on, why don't you?' I challenged him. 'You want your revenge so bad, why don't you have a go at *me*!'

'I will, you can be sure of that,' the man in black whispered. 'But before I do, I want you to witness your people laid low, as mine were. You are a fool, and a blusterer, and you have no magic. But your meddling has thwarted me from taking my revenge, until now.'

'Oh, I thwarted you, did I?' I retorted. 'Well, let me tell you something, Misquamacus, I'm going to thwart you again. You're going to be so goddamned thwarted you won't know what hit you. I'm going to be the very thwart of you, dude!'

The man in black didn't take his eyes off me, but now Singing Rock suddenly cried out – an echoing, hair-raising wail that sounded as if he were screaming in a tunnel. I heard a crackling noise, and a wide parting appeared in Singing Rock's hair, revealing his red-raw scalp underneath. There was a momentary pause, and then his scalp started to peel away from the top of his head, like a red tulip slowly opening its petals.

He screamed again, in unbearable agony, but his skin continued to unroll from the top of his head downward, exposing his eyeballs and his cheek muscles and his nose. His lips were turned inside-out, exposing his tongue and his grinning, tobacco-stained teeth.

I launched myself at the man in black a second time, but again he jerked his head and spat at me, and I was thrown back so hard that I felt as if I had been hit by a car. I knocked the back of my head against the wall and fell awkwardly onto the floor, and a framed print dropped on top of me. Winded, bruised, I tried to get up again, but Amelia knelt down beside me and said, 'Harry – no – there's nothing you can do!'

Singing Rock screamed again, as shrill as a tortured cat. His skin was now peeling down his neck, revealing his carotid artery and his Adam's apple, bloody and glistening I could actually see his Adam's apple rising and falling as he cried out in pain.

'For Christ's sake!' I said. 'I can't let him do this! *Misquamacus! Misqua-goddamned-macus!*'

The man in black was still gripping Singing Rock's wrists, while Singing Rock's skin unrolled from his shoulders, unrolling his coat and his shirt along with it. His chest muscles and his tendons and his veins were exposed, and all the bubbly connective tissue that held his body together. He looked now like one of those anatomical models, with all of their insides showing, except that his muscles and his tendons were twitching with pain, and his lipless mouth was dragged down in a silent howl of despair.

'Harry – *don't!*' Amelia insisted. 'Singing Rock is dead already! Misquamacus is making him suffer, but he can't kill his spirit!'

'That's not the goddamned point! Singing Rock saved our lives! I'm not going to let that bastard hurt him – even if he *is* dead!'

I pulled myself onto my feet, and lunged toward the dining table. Immediately, I was struck but yet again by something or somebody that I couldn't see. The blow caught me right on the side of the head, so that my ears sang. But I managed to fall forward, and sprawl across the top of the table, and reach out for the candle and the black-pebble bracelet.

'Ecúnsniyo!' barked the man in black, and the candle flame roared up into a white-hot jet of fire, which reached right up to the ceiling and set fire to the lampshade. The heat scorched my face, and I smelled my hair burning. I had no choice but to back away, shielding my face with my hand, and as I did so I was hit yet again, across the shoulders, with a crack that almost broke my spine.

I fell down onto my knees, coughing. But it was then that I saw the broken chair leg, easily within reach. I picked it up, and gripped it as tight as I could.

I looked up. Singing Rock had stopped screaming now, but he was shuddering violently. By now the man in black had unrolled both his clothes and his skin almost down to his knees, baring his stomach muscles and his thigh muscles. All of the skin had been peeled off his penis so that it was only a thin, bloody string.

Amelia was standing in the corner with her hand clasped over her mouth, her eyes wide with horror.

I stood up and lurched toward the dining table again. The candle flame roared even higher, and even hotter, but I swung the chair leg and knocked it onto the floor. It fell onto the rug, where it kept on burning, its white flame playing against the wall as fiercely as an oxyacetylene torch. But I wasn't worried about that: I reached across the dining table and snatched the black-pebble bracelet, and slipped it back onto my wrist.

I held my fist up, and shouted out, 'John Singing Rock! *John!* Here!'

The man in black spat at me, again and again, and I was thrown from one wall to the other. But I kept on staggering back onto my feet, and brandishing Singing Rock's bracelet, and I could see that Singing Rock's skin and clothes were rolling back up again, to cover him. The man in black let go of his wrists, and stalked toward me, tossing an armchair out of his way, his face contorted with anger. But Singing Rock, released from his grasp, immediately began to fade. His color was leached away, until he was translucent, and he looked like the ghost he really was. Silently, his ectoplasm twisted around, like a long white chiffon scarf, and rose up into the air, and floated away. It flew out of the open door that led to the balcony, and upward, into the sunshine, out of sight.

All that was left was smoke, and that began to shudder, and curl, and blow away, too. As it vanished, I felt the bracelet tighten and tingle, and I knew that Singing Rock's spirit was back inside the black pebbles that he had carefully picked from the bed of the Okabojo, when he was only a young man, and first learning the art of Native American shamanism.

The man in black stormed right up to me, and stood over me like a angry bull, his chin tilted aggressively upward.

'You want Singing Rock?' I asked him. He was so close that I could feel his chilly breath on the back of my upraised fist. 'He's *here* now, where you can't hurt him any more. His spirit's inside this bracelet, Misqua-smartass-macus, and you can't go after him because you don't

229

happen to *have* a spirit any longer, now do you?'

'I could destroy you where you stand,' whispered the man in black. 'I could turn your heart into a stone, or boil your brain. I could fill your stomach with venomous snakes and your lungs with fire-ants. I could flay you alive, like your treacherous friend.'

I didn't answer him. To be totally truthful, I was too scared to open my mouth. Amelia was looking at me from the other side of the room, and from the expression on her face I could see that she was just as frightened as I was. The candle flame had gone out now, but the rug was still smoldering, and fragments of glowing ash were still floating down from the skeletal remains of the lampshade.

The man in black stayed in front of me, breathing hard, for what seemed like an hour, even though it was probably no longer than twenty seconds. Then he said, very softly, 'I promised you that I would show you your people scattered and blown to the winds, and I shall keep my promise. But when the sun sets on that day of destruction, you will pay for what you have done to me, both you and this woman, and the pain that I inflicted on your treacherous friend will be as nothing compared with the pain that I will inflict on you.'

I still couldn't find the words to answer him. The last thing I wanted to do was provoke him into changing his mind so that he peeled *my* skin off, like some kind of gory banana. I couldn't even work out how to nod.

At last he turned away from me, and as he

turned away he vanished, as if he had never been there. I *felt* something, like a door opening and closing, and a momentary draft, but that was all. Wovoka had more substance than Misquamacus. At least he could make himself visible. But he was still no more than a spirit, and every spirit has to return to the other side, sooner or later.

'Has he really gone?' I asked Amelia.

She closed her eyes for a moment, and raised one finger, as if she were trying to feel which way the wind was blowing. Then she opened her eyes again and said, 'Yes ... he's gone.'

I came over and stamped on the smoldering carpet, until I had extinguished the last of the glowing orange sparks. The smell of burned wool made me sneeze, three times, which my grandmother always told me was bad luck. Sneeze once, you wake up the Devil. Sneeze twice, he realizes where you are. Sneeze three times and he comes to get you.

'What Singing Rock said about Misquamacus was right, then?' I said. 'He's borrowing the spirits of other medicine men so that he can come back into the real world and get his revenge.'

'It looks like it,' said Amelia. She was looking nervy and shaken, and she kept folding and unfolding her arms and touching her cheek, like somebody who badly needs a cigarette. 'And of course there used to be *hundreds* of medicine men and wonder-workers, all across the country, so he has plenty to choose from.'

'Well, Singing Rock told us a few of them, didn't he? Infernal John and Chief Hot Dog or

231

whatever his name was.'

Amelia said, 'Every tribe had at least one medicine man. Sometimes more than one. They all had their different ways of making magic, but their powers were pretty similar. Healing people, or making their enemies sick. Making it rain, or making it stop raining. Filling up lakes with plenty of fish. Shape-shifting, into coyotes. Turning into eagles, and flying.'

'What about making people go blind?'

'I don't know. I really don't know about that. And of course Singing Rock didn't get the chance to tell us.'

'Can we bring him back?'

'If we do, that will probably bring Misquamacus back, too, to finish what he started. Do you really want to risk it?'

'Unh-hunh. I don't want Singing Rock to get skinned again. And I don't want *us* to get skinned, either. I don't much care for the raw look.'

'I suppose I could try to communicate with him by thought-dowsing,' said Amelia.

'What the hell is that when it's at home?'

'It's like dowsing for water, only you're trying to find thoughts instead of hidden springs. Actually it's more like tuning in to radio signals than dowsing, but you use a hazel twig, just the same. You can pick up thoughts right out of the air. You can hear them.'

She went over to her woven bag, rummaged inside it, and eventually produced a dry, Y-shaped twig, only about six inches long, and showed it to me.

'It's not always successful,' she said, 'especially when somebody's been dead for quite a long time. It works best when the subject has only just passed away, and their thoughts are still in the room. But Singing Rock's *spirit* was here, wasn't it, so I might have an outside chance to getting in touch.'

I took the twig from her and turned it this way and that. I even sniffed it but it didn't smell of anything except Amelia's musky perfume. I have to admit that I was skeptical, but there was no harm in giving this 'thought-dowsing' a shot. Until we found out how Misquamacus was striking people blind, we would be groping around in the dark, just like they were.

At that moment, we heard a loud bang in the street outside – then shouting, and a woman calling out for help. We went out onto the balcony and saw that a Shogun had collided into the back of a trolley car, and that a man had been pinned against its rear bumper. He wasn't yet dead, but I wouldn't have put serious money on his chances of surviving.

A crowd had gathered, and three or four men were trying to open the Shogun's doors. The woman driver didn't seem to be making any attempt to get out, even though one of the men was hammering with his fist on her window.

'You have to back up!' he shouted at her. 'Come on, lady, you have to back up!'

Amelia and I stood on our balcony watching this scene for a few minutes. A police car arrived, and two cops got out and tried to get the woman to back up, too. She turned her head and

233

stared at them, but she didn't seem to see them.

'She's *blind*,' said Amelia. 'Look at her, the way she's pressing her hand against the window.'

An ambulance drew up, and after the paramedics had examined the man who was crushed against the back of the trolley car, they talked to the cops and one of the cops smashed the Shogun's passenger window with the butt of his gun. The cops and the paramedics opened the driver's door and helped the woman out. From the way she was holding her head it was plain that she couldn't see.

'We have to do something,' said Amelia. 'Misquamacus is going to make us *all* go blind if we don't.'

We watched the street scene for a few moments more, but then Amelia said, 'I feel like a rubber-necker. Let's go back inside.'

'So, you're going to try this thought-dowsing thing?' I asked her.

She nodded. She crossed over to the couch and without any hesitation she crossed her arms and pulled off her pale gray sweater. She was wearing a white lacy bra with rosebuds embroidered on it. She was very big-breasted and it didn't leave a whole lot to my imagination. Next she unbuttoned her jeans, sat down on the couch, and took those off, too, revealing a white lacy thong that matched her bra. I had guessed the thong correctly, but not the color. White, not black. Saintly, rather than Satanic.

'Hey – you have to do this in your *under-wear*?' I asked her, trying to sound all jovial and

234

offhand.

She reached behind her back and unfastened the catch of her bra, and slipped it off. Her nipples were very pale pink, and they crinkled in the warm breeze that was blowing in from the open balcony door. I tilted my head away and half-covered my eyes with my hand. When I looked back she had taken her thong off, too, and was sitting on the couch completely naked, except for her short white socks.

'You have to do this in the nude?'

Amelia nodded. 'The hazel twig acts as the antenna, but my skin will actually be the receiver. If I wore clothes, any thoughts that I picked up would be so muffled that I probably wouldn't be able to understand them.'

She paused, and then she said, 'If you're embarrassed, Harry, you can always go out on the balcony, or shut yourself in the bedroom.'

'Embarrassed? *Moi?* Of course not. You go ahead.'

She peeled off her socks and then sat cross-legged in the center of the couch, with her back very straight, almost as if she were practicing yoga, except that she held up the hazel twig in front of her, at eye-level.

I straddled one of the dining chairs and watched her and thought how much I liked everything about her. Her face, her body, her aura. The way the heel of her right foot was tucked up between her legs. In fact I was in love with her, and I wished to more than anything that she had never married Bertie.

She looked at me, her forehead furrowed in a

mock-frown. 'I love Bertil,' she said. 'He's a wonderful husband. But that doesn't mean that I don't love you, too.'

'You heard what I was thinking,' I said. I couldn't believe it.

'Of course I did. I wouldn't waste my time doing this if I couldn't.'

'Jesus, I'm embarrassed.'

Amelia smiled. 'Don't be. Hasn't it ever occurred to you that I might feel the same way about you?'

SEVENTEEN

She slowly waved the hazel twig from side to side. 'Hazels used to be called "wishing sticks,"' she said.

'Oh, really?' To tell you the truth, I wasn't really concentrating on the twig.

'The first hazel was brought to America by the Pilgrim Fathers, because they believed the story that God gave Adam a hazel branch so that he could strike the surface of a lake with it, and produce any animal he wished for. They thought it would save them from having to carry too many sheep and pigs with them, on their ships.'

'Hey – that would have been really neat if it had worked.'

'Another magical thing about hazel twigs ... if you tangle some into your hair, they make a

236

"wishing-cap" and you'll soon be granted everything you ever wished for.'

'Either that, or get locked up in the nuthouse for walking around looking like a scarecrow.'

Amelia raised the hazel twig a little, and closed her eyes.

'Do you hear something?' I asked her.

'Shh, there's a very faint resonance. Somebody's talking.'

'Who is it? Does it sound like Singing Rock?'

'*Shh!*' she insisted.

I shut my mouth and kept it shut. Amelia slowly waved the hazel twig in ever-widening circles, and then held it up high above her head, and very still. She closed her eyes and then she said, '*I kill us.*'

I was bursting to ask her what she meant, but now she was listening even more intently, nodding her head slightly and moving her lips. '*I kill us. Car winner.*'

Almost half a minute went past, and she kept on nodding and murmuring, '*Car winner and shy lower.*'

I waited for more. If this gibberish was all she could pick up from the Great Beyond, then her 'thought-dowsing' wasn't going to help us very much.

'*I kill us,*' she repeated.

Another half-minute went by, and then she abruptly opened her eyes. 'I'm sure that was Singing Rock,' she said. 'He was very faint, and there was so much white noise – probably some of the psychic static that Misquamacus left behind him. But it was definitely him.'

'Well, I'm glad he told us something useful – *not*,' I said. '"I kill us"? "Car winner"? "Shy lower"? What the hell did any of that mean?'

Amelia pulled her socks back on, and then her thong and her bra. 'Whatever it was, it must have been important. He kept on saying it over and over. "I kill us," "I kill us."'

'Well, maybe it is important,' I complained. 'But don't you think that spirits can be a right royal pain in the ass? Why don't they just speak-a da English, like living people do? Oh, no. They have to communicate in signs and portents and mysterious mutterings.'

Amelia was buttoning up her Gloria Vanderbilts and buckling her leather belt. While she was doing so, however, I suddenly saw a dark blue spot appear on the pale blue wall behind her. Almost immediately, it started to grow, creeping around counterclockwise until it described a semicircle. I pointed to it and said, 'Would you take a look at that? What the hell do you think that is?' But by the time Amelia had turned around it had formed almost a complete circle, around nine or ten inches in diameter.

I went up to it, and rubbed it with my fingertip. 'It's not Magic Marker or anything like that. It's not wet, anyhow.'

I was still peering at it when another dark blue mark appeared to the right, and that, too, started to form a circle. We watched it in bemusement. It was like somebody was drawing on the wall from the *inside*.

As soon as the second circle was complete, a third circle started to appear, and then a fourth.

We waited for more, but it looked as if four circles were all we were going to get.

I folded my arms. 'OK. These are a sign from the Great Beyond, unless I'm mistaken.'

Amelia cautiously touched each circle with her fingertips. 'I'm sure of it. Singing Rock must have realized that we might not have understood what he was saying. So he's given us a clue.'

'Four circles? What kind of a clue is that? Why doesn't he just tell us straight?'

'Because he *can't*, probably. Misquamacus could be running interference. Stopping Singing Rock from speaking to us direct.'

We were still staring at the circles when a large turquoise butterfly came flickering in through the balcony door. It fluttered around the living room for a while, and then it perched itself in the center of the left-hand circle, and stayed there, its wings rising gently up and down.

'So is this a clue, too? Or just some stray lepidoptera?'

'I don't know, Harry. Really I don't.'

As we were watching, however, the butterfly suddenly took off, and perched itself in the center of the second circle. Then, a few seconds later, it flew to the third circle, and perched there, too. This had to be a message, although I didn't have the foggiest notion what it was.

The butterfly landed on the fourth circle, and there it seemed content to stay.

I went up close to it, but it made no attempt to fly away. It had dark brown ovals on its wings that almost looked like human eyes staring back at me, and a crimson head, like a large drop of fresh blood. 'This is some butterfly,' I said. 'It doesn't look Portlandian, or Oregonish, does it? It looks tropical.'

'I never saw a butterfly anything like it before.'

'Oh, I did. When little Lucy came down to spend the weekend in Miami, and I took her to Butterfly World. It's probably a greater green cross-eyed squinter, or something like that.'

'Butterfly World,' Amelia repeated. She came up to the wall and touched the circles again, one by one. 'Butterfly World. That's it! That's what these are! They're *worlds*.'

'Worlds? How do you work that out? They could be hula hoops for all we know.'

'No, Harry, they're worlds, I'm sure of it. I *feel* it.'

'OK. You're the genuine authentic psychic. Who am I to argue?'

'Four worlds, that's right. And you can go from one world to the next, just like that butterfly.'

'So what does that tell us?'

'That tells us that we have to find ourselves a PC.'

'OK ... they have one downstairs, in reception. They'll probably let you use it for free if you offer to do it in your birthday suit.'

Amelia gave me one of her old-fashioned looks. 'OK, sorry,' I said. 'But any time you're thinking of trying any more thought-dowsing, and you need moral support, or even if you need *im*moral support, I'm your man.'

She reached up and gave me a playful pat on

the cheek. 'I'll take that as a compliment,' she said. At the same time, the butterfly suddenly flickered away, and vanished out through the balcony door.

Down in the hotel lobby, the Art Garfunkel lookalike ungraciously allowed us to use one of the hotel's laptops. The fuss he made about it, you would have thought we wanted to play Cajun fiddle music on his prize Stradivarius.

We sat close together on one of the bright red Bugs Bunny-style couches and Amelia tapped in 'Four Worlds.'

Our answer came up instantly. Neither of us had ever heard of the Four Worlds before, but here on the Internet was everything we needed to know.

It turned out that the Four Worlds were part of the belief system of some of the Pueblo Indians of New Mexico. Their legends said that Tawa the Sun Spirit had created a world where his people could live together in peace and harmony.

In his First World, however, the Pueblos began to misbehave themselves – stealing and lying and fighting and indulging in all kinds of sexual shenanigans. So the least badly behaved were taken by Tawa's messenger, the Spider Grandmother, to a Second World, and those who were left behind in the First World were promptly incinerated. Well, that's life. You steal, you lie, you fight, you indulge in sexual shenanigans, you're toast.

After a while, though, the inhabitants of the

Second World began to conduct themselves just as disgracefully, and so they were moved by Spider Grandmother to a *Third* World – and at last to a Fourth World. By the seventeenth century, the Pueblos had reached a state of physical grace and social harmony – just in time to be invaded by the Spanish, who built Catholic missions all across New Mexico and tried to wipe out their native beliefs altogether, Four Worlds and all. Five hundred Pueblo Indians who refused to convert to Roman Catholicism each had one foot cut off.

To their credit, the Spanish taught the Pueblos how to farm wheat and barley and grow fruit trees, but the Pueblos' new prosperity brought more and more attacks from wandering Indian tribes, like the Navajo and the Apache, who seriously coveted their neighbors' oxes and their asses, not to mention their apples and their stores of grain. Apart from being continually raided by other Indians, the Pueblos contracted all kinds of European diseases from the Spanish, and hundreds of them died of smallpox and scarlatina.

Eventually they rebelled against the Spanish and the Roman Catholic religion and returned to their old gods like Tawa and Spider Grandmother. To punish them, General Juan Trevino arrested forty-seven Pueblo medicine men on charges of witchcraft. He had three of them hung and the rest publicly flogged. Big mistake. In 1680, a rebellious San Juan Indian called Popé organized a mass revolt. Houses and missions were burned, and over four hundred Europeans were hacked to pieces. The Spanish were driven out of New Mexico and it was fifteen years before they were able to fight their way back.

It was General Trevino's letters that gave me and Amelia the answer we were looking for. In fact, when Amelia brought up a translation of his last letter to the royal court in Spain, we just turned and looked at each other and said, almost simultaneously, '*I kill us.*'

'Your Reverence, having been murderously attacked by Taos, Picuris, and Tewa Indians in their respective pueblos, we retreated with an hundred and fifty settlers to Isleta Pueblo, which was the only pueblo where the natives had not turned against us.

'As dusk fell, however, three Tewas approached the pueblo from the southwestern side, along a dry arroyo. I recognized two of them as medicine men who had been imprisoned at Santa Fe for practicing witchcraft.

'Accompanying them were at least twenty strange figures. They were wearing expressionless white masks with slits for their eyes. They were dressed in some manner of armor, which appeared to be crudely constructed of wood, and painted in red and black. This creaked and rattled as they approached us, and for some reason we began to feel deeply apprehensive.

'In the dim light, I found it difficult to ascertain precisely how many of these strange figures there were. At times it seemed as if there were more than two score. Then there seemed to be no more than six. They altered their positions as if they were chess pieces upon a board, and one moment they appeared to be extremely tall, and

243

the next moment as small as children, and far away.

'Te'E, one of the older Indians, was standing close to me. I asked him what these figures were, and if they had any connection to witchcraft. Whereupon he covered his face with his hands, *so that only his eyes looked out*, and he explained that these were Eye-Killers, the demons produced when Pueblo girls became impregnated with the offspring of foreign objects, such as prickly cactus prongs.

'He said that they were sometimes known as *shilowa*, which is the Zuni Indian word for red; and sometimes as *k'winna*, which is the Zuni word for black. He said that we should retreat from the pueblo with all haste, because the Eye-Killers were capable of blinding us with a single look.'

'"Car winner" and "shy lower,"' said Amelia. 'Black and red, in Pueblo Indian-speak.'

'That's what Singing Rock was trying to tell us, then. Misquamacus has called up these Eye-Killer things.'

We read on. General Trevino had taken old Te'E seriously, and ordered the settlers and the Isleta Indians to evacuate the pueblo and make their way northeastward. At the same time he directed twelve of his soldiers to take up positions at the top of the arroyo and prevent the Tewa medicine men and their scary collection of Eye-Killers from entering the village.

'As the strange figures came closer, I called upon the Tewas to stay where they were, but even if they heard me they did not respond, and continued to climb toward us. I gave the order to open fire, but the first volley of harquebus shot inflicted no casualties on the Tewas and their strange companions.

'My men prepared to engage them with sword and pike, but as they advanced, the eyes of the white-faced figures flashed as brightly as summer lightning. One after the other, my men fell to the ground, each of them crying out that he had been blinded, and calling on the Lord for help.

'I realized that it would be futile for me to stay, and that if I, too, were to be blinded, I would be of no service to those settlers who depended upon me for their protection. Therefore I left the pueblo without further delay.'

'So the gallant general skedaddled,' I said. 'Mind you, I can't say that I blame him.'

Amelia closed the laptop. 'What are we going to do now?' she asked me. 'We should really tell somebody about this, shouldn't we, and as soon as we possibly can.'

'The trouble is, who? And who's going to take us seriously? You can imagine what they'd say if we tried to call the Pentagon, or the FBI.'

'We need to know more about these Eye-Killers,' said Amelia. 'What they are, where they come from, and if there's any way we can stop them.'

'Maybe we could try asking Singing Rock again.'

Amelia shook her head. 'It's much too dangerous. For Singing Rock, as well as for us. What we need is somebody who knows all about

245

Pueblo shamanism, but who isn't on Misquamacus' radar.'

'Oh, simple,' I said. 'Maybe we should look in Yellow Pages.'

I took the laptop back to the desk. The Art Garfunkel lookalike wasn't around, so I put his precious computer on a shelf underneath the register.

Amelia and I went back upstairs. As we walked along the corridor toward our room, we saw that our door was open and the Ersatz Art was standing there talking to the maid.

'Excuse me, sir! Madam! What exactly have you been *doing* in here?'

I raised both hands in surrender. 'We had a little accident with a candle, that's all. I swear to God we haven't been smoking.'

He opened and closed his mouth several times. Eventually, he said, 'You'll have to leave. Like, *now*. And you can expect a bill for all of the damage you've done.'

'Believe me, Mr. Garfunkel,' I told him, 'a burned rug is the least of your worries.'

As if to emphasize what I was trying to tell him, we heard a loud collision from out in the street, and a woman screaming, and then another collision, and another.

The hotel receptionist stared at me in bewilderment, as if I had somehow caused those accidents myself, by remote control. Then he said, 'My name's not Garfunkel. Why did you call me "Garfunkel"? My name's Resnick.'

246

EIGHTEEN

Ladera Park, Los Angeles
Jasmine was woken up by a loud banging noise, followed by another, and another, and then people furiously shouting. She sat up on the couch. It was almost dark outside, and the sky was a dusky purple, with only a narrow streak of orange where the sun had gone down.

She heard more shouting, followed by a shot. A man started screaming, and a door slammed. Feet came cantering and squeaking along the corridor, maybe ten or eleven people, and it sounded like they were all wearing sneakers. Somebody kicked at the door of Auntie Ammy's apartment.

The baby boy was sleeping in one of Auntie Ammy's armchairs, but now he woke up too, and started to cry. Jasmine went over and picked him up. He was still hot, and his hair was stuck up in a lopsided plume, and he smelled of warm pee.

Somebody kicked the apartment door a second time, and then a third. Jasmine held the baby close to her chest to muffle his crying. 'Shush, honey. Shush.'

There was another bang, further along the corridor. A young man shouted, 'Here, bro! Forget about that one! We got this one open!'

More shouting, more scuffling. A voice that sounded like an elderly lady. 'Get out! Get out! I'll call the police!'

'You can't call nobody, Granma! Get out of my way!'

Auntie Ammy came in from the bedroom. 'What's happening?' she asked. 'I just dozed off for a moment and then I heard all of this hollerin'.'

'I don't know,' said Jasmine. 'It sounds like some gang's broken into the building.'

The baby boy had stopped crying now. He leaned his head against Jasmine's shoulder and softly snuffled. Jasmine lifted her hand to him and he clutched her fingers. Little, and damp, but so vulnerable.

Auntie Ammy went across to the light switch but when she flicked it, nothing happened. 'Power's out,' she said. 'The air's off, too. I thought it was hot.'

She went into the kitchen, pulled open one of the drawers, and took out a large black-rubber flashlight. She switched it on and shone it upward, into her face, so that she looked like a Hallowe'en witch. Then she came back, slid open the door to the balcony, and stepped outside. Jasmine followed her. There was a strong smell of smoke in the air, and more than half of the city's lights were out. Jasmine was so used to seeing the glittering lights of Los Angeles at night that she stood holding the baby boy and staring at the blackness with a terrible feeling of dread. Auntie Ammy leaned over the balcony and said, 'I think there's a fire down there. A fire burning on the first floor, God help us. That's old Mr. Petersen's apartment.'

They heard more screaming, and another shot. Jasmine said, 'I think we need to get out of here, Auntie Ammy. It's like they're breaking in everywhere.'

'I ain't leavin' my apartment to get lootified. I'm goin' to stay here and fend 'em off.'

'Auntie Ammy, we have to go. Let's go down to the parking level and get your car and hightail it out of here. We can stay with Hubie until this rioting is all over.'

'S'posin' they riotin' in Maywood, too? I tell you, Jazz. I'm real reluctant to leave all my stuff unperfected. These pictures, these statuettes. They're my *holy* things.'

But then they felt a deep, thumping explosion somewhere in the basement. They looked over the balcony and saw that smoke was pouring out of the ventilator grilles which surrounded the parking level. There was another explosion, and then a third, and tongues of flame licked lasciviously out of the grilles and shriveled the bougainvillea that grew up the walls.

'They're blowing up the cars,' said Jasmine. 'Come on, Auntie Ammy. We have to get out of here before this whole building goes up.'

In frustration, Auntie Ammy picked up the phone. She jabbed 911 with her long red-polished fingernails, and then listened, but the phone was dead.

'OK,' she said. 'Looks like we don't have no option. Give me a couple of minutes to get dressed, and while I'm doin' that I'll say a prayer to Changó, because Changó can pertect us against fire.'

'Just hurry,' Jasmine urged her.

Outside, in the corridor, they heard the old woman shrieking, and somebody laughing at her – a loud coarse laugh followed by whooping and shouting and repeated door-slamming.

'Wass wrong wichyou, Granma? You doan like dancin'? How's about I set fire to that ugly old dress of yours? Maybe you'll dance better then?'

Jasmine pressed her hand against her mouth. Her natural instinct was to go out and confront the old lady's tormentors, but she knew what would happen if she did. She and Auntie Ammy and the little baby boy would all be hurt, too, or even killed.

Quickly, she changed the baby's diaper, and dressed him in his romper suit. She took a maroon shawl from the back of Auntie Ammy's couch, and wrapped it around him until only his face was showing. He didn't cry, but he blinked at her unhappily, as if he were thinking about it.

Auntie Ammy came out of her bedroom in a black ankle-length dress. Around her neck she was wearing at least a half a dozen brightly colored bead necklaces, each of them representing a different Santería orisha. Red and white beads for Changó, green and yellow beads for Orunla, blue and crystal beads for Yemayá.

'I called on Changó,' she said. *'Kabio, kabio sile*, come to my house and pertect us, Changó! Now we can go.'

They heard more screaming, coming from the next apartment. 'Let's use the fire escape,' said Jasmine. But as soon as they stepped out onto the balcony again, they heard laughter and shouting from the square paved area below. Jasmine looked cautiously over the railing. In the half-darkness she could see six or seven youths, some of them white, some of them Latino. They were pushing a fortyish man and woman from one side of the square to the other, taunting them and spitting at them.

'Who's the big man now? Who's the big man now, huh? Bet you're pissing in your pants, *amigo*! You want to see me screw your wife? How about that? You want to see your wife suck my *nabo*?'

Jasmine pushed Auntie Ammy back inside.

'*Now* what we goin' to do?' asked Auntie Ammy, clutching at her necklaces.

Jasmine went across to the front door and placed her ear against it. All wrapped up in his shawl, the baby shook his head from side to side and said, '*Wum wum.*'

The corridor outside Auntie Ammy's apartment sounded quiet now. No screaming, no shouting, no running sneakers.

'I can't hear anything,' said Jasmine. She peered through the peephole but all she could see was the cream-painted door to the opposite apartment.

'*Wum wum,*' the baby repeated.

'Sorry, sweet thing, I don't know what you mean. A *gah*, yes. *Mmm-mmm*, yes. But what on earth is a *wum wum*?'

'*Wum wum*,' said the baby, and smiled at her.

'Maybe he's tryin' to tell us that it's safe to go out,' Auntie Ammy suggested. 'After all, this little fella can see things that nobody else can see. He got the perception.'

'I don't know,' said Jasmine. 'What if "*wum wum*" means there are half a dozen young hoodlums right outside the door, waiting to jump on us, and we're better off staying where we are?'

From the square below the balcony came the sound of breaking glass, and the fortyish man shouting, 'No! *No!* Get away from her, you animal!'

'Don't think we have a whole lot of choice, do we?' said Jasmine.

She passed the baby over to Auntie Ammy. Then – as quietly as she could – she drew back the heavy security chain. Next she turned the keys in the three steel deadlocks, and eased the door open.

Outside, it was still comparatively quiet, although she could hear water running somewhere. She could also smell smoke, much stronger than before. She waited for a few seconds, and then she put her head out, shining Auntie Ammy's flashlight left and right. The green-carpeted corridor was deserted, although the door of the next apartment but one was wide open.

'Come on,' she said to Auntie Ammy. 'It looks like they're gone.'

Auntie Ammy was holding the baby tight against her shoulder. 'If they're gone, maybe it's safe for us to stay?'

But as if to answer her, there were two more muffled explosions from the parking level. 'We have to go,' Jasmine insisted. 'This whole apartment block is going to burn down, and I don't exactly hear the fire department speeding this way to put it out, do you? Hurry up, Auntie Ammy, otherwise we're going to be barbecued.'

She took the baby. Auntie Ammy closed her apartment door behind her and made an elaborate performance of locking every lock. While she was doing so, Jasmine walked along to the open apartment door, and peered inside.

'Hallo?' she called out. 'Is anybody in there?'

There was no answer, so she stepped inside. The bathroom was off to the right of the open front door, and it was one of the bathroom faucets that was splashing. The door was two or three inches ajar.

Jasmine said, 'Hallo? Is anybody in there? If there is, you really need to get out of here now. The whole building's on fire.'

There was still no answer, so she pushed the door a little wider, shining the flashlight through the gap. At first she saw only the washbasin, and the mirror above it, which reflected nothing but the shower curtain, with a pattern of white seagulls on it. But then she looked around the door, and shone the flashlight toward the bathtub. 'Oh my God,' she said, and jerked backward, jarring her shoulder on the door frame.

An elderly woman was lying in the tub, both of her arms upraised as if she were reaching up for someone to pull her out. But her arms were burned scarlet, and her face was burned scarlet, too, her pale blue eyes staring furiously at the ceiling. She looked like an African ju-ju mask, her mouth dragged downward in agony, her hair sticking up in blackened spikes. Her dress had been reduced to rags and ashes.

She must have climbed into the bath and turned on the cold water to numb the pain of her burns, but the shock had been much too severe, and her heart had stopped.

Jasmine turned away. Auntie Ammy was standing right behind her. Auntie Ammy could obviously tell what Jasmine had seen, by the look on her face.

'Is she gone?' she asked.

Jasmine said, 'Yes.'

'Dottie Feinstein,' said Auntie Ammy, as if the name itself were a prayer, and crossed herself. 'She was a dear, kindly woman.'

Another *boom!* from the parking level. 'Let's go,' said Auntie Ammy. 'If I lose all of my holy things, that's the will of the orishas. I know they'll make it up to me.'

They walked quickly along the corridor. Jasmine stopped to knock at every apartment they passed, and shouted out, 'Fire! You need to get out of here!' Strangely, though, not one door opened up, and nobody answered, except for one Hispanic-sounding woman who called back, 'Go away! *Vamos!* You leave me alone!'

The residents had locked and bolted themselves in their apartments as if they were all in denial. This couldn't be real. How could airliners drop out of the sky? How could the whole city go dark? How could the TV go blank and the phones go dead and the air-conditioning clatter to a stop?

They reached the door that led to the stairs, and pushed it open. The staircase was almost completely dark, and filled with eye-watering smoke. It echoed with shouts and screams from the square outside so that it sounded like the staircase down to hell. Jasmine gave the flashlight back to Auntie Ammy and began to make her way downward, holding onto the handrail so that she wouldn't lose her footing. The baby started to cough, and then he let out two emphatic sneezes.

When they reached the door to the front hall, Jasmine again handed the baby to Auntie Ammy. She opened the door very slowly, and then she peered out. The hallway was smoky, but there was nobody there. The door to the super's office was open, but there was no sign of him, either. His chair lay tipped over on the floor, and a Styrofoam coffee cup had been spilled across the newspaper on his desk.

Jasmine beckoned to Auntie Ammy and they hurried across the hall and pushed their way out through the revolving doors. The baby said, '*Wum wum,*' and looked up at Jasmine as if he were trying to tell her something really serious.

'Yes, darling,' said Jasmine. 'You're absolutely right. *Wum wum.*'

Outside, the night sounded like a zoo crowded with panicking animals. As they walked as quickly as they could down Ladera Avenue, they heard howling and screaming and desperate shouts for help. A young Hispanic man in a T-shirt stained dark with blood came staggering across the street, his arms held out in front of him, sobbing. He passed within less than fifteen feet of them, but he was blind, and he wasn't aware that there was anybody so close.

'Where we goin' to go?' asked Auntie Ammy. 'Seems to me like every place is just as dangerous as every other place.'

'We need to find ourselves some wheels,' said Jasmine. As if to emphasize her point, they heard two more loud explosions behind them, from Auntie Ammy's apartment block, and they turned around to see fire jumping out of the basement windows.

There were three automobiles parked in the street just ahead of them. Jasmine tried their door handles, but they were all locked.

'Can't you jimmy them open, or somethin'?' asked Auntie Ammy.

'What do you take me for, some carjacking expert? I wouldn't know how.'

They continued to hurry down Ladera until they reached South La Brea. Not far away they heard more baboon-like screaming, and the smashing of glass – dull, repetitive crashes as if somebody were using a sledgehammer to break every window in a whole apartment building. Sirens whooped in the distance, but there was no sign of any squad cars.

About three blocks to the south, Jasmine saw a sudden flicker of intensely bright lights. They didn't look like lightning: more like camera flashes.

'Think we'd better head in the opposite direck-shun,' said Auntie Ammy, nodding so emphatically in the direction of the lights that her earrings swung.

'Any special reason?'

'They ain't natural, those lights. That's reason enough.'

'What do you mean? What are they? They're cameras, aren't they?'

Auntie Ammy shook her head. 'They ain't no cameras. I seen somethin' similar when I was a girl. They *devils*.'

'Oh, come on, Ammy. You don't believe in devils, do you?'

Auntie Ammy looked up at Jasmine with her mouth pursed defiantly, so that she looked as if her lips had been sewn together by a headhunter.

'Anybody who believe in good spirits gotta believe in the opposite. You wouldn't have to say prayers to God if there weren't no Satan, now would you?'

'I guess not. But I don't believe that *those* are devils.'

'What do you want to do, then? Go find out for yourself?'

Jasmine hesitated. The lights were still flashing, like strobe lights. Then, carried on the wind, she heard the sound of people screaming, both men and women. A dreadful *low* screaming – more like moaning than screaming – the way that airline passengers moan when they think that their plane is going to crash.

'OK, you win,' said Jasmine. 'But I still don't

believe they're devils.'

They started walking northward. A little further on, they came across two abandoned cars by the side of the street, a Buick LaCrosse and a Honda SUV, but both of them were badly damaged. The Buick's windshield was shattered and the driver's seat was glistening with blood. Jasmine saw an erratic spattering of blood all across the blacktop, but there was nobody in sight.

Auntie Ammy looked down at the blood trail. 'May the saints take care of whoever that was.'

They walked on further. As they did so, more lights began to go out, up in the hills, and over to the east, toward Pasadena. The only other person they passed in the street was a gray-haired woman in a gray dress standing in the darkness in front of a single-story house. She was slightly stooping forward as if she were trying to focus on something in the middle distance.

Jasmine called out, 'Are you all right, ma'am? Are you OK?'

The gray-haired woman didn't answer, didn't even wave her hand.

Jasmine said, 'Maybe I should go across and see if there's something wrong.'

'Let's take care of ourselves first,' Auntie Ammy cautioned her.

A net curtain in the front window of the house was drawn aside, and a pot-bellied man in a white T-shirt stared out, although he didn't seem to be looking in their direction.

'I don't think they can see, neither of them,'

said Jasmine.

'Well, there's nothin' we can do about that,' Auntie Ammy retorted. 'Let's keep going. Maybe we should try to *walk* to Hubie's house.'

'Wait up a minute,' said Jasmine. 'Do you see what I see?'

Up ahead of them, South La Brea curved to the left slightly, but a huge red-and-white truck had carried on going straight ahead. It had mounted the sidewalk and jackknifed into the white-washed cinder-block wall in front of some-body's house, and here it still was, its tractor facing toward them, its trailer angled halfway across the road. Its headlights were still on, but the driver's door was open, and there was nobody in the cab.

Jasmine jogged toward the truck and gave it a slap of appreciation on its shiny chrome wheel arch. It was a Mack Titan, the largest and most powerful truck on the road. It was loaded with steel construction girders – over a hundred tons of them, in Jasmine's estimation.

She looked around. There was no sign of the driver, and behind the cinder-block wall the house was in complete darkness. She went up the steps and knocked at the front door. There were no candles burning inside the house, no flashlights. She called out, 'Hallo! Is there any-body home?' but nobody answered.

Auntie Ammy was waiting for her outside the front gate, holding the baby.

'Nobody home,' said Jasmine. 'Or if there is, they're too chicken to open the door.'

She tried the next house, but that, too, was in

darkness, although she thought she could hear somebody stumbling around inside, and somebody say, *'Ssshh!'*

'Hallo?' she shouted, and knocked again, and yet again. But half a minute went by and there was no response. She came down the steps and walked back over to the abandoned Titan.

'Looks like finders keepers, losers weepers,' she said.

She climbed up into the cab. The keys were still in the ignition, with a bare-breasted hula dolly dangling on the key ring.

'What you think you *doing*, girl?' Auntie Ammy called up to her. 'You can't take this monster!'

'Why not? Don't look like nobody else wants it.'

She swung herself into the driver's seat. Scotch-taped to the sun visor in front of her were two photographs of the truck driver and his family: a broad-faced, suntanned man in a Mack Trucks cap, and a plump peroxide blonde in a sleeveless top, with a barbed-wire tattoo around her upper arm. Two plump little boys were sitting in front of them, one of them giving Jasmine a toothless grin.

Jasmine turned the key and the truck immediately rumbled into life.

'It's working fine!' she shouted down to Auntie Ammy. Then she switched off the engine and swung back down to help her.

Auntie Ammy scaled the side of the truck as slowly and cautiously as if she were climbing the north face of the Eiger. 'Don't hurry me,

Jazz! Don't you go pushing me, neither!'

She went through an inelegant struggle to pull herself into the cab, her black-stockinged legs waving like an overturned stag beetle, but she eventually managed to settle herself into the passenger seat. Jasmine lifted the baby up to her, and as she did so, the baby gave her another one of his grave, slightly frowning looks, as if he knew that something bad could happen to all of them, but couldn't tell her what it was.

Jasmine climbed back into the driver's seat and restarted the engine. She put the Titan into reverse, and slowly backed up, using the rear-view TV monitor to see where she was going. The tractor's fender made a thick scraping noise against the wall, but gradually she managed to steer it off the sidewalk and maneuver it back into line with its trailer.

She shut off the trailer air-supply to lock its brakes, and eased the pressure on the fifth-wheel locking jaws by gently backing up a little more. Then she switched off the engine again and opened the door.

'What now?' asked Auntie Ammy.

'I'm just going to lose the trailer,' Jasmine told her. 'We're not going to get very far hauling a whole load of steel, are we?'

She walked back to the trailer. Usually, she would have made sure that its wheels were chocked, but tonight she didn't have the time or the chocks. She wound down the trailer's landing gear, and once it had made contact with the road, she gave the crank a few extra turns so that it would be easier to unlatch the trailer's kingpin from the cab's fifth wheel. Then she disconnected the air lines and coupled them up with the dummy couplers at the back of the cab, and pulled out the electric plug. There was a smoky-smelling breeze blowing from the southwest, and from far away she could still hear people wailing, like damned souls in hell.

She tugged the release handle to unlock the fifth wheel. A yellow taxi drove past, very slowly, and she saw the driver staring at her, but he didn't stop. In the ten minutes since they had escaped from Auntie Ammy's apartment block, only three other cars had passed them by, and none of them had stopped, either. South La Brea was lined on both sides with single-story houses and apartments, but candles were twinkling in only a few of them, and the gray-haired woman in the gray dress was the only person they had seen on the street.

She hauled herself back into the cab. Before she closed the door, she looked back down the street, and she could still see the bright flashes of white light – the lights that Auntie Ammy called 'devils.' She wondered what they really were.

'OK,' she said. She adjusted her seat with the foot pedal, and then she started up the Titan's engine. 'Let's see what this baby can do.'

She slowly drove the tractor unit forward until it was clear from its trailer. Then she put her foot down, and the Titan bellowed up South La Brea toward the intersection with West Slauson. The traffic signals were out, so Jasmine slowed down. A single SUV with darkened windows appeared from the left, but it stopped for them, and flashed its lights. The driver obviously didn't want to get into an argument with a sixteen-liter ten-wheeled truck that weighed something over nine and a half tons.

Jasmine took a right and headed east toward Maywood. She had never driven a Titan before, and at any other time she would have found it exhilarating. It was hugely powerful, its engine producing over six hundred horsepower, and now that it was bobtail, without a hundred tons of steel girders to pull around, the tractor unit surged forward eagerly every time her foot touched the gas pedal.

'I'll tell you something, Auntie Ammy. If we ever get out of this mess, I'm going to save up and buy me one of these.'

It took them less than twenty minutes to reach Maywood, although East Slauson was littered with abandoned vehicles, several of them burning. South La Brea had been almost deserted, but as they drove further east, they came across more and more people wandering blindly around the streets.

'Jesus,' said Jasmine. 'It's *The Day of the Dead*.'

Again and again she had to slow down and let out a deafening blast with the Titan's double airhorns. Some people stumbled out of their way, but others milled around in the middle of the road, their arms lifted in a vain appeal for help.

One man stood right in front of them, holding up a little curly-headed girl. 'She can still see!' he shouted. 'She can still see! Please – take care of her for me!'

Jasmine blew the Titan's horns again and again, until the little girl was screaming with fright. At last the man clutched the little girl tightly against his chest and weaved his way back to the sidewalk, almost tripping on the curb as he did so.

'God, I hate myself,' said Jasmine.

Auntie Ammy reached over and touched her arm. 'Don't you feel bad, Jazz. You didn't have no alternative. The saints will forgive you, when you get to heaven.'

'Well, I hope that's not too soon.'

They turned north toward East 56th Street, where Hubie lived. It was a scrubby area of small one-story houses, close to the railroad line, but most of the fences and front yards were well kept, with roses intertwined into trellises, and brick pathways, and concrete garden statues.

However, they were still a block away from Hubie's house when Auntie Ammy pointed ahead of them and said, 'Look!'

Dense black smoke was rolling across the street. Jasmine put her foot down and pulled up in front of Hubie's house so hard that the Titan's wheels locked. Through the smoke she could see that the house was burning fiercely, with flames dancing inside the living room like some hellish house party. The house next door was beginning to burn, too, with smoke pouring out from under its shingles.

'Where's Hubie?' asked Auntie Ammy. 'I can't see Hubie nowhere!'

The baby sensed her anxiety, and started to cry.

Jasmine said, 'Wait here. I'll see if I can find out where he's at.'

'O Changó, pertect him,' said Auntie Ammy, fingering her necklace of red and white beads. 'O Changó, please pertect him.'

Jasmine jumped down from the Titan's cab. She opened Hubie's front gate and stepped into his concrete-paved yard. His Toyota was still parked in front of the garage, although its windshield had been cracked and its yellow paint was blistering. As she approached the front porch, she had to lift her arm to protect her face. The heat was overwhelming, and she couldn't get close. Blazing fabric from the living-room drapes was flying up into the darkness, and even the wooden swing-seat was alight.

She looked up and down the street. About a hundred yards away an elderly man and a woman were shuffling along the sidewalk, but the man was touching every fence and every wall to guide him, and the woman was holding on to his belt. It was no use asking them where Hubie was. They probably didn't even know where *they* were.

She climbed back into the cab. The baby was still crying and Auntie Ammy was rocking him and shushing him.

'Hubie's not there?'

'I'm sorry, Auntie Ammy. But you know Hubie. He's a survivor. Remember that time at Venice Beach when he almost drowned? And that time he rolled his Jeep over? I'll bet you whatever you like that he got himself out of there.'

265

Auntie Ammy said, 'His car's still here. He wouldn't never have gone no place on foot. Not Hubie.'

'You don't know that for sure. He could be with one of his friends. Or – I don't know—'

'—or he could have been blinded and gotten himself lost?'

'I didn't say that.'

'Maybe you didn't but you thunk it.'

They sat for a while, watching the roof of Hubie's house collapse. The single stone chimney was left standing, with smoke pouring out of it, in a grim parody of a happy home.

The baby had stopped crying. He, too, was watching the house burning, with one hand held out, opening and closing his fingers as if he were trying to catch hold of the flames that were reflected on the window. 'A *gah*,' he said. 'A *wum wum*.'

'So what do we do now?' asked Auntie Ammy. 'Do you think we should drive around for a while, see if we can find Hubie someplace?'

'Don't think there's a whole lot of point,' said Jasmine. 'We'd only be wasting diesel, and if the power's still out, none of the gas-station pumps are going to be working.'

'But if we don't go looking for Hubie, where else are we going to go?'

'I don't know. I guess we could try going back to my place but it sure didn't look too healthy around Inglewood, did it, with all those planes crashing? I don't know if *any* place is safe.'

She was still thinking what to do next when – behind the dark brown smoke that was rolling across the street – she glimpsed three or four bright flashes. Only a few seconds later, she saw at least six more, much clearer this time.

'*Hey* – lookit!' she said. 'There's those lights again.'

Gradually, the flashes grew faster and faster, and Jasmine could see that they were coming nearer, too. She could also make out the silhouette of somebody walking toward them.

'I don't like this,' said Auntie Ammy. 'I don't like this one teensy little bit.'

The baby twisted around and pointed at the flashes in excitement. 'A *gah*!' he said, excitedly. 'A *gah*!'

Out of the smoke, a stockily built man appeared. Jasmine flicked on the Titan's full halogen headlights. The man stopped, dazzled. On his head he carried a strange lumpy hat that looked as if it had been sewn together out of half a dozen squirrel skins, complete with dangling tails. A dark red blanket was fastened across his shoulders with a long pin that looked like a bone, and underneath it he was wearing a yellowish leather jerkin and leggings that were bound around with leather thongs.

In one hand he held a stick decorated with feathers and beads and birds' skulls.

He squinted at the headlights with his brow furrowed, but he didn't make any attempt to shield his eyes. He looked irritated, and contemptuous, rather than angry.

'So who the hell is *this* whacko?' said Jasmine. 'Look at him, he looks like Geronimo.'

But Auntie Ammy pulled at her sleeve in a

breathless panic. 'Jazz – get us out of here, quick!'

'Come on, what's the matter? He's probably escaped from some nuthouse.'

'*Get us out of here!*' Auntie Ammy screamed at her. She sounded terrified. '*I'm serious! Get us out of here now!*'

'OK! OK! Keep your darn wool on!' Jasmine started the Titan's engine, and gunned it. As it roared into life, three more figures emerged from the smoke and assembled around the man in the squirrel-tail hat, and then another two.

'*Whoa,*' said Jasmine. The five figures were very tall, with dead white faces – more like *masks* than faces – and bodies like rectangular wooden boxes, crudely hammered together and painted black. For some reason Jasmine couldn't work out how near they were, or how far away, or even if there were only five of them. One second they seemed to be clustered close to the man in the squirrel-tail hat, but when she blinked they seemed to have jumped away, to stand ten feet in front of him, almost close enough to touch the Titan's front bumpers. Another blink, and they were standing behind him, half-hidden by smoke. She blinked again and she could see seven or eight of them, or even more.

She yanked the Titan's gear shift into reverse, and backed up faster than she had ever backed up before. Instantly, a dazzling array of lights came flickering out of the figures' eye slits, but Auntie Ammy kept her head turned away, and covered the baby's face with her hand.

'Don't you turn around and look at them!' she

warned Jasmine. 'You look at them just once, that'll be the last-ever thing you ever get to see!'

Jasmine kept her eyes fixed on the Titan's rear-view TV monitor, and sped back nearly three blocks. Then she spun the wheel and the tractor slewed around, its ten tires howling in a rubbery chorus.

She jammed her foot on the gas, and they roared away, turning south. At speed, the bobtail tractor was much more difficult to handle than a tractor with a loaded trailer, and when Jasmine reached the intersection with East Slauson, it went into a wide sliding skid, and sideswiped a parked car with a thunderous bang. She straightened it out, and headed east, toward the Long Beach Freeway.

'Those *things*,' she said. 'What were they?'

'I don't rightfully know,' Auntie Ammy told her. 'But I know that they're evil and I know that they ain't of this world. I also know that they can strike you stone blind.'

'So who told you that?'

'My orisha told me, Changó. He was taking real good care of me. I take real good care of him, with offerins, and with sacrifices, and I call him with invocations, and in return he speaks to me, and warns me of any danger, and 'splains in a way what it is.'

'Maybe *I* should convert to Santería.'

'It's what you truly believe, girl. That's what counts.'

They reached the Long Beach Freeway, which crossed over the Maywood district on grimy concrete pillars. The left-hand side of the on-

269

ramp was cluttered with burned-out cars and SUVs, but Jasmine drove up on the right-hand side, with the Titan's wheel arches scraping against the retaining wall, and throwing up fountains of orange sparks. In low gear, the Titan was powerful enough to push aside any vehicles that obstructed them, with a loud crunching and squealing of metal.

The freeway itself was deserted, although a few cars and vans had been left abandoned in the middle of the road, including a police squad car and a burning ambulance.

'Where we headed?' asked Auntie Ammy. 'I think this little fella is getting hungry.'

'I don't know,' said Jasmine. 'But I think we need to get away from LA, don't you? We're heading north, so let's keep on heading north.'

They drove for a few minutes in silence, and then Jasmine turned to Auntie Ammy and said, 'That was an Indian, wasn't it? Like a real cowboys-and-Indians Indian.'

'I don't know how real he was.'

'What do you mean by that? He was just wearing fancy dress?'

Auntie Ammy looked across at her with a strange expression that Jasmine couldn't read.

'No, I don't mean that. I mean he had no *aché*. No power in him, no life.'

'I still don't understand what you mean.'

Auntie Ammy held the baby closer, as if she didn't want him to hear what she was going to say next.

'I mean, girl, that he was long dead. I mean that he was what you might call a spirit, of sorts.

But he was wearing a disguise. He wasn't wearin' the face that he wore when he was alive. He was wearin' somebody else's face. Like as if you looked in the lookin'-mirror one morning and saw that you was me.

She gave a deep, dry sniff, and then she said, 'I could tell by his eyes, Jazz. The eyes that were lookin' out of that face didn't rightfully belong to that face at all. And there was so much hate in those eyes. That was the scariest man that I ever saw, ever.'

NINETEEN

Washington, DC

The President was asleep, and he was dreaming about his parents' house in Cincinnati. He could see the orange beady-eyed cicadas crawling out of the soil in his parents' backyard, and clustering in the trees, endlessly chirruping. They had always frightened him when he was a child. They had been like an alien invasion, thousands of insects struggling out of the earth and nothing that anybody could do to stop them.

His mother had driven him to school and there had been so many dead cicadas on her windshield that the wipers had eventually stuck, and she could barely see where she was going for beige cicada slime and broken wings.

He felt a cicada on his cheek. He jerked his hand up and tried to flick it away. But it wasn't a cicada, it was a man's fingertips, touching him. Cold, dry fingertips.

'Have you decided?' the man whispered, so close to his ear that he could feel his chilly breath.

The President opened his eyes. Misquamacus was leaning over him, a negative black-and-white image, just as he had been yesterday evening. The President didn't move at first; or speak; even though he could hear insects dropping onto his pillow.

'You know that you could save countless numbers of your people, if you so chose. And perhaps, if your people learned our ways, and observed our beliefs, we could live together in harmony, as children of the same gods.'

An insect that felt like a cockroach dropped onto the President's cheek and scuttled underneath the collar of his pajamas. Abruptly, he sat up, slapping at his neck.

'Am I dreaming this?' he demanded. 'Tell me – this can't be for real, can it?'

'What do you mean by "real"?' asked Misquamacus. 'Everything that can be seen and heard and felt is real. You are real. I am real. The Great Old Ones who wait in exile beyond the limits of the stars, they are real, too, and it is time for their return, whatever you decide.'

The President said, 'What you're asking, it's impossible. People simply won't do it.'

'If they refuse, I will have no choice but to force them, and those who refuse will have to die.'

'You can't expect a whole nation to give up its way of life, just like that.'

'Why not?' asked Misquamacus. *You* did. Or at least your forefathers did. And they massacred all those who stood up to them. I am simply doing the same.'

The President pressed his call button, and shouted out, 'Johnson! Kaminsky! Get in here!'

'That will do you no good,' said Misquamacus. Even though he was a negative image, the President saw him smile.

The door opened, and he heard Johnson and Kaminsky come into the room.

'Something wrong, Mr. President?'

'He's here. He's right here in front of me. Don't you *see* him?'

A lengthy pause. Then, 'Who exactly do you mean, sir?'

'The goddamned Indian! He's right here!' The President jabbed his finger at Misquamacus, standing in the blackness of his blindness. 'Him and his goddamned bugs! I can even *smell* him, goddammit!'

Another pause, punctuated by a cough. 'I'm sorry, sir. I can't see anybody. Maybe I should call your doctor.'

The President dragged back his bedcovers and swung his legs out of bed.

'Mr. President, sir – for Christ's sake be careful!'

But the President lunged at Misquamacus, and seized the lapels of his coat. Misquamacus made no attempt to pull himself free, but looked down

273

at the President with pity.

'He's here, goddammit! He's real! I can feel him! I can feel his coat!'

Kaminsky came up to the President and gently but firmly laid a hand on his shoulder. 'There's nobody there, sir. Why don't you get back into bed and let me call Dr. Henry?'

'It's probably shock, sir,' Johnson put in. 'After what happened yesterday we talked to Dr. Cronin. I'm sorry, we didn't mean to overstep our authority. But Dr. Cronin told us that people who suddenly lose their sight can suffer all kinds of delusions. It's like the rest of their senses go into overdrive.'

'Come here,' said the President, his voice trembling. 'Give me your hand.'

Kaminsky held out his hand and the President grasped his wrist. Then he lifted Kaminsky's hand toward Misquamacus' face, so that his fingers appeared to be touching Misquamacus' cheek, and then his nose.

'Don't tell me you can't feel him now.'

Kaminsky said, 'Sorry, Mr. President. Like Dr. Cronin said, it's probably some kind of self-suggestion. Your brain overcompensating for your eyes.'

'You can't feel him? Why can't you feel him? You're *touching* him, for Chrissakes!'

Kaminsky guided the President back to his bed. The President sat down, and then looked up at Misquamacus, shaking his head in bitterness and bewilderment. Misquamacus was right there, the President could see him. He could hear him, he could even smell him. Why couldn't anybody else?

Maybe Dr. Cronin was right. Maybe 'Misquamacus' was nothing but a delusion caused by the trauma of losing his sight. Maybe his brain was simply inventing this Native American spirit, in the absence of any input from his optic nerves. After all, amputees could still feel the ghost of their severed limbs. They could even feel excruciating pain in a foot that was no longer there. Maybe this image of 'Misquamacus' was the same kind of ghost.

As if he could read the President's thoughts, Misquamacus whispered, 'I exist only in your darkness, my friend. You see me because I want you to see me. But you can see nothing else, and nobody can see what you see.'

'I want you to go away,' the President told him, turning his face away.

'Don't you want us to call Dr. Henry?' asked Kaminsky.

'No, Kaminsky, I don't. But I wasn't talking to you.'

Johnson said, 'Maybe we should call Dr. Cronin, too. With all due respect, sir, we don't want you to suffer some kind of a breakdown.'

'I am not suffering from any kind of breakdown. I'm fine. I'm perfectly fine. Now why don't you leave me alone for a while? Thank you.'

There was another long pause, as if Johnson and Kaminsky were conferring with each other by pulling faces and making gestures.

'You *deaf*?' snapped the President. 'I could have been suffering some kind of delusion or something, but now I'm OK. So leave me alone. And I don't want to see any doctors. *Comprendo?*'

'Got it,' said Kaminsky. 'But please don't hesitate to call us if there's anything else you need. Mr. President. Sir.'

They left the room. The President remained where he was, sitting on the edge of his bed in his blue-and-white-striped pajamas. He looked up at Misquamacus and said, 'You're not a delusion, are you? You're real. At least you'd better be real, or else I'm a loony.'

He could see Misquamacus in even sharper detail now, even though he was still a negative image. He could clearly see his face, even though his skin appeared black and his eye sockets appeared white, with white crows' feet around them. He could see the necklaces around his neck, and the bracelets around his wrists. He could see the black-and-white feathers hanging from his buffalo-horn headdress, and the black skulls of animals, too.

Misquamacus whispered, 'The day is coming very soon for the final reckoning. Many thousands of your people have been blinded and they will be defenseless when we start to slaughter them, just as our people were defenseless all those years ago when you came from the east and started to slaughter us.'

'Please,' said the President. 'I'm asking you not to do this. I can make your people an offer.'

'An offer? What manner of offer?'

'Listen, I've been thinking about this. For beginners, I can set up a federal commission to

276

return some of the land your people lost. Then I can arrange for millions more dollars in federal and state funding for Native American education, and hospitals, and recreational facilities.'

Misquamacus let out a hiss of amusement, like a snake. 'You think that you can bribe us with our own forests? You think that you can teach us our own legends, and our own religion, and for that we should be grateful? You think that you can treat us with your drugs and your chemicals, instead of the sacred healing magic that we learned from the gods?'

He swept his skull-topped medicine stick from side to side, to show his contempt. 'This is our land, and your people stole it from us with lies and with cruelty and broken promises. We will take it back from you, by fighting again all of those battles in which you defeated us. But this time you will be the losers. This time, it will be *your* blood that soaks the ground at Sand Creek and Wounded Knee, and up in the Infernal Caverns.

'We will start with Memory Valley, where you massacred so many Hupa, and then we will make our way eastward, turning back time, battle after battle, and we will reclaim every plateau and every forest and every lake that you stole from us.'

The President lowered his head. 'I think I'm going mad,' he said. 'Tell me this isn't happening.'

Misquamacus came up close to him, and laid a hand on his shoulder. His fingers were so cold that the President gave an involuntary shiver.

'Tell your people that their time of supremacy is over,' Misquamacus whispered. 'Tell them, and I will spare as many as I can.'

'I can't,' said the President. 'This country was founded on freedom. Religious freedom. Political freedom. Maybe racial freedom came later than it should have done, but now we have that, too.'

'You talk of *freedom*?' said Misquamacus. 'What freedom did you grant to the Apaches you murdered, at Salt River Canyon, and Turret Butte? What freedom did you give to Chief Joseph, when you pursued his entire community of Nez Percé for nearly two thousand miles? Where was your freedom when Dull Knife's people escaped from Fort Robinson, and your soldiers went after them, and killed them – men, women, and little children? I spit on your freedom, and I will spit on your grave.'

'Well, if you really think that you can beat us, that'll be your privilege,' said the President. 'But I'm still not going to tell my people to give in to you. Americans – and that's us – we *never* give in.'

Misquamacus lifted up his medicine stick, and tapped it against the President's forehead. 'There will be much blood, then. And much darkness. And it will all be on your head.'

The President said nothing. In his heart, he found it impossible to believe that this was really happening, in spite of all the airplane crashes and the highway pile-ups and the hundreds of people who had drowned or fallen off buildings or stepped blindly into traffic.

Misquamacus said, 'I will grant you one favor. I will restore your sight to you, so that you can witness the destruction of your society and the scattering of your people, just as I did, and Chief Joseph did, and Tecumseh and his brother Tenskwatawa, and Crazy Horse, and all of my brothers and sisters, and all of our children, too.'

He held out his right hand and said, 'Close your eyes, my friend.'

The President hesitated, but then he did what he was told. Misquamacus touched him with a cold fingertip on each eyelid, and said, *'Wàbi, wàbi.'*

The President opened his eyes. Gradually, the negative image of Misquamacus began to grow darker, until he was absorbed into the overwhelming blackness altogether, and disappeared. There was a long moment when the President thought that Misquamacus must have been deceiving him, and that he was going to stay permanently blind. But after a while, he realized that he could see a faint misty light, and then the blurry rectangle of a window, and a red armchair, and a bureau with a large vase of orange roses on it.

He looked around him. Now he could see the end of his bed, and the doors of a pale oak closet, and a large framed print of the seashore, with yachts.

His heart thumped with exhilaration. He blinked, and he blinked, and with every blink his vision became clearer. He was just about to call out for Johnson and Kaminsky when he became aware that there was somebody standing close

279

behind him. He turned, and shouted out in surprise.

There was an Indian there, in an old-fashioned frock coat, with leggings underneath. He had gray shoulder-length hair and a faded red bandanna, decorated with animals' claws. His face looked like crumpled brown leather, and it was obvious from the way that his lower lip protruded that he had no teeth.

Around his neck he was wearing at least seven necklaces, all made of bones and beads and painted clay.

'What the hell are you doing here?' the President demanded. 'You're not Marcus.'

The elderly Indian gave an almost imperceptible shake of his head. 'You speak of Misquamacus, The One Who Went And Came Back.'

'That's right. But who the hell are you?'

'I am Graywolf, but I am also Misquamacus. Look into my eyes. The memory of Misquamacus lives inside me.'

The President stood up. 'Whoever you are, old man, I think you need to get out of here. Kaminsky! Johnson! Come in here, will you?'

Johnson and Kaminsky came into the room. Johnson was eating a baloney sandwich but his mouth dropped open when he saw Graywolf standing right next to the President. Kaminsky immediately tugged out his gun.

'You want to tell me how this clown managed to get in here?' asked the President.

'You can *see* him?'

'I can damn well see him all right. I just got

280

my sight back.'

'You mean, just like that?'

'That's right. Just like that. And that's when I saw—' He waved at Graywolf dismissively. 'Get him out of here, will you? And lock him up. And have Gene Schneider interrogate him. And the FBI, too. I want to know how he managed to get past you two hotshots without you seeing him. And I urgently want to know what he knows about this blindness.'

Kaminsky said, 'We should call in your doctors, too, Mr. President. Have you checked over.'

'Let's leave that till later. I want you to deal with this guy first. You can call Doug Latterby, though. And John Rostoff. And General McNamara, too. I want them all here in twenty minutes flat. And call Mrs. Perry, as well.'

'That could be a problem, sir.'

The President had opened the closet and was taking out a clean white T-shirt and shorts. 'Why? Where is she?'

'Not just the First Lady, sir. All of them. All of our communications are out. Telephones, cellphones, Internet. TV and radio are all out, too.'

Graywolf said, quietly but very clearly, 'To defeat your enemy, first you must take away his eyes, and then his ears.'

'Get him out of here!' snapped the President.

Kaminsky went up to Graywolf and tried to take hold of his arm, but as he did so Graywolf gave a sideways jerk of his head and Kaminsky shouted out, 'Jesus! My wrist!'

Johnson tossed aside the crust of his sandwich

and pulled out his gun, too, holding it with both hands and aiming it at Graywolf's head.

'What's the matter, Joe? *Hey!* Hey, buddy, don't you move a muscle!'

'Felt like my wrist was being twisted. Hurts like hell.'

'OK, wise guy,' said Johnson, edging around Graywolf, until he was standing close behind him. 'Put your hands behind your head and walk toward the door, and don't try anything clever.'

Graywolf turned to the President. 'You and I will see each other again, my friend, when this is all finished, and the smoke has cleared. We will have the greatest scalp dance that this land has ever seen.'

'Just get the hell out of here, whoever you are,' the President retorted.

'*I said hands behind your head!*' Johnson barked out.

Graywolf unhurriedly raised both hands and ran his fingers into his shoulder-length hair.

'Now, move!' Kaminsky ordered him.

Graywolf started to walk toward the open door, with the two Secret Service men following him. As they neared the door, however, they turned to face each other and collided.

Both of them shouted *'Hey!'* in surprise. But then – immediately afterward – they both let out screams of pain. Somehow they had not only collided, but stuck together, chest to chest, and they were staring at each other in horror. The front of their white shirts was suddenly flooded with dark red blood, and the cotton fabric ripped apart.

'Aaah!' cried Kaminsky. *'Christ Almighty! Aaaah! Christ that hurts!'*

At first the President couldn't work out what was happening. But then he saw the two agents' skin tear open, so that their chest muscles were exposed, as scarlet as freshly butchered meat. Their breastbones audibly cracked apart, and their ribs splayed out of their chest cavities, wider and wider, like four skeletal hands opening up, and he could see their lungs swelling, and their frantically pumping hearts.

'Oh, God!' screamed Johnson, and his voice was so high that it could have shattered glass.

Graywolf turned around. His dried-up face was expressionless, but he appeared to be muttering under his breath, and every now and then he closed his eyes and nodded his head, as if for emphasis.

'What are you doing, you bastard?' the President shouted at him. *'Stop it! You're killing them!'*

But Graywolf didn't acknowledge him. Instead, he took his hands away from the back of his head, and held them up in front of his face, lacing his fingers together like a cat's cradle.

Johnson's ribs and Kaminsky's ribs slid together, too, just like Graywolf's fingers, and the two of them were drawn closer and tighter together, until they were screaming in each other's faces, their noses less than three inches apart. Graywolf had turned them into conjoined twins, two men whose insides were now inextricably interlocked.

'Get them apart!' the President shouted at

283

Graywolf. By now, several nurses and orderlies had heard the screaming, and had gathered in the reception room outside the door. They all looked shocked, but it was clear that they couldn't understand what they were looking at, or what they could do.

'You heard me, you bastard! Get them apart!'

Graywolf unlaced his fingers, but Johnson and Kaminsky stayed fastened together, screaming until they were hoarse. They staggered from one side of the doorway to the other, their arms around each other like drunken dancers, trying to keep their balance.

Graywolf said something, but the President couldn't hear it. Then he tilted his head back and let out a long eerie howl.

Johnson lifted his right hand and tried to angle his automatic to point at his own forehead, but Kaminsky's shoulder made it impossible for him to twist his hand around far enough. Gasping with pain, he said, 'Shoot me! Shoot me! And I'll shoot you!'

'No!' the President shouted, and tried to step forward, but Graywolf lifted one hand, with his palm facing toward him, and the President felt as if he had been pushed in the chest, hard.

Johnson pointed his automatic at Kaminsky's ear, and Kaminsky managed to raise his gun so that the muzzle was pressed against Johnson's left temple.

'Don't do it!' the President pleaded. 'Joe! Dennis! Don't do it! We can find a way to help you!'

But Johnson hysterically shouted out, 'One!

Two! *Three!*' and the two of them fired together. The double bang of their guns was deafening, and blood was sprayed up the walls and halfway across the ceiling, in the shape of a monstrous red flower.

The President closed his eyes, and took a single staggering step sideways, and sat on the bed. Johnson and Kaminsky collapsed together onto the floor, their arms and legs tangled together. Outside, in the reception room, a hospital security guard shouted at Graywolf, 'Stay there! Stay there! Keep your hands where I can see them!' One of the nurses was sobbing in shock and a doctor was shouting again and again for a paramedic, as if Johnson and Kaminsky were not far beyond human help.

'Stay there! Don't you move!' shouted the security guard.

The President opened his eyes and saw that Graywolf was continuing to cross the reception room, heading for the opposite door. The security guard moved sideways to block his path, but Graywolf seemed undeterred. He carried on walking, and walked right through the security guard and vanished.

The security guard whirled around, as if he expected Graywolf to reappear behind him, but the medicine man was gone.

'Did you see that?' said the security guard. His eyes were bulging in disbelief. 'Did you *see* that?'

The President stood up. 'Listen to me!' he said, in his clearest, presidential-address voice. 'I want you all to stay calm, and clear-headed.'

'The guy just disappeared!' jabbered the security guard. 'He was coming right for me and then he walked right into me and disappeared!'

The President raised his hands for silence. 'Please – don't let's panic! You need to know that there are some pretty strange influences at work here. I guess you can call them supernatural if you want to. But everything that's happened here in the clinic – and the blindness that so many people have been suffering all across America – they're all part of the same phenomenon.'

The doctor came forward and hunkered down beside Johnson and Kaminsky. He was young and red-faced, with a sandy moustache. He examined the two Secret Service men quickly, and then he looked up at the President and said, 'What could possibly cause anything like this? I *see* it. I see it with my own eyes, like I saw that old guy vanish just now. But I don't believe it. It's impossible.'

'We'll have to believe it if we want any chance of surviving it,' said the President. 'Since I've been here, I've seen things – visions, if you like. Ghosts. And there was one in particular, who told me what's been happening to us, and why.'

The doctor slowly stood up. 'Ghosts,' he repeated.

'What do you think that was? That guy who just disappeared?'

'I don't know. Some kind of hologram?'

The President said, 'Can somebody cover up these two poor bastards, and bring a gurney to take them away?'

286

'Shouldn't we leave them here, sir, for the police to look at?'

'This isn't a police matter, Doctor. This vision I saw, this ghost, he said he was a Wampanaug medicine man. He said that we had a choice. Either we tear down our buildings and dig up our roads and go back to living the way the Indians used to live, or else we'll all be massacred.'

'With all due respect, Mr. President – that's crazy.'

'That's what I told him. But it seems like our past has caught up with us. What we did to the Indians, they're going to do back to us, in spades.'

The doctor carefully negotiated his way around the two dead Secret Service agents, and came up close to the President and looked him in the eyes. 'Mr. President ... this blinding, it isn't being caused by ghosts. We haven't yet been able to identify why so many people are losing their sight, but the most likely culprit is some type of virus, like the Spanish flu pandemic in nineteen-eighteen.'

'So what are you saying? That I've been hallucinating?'

'No, sir, I'm not necessarily suggesting that. But the trauma of sudden blindness can play all kinds of strange tricks on your mind.'

The President waved his hand backward and forward in front of his face. 'This Wampanaug medicine man said that he would give me my sight back, so that I could watch our whole society being taken apart. And he *did* – you can't argue with that.'

The doctor looked uncomfortable. 'You can see again, sir, that's for sure. And I find that really encouraging. It indicates that this blindness is reversible, and maybe only temporary.'

'But nothing to do with Indian spirits? In spite of what happened to these two guys here? And the guy who disappeared into thin air, right in front of your eyes?'

The doctor pouted, so that his moustache bristled out. 'I wouldn't like to contradict you, Mr. President. And I'm not pretending that I can understand any of this. But there has to be some explanation, even if it's mass delusion.'

The President laid a hand on his shoulder, firm and paternal. 'OK. Maybe it *was* a delusion. But until you can convince me it was a delusion, I'm going to treat it like it really happened. Go downstairs and tell the Secret Service detail what's happened up here, and also tell them that I want the Vice-President brought here as soon as possible, as well as the Secretary for Homeland Security, and General McNamara from the Pentagon. And Mrs. Perry.'

'Yes, Mr. President.'

'Oh – and one more thing. Tell them to find the Assistant Secretary for Indian Affairs, and make sure that they bring *her* along, too.'

The doctor said nothing, but the President was canny enough to guess from his expression what he was thinking. *Why don't you ask for a psychic, for good measure?*

TWENTY

Eugene, Oregon

Less than two hours after we left Portland we were driving south through the Willamette Valley toward Eugene. It was a bright afternoon, with a sky so blue that it was almost violet, and way off to our right we could see the rumpled gray peaks of the Cascade mountains, dusted with snow.

I counted fewer than twenty other vehicles on our way down Route 5 from Portland – SUVs and crossovers, most of them, with suspiciously staring families inside, and precarious piles of suitcases on the roof. Some were headed north and some were headed south, but I had no idea where they were going, or why they thought that where they were going would be any safer than where they had come from. Although the Willamette Valley is so idyllic, all cherry trees and vineyards and lazily winding river, there was an almost tangible feeling of foreboding in the air, as if war had been declared, and we were expecting an H-bomb to explode at any moment, like a scene out of *Dr. Strangelove*.

We turned off Route 5 onto 126 and drove into the suburbs of Eugene.

'Eugene, tree-hugging capital of the world,' I

remarked.

'Nothing wrong with hugging a tree or two,' Amelia retorted. 'You'd be surprised how much psychic energy they can absorb.'

'*Trees* are psychic? You're pulling my leg.'

'No, I'm not. Sometimes I can hug a very old tree and I can hear the voices of people who sat under it over a hundred years ago. Only faintly, but it's almost like a long-playing record, with tree-rings instead of grooves.'

'Is that what they call "keeping a log"?'

Amelia smacked me on the shoulder. 'Your jokes get worse, you know that?'

After they had unceremoniously kicked us out of the Inn at Northrup Station, we had rented a blue Ford Escape from Hertz and headed for civilization – or what we thought would be civilization. We didn't know then that the power blackout had already crept all the way northward from San Diego to San Francisco, with the lights blinking out in one community after another, and as far east as St Louis. We *did* know that neither of us could get a signal on our cells, and that the Escape's radio gave out nothing but a soft hiss of white noise, but we didn't yet realize that *all* communications were rapidly closing down – phones, faxes, emails, everything. By now, the only way to get messages across the country was by carrier pigeon, or heliograph. Or maybe smoke signals, if you were a Native American and understood how to read them. Singing Rock had tried to teach me a few, but all I could remember was: if you see smoke halfway up a hill, everything's hunky-dory – but if you see smoke on the summit, watch out, General Custer's coming.

'*Trees*,' I repeated, as we drove slowly through the center of Eugene. It looked like most of the stores and cafes were closed, and the sidewalks were almost deserted. However there were squad cars parked at almost every intersection, and there were even cops with rifles on the upper deck of the Fifth Street Public Market, leaning against the railings with their sunglasses glinting in the afternoon sun.

'What about trees?' Amelia asked me.

'Don't you remember when Misquamacus first got himself reborn inside of Karen? We went to visit Dr. Snow, and Dr. Snow told us all about Native American medicine men and the different ways they reincarnated themselves? He said that after they were dead, Kiowa medicine men could reappear as trees, and they could even move from place to place, and talk.'

'I remember, sure. But how does that help us with these Eye-Killers?'

'It doesn't. Not in the slightest. But Dr. Snow could. He's the greatest expert on Native American superstitions in the whole damned country. If anybody will know about the Eye-Killers, he will.'

'Stop,' said Amelia. 'There's a restaurant right across the street and it's open and I'm hungry and I need to visit the bathroom.'

I U-turned and parked in front of a brick-fronted building that announced itself as the Steelhead Brewery and Cafe. We climbed out of the Escape and went in through the open front doors. Inside, the place smelled of glass polish and stale beer, and the only person in there was the bartender, who was shining up the mirrors behind the bar.

'You open?' I asked him.

He didn't turn around, but he didn't need to, because I could see his face in the mirror. He looked like a spotty version of Ron Howard, in the days when Ron Howard still had hair.

'You kidding me?' he said.

I looked around. In one corner of the bar stood a red London telephone booth. 'That work?' I asked him.

He sprayed more Spic & Span on the mirror, and carried on polishing. 'You kidding me?'

I went up to the bar and watched him polish for a while. 'OK,' I said, 'I'm kidding you. But are you planning on opening any time soon?'

'Nope. Well, not until the power comes back on.'

'Everything's out? Even the phone?'

'Yup.'

'Anyplace in town where it isn't?'

'Nope. Not so far as I know. And no place else, neither, not from here to Myrtle Creek.'

Amelia came out of the women's bathroom. 'There was no light in there,' she complained.

'Power's out,' I told her. 'All the way from here to Myrtle Creek. Phones are out, too.'

We left the bar and climbed back into our Escape. 'What do we do now?' asked Amelia. 'I'm absolutely starving.'

'We stock up on Hershey Bars and Whatcha-macallits and go visit Dr. Snow.'

'Be serious, Harry. Dr. Snow lives in Albany. It's going to take us *days* to drive to Albany.'

'Aha – that's where you're wrong,' I told her. 'When he turned eighty, Dr. Snow moved to California to live with his daughter's family in Memory Valley.'

'I didn't know that.'

'Neither did I, until our last run-in with Misquamacus. I called him up a couple of weeks later because I wanted to tell him what had *really* caused that so-called blood infection.'

'Did you talk to him?'

I shook my head. 'The woman who bought his house gave me his number, but I never got around to it. To tell you the truth, I wasn't sure that he would believe me.'

'Why not? It was true.'

'I know. But Dr. Snow always insisted that Indian spirits were so much more powerful than European spirits, didn't he? He wouldn't believe that Misquamacus would have needed to raise up those *strigoi* things to help him.'

'Those *strigoi* things were absolutely terrifying.'

'Sure they were, but they were Romanian, and Dr. Snow thinks that compared with Native American demons, Old World demons are no more frightening than a pack of rabid dogs.'

'Rabid dogs are frightening. They sure frighten me.'

'Yes, but a rabid dog can't strike you blind just by looking at you, can it? And you can shoot a rabid dog. But these Eye-Killers ... God alone knows how we're going to find a way to stop them.'

Amelia said, 'Harry, we don't have to stop them ourselves. All we need to do is find out what they are and how to send them back to wherever they came from, and convince somebody in authority that we're not lunatics.'

'Oh, simple.'

'Harry, you can't save the whole country single-handed.'

We were back on Route 5 now. I turned into a Shell gas station and pulled up.

'Listen, Amelia,' I told her, 'I may not be the most selfless guy you ever met. I may have dishonestly extracted a whole lot of money from some very gullible old ladies by making them believe that they were going to get lucky in the sack. And, believe me, I'm not trying to save the whole country single-handed. But whether I like it or not, this country happens to contain you, and Lucy, and Karen, and a lot of other people I really care about, and if the only way for me to protect you from these Eye-Killer things is to face up to them myself personally, then face up to them myself personally I will.'

Amelia sat and looked at me for a long moment. Then she leaned across and kissed me.

'I love you, Harry Erskine. But look.'

She pointed to an improvised cardboard sign hanging from the gas pumps. *Sorry no gas Pumps non-operashanul.*

'Actually I didn't stop here for gas. I came here for candy and soda.'

'In that case, get me some Three Musketeers, would you? And a bottle of Mountain Dew.'

'Your wish is my command,' I said, and I kissed her back.

Memory Valley may have been a whole lot closer to Eugene than Albany, but it was still more than five hundred thirty miles due south, through Yreka and Weed and the Whiskeytown–Shasta–Trinity National Recreation Area, and all the way down the Sacramento Valley.

Great scenery, I expect. But we drove through the night, taking it in turns to sleep on the back seat, and all that either of us saw were bushes turned into cardboard by the light of our headlamps, and deer's eyes gleaming at us out of the darkness. Apart from changeovers at the wheel, the only stop we made was at the 76 gas station in Williams, at about one-thirty in the morning. I cut a length of hose from the airline and siphoned a tankful of gas from a Jeep that was parked at the side of the forecourt. Amelia kept watch in case an enraged proprietor came out with a shotgun, but the gas station was locked, and silent, and all I heard was a dog barking in the distance.

Altogether the drive took us over nine hours, and when we finally rolled into Memory Valley it was quarter after three in the morning, and we were exhausted.

'Maybe we could find a motel,' said Amelia, as we crept along Main Street. Of course the power was out, but a cold white moon was still high in the sky, and I could see what a neat, prosperous community this was. There were potted yuccas along the center of the street, and an ornamental fountain, even though it wasn't working, and bookstores, and craft shops, and a wholefood restaurant called Earthly Origins.

'How are we going to find Dr. Snow?' asked Amelia. 'Do you still have his number?'

'Unh-hunh. But I don't suppose it'll be difficult. This is the kind of town where everybody knows everybody else's business. Look at that. Even that gym is called Busybodies.'

Main Street ended in a brick-paved square surrounded by cafes and the Memory Valley library. We turned off left and drove down a shadowy, tree-lined avenue until we passed a sign saying Sweet Memory's Bed & Breakfast. It was a fine old colonial-style house with a porch and a gambrel roof, and even a turret with a weathercock on top. I parked the Escape outside, and Amelia waited for me while I went up to the front door. The doorbell didn't work, so I took hold of the knocker and gave a few sharp raps.

No answer, and the windows remained in darkness, so I knocked a second time. Still no answer. Amelia put down her window and said, 'Forget it, Harry. There's probably a Howard Johnson's on the outskirts of town.'

'OK,' I agreed, and turned away, but as I did so I heard a shuffling noise inside the house, and then a banging, as if somebody had knocked over a chair. A querulous woman's voice called out, 'Who is it? What do you want?'

I went back up close to the door and said, 'Me and my friend, we're looking for someplace to stay. We just drove all the way from Oregon.'

'I can't let you in. I'm sorry. We've all been told not to.'

'All we want is a bed for a couple of hours, and maybe a bath, and something to eat.'

'There's no power.'

'Yes, ma'am. I understand that. A cold bath and a couple of baloney sandwiches would do it.' I had eaten so many Whatchamacallit bars that I felt sick, and I was sure that I had put on ten pounds.

'I still can't let you in.'

I beckoned to Amelia. She climbed out of the Escape and came up to join me at the door. 'She won't let us in. Can you persuade her that we're not a couple of yeggs?'

'I'll try,' said Amelia. She rapped gently on the stained-glass window at the side of the door and called out, 'Ma'am? Ma'am? My name is Amelia and all we need is someplace to rest up for a while. We won't bother you at all, I promise.'

'They told us not to let anyone in.'

'Who told you?'

'Deputy Ramsay. He said to keep our doors locked and not to let anyone in, and that he'd come around and check up on us in the morning. But I don't know whether it's morning yet. What time is it? I tried to find out the time from the phone but the phone's dead.'

'It's three-thirty-five, ma'am. It's still not sunrise yet.'

There was a very long pause, and then the woman said, 'What did you say your name was?'

297

'Amelia. Mrs. Amelia Carlsson. I'm from New York City. My friend here is called Harry. I can swear to you that all we want is a bed to sleep in. We won't give you any trouble.'

We heard the woman shuffle up to the door. Then we heard the bolts drawn back, and the chains rattle. Eventually the door opened, and there was a skinny woman in her late sixties with a silver pudding-basin haircut and a knee-length black dress, with three strings of pearls around her neck. She stared at us with her chin slightly raised, but she didn't seem to be focusing on us at all.

'Can I really trust you?' she asked us.

Amelia said, very gently, 'You can't see us, can you? You're blind.'

The woman nodded. 'Me and half of the population of Memory Valley, from what they tell me. That's why Deputy Ramsay told us all to stay indoors. They're trying to get help, but it doesn't look very likely that anybody is going to come. Not anytime soon, anyhow.'

'The same thing has happened to my sister Lizzie, and her family,' said Amelia. 'It's been happening everywhere, all across the country.'

'Is it OK if we come in?' I asked her.

'I guess so. You haven't come to rob me, have you? Even if you have, there isn't much for you to steal, apart from bathrobes, and my guests steal those anyway.'

We stepped into the hall. Although it was very gloomy, we could see that it was furnished with antique side tables and vases of dried flowers, and on the wall hung a large oil painting of a fetching young woman with very red lips, wearing a brown bonnet and a brown riding coat.

'I'm Belinda Froggatt,' the woman told us, groping her way toward the living room. I closed the front door behind me, and then I went across and took hold of her arm. She looked up and tried to smile. Her eyes didn't appear to be blind, but she was staring at my left shoulder as if I had a second head.

'When did this happen?' asked Amelia. 'When did you all go blind?'

I guided Belinda Froggatt over to one of the big old-fashioned armchairs and helped her to sit down. Amelia and I sat down opposite her, on the couch. The living room was decorated with floral wallpaper, and gilt-framed mirrors, and thick crimson drapes with swags and tie-backs. I had always fantasized about a nineteenth-century living room like this, with a bell to tinkle so that my French serving-maid could bring me a large Jack Daniel's on the rocks, and then leave the room to reveal that she was wearing nothing but a lace cap and a frilly apron and a pair of very high stiletto heels.

'It was the day before yesterday, at the craft fair. We hold a craft fair every year and it's always crowded. I take my quilts to sell. I don't get much time for sewing quilts, what with this place to run, but this year I had three.'

She touched her fingertips to her cheek, as if to reassure herself that she was still there, even though she couldn't see. Looking at her now, I realized that the oil painting of the girl in the hall was probably her, or maybe her mother. She had

299

once been very attractive, and she still hadn't lost her well-defined cheekbones, and her dark brown eyes, blind though they were.

'All I can remember is that some photographers were taking pictures. I recognized one of them, John Leppard from the *Marin Scope*, but there were six or seven others, too, and their cameras were flashing so bright that I was dazzled, and then suddenly I couldn't see.

'I could hear people shouting that they couldn't see, either. There was a whole lot of confusion, and people bumping into me, and the stand right next to me was tipped over altogether. It was all home-made jellies and preserves and the glass jars smashed all over the floor.

'I found my chair and I sat down and I decided it was safer not to move. I sat there and sat there with all of this pandemonium going on around me, and after what seemed like a very long time, a paramedic came up to me and asked me if I was OK, and then a very kind man drove me home. I don't know who he was. All I can remember was that he smelled of cigarettes.'

I said, 'These other people who were taking photographs ... can you tell us what they looked like?'

Belinda Froggatt frowned. 'That was the strange thing. I saw them out of the corner of my eye, and I saw the flashes from their cameras. But I couldn't really describe them to you. It was like – when you turned your head to look at them – they were someplace else. I do remember, though, that their faces were very pale. It was almost as if they were wearing hockey masks.'

'Was there anybody else there you didn't recognize?' asked Amelia. 'Maybe some character wearing black, with a hat on, and necklaces?'

Belinda Froggatt thought about that, biting her lip, but then she shook her head. 'The only person who caught my attention was an old man who was standing by the entrance, wearing a very odd hat like a pirate's hat, and a furry wrap, deerskin, I'd say – and, yes, he was wearing necklaces, lots of them. And he had marks on his face, two marks on each cheek. I don't know whether they were scars or make-up.'

'Could he have been an Indian?'

'I'm sure I don't know. I don't think I've ever seen an Indian that looked like that before. I just remember pointing him out to my friend Lily on the jellies and preserves stand, and thinking how eccentric he was. She said he looked like Long John Silver's grandmother. She did make me laugh.' She paused. 'She went blind, too.'

I said, 'How are you feeling now, Belinda? Is there anything we can do for you? Make you something to eat, maybe? How about a drink?'

'I'm all right, thank you for asking. I had a cold chicken leg earlier, and a glass of milk. I think I can survive until Deputy Ramsay comes to rescue me. Everybody else will have to, won't they?'

'Only one thing more. Do you happen to know a Dr. Ernest Snow? He moved out here from the east coast a couple of years ago to live with his daughter and her family. Old guy, white hair, very upright.'

Belinda Froggatt nodded. 'Dr. Snow? Of course I do. Well, I know just about everybody in Memory Valley. I should do. I've been living here since nineteen sixty-two, and opened up this place in nineteen seventy-eight.'

'Can you tell us where he lives?'

She sat up straighter, cocking her head to one side. 'Why do you want to know? You're not debt collectors or anything like that, are you?'

Amelia said, 'Of course not. Dr. Snow is a long-time acquaintance of ours. You probably know that he's an expert on Native American anthropology. We – ah – we did some research together on Indian rituals.'

Belinda Froggatt took out a crumpled-up Kleenex and fastidiously wiped her nose. 'I'm not sure. So long as you're telling me the truth, and Ernest isn't going to give me a hard time.'

'Belinda,' I said, 'You don't seriously think that *anybody* would be out here at four A.M., with the power out all over the country and everybody going blind, dunning an eighty-year-old man for a couple of Diners Club payments?'

'No, of course not. You're right. Dr. Snow lives with his daughter on Jumping Dance Lane.'

'Thank you,' said Amelia. 'What's his daughter's name?'

'Meredith – Meredith Burgess. I don't know the number of the Burgess house but Jumping Dance Lane is right across the main square and second on the left, or is it third? They live about a third of the way along, and they have a yellow-painted house with a very large white oak in front of it. Jack Burgess, he's a local attorney. Very nice man. Maybe a little smooth-talking for my liking, but very nice.'

I stood up, took hold of both of her bony hands with all of her rings on, and kissed her on each cheek. She smelled faintly of some perfume that reminded me of my mother, Joy maybe. 'Let me tell you something, Belinda. When they come to write the history of what happened in America this morning, – that's if there's anybody left to write it, and anybody left to read it – then the true heroine will be you.'

Belinda smiled. 'So long as they spell my name right. There's two "g's" in Froggatt.'

Nationwide crisis or no nationwide crisis, it was far too early to wake anybody up, especially an elderly geezer like Dr. Snow. Besides, I was so tired that the carpet kept rising and falling, as if I had jet lag. Belinda directed us to a room upstairs, where there was a huge four-poster bed. She didn't ask if we wanted separate bedrooms. Either she thought that we were too exhausted to care, or else she sensed in her blindness exactly what our relationship was all about, which to tell you the truth was more than I could.

We stripped to our skivvies and climbed under the home-stitched quilt and slept like two dead people for over five hours. When I awoke, the first thing that I was aware of was sunshine, and a heap of snow, but it wasn't a heap of snow, it was an intensely white cotton pillow, smelling of starch. For a few moments, I couldn't understand where I was. I didn't have an antique mahogany night table, with a brass clock on it, and a porcelain statuette of a Pierrot, and neither did anybody else I knew.

But then Amelia stretched and said, 'Urrrggg-hhhhhhhh, don't tell me it's time to get up?' and I remembered where we were and what we were doing here.

She threw back the quilt, climbed out of bed, and drew back the drapes. I don't exactly know what the word is to describe the way you feel when you can't take your eyes off someone, even if you're not lovers. The way you feel that every curve of their back is perfect, every mole on their arms, as if everything about them was specifically made to please you. When she turned away from the window and I saw that little crease in the front of her pale-green ribbony panties, I could have written a symphony about it. Or a country-and-western song, at worst.

'Cold shower?' asked Amelia, and I thought, yes, I probably need one.

TWENTY-ONE

Memory Valley, California
We raided Belinda's icebox (even though it wasn't working, and it was dark inside) and made ourselves a feast of cold chicken legs and holey Swiss cheese and red apples and stale bagels. We were still sitting at the kitchen table when Belinda came in, running her hand along the counter to guide herself. Outside the leaded-glass window, her small orchard was brilliant with sunshine. She couldn't see it, but she stopped and cupped her hand to her ear for a moment and said, 'The wind is getting up. I can hear it!'

'Listen, we've helped ourselves to some of your food, but we'll replace it,' I told her. 'Is there anything else you want us to bring you?'

'I would love some pecan pie, if you can find any. I don't know what it is about going blind. I keep feeling like something sweet.'

'Well, you stay here and keep your door bolted. We're going over to visit Dr. Snow.'

'You're welcome to stay here as long as you like,' said Belinda. 'It's a little frightening, being on my own here, not even knowing if it's day or night.'

'Don't worry,' said Amelia. 'After we've seen Dr. Snow, we'll come right back.'

Once we had washed our plates, we left Belinda's bed-and-breakfast and headed back toward Memory Valley's main square. Two white-and-green-striped Fords from the Marin County Sheriff's Department were parked at angles by the ornamental fountain, and a group of very fat guys in deputies' uniforms were standing around talking to half a dozen lean and ascetic-looking locals. As Amelia and I drove past, they all turned their heads and stared at us, and one of the deputies waddled toward the curb as if he intended to flag us down, but I kept on going – not *too* fast, but fast enough to leave Deputy Lardbutt standing in the middle of the road with his hands resting on his podgy hips, frowning after us.

'Here it is, Jumping Dance Lane,' said Amelia, and we took a left. Three hundred yards along and there it was, the yellow-painted house with the giant white oak outside. We parked and climbed out, and as we walked up the drive we could see a woman staring at us out of one of the bedroom windows. The wind was rising and the pages from a newspaper tumbled across the street, as if they were chasing each other.

Again, the doorbell didn't work, but there was a heavy brass knocker in the shape of a glaring wolf's head. Singing Rock had once told me that if your front door faces to the east, you should be sure to hang a wolf's-head knocker on it to keep out the evil demons who always come from that direction, especially when it starts to grow dark. My front door on East Seventeenth Street faced east, but the only apparitions who ever approached it were white-haired ladies looking for a Tarot reading, or Velma from across the landing, wanting to borrow a cup of Jack Daniel's.

I knocked twice, and the door was opened so quickly that it took us by surprise. We were confronted by a small freckly woman with vivid red hair, wearing the redheads' uniform of green cardigan and green sweater to match, and black elasticized slacks that were two sizes too big for her.

'Yes?' she demanded. It was obvious that *she* hadn't gone blind. She looked aggressively from me to Amelia and back again, like an attack dog trying to decide which one of us to bite first.

'Hey, we're sorry. We didn't mean to alarm you. We're looking for Dr. Ernest Snow, and Belinda Froggatt at the bed-and-breakfast said we might find him here.'

'Who are you? What do you want? You know what's happened in this community, don't you?'

'Yes, we do, ma'am, and that's one of the reasons we're here. You must be Mrs. Burgess, am I right? Dr. Snow's daughter?'

She didn't get the chance to answer before a dry, patrician voice said, 'That's absolutely correct, sir! And if my eyes don't deceive me, *you* must be Mr. Harry Erskine, and this lovely lady must be the delightful Ms. Amelia Crusoe!'

Flustered, the redhead turned around. Standing in the hall behind her was Dr. Snow. He looked as elegant as ever, in a green quilted smoking-jacket, although his white pompadour was very much thinner now, and his cheekbones were much more prominent, and he was altogether *bonier*. He was carrying a silver-topped walking cane, and he came toward us with a limp.

'Arthritis,' he said. 'One of the reasons I left Albany and came out here to California. Mind you, when it's foggy, my knees still seize up. How the devil are you both?'

'Good,' I told him. 'Amelia is Mrs Carlsson these days, but I guess you can't have everything.'

Meredith immediately melted. 'So you're *Harry*, and you're *Amelia*! I am so, *so* sorry! But after what's happened here, we can't be too careful. Do you know, we heard gunshots last night, and I *never* heard gunshots before, not here. Not in Memory Valley.'

She beckoned us to come inside and led us through to a large conservatory at the back of the house. The conservatory was furnished with white wicker chairs with heaps of hand-embroidered cushions and aspidistras in porcelain planters. Through the windows, we could see a swimming pool, and a sloping green lawn, and a small gazebo. It would have been middle-class idyllic, if the whole country hadn't been collapsing all around us.

'I can only offer you juice, or a Coke,' said Meredith. 'They still haven't told us when the power might be coming back on.'

I didn't say anything. It wasn't my job to frighten her. But I looked across at Dr. Snow and I hoped he could tell by my expression that we hadn't come here for a Facebook reunion.

'Merry, sweetheart,' he said, 'why don't you give me a little time alone with Harry and

Amelia? I get the feeling that they have one or two rather *personal* questions that they want to ask me.'

'Oh. OK, Daddy. Right.' Meredith looked disappointed, but all the same she got up and left the conservatory, and closed the door behind her.

Dr. Snow stretched his right leg out straight, and winced. 'It's been a long time, hasn't it, Harry? Hard to believe it ever really happened.'

'He's back,' I said.

'He's *back*?' Dr. Snow looked at us with his watery, solemn eyes, like an old spaniel that somehow knows that it doesn't have very much longer to live. 'Are you sure about this? I thought you told me that he could *never* come back.'

'All of these planes and cars crashing. All of these power outages. All of these people going blind. It's him.'

'Do you have any evidence that it's him? I suppose you must, or you wouldn't have come here, would you?'

'Amelia has a sister Lizzie. She and her family were on vacation in Hell's Canyon when they went out cycling and met these really weird characters standing in the road. The family couldn't agree if these characters looked like boxes, or mirrors, or puppets. But they all agreed one thing: the characters' eyes flashed and they all got instantly blinded.'

'Go on,' said Dr. Snow.

I glanced at Amelia, and then I said, 'We wouldn't have known who these characters were, or *what* they were. But when she was in the eye clinic, Lizzie kept on ranting about The One Who Went And Came Back.'

'*Misquamacus.*'

I nodded. 'Amelia did her seance thing and got through to John Singing Rock, and John Singing Rock confirmed it. It's Misquamacus, and this time he's determined to pull the rug out from under the whole of our society.'

'Funny, isn't it?' mused Dr. Snow, shaking his head from side to side.

'*Funny?*'

'Well, funny peculiar, not funny ha-ha. I had my own suspicions, you know, but I thought I was being paranoid. But there isn't a terrorist organization in the entire world that's capable of wreaking such havoc on such a scale. Not even the Russians could do this, and that's supposing they would *want* to do it, or dare. The Russians depend on our economic stability for *their* economic stability, and they depend on us to maintain the balance of power between East and West. *They* don't want to police Iraq, or Iran, or Afghanistan, they'd rather leave it to us. They tried in Afghanistan and look what happened.

'Only the magic of the First People is powerful enough to turn our whole country upside down. It is, after all, *their* country, not ours.'

Dr. Snow thought for a moment, and then his brow furrowed.

'*Misquamacus,*' he repeated. 'But didn't you say that you had exorcized him – *utterly*? You told me, didn't you, that you had annihilated his very *substance*? His spiritual energy, his ectoplasm. You made it impossible for him to return to the living world, even as a ghost.'

'That's what I thought, yes. But John Singing Rock said that so long as he's remembered – even if he's only remembered by other spirits – he still exists.'

'I see. I see. And he's obviously found a way to come back to life?'

'He's possessed the spirits of other dead medicine men – *hundreds* of them, from every tribe you can think of, all across the country. From Apache to Zuni.'

'A spirit who possesses other spirits. I never heard of such a thing, even in Indian mythology.'

Amelia said, 'It's true, Dr. Snow, believe me. Misquamacus appeared in our hotel room in Portland. He didn't *look* like himself, not outwardly. He looked like some other shaman, and he called himself Wovoka. But it was him all right. He started to torture Singing Rock but we managed to put a stop to that. He told us, though, that this was going to be the finish, as far as we were concerned. He's going to blind us, and then he's going to slaughter us, and then he's going to tear down our cities, brick by brick.'

'Of course it's impossible,' said Dr. Snow. 'In fact it's quite absurd. Native American magic may be strong, but it's not *that* strong.'

'That's not the point,' I replied. 'It's the damage he's going to do, the innocent lives that are going to be lost. He's massacred thousands already.'

Amelia said, 'We think we've found out how he's doing it. Blinding people, I mean. Singing

Rock gave us some clues, and we believe that he's been using some kind of Pueblo Indian spirits called Eye-Killers.'

Dr. Snow lifted one finger in excitement. 'Eye-Killers! *Eye-Killers!* Of course! I should have thought of that myself!'

'You've heard of them? You know what they are?'

'Oh, *yes*! They're a very interesting part of Pueblo Indian mythology – mainly Zuni, although the Hopi and the Acoma also have stories about similar demons.'

'We Googled them,' said Amelia. 'Apparently they were created when girls got themselves pregnant with foreign objects, like cactus prongs.'

'Cactus prongs, yes. Or enormous phalluses fashioned out of clay. The Pueblo Indians have always been brilliant potters. I have a wonderful clay bird effigy made by Cicuye Indians. And some Acoma bowls. Would you care to see them?'

'Maybe later. What we really need to know is, are these Eye-Killers real? And if they are, what can we do to stop them?'

Dr. Snow stood up, and began to circle around us, the brass ferrule of his cane tapping on the marble floor. 'Sorry to be so restless. If I sit still for too long, my knee locks.' He tapped around us three times, and each time he looked as if he were just about to say something, but couldn't quite find the right words.

Eventually, he said, 'The thing about it is – the thing about it *is* – the Eye-Killers themselves were real, but the popular myth about how they were created – that was almost certainly erroneous. About fifteen years ago a fascinating paper was published by the University of New Mexico Press, by a Zuni scholar, George Lonan. Lonan, incidentally, is the Zuni word for "cloud."

'Lonan talked to a very old Zuni medicine man, and discovered that when Zuni girls became pregnant by a boy that their families did not approve of, they would protect the identity of their lovers by pretending that they had been pleasuring themselves with a cactus or a corn cob or a clay phallus, and that is how they had fallen for a baby.

'The family would of course assume that the baby was some kind of unnatural being, and when it was born they would immediately put it into a makeshift wooden coffin, with only a slit for its eyes, so that they could tell when the baby had died.'

'The babies were put into these coffins when they were still alive?' asked Amelia.

Dr. Snow stopped circling. 'The Zunis believed that if they killed the babies themselves – by strangling or by drowning or tossing them into a fire – then the demons which possessed each inanimate object would take their revenge on them.'

'Revenge of the cactus prongs,' I put in.

'Ha! You may find it amusing,' said Dr. Snow. 'But the prickly cactus was said by the Zuni to be capable of terrifying change, and to turn itself by night into a shapeless creature like a giant slug, covered with bristles, which would crawl

313

into a man's mouth and down his throat and choke him.'

I kept my flippant comments to myself after that. Ever since I had first encountered Misquamacus, I had been threatened by mythical Native American creatures just as horrifying as a giant cactus slug, and I knew that in some parallel dimension they really existed. I knew, too, that any shaman with the necessary skills could summon them through to the world of the living, and cause indescribable mayhem. There was the Lizard of the Trees, for instance, which had looked like a giant Komodo dragon. It had been semi-transparent – half-reptile and half-apparition – but it had still taken a man's fingers off with one crunchy bite.

Dr. Snow said, 'One day, twin babies were born to the daughter of a Zuni chief, a boy and a girl. The girl claimed that they were the children of a clay phallus, so they were put into makeshift coffins and carried out to a sacred place in the desert, and left to die. But the story says that when Tawa the Sun Spirit saw what his people had done, he was enraged. He had tried for centuries to teach them to be tolerant and forgiving, and here they were, abandoning two newborn infants in the midday heat. To Tawa, it didn't matter how the babies had been conceived. Even the child of a demon is helpless, and to leave a helpless child to die is unforgivable.

'So – Tawa stared from the sky into the slits in the coffins. He stared all day, from dawn until dusk, and filled each baby's eyes brimful with

314

dazzling sunlight. When the Zuni came to see if the babies were dead, the babies stared back at them, and blinded them. They had become Eye-Killers.'

'From what Lizzie and her family told us, they could walk,' said Amelia. 'They had bodies like boxes, but they had arms and legs, and faces, too.'

Dr. Snow sat down again, gritting his teeth because of the stiffness in his knee. 'That is because – after at least *five* of the Zuni men had been blinded – the coffins were carried hurriedly back to the pueblo, and shown to a shaman, who went by the name of Talking Hawk. Talking Hawk went into a seeing-trance, and in his see-ing-trance, Tawa told him that the babies were no longer human babies (which they had been) but sun-devils. If Talking Hawk took good care of them, they would protect the Zuni people against all of their enemies, of which the Zuni had many – and this was long before the Spanish had made their appearance. The word "apache" is Zuni for "enemy" or "stranger" or "people of the other side." The Apache themselves call their tribes "Ende," which simply means "Our People."

'Anyhow, Talking Hawk instructed the pueblo woodworkers to make jointed arms and legs for the coffins, and potters to mold masks out of white clay. Some of them were given head-dresses made of deer antlers, too. When they were finished, the Eye-Killers could stand, and walk. Beyond a doubt, *those* were the creatures that your sister and her family saw, in Hell's

Canyon.'

'But there must be more than two Eye-Killers,' I said. 'People have been going blind all over the country.'

'Of course there are more than two. There are probably *thousands*. Remember that the first Eye-Killers were a boy and a girl, and somehow they reproduced. I'm afraid that I don't know the intimate details, but Native American spirits multiply in many different ways. They can temporarily possess animals, like wolves or deer, and reproduce when the animals reproduce. Some of them can increase their numbers simply by reflecting their image in a lake. Who knows what these two got up to.'

Amelia said, 'They've blinded some people instantly, haven't they? Like Lizzie and her family. One flash and they couldn't see. But for other people, it must have been delayed. Like airline pilots. They were able to take off, but then they went blind in midair.'

'Of course,' said Dr. Snow. 'This blinding is not a *physical* reaction, you understand, like being blinded by the sun. The flash of light that comes from an Eye-Killer's eyes is very bright, I'll grant you, but it doesn't irreversibly damage your sight. It's more like hypnosis – like putting you into a trance, and telling your brain that you simply can't see. And just like hypnotists, the Eye-Killers can implant a suggestion into your mind that you're going to lose your sight in twenty minutes, or two hours, or whenever – and, hey presto, you do.'

'That sounds very sophisticated for a spirit,'

316

said Amelia.

'Yes. But I suspect that's why the Eye-Killers are all accompanied by medicine men. The medicine men decide who should be blinded, and when, and for how long, and give the Eye-Killers instructions.'

'Then this blindness may not be permanent?' I asked him.

'I'd say that largely depends on Misquamacus, wouldn't you? Once he's defeated us, he may magnanimously decide to give us our sight back. On the other hand, he may not. He may consider that – after what we did to his people – we deserve to spend the rest of our lives in darkness.'

'Which brings us to the sixty-four-zillion-dollar question, doesn't it? How can we *stop* these walking boxes?'

Dr. Snow looked at me for a very long time without saying anything, until I began to wonder if he had actually heard me.

I was about to repeat the question when he said, 'To be absolutely honest with you, Harry, I don't have the first idea.'

'There must be something in one of your books, surely?'

'Most of my books are in storage, I regret.'

'Isn't there somebody you can talk to?'

'In New Mexico, certainly.'

'OK. If that's what it takes. We'll drive you to New Mexico.'

'Harry, I'm eighty-three years old. I have chronic arthritis. I'm also a diabetic. You can't possibly drive me to New Mexico.'

'But it wouldn't take much more than a day – well, a day and a half. And we're talking about the survival of our whole way of life here. We're talking about millions of lives. Look around you. Look around this house. None of this is going to last. Before you know it, we'll all be living in tepees and wickiups. Or caves, even.'

'Harry, I'd be dead before we got as far as Phoenix.'

'So what we are going to do? Wait for the Eye-Killers to show up, go blind, and then let Misquamacus do whatever he wants with us?'

'Of course not. Amelia here is a talented psychic, is she not?'

I glanced at her. 'Absolutely. She's the best there is.'

'Then she must try to contact somebody who can tell us what we need to know. Some Native American shaman who knows his onions.'

Amelia said, 'I couldn't get through to any spirits in New Mexico. Unless I know them personally, like Singing Rock, and I know the way through to them, they have to be spiritually close. They have to have died in this house, or someplace nearby.'

'In that case, I don't think you'll have too much trouble, dear girl. This is Memory Valley, remember.'

'What about it?'

'Oh, come on. Have you never heard of Memory Valley? It was here in eighteen ninety-one that General Henry Lawrence eliminated the last coherent group of Hupa Indians. Since eighteen twenty-six they had been steadily

318

driven south from their traditional lands by gold prospectors, and at last they had settled here, in this valley, which they called the Valley of the White Moon.

'There were fewer than a hundred of them – men, women, and children. They had been told to leave Memory Valley and relocate on a reservation further inland, but they had resisted. One night in early January, General Lawrence and two hundred soldiers surrounded them, and killed them all. In his report, General Lawrence said that the Indians had fired first, and for the protection of his men he had been obliged to open up with Hotchkiss guns. There were no Indian survivors to say otherwise.'

'I never heard about that,' I admitted.

'It was the month after the massacre at Wounded Knee, and I think the Government was anxious to keep it as quiet as possible. It was, in fact, the very last conflict in the Indian Wars. The very last night of a civilization that had lasted for thousands of years.'

Amelia touched her fingertips to her temples. 'I don't know, Doctor. I can't *feel* any presences. And we've been talking about them, too. Usually they respond when they become aware that living people are talking about them.'

'Why don't you try the whole candle thing?' I suggested. 'All that spooky chanting you used to do? *Venora, venora, spiriti venora.*'

'I could, I suppose. But even if I managed to contact one of these Hupas, what would they know about the Zunis?'

'Probably nothing at all,' said Dr. Snow. 'But

319

almost every Native American tribe has a similar story about demons who can blind you or even kill you just by looking at you. Each tribe may call them by different names, and tell different stories about where they came from, but they're more or less the same demons.'

'I could try, I guess. But it would probably be better to do it at night. The spirits are always more receptive when it's dark – and besides, these people were killed at night, weren't they?'

Dr. Snow said, 'Come back around seven, then. I'm sure that Merry will be able to rustle us up something to eat. And I still have a few bottles of Arrowood Syrah-Shiraz left to get us in the mood.'

Meredith showed us to the door. 'I gather you're coming back this evening,' she said. She didn't look too happy about it. 'I don't know what this is all about, but I have to warn you that Daddy hasn't been well. His heart, as well as everything else. I don't want him getting over-excited.'

'We understand that,' said Amelia. 'We'll keep everything as low key as possible, we promise.'

We walked back to the Escape, with Meredith standing in the open doorway, watching us. As soon as we were safely out of earshot, I said, 'Low key? How are you going to summon up the spirit of a massacred Hupa in Dr. Snow's dining room and keep it low key?'

Amelia opened the car door and climbed in. 'I don't think I can. But, like you said, we're talking about the survival of our species here.'

TWENTY-TWO

San Fernando, California
They sped northward out of the city, weaving left and right between more and more crashed and abandoned vehicles, many of them still smoking. Perched on the pillion of his Electra Glide, Tina clung on to Tyler as tightly as she could, and kept her head pressed against his back. They had passed a seven-vehicle pile-up at the intersection with the Golden State Freeway, and she had made the mistake of looking. A whole family of cinder-people had been sitting in a burned-out Bravada, husband and wife and three small children, even their dog, with its blackened head stiffly raised as if it were still howling.

Tina could hear hardly anything over the aggressive burbling of the Electra Glide's engine, and the buffeting of the slipstream past her ears, but two or three times she was conscious of a deep, compressive thump, somewhere behind her, and when she looked back she could see gray cauliflowers of smoke rolling up into the sky.

'We'll stop when we get to Wheeler Ridge!' Tyler shouted.

'How long will that take?'

'About an hour, if we're lucky!'

'Then how long to Memory Valley?'

'Another four hours on top of that!'

'Great! I wish my fanny was better upholstered!'

Twenty or thirty cars passed them on the opposite side of the highway, traveling south toward the city, but they passed only one moving vehicle on their own side – an ancient VW Combi, decorated with faded sunflowers, chugging along at less than twenty, with oily smoke pouring out of its exhaust. Inside they saw a gray-bearded man with long gray hair and a red bandanna, and a gray-haired woman with tattoos on her shoulders. As they roared by, Tyler gave them the peace sign, and they replied with an asthmatic toot on their horn.

They passed the Los Angeles Reservoir on their left, and the sun was shining on the water like a polished silver ingot. There was no sign of any Highway Patrol cars, and no helicopters flying overhead, so Tyler opened up the throttle until they were speeding along at nearly ninety. After only four or five miles, though, they saw smoke up ahead of them. Tyler slowed down.

'Jesus,' he said.

A concrete bridge crossed diagonally over the highway about a half-mile in front of them, but beneath it all four lanes were blocked with burning vehicles. They were smashed together so comprehensively that Tyler couldn't even guess how many there were, but there was nobody standing by the side of the road, so it looked as if there were no survivors.

He stopped, and put his feet down on the roadway. He could feel the heat from the burning vehicles on his knuckles and his face, and the warping noise of overheated metal played an eerie, melancholy tune.

It wasn't difficult to see what had happened. A huge white semi had careered off the bridge and crashed across the highway. Another semi, southbound, had collided with it, and its trailer had overturned. After that, a shoal of cars and vans and SUVs had all crashed into them.

'What do you think?' asked Tina. 'Anybody left alive?'

Tyler shook his head. 'After a fire like that, they won't even be able to tell who they were.'

'Those poor people. I hope God takes care of them.'

'Let's hope so. I don't think that anybody else will.'

Tina twisted around and looked behind them. 'We'll have to make a detour.'

'No way. It's over ten miles back to the nearest intersection. We're low on gas, too.'

'Well, what else can we do?'

'We can go up and over.'

'What?'

'Up the embankment, across the bridge, and down again.'

Tina looked up at the sloping concrete walls on either side of the highway and said, 'You're out of your *mind*! Look how *steep* that it is! You couldn't even climb up there on *foot*! You couldn't even climb up there with a *ladder*!'

Tyler spread his arms out wide. 'Ex-squeeze

me? What do I do for a living? I'm a stunt person. Can we go up the embankment, across the bridge, and down the other side? Yes, we can!'

'I thought you worked your stunts out in advance. Like really meticulously, to make sure that nobody got hurt.'

'Unfortunately, we don't have time for that.'

Tina said, emphatically, 'I'm not doing it.'

'So how else are you going to get past this inferno?'

'I'll find a way. I'll walk.'

'Listen, Tina. I've done this kind of thing dozens of times. I've even ridden a motorcycle straight up the side of a trailer.'

'I'm sure you have. Is that how you smashed your kneecap?'

'No, I did that jumping off a horse and onto the back of a flatbed truck. When I did the trailer thing, I only fractured my wrist.'

'That settles it! I'm not doing it!'

She started to climb off the pillion but Tyler gripped her arm. 'I was only kidding. I didn't get hurt at all. And we won't get hurt now, I swear to you. Come on. You're Tina Freely, tough-nut lady reporter. You broke the Culver City vice-ring story, even when they threatened to break your arms.'

There was a moment of high tension, when Tina was still trying to lift herself off the pillion but Tyler was holding her down. They stared into each other's eyes but it wasn't so much a battle of wills as a mutual search for understanding.

I've never done anything like this. I'm scared.

I know you are, but I promise to take care of you, OK?

Gradually, she relaxed, and eased herself back down. 'OK,' she said. 'So long as you're sure, let's go for it.'

Tyler settled himself into his seat and revved up the Electra Glide's engine until Tina was almost deafened. Then he turned around and shouted, 'Hold on to me like grim death, you got it? Lock your hands together. Don't even think about letting go of me, even if we fall off!'

'What? You didn't say anything about falling off!'

'Oh, didn't I? Too late now!'

He steered the motorcycle in a wide, slow circle, until they were positioned on the south-bound side of the highway, facing east. The flames from the wreckage under the bridge had died down now, apart from an occasional orange lick, but the smoke was pouring out even thicker. Keeping the brakes on, Tyler gunned the engine up to 3,000 rpm, until their saddles were quaking between their legs.

'You ready for this?' he shouted.

Tina had her eyes squeezed shut. 'No! Absolutely not!'

'OK, then. *Geronimo!*'

The motorcycle burst across the highway with an angry scream. As they rushed toward the concrete embankment, Tyler heaved up the handlebars, as if he were doing a wheelie. There was a loud thump and both of them were nearly jolted off their saddles, but then they were roaring up the forty-five-degree incline as if they were riding an Apollo rocket.

As soon as they came level with the railings on top of the bridge, Tyler tilted himself to the left and they flew over the retaining wall and landed on the overpass with another loud bang. The motorcycle wobbled wildly, and for a split second Tyler thought they had lost their balance, but they were hurtling so fast toward the retaining wall on the opposite side of the road that there was nothing he could do but yank up the handlebars again and hope that they wouldn't hit it head-on.

As one grizzled old stuntman had once told him, 'If in doubt, do it anyhow.'

They cleared the retaining wall and flew out over the embankment on the other side of the bridge. Tina screamed out, *'Aaaaahhhhhh!'*

Now Tyler knew why they sometimes played action scenes in slow motion. He felt as if the air had turned into glue, and they were flying through it very slowly, with plenty of time to consider everything that was happening around them. They fell through a blur of smoke, and for a few seconds he was blinded, but then he could see the highway, stretching all the way north-westward, and green forested hills.

The motorcycle's front wheel touched the concrete with a sharp, rubbery scream, and Tyler thought: *We've made it.* But then the rear wheel kicked up like a bucking bronco, and Tina was thrown from the pillion, still holding him tightly around the waist. Both of them tumbled down the embankment, over and over, and all Tyler could see now was a blur of arms, legs, concrete, and sky.

The Electra Glide missed them by inches, crashed onto the highway and bounced. Tyler ended up face down on the blacktop with Tina on top of him. He lay there for a moment, completely still, as he had been taught to do after a stunt accident. If any bones were broken, trying to move would only make the injury worse.

After a few moments, Tina climbed off him. He twisted himself around and looked up at her. She had a large red bruise on her left cheek, but otherwise she didn't appear to be hurt.

'Are you OK?' he asked her.

'*No*,' she said. 'I knew this was a bad idea.'

He climbed to his feet. His artificial kneecap had hit the road at an awkward angle, and he grunted with pain.

'How about you?' she asked him. 'You haven't broken your leg, have you?'

'No, no. I'm great.'

He limped over to the Electra Glide and heaved it upright. It didn't look damaged, but when he pushed the starter button, there was no *whump* from the starter dampers, only an irritable clicking. He tried again, and again, but the engine refused to turn over.

'What's wrong?' asked Tina. 'Can you fix it?'

'Could be almost anything. Fuses, connections. Maybe the ECM has been damaged.'

'So what do we do now?'

'Find ourselves some alternative means of transport, I guess.'

Tina touched the bruise on her face 'I hope the bone isn't broken.'

Tyler came up to her and said, 'Here,' and gently felt it with his fingertips. 'No, you're OK,' he told her. 'It's just a contusion.'

'Oh, wonderful. It's a good thing I'm not appearing on TV tonight.'

Tyler tried to start the Electra Glide again, but it still wouldn't fire up. He climbed out of the saddle and said, 'Guess we'd better start walking. So long, old girl. I'll come back and rescue you, if I get the chance.'

They had walked only about a hundred yards, however, when they heard the distant bellowing of a truck. It was approaching from the south, from behind the chaos of burning vehicles beneath the overpass.

They stopped and listened. The truck came nearer and nearer, and then stopped. They could see it intermittently through the drifting smoke, a big red tractor with shiny chrome bumpers.

'Come on,' said Tyler. 'It won't be any use to us. It'll have to turn back.'

'Yes, same as *we* should have done.'

'OK. You're right. I admit it. We nearly made it, though, didn't we?'

'Oh, sure. We're still having to hoof it, though, aren't we?'

The truck slowly started to back up, but it didn't turn around. Instead, it reversed for more than a quarter of a mile, and then stopped. Twin blasts of dirty brown exhaust blew out of its smokestacks, and they heard its engine revving.

'I don't believe this,' said Tyler. 'I hope he's not trying to do what I think he's trying to do.'

But the driver released the truck's brakes, and it came blaring along the highway toward the bridge, faster and faster, until it was traveling at nearly sixty miles an hour. It collided with the wreckage with a bang like a bomb going off. Three burned-out cars came exploding out from under the bridge, and the truck followed them. Immediately, the driver slowed down, and with a long-drawn-out screech of protesting metal, it pushed the wrecks onto the median strip, and then stopped.

Tyler walked over to it, and Tina followed him. In the passenger seat he could see an elderly black woman with a bright red scarf on her head, holding a small baby. The driver's door opened and a young black woman jumped down, wearing tight black jeans and a tight black sweater. She came around the front of the truck and said, 'Hi, there. Hope that didn't shake you up too much.'

'Are you OK?' Tyler asked her. 'That was one hell of a stunt.'

The woman inspected the Titan's bumpers. One of them was dented, and the paintwork over the nearside wheel arch was scratched, but otherwise the truck was undamaged.

'Six hundred horsepower,' the woman said. 'Take a whole lot more than a few wrecked cars to stop *this* rig.'

All the same, she turned around and looked at the wrecks and said, 'Not that I wanted to do that. All those poor souls. It makes you weep, don't it? It really makes you weep.'

The cars that she had pushed aside with her truck were so badly burned that they were all the same dead gray color, and their windows were blackened with smoke, so that their incinerated occupants were hidden from sight.

'You guys on *foot*?' the woman asked them.

'That's my Harley over there. We had a kind of a mishap.'

Tina pointed to the bruise on her cheek. 'Somebody tried to be a little too clever, and we crashed.' She held out her hand. 'My name's Tina, by the way. This is Tyler.'

'Jasmine,' said Jasmine. 'And that's my Aunt Amadi, but I always call her Auntie Ammy.'

'And the little guy?' asked Tyler.

'I don't know who he is. There was a pileup on the freeway and I rescued him. His mom was killed. I tried to get in touch with Children's Services to take care of him but nobody showed.'

'It's Armageddon,' said Tyler. 'End of the world as we know it. Where are you headed?'

'I don't know. North. We thought it would be safer if we got out of LA, that's all. We didn't want to go blind.'

'We're trying to get to San Francisco. Well, Memory Valley, near Sausalito. But the same thing's been happening there, too. My mom and my dad and my sister have lost their sight, and so have a hundred other people. I don't think any place is safe.'

'Do you have any idea what's actually *happening*?' asked Jasmine. 'We went to find my brother in Maywood but then we saw these

330

weird characters with white faces and these bright flashing lights coming out of their eyes and Auntie Ammy thinks it's *them* that's making everybody blind, whoever they are. I don't know. It sounds crazy, don't it?'

But Tina shook her head and said, 'No, it doesn't. We've seen them, too, Tyler and me, in Hollywood. We actually saw them blinding some kids who were trying to steal stuff from people's houses.'

'Do you know who they are? Or what they are?'

'Not at all.'

'Maybe they're like aliens or something,' said Jasmine. 'You know, like *War of the Worlds*.'

'I guess they could be,' said Tyler. 'They sure don't *look* human, do they?'

Auntie Ammy put down her window and called, 'Little fella's gettin' hungry, Jazz!'

Jasmine said, 'OK.' Then she turned back to Tyler and Tina. 'We could give you a ride, if you like. It's not like we were heading anyplace special.'

'We'd really appreciate that,' said Tyler. 'With this knee, I don't think I could have made it to the next town, let alone San Francisco.'

They climbed up into the cab. It was cramped, with the four of them, and baby, too, but Tina shared the passenger seat with Auntie Ammy and Tyler sat on the floor with his back against the dash. Jasmine started the engine and they drove off northward.

'Does the little guy have a name?' asked Tina. The baby was staring up at her, fascinated, and playing with the button on the front of her sweater.

'I didn't think it was my place to name him,' said Jasmine. 'If I can't find out who he is, though, I guess I'll have to.'

'He looks like a Mikey to me,' Tina suggested.

'Mikey?' said Tyler. 'That's a terrible name. Give the poor little fellow a break, will you?'

'All right, what would *you* call him?'

'Frank.'

'Frank! That's even worse!'

Auntie Ammy said, 'If we are to give him a name, we should call him Peter, after Oggún.'

'Excuse me?'

'Oggún is a Santería god – what we call an orisha.'

'So why are we going to call him Peter?'

'Because that was Oggún's secret name. When the slaves from West Africa were first brung to this country, they were forbidden by their masters from worshippin' their own orishas, so they gave them the names of Catholic saints instead. Oggún was worshipped under the name of Saint Peter. Oggún is 'specially suitable for this poor little fella because Oggún is always there when cars crash, and blood is shed.'

Tyler said, 'I never heard of that before. But Peter, that's a good name. What do you think, Petey?'

'Petey' abruptly burst into tears.

TWENTY-THREE

Modoc County National Forest, California

'Would you fasten your seat belt, please?' said Ranger Butowski.

'I can't find my buckle,' said Cayley.

'It's right there, honey, down by the side of your seat.'

Cayley groped for it but she still couldn't find it.

'Right there,' said Ranger Butowski, growing impatient.

'I can't see it,' Cayley told her. 'I can't see anything. I'm blind.'

'What?'

'We're *all* blind, all four of us.'

Ranger Edison turned around in his seat. 'What do you mean, you're *blind*? Are you kidding me?'

'It's true,' said Charlie. 'It happened to us yesterday.'

'Hey, get serious. You could see us clear enough when we were landing.'

'We could, yes. But we don't know how that happened. We all held each other's hands, and while we were holding hands we could see. But as soon as we let go, we went blind again.'

'Hard to believe, isn't it?' said Remo. 'I don't

even believe it myself.'

'You know that people have been going blind, all over the country, coast to coast?' Ranger Edison asked them.

'You mean it's not just us?'

'Unh-hunh. It's been a pandemic. Airliners have been crashing 'cause the pilots have gone blind. People have been stepping into traffic and getting themselves killed, and there's been literally thousands of auto wrecks. We picked up three other anglers yesterday afternoon, and some birdwatcher just after sunrise this morning, and *they* were blind, too.'

He picked up his radio microphone and clicked it on and off. 'Not only that, all communications have gone down. We lost all radio contact with our headquarters in Alturas about a half-hour ago, and we can't raise any of the ranger stations. I don't know. Myself – I reckon it's solar flares that's responsible. Unusual surface activity on the Sun.'

He pressed the LongRanger's starter button and the rotors began to turn. 'Don't you worry,' he added. 'We'll soon get you to a doctor.'

The helicopter tilted upward, and Ranger Edison angled it over the river. They were less than fifty feet above the ground, however, when three figures appeared through the smoke from the smoldering wreck of the Winnebago.

'Hey, Jim – there's some more people down there!' said Ranger Butowski. 'We should make sure they're OK!'

'How many?' Remo shouted, over the noise of the engine.

'Three! Why, did you see them before?'

'Guy in a black suit, with a hat, and two funny-looking dudes with white faces and horns on their heads?'

'That's right. Jim – why don't you take us down again, so that we can check they're not injured?'

'No!' yelled Remo, and he was almost screaming. Then, 'Mickey! Charlie! Cayley! Give me your hands! Give me your hands!'

They flailed around, trying to find each other's hands.

'What's the problem?' asked Ranger Edison.

'It's them!' Remo shouted at him. *'They're the ones who made us go blind!'*

'What? What are you talking about?'

Remo found Cayley's hand, and then Mickey's, and Mickey found Charlie's hand. They gripped each other tight, but they all remained sightless.

'Shit!' said Remo.

'It's not working!' wailed Cayley. 'I still can't see!'

'Listen,' said Ranger Edison, 'don't panic. This won't hold us up for long.'

'Just get out of here, man! Quick!'

But Ranger Edison said, 'I'm sorry, son. It's our duty to take care of anybody in the park who might be in trouble. We have to talk to them, at least – check out they don't need any assistance.'

'Don't!' shouted Mickey. 'They could make *you* go blind, too!'

'Hey, just calm down, OK?' said Ranger

Edison. 'This won't take long.'

He tilted his cyclic stick and the helicopter made a tight turn over the river, kicking up concentric circles of spray.

'Please!' begged Cayley. 'You have to believe us! How are we going to get out of here if they make *you* blind, too?'

But the helicopter was now sinking slowly back down to the parking lot, and Infernal John and his two stilt-legged companions were walking toward it.

'Are they still there?' asked Remo, anxiously.

'They're still there,' said Ranger Edison. 'But don't panic. We'll just check that they're OK and then we'll hightail it right out of here. And if they give us any trouble – I have a Remington Model Seven right under my seat here.'

'For Christ's sake, dude! A gun's no goddamned use! All they have to do is *look* at you.'

The helicopter was only ten feet off the ground now. Infernal John raised both his arms, and dazzling blue-white lights started to jump out of the eyes of his two companions.

'What the Sam Hill –?' said Ranger Edison.

Ranger Butowski clapped her hands over her face. 'I can't see! Jim, I can't see!'

Remo banged his fist on the side of the cabin and yelled, *'Go-go-go-go-go! Go!'*

This time Ranger Edison didn't hesitate. He swung the helicopter around on its axis and simultaneously lifted it almost vertically upward. He carried on climbing until they were almost level with the top of the promontory, and then he turned it northward, following the Pit

River. They all clung tightly to their seats, feeling as if they had left their stomachs down in the parking lot.

'Margot?' said Ranger Edison. 'Margot, are you OK? Tell me you're OK!'

'I can't see!' wept Ranger Butowski. 'I can't see anything! Only black!'

'Jesus,' said Remo. 'Didn't I *tell* you to get out of there?'

'Just keep it shut, son,' snapped Ranger Edison.

'Oh God,' said Ranger Butowski. 'What am I going to do?'

'Stay calm, OK?' Ranger Edison told her. 'Soon as we get to Alturas, I'll find you an eye doctor. These kids managed to see us momentarily, didn't they? That means you haven't lost your sight for good.'

But Ranger Butowski continued to sob as they flew northward, with their shadow leaping and jumping ahead of them over the hills. Mickey and the rest of them stayed quiet. They were all bruised and exhausted, and there was nothing they could say that would make Ranger Butowski feel any better.

After they had been flying for about five minutes, Ranger Edison said, 'Who were those guys? And what were those flashing lights? Were they lasers?'

Mickey said, 'The guy in the black suit told us his name was Infernal John. He's an Indian.'

'An *Indian*? So who were the other two guys?'

'We don't know. The guy in the black suit told us their names. Tuddy-something and Tubbysomething. But they weren't real people.'

'What do you mean, they weren't real people?'

'They just weren't. It was like they were made out of wood.'

'I see,' said Ranger Edison. He glanced back at Mickey over his shoulder. 'Sure they were.'

He didn't ask Mickey any more questions but tried his radio. 'State Park Ranger Edison, calling Alturas HQ! State Park Ranger Edison, calling Alturas HQ, come back!'

He waited, but there was no reply, only a loud, persistent hiss. Ranger Butowski was whining now, in the back of her throat, like an injured puppy. 'I won't be able to see my sister's kids any more. I won't be able to work, or drive, or watch TV or *anything*.'

'Hold on, Margot. We'll be there in another ten minutes.'

They kept on flying in silence. It was obvious that Ranger Edison wasn't interested in discussing Indians in black suits or wooden people with white faces and antlers. Either he thought they were lying or delusional; or else he simply refused to think about it.

'Alturas Municipal Airport dead ahead,' he said, at last.

But just as he began to angle the LongRanger toward the airport, he said, almost inaudibly, *'No!'* and the helicopter lurched and bumped and spun around, its engine-note rising and falling with a screech like a bandsaw cutting through trees. Cayley and Ranger Butowski both screamed, and the boys shouted out, too.

'What's happening?' Cayley squealed. *'What's*

338

happening?'

The helicopter spun around a second time, but then it steadied, and the engine note returned to normal. Ranger Edison said, 'It's OK, it's OK! Don't panic! We're going to be fine!' but he was gabbling and he sounded close to hysteria.

'What's happening, dude?' Remo shouted. 'What the hell's wrong?'

'It's OK! I've gone blind, too, but I think I can get us down!'

'What? You've gone blind, too? Jesus!'

'We're all going to die!' wailed Cayley. 'We're going to crash and we're all going to die!'

Ranger Edison said, 'Listen, listen! Alturas airport was right up ahead of us, less than two miles. I can fly forward for a couple of minutes and then take us down. If I take it real slow, we should be OK.'

'But we were spinning around and around in circles,' Charlie protested. 'How do you know we're still flying in the same direction?'

'I'm pretty sure we went all the way through three hundred sixty degrees. So we should be heading roughly the same way.'

'How sure is "pretty sure"?' Charlie asked him, his voice so high that he sounded almost like a girl. 'How roughly is "roughly"?'

'I don't know. Pretty sure, that's all. And pretty roughly, too.'

They flew unsteadily forward, with the helicopter dipping and waltzing as Ranger Edison tried to keep it headed in a straight line. Ranger Butowski counted out loud to a hundred, and then she said, 'That's it – two minutes! We

339

should be over the airport now!'

Ranger Edison adjusted his collective lever until the helicopter was hovering, and then, very gradually, he took it down. Cayley said, 'Dear God, please don't let us die. Dear God, please don't let us die. Especially don't let us get burned to death. Whatever happens please don't let us get burned to death.'

'Will you do us all a favor and shut the fuck up?' Remo told her.

The helicopter sank lower and lower until Mickey thought that they must be nearly down on the airport runway. Ranger Edison took it down a few feet more, but then there was a loud scraping noise underneath the helicopter's belly, and they were all thrown violently to the left. With a scream of power, Ranger Edison took them up again.

'What was that?' said Cayley. 'I thought we were going to crash.'

'Tree,' said Ranger Edison, tersely.

'We can't be over the airport, then?' said Charlie.

'No, son. We're not. To be honest with you, I don't know where the hell we are. But hold on, I'm going to try again.'

He flew ahead for another hundred-second count, and then he took the helicopter down again, even more cautiously this time. Even though he was blind, Mickey closed his eyes tightly and tried to picture his home and his family and his black Labrador, Jet. For some reason, he had believed when they threw themselves off the promontory at Infernal Caverns

340

that some miracle would save them, but now he was totally convinced that they were all going to die.

Ranger Edison took the helicopter down so gradually that it hardly felt as if they were descending at all. But then they felt a bump as the right-hand skid hit the ground, and Ranger Edison immediately took them back up.

'That was a slope,' he said. 'Felt like a hillside, or maybe a roof.'

He flew on further, and tried to land for a third time. This time, with an ear-splitting creak and a splintering of branches, the helicopter came down on top of another tree. Cayley was openly crying now, and Remo said, 'Come on, man, for Christ's sake. Just get us down, will you?'

'We're still full of fuel,' said Ranger Edison. 'If we crash-land, then your girlfriend here has every right to be worried that we're going to burn up. What I suggest is, we keep on flying until we run dry.'

'That doesn't make any sense,' Remo retorted. 'We don't even know how high up we are. We could run into a mountain, anything. How far can this thing fly?'

'About three hundred fifty miles, a little over.'

'We could end up in the ocean, for Chrissakes!'

'Look,' said Ranger Edison, 'we're all blind, so we don't have very many options open to us, do we? I could keep trying to land, but it's way too dangerous with nearly a hundred gallons of fuel on board.'

'But when all of that fuel runs out, we'll still

crash!'

'We won't just drop out of the sky, son. I'll put the rotors into autorotation and we should be able to glide down.'

'I think it's the least dangerous alternative,' put in Ranger Butowski. 'If we come down on a tree or a mountainside, and the tanks are still full, we won't stand a chance.'

Cayley said, 'Please. Let's do that. I don't want to get burned alive. One of my boyfriends was in a car wreck and he got burned alive.'

Ranger Edison took the LongRanger up higher and then increased their forward speed. Mickey knew that at any second they could collide with a tree or a hill or a power-line pylon, but he took some morbid comfort in thinking that they would all die instantly.

'Us rotorheads have a formula,' said Ranger Edison. 'We call it the Pucker Factor. The more risky the situation, the more of the seat cushion gets sucked up your ass. The formula is, S equals Suction, H equals Height Above Ground, I equals Interest in Staying Alive and T equals Technical Trouble.'

'Thanks,' said Remo. 'I really needed to hear that.'

'I'm trying to lighten things up a little,' Ranger Edison replied. 'We're all still alive, aren't we? We're all in one piece. Let's try to stay that way.'

They kept on flying for nearly three hours. The Emperors of IT tried holding hands again, four or five times, but they stayed completely blind. In the end, they gave up.

Charlie said, 'Maybe we need to be down on the ground. You know, like maybe we need to be *earthed*. Like, when you get struck by lightning.'

'I don't know,' said Remo. 'Right now, I just want to get down on the ground in one piece.'

Even though they were aware that they could be unexpectedly killed at any second, the monotonous beating of the LongRanger's rotors eventually lulled Cayley and Charlie and Mickey into sleep. Remo couldn't sleep at all. He sat with his head bowed in case he had to assume the crash position, wishing that this nightmare were all over, one way or another. It was the endless, seamless darkness that depressed him the most – the thought that even if they did survive, he would be totally blind for the rest of his life.

Without warning, the helicopter's engine began to stutter and blip. 'That's it!' said Ranger Edison. 'We've run out of gas! We're going down!'

Cayley and Charlie and Mickey all woke up. The engine had cut out altogether now, and Ranger Edison disengaged the main rotor so that it would windmill, and start the helicopter on a downward glide. They were jolted and buffeted by the slipstream, and it felt to Mickey as if they were dropping out of the sky like a brick, but Ranger Edison shouted out, 'We're coming down good! Textbook autorotational landing, less'n we hit something untoward!'

None of them answered him. They were all clutching the edges of their seats, and if they hadn't been blind, they would have been able to see how white all their faces were. As the helicopter fell out of the sky, the rotors made a sweeping, whistling noise, almost melancholy, as if it were singing them a sad song as it carried them down to die.

'Don't you worry,' said Ranger Edison. 'One French guy came down from forty thousand feet without any power!'

'Please, God!' said Cayley. 'Please, God, help us!'

They had no idea how high they had been flying, but their descent seemed to take forever, as if they would never reach the ground at all. The sweeping, whistling noise went on and on. But then there was a devastating bang, like a giant metal door being slammed in their faces, and they were tossed from one side of the helicopter to the other. Mickey's shoulder collided with the bulkhead, and then he knocked his head against Remo's knee, so hard that it stunned him. He felt Cayley seize his shirt, and tear away one of his sleeves, and then Charlie dropped with his full weight onto his spine.

The LongRanger tipped over onto its starboard side and then rolled over again and again, so that they felt as if they were being tumbled around in the drum of a giant dryer. At last, with a metallic groan, it gave a last rocking motion and came to a stop.

'We're down!' shouted Ranger Edison. 'Anybody hurt?'

'I'm OK,' said Remo. 'Cayley, how about you?'

'I hurt my arm again.'

'But you're alive, that's all that matters. Charlie? Mickey?'

'I'll be OK, once Charlie gets off of me.'

'Charlie?'

'I hit my head. I think I'm bleeding.'

'Margot? How about you?'

There was no answer from Ranger Butowski. 'Margot!' Ranger Edison repeated. 'Margot, are you all right? Margot!'

He must have been groping to find out what had happened to her, because he suddenly said, 'Oh, God. Oh, God. Margot.'

'What's wrong?' asked Remo. 'Maybe she just got knocked unconscious.'

'I don't think so,' said Ranger Edison. 'Feels like a piece of the airframe went right through her chest. There's blood, I can feel it. She doesn't have a pulse.'

'Oh, Jesus.'

The helicopter was lying on its side, and they were still struggling to find out where the door was when they heard voices, and knocking.

'Are you people all right in there? Hold on – we'll get you out!'

There was a lengthy pause, and then they heard people climbing onto the helicopter's fuselage, and trying to open the door. 'Michael, hand me that crowbar will you? Dave, give me a hand here!'

At last, the door was pried open, and hands reached down into the cabin to help them climb out.

'You folks are darned lucky you wasn't all

killed.'

'My partner,' said Ranger Edison. 'I think she's pretty badly hurt.'

'Paramedic!' shouted one of the voices. 'Paramedic – there's a woman injured here!'

Still shaking with shock, the Emperors of IT sat down on the ground. It felt like neatly mown grass, and it felt as if the sun were shining. 'Here,' said Mickey. 'Let's hold hands.' He reached out for Charlie's hand on his left and Cayley's on his right. Remo held Charlie's other hand and almost immediately their eyes were filled with light and color.

'Oh my God,' said Cayley, and burst into tears. 'Oh my god, it works!'

They were sitting in a bright green park, under an intensely blue sky, and they were surrounded by a crowd of twenty or thirty people. An ambulance was already parked on a path nearby, as well as two squad cars from the Marin County Sheriff's Department.

Two deputies were trying to lever out the LongRanger's front windshield. One of the helicopter's main rotors had been torn off and its tail was sticking up like a crushed cricket. It had left a fifty-yard trail of wreckage and torn-up grass behind it, but they could see that it had only just cleared the tops of the tall chestnut trees that bordered three sides of the park.

'We've all been blinded,' said Ranger Edison. 'These kids – me and my partner, too. That's why we crashed.'

'Well, the Lord was sure taking care of you today, my friend,' said a gray-haired man in a white Giants jersey. 'It's happened here, too. Over a hundred local people gone blind.'

'Where are we?' asked Remo, looking around. 'We've been flying for ever, trying to use up all of our gas.'

'Dan Johnson Memorial Gardens, in Memory Valley.' Then, 'Are you *sure* you kids can't see?'

'Memory Valley? I don't believe it! We flew that far? And that's almost due south!'

With a grinding crack, three men lifted out the LongRanger's front windshield and laid it on the grass. The Perspex was spattered with blood. A blue-uniformed paramedic leaned inside the cockpit, and they could just see Ranger Butowski's head tilted back. After a short while, the paramedic stood back, and helplessly raised both hands.

'That's just terrible,' said Charlie. 'That could have been any one of us.'

'I don't know about you,' said Remo, 'but I could sure use a drink. Then we can find our way back home. I sure hope my parents are OK.'

Ranger Edison was sitting a few feet away. The paramedic came over and hunkered down beside him and spoke to him, and they saw him nodding his head and wiping his eyes. Cayley said, 'Let's go hold his hand. Maybe he'll be able to see, too.'

They walked over, in a human daisy-chain. Several onlookers turned around and gave them a curious look, but they ignored them. They were too pleased that they were able to see.

'Ranger Edison, sir?' said Mickey. Ranger Edison lifted his head and stared blindly in his direction. 'We're holding hands again. We have our sight back.'

Ranger Edison slowly climbed to his feet. 'You can see? Did you see Margot?'

'Yes, sir. I guess she must have been killed outright. But here – why don't you hold hands with us, too?'

Ranger Edison hesitated for a moment, and then held out his hand. Remo took hold of it, and almost immediately Ranger Edison blinked at them, and turned his head around, left and right. 'I can see again! What about that? That's amazing!'

He looked over at the wreckage of the Long-Ranger. The deputies were covering one side of the cockpit with a blue blanket. *'Margot,'* he said. 'Why did it have to be Margot? She was such a terrific girl, you know? Smart, funny. And she really cared about the park service. Not like some of those horses' asses that call themselves rangers.'

Two of the deputies came over and said, 'You folks should really get yourselves checked out. Only trouble is, with so many people going blind, and so many accidents, the hospitals are all full to busting.'

'I think we're OK, deputy,' said Ranger Edison. He patted his chest with his left hand. 'I don't feel like there's nothing broken.'

'We really need to get home to Palo Alto,' said Mickey. 'We could see our own doctor, couldn't we?'

'I guess,' said the deputy. 'Don't know how you're going to get there, though. There's no bus

348

service, and no taxis, and the trains aren't running, neither.'

A black Labrador just like Jet came running across the grass toward them. 'See that dog?' said Mickey. 'I got one at home, exactly the same. Could be the same darn dog.'

One of the deputies frowned behind his sunglasses and said, 'Thought you people were blind.'

'It comes and it goes,' said Remo. 'One minute we can see, the next we can't. Don't ask us. We don't understand it, either.'

The deputy looked as if he were on the verge of asking them why they were holding hands, but then another deputy whistled to them and beckoned them back to the helicopter wreck. 'We'll talk to you later, OK? Why don't you go over to the main square, it's right over thataway. The power's all out, but the cafe's open, and you can get yourselves a drink and clean yourselves up.'

They left the wreck of the LongRanger and walked hand-in-hand across the park. They had nearly reached the gate that led out onto the main square when Remo stopped and said, 'Look.'

Standing deep in the shadow of the chestnut trees on the other side of the park they saw more than two dozen men, at least six of whom were sitting on horses. Some of them wore wide-brimmed hats and ankle-length coats. The horsemen wore dark blue jackets and blue pants with a single stripe down the side, and pale yellow gauntlets. They weren't moving, any of them, but the horses were restless, and they could hear harnesses jingling.

Mickey said to Charlie, 'They look exactly like those guys we saw before we got in the helicopter. Like old-style Seventh Cavalry.'

'Maybe this is some kind of an anniversary,' Charlie suggested. 'Maybe they're re-enacting some famous battle or other.'

'You think?' said Remo. 'The whole country's going blind and they're all messing around in fancy dress?'

They stood and stared for over a minute, and as they did so the shadows under the trees seemed to grow darker and darker, and the men and their horses became more difficult to see. Eventually it was so impenetrably dark that they couldn't make them out at all.

'Well, what the Sam Hill do you make of *that*?' asked Ranger Edison. 'I wouldn't like to say that they were ghosts, but they sure *looked* like ghosts.'

'Do you believe in ghosts?' Mickey asked him.

Ranger Edison emphatically shook his head. 'No, absolutely not. But if they weren't ghosts, then what the hell *were* they?'

TWENTY-FOUR

Washington, DC

Sitting behind his desk in the Oval Office, the President said, 'There are times when a leader has to lead from the front, regardless of the risks, and this is one of those times.'

'I don't exactly understand what you're proposing, sir,' said General McNamara.

'I'm proposing to go to Memory Valley myself. If that's where the first attack on our society is going to be, then I believe that I should be there in person to defend it.'

'With every respect, Mr. President,' put in John Rostoff, the Secretary for Homeland Security, 'your information that Memory Valley is going to be targeted first by this terrorist faction – well, you said yourself that it came to you in a vision of sorts. If you fly out to Memory Valley you'll be putting yourself in considerable jeopardy, if only through the risk of your helicopter crew losing their sight en route. And even if your information does prove to be correct, the Lord alone knows what acts of terror these people have in mind.'

The President stood up and walked over to the window. In spite of his recent ordeal, Marian Perry thought that he had regained almost all of

351

his previous energy. He was standing straighter, and his eyes were bright, and his jaw was set aggressively. This was the old 'Pug Dog' Perry, who always relished a fight, especially if the odds were stacked against him.

'These "terrorists," John, are Native Americans, or the *spirits* of Native Americans, and they want their country back. I don't know how they think they're going to achieve it, but I've seen some of their supernatural power for myself, first hand, and I think that if we dismiss it as hocus-pocus, or some kind of conjuring trick, we'd be making a very grave mistake.'

'You realize, Mr. President, that this is all extremely difficult for us to believe,' put in General McNamara. 'Whatever their ethnic origins happen to be, these people are either terrorists or a hostile invasion force, and we have to treat them as such.'

'General,' said the President, 'you have to fight fire with fire. From what I've seen, they can vanish and reappear at will. They can take on different identities. Christ Almighty, General, they physically welded two of my Secret Service agents together, right in front of my eyes, and in front of plenty of other witnesses, too.'

'So what do you propose?' asked the general, wearily.

'We have no radio or other communications, so I want you to send aircraft out to the Presidio at San Francisco and mobilize the Sixth Army, and also the Ninth Infantry Division from Fort Lewis in Washington. Send back-up messengers by road, too, in the event that the aircraft don't make it. But that will take care of our conventional response. Leila – what about the supernatural aspects?'

Leila Whitefeather was the Assistant Secretary for Indian Affairs. She was a full-blooded Navajo – a handsome forty-five-year-old woman with her long dark-gray hair pinned up in a pleat, and a gray business suit. The only concessions in her dress to being a Native American were her turquoise-and-silver earrings, and her turquoise-and-silver brooch in the shape of a turtle.

'I'm sorry, Mr. President,' she said, 'but Native American magic is not what it was – even if it *ever* was. Each tribe has a rich and complicated belief system, which includes so-called magical healing and the power to change the weather or strike down one's enemies. But these days, to be perfectly frank with you, these belief systems do very little more than preserve a tribe's history and identity. They're very valuable, in this respect. But I don't think that we're talking about real magic here. When people die, they're dead, whatever their religion. They don't come back and try to reclaim the land they lost, no matter how romantic that may sound.'

The President steepled his hands and looked at her seriously. 'That's a very pragmatic point of view, Leila. But how do I account for the visions I saw when I was in the clinic? How do I account for Graywolf, walking right through a security guard like he had no substance at all? How do we account for all of the thousands of Americans who have been blinded, and killed?'

'I believe we have to look for high-tech

weaponry, Mr. President. Not magic. And I seriously believe that the visions you saw were just that – visions.'

The President looked around the Oval Office. It occurred to him that if he went to Memory Valley today, he might never stand here again.

'If I can't trust my own judgment, and my own sanity, then whose judgment and whose sanity can I trust? I'm the President, ladies and gentlemen, and I'm going to Memory Valley to protect our way of life. Have Marine One ready to leave for San Francisco in twenty minutes.'

TWENTY-FIVE

Memory Valley, California
As we crossed the main square on our way back to Sweet Memory's Bed & Breakfast, we saw that the Aspen Cafe now had its doors open, and was filled with people. It had a wide glass frontage, with fluted oak pillars, and inside it had a polished oak floor and about twenty circular tables, with bentwood chairs. The back wall was lined with mirrors, so that it looked as if it was twice as crowded as it really was. On the ceiling there were two large fans, but there was no power to make them turn, so the atmosphere in the cafe was hot and stifling.

A red-haired young woman in a red-striped apron had set up a camping stove on the marble-topped counter, and was brewing up coffee. There was a long line of people waiting to be served. At least a third of them were blind, with other people guiding them – wives and husbands and friends, and even some children guiding their parents.

'How about a cup of coffee?' I asked Amelia. 'Looks like they have food, too. Well, Oreos, anyhow. And KitKats.'

I bought us two mugs of black coffee, and took them over to a table close to the window, where five people were already sitting – three young guys in jeans and sweatshirts and a pretty girl in a very short denim skirt, plus (oddly) a state park ranger with a bristly brown moustache, still in his khaki uniform. What was even odder about them was that they were all bruised and scratched as if they'd been fighting, even the ranger. The girl had her left arm strapped up with a belt and one of the young guys had the right sleeve of his shirt missing. But oddest of all was the way that they were all holding hands.

There were five of them, but there were still three spare chairs at the table. 'OK if we sit here?' I asked them.

They looked at each other uncomfortably. Then one of the young guys said, 'The problem is, we don't really want to break the circle.'

'What are you doing here, holding a seance?'

'No, nothing like that. But all of us were struck blind, and we found out that if we hold hands together like this, we can see.'

Amelia's interest was aroused immediately. 'You can *see*, just by holding hands?'

'That's right. But we don't know how long it's going to last.'

'How were you struck blind?'

'We were fishing up at the south fork of the Pit River. Like the Modoc County National Forest? Then this Indian guy comes up to us all dressed in black, and he has these two weird kind of life-size dolls with him. I don't know – dolls, or robots.'

'These dolls, or robots, or whatever,' said Amelia. 'Did they both have white faces, and bodies like rectangular boxes, painted black and red? And really bright lights that flashed out of their eyes?'

They all nodded, furiously. 'That's right, man! That's right! Have you seen them, too?'

'Haven't seen them for ourselves,' I said. 'But we've sure heard about them. Amelia here – her sister and her family were blinded up at Hell's Canyon Recreation Area, in Oregon.'

The ranger said, 'I can vouch for these kids because those things blinded me, too, whatever they were. I flew us all the way down here to burn up our fuel, three hundred miles and more, and then we crashed. My partner was killed, God rest her soul.'

Amelia said, 'This holding hands thing?'

'We found out about it by accident. We just held hands when we first heard the helicopter and we could see.'

Amelia glanced around the cafe, at all the blind people shuffling up to the counter. 'Have you told anybody else about it?'

'Not yet. We thought about it, but we didn't

want to upset anybody in case they tried it but they *still* couldn't see. We thought we'd better wait for the sheriff's deputies to come see us, maybe they could organize it. We didn't want to cause a riot.'

Outside the cafe, the afternoon was growing steadily gloomier. A charcoal-gray bank of cloud had blotted out the sun, and the main square seemed to have had all the color drained out of it. Even the leaves on the aspen trees had turned to gray, and they began to shiver.

'Looks like rain,' the ranger remarked.

Amelia said, 'Do you mind if *I* join hands with you?'

The five of them looked at each other. They were obviously wary of breaking the chain, in case they lost their sight again.

Amelia said, 'I'm a psychic. I'm very sensitive to circles like these. I'd like to find out if there's any psychic energy passing between you, which I strongly suspect that there is.'

'She's very good,' I reassured them, giving them the thumb's-up. 'She can talk to spirits, and dead people, and make wooden heads rise up out of tabletops, and talk to *them*, too.'

'How about it?' said one of the young guys, a dark Italian-looking character with stubble.

One of the other young guys, a chubby fellow with curly hair and flaming red cheeks, said, '*No*, man! ... what if we lose our sight again for good?'

'I think we ought to give it a try,' said the girl. She looked up at Amelia and I could see that there was an immediate rapport between them.

Some people you just like the look of when you first meet them, and for some reason you trust them, too. I could see that this girl had immediately taken to Amelia. Maybe it was her hoopy earrings and all of her jangly bracelets. 'What if she can give us our sight back permanent, so we don't have to hold hands all the time? No offense, Charlie, but you have *so* sweaty palms.'

They all hesitated for a moment, and then the ranger released his grip on the Italian-looking guy's hand, and we pulled out two of the spare three chairs and sat down. Amelia held hands with the ranger and I held Amelia's hand and the Italian-looking guy's hand, too.

'We don't actually have to be in a complete unbroken circle,' explained the young guy who had lost his sleeve. He was skinny, with thick-rimmed eyeglasses, and he was so pale that he looked as if he had spent his entire life locked in a linen closet. The left lens of his eyeglasses was crazed, so that I could hardly see his eye through it. 'We got our sight back when we just held hands in a line, but it seems a whole lot better when we sit in a circle. Brighter, you know. Sharper. And I guess we feel safer, too. We feel like we're kind of sharing the experience, you know?'

Amelia looked at them all, one after the other. 'You're Charlie,' she said to the red-faced young guy with the curly hair. 'Your parents called you Clarence, didn't they, but you prefer your friends to call you Charlie.'

'*Clarence?*' exclaimed the Italian-looking guy.

'You never told us your real name was Clarence!'

'After Clarence Darrow,' Charlie protested. 'My dad always wanted me to be a lawyer.'

'*Your* name is Remo,' said Amelia. 'You were named for San Remo, the city, where your grandparents originally came from, because there isn't actually a saint called "Remo." And you – you're Mickey. That was your father's second name, after *his* father. Cayley – your parents just liked the sound of "Cayley." And Jim, you were christened Robert James Edison but you never liked anybody calling you "Bob-Jim." You thought it sounded too much like *The Waltons*.'

The five of them stared at Amelia, deeply impressed. I had seen her do her name-guessing trick before, at parties, but it still amazed me.

'Now,' said Amelia, 'I'm going to close my eyes and I'm going to discover what kind of psychic power is running through you. I can sense it already, it's like a generator humming, but it's very, *very* strong.'

She said nothing for almost a minute, and we all looked at each other and tried to be serious about what we were doing. I usually found it hard not to laugh during seances, but this time it wasn't difficult to keep a straight face. We all knew what would happen if Amelia couldn't discover why these young people and this park ranger had lost their sight, and how they could get it back. They couldn't sit at this table for the rest of their lives, holding hands.

The inside of the Aspen Cafe was growing

increasingly dark, and when I turned around and looked out of the window I saw a flicker of lightning behind the trees. The wind was getting up, too. Dry leaves were scurrying across the sidewalk and the sheriff's deputies in the main square were holding onto their hats to stop them from blowing away. A large red truck appeared at the far end of the square, and came slowly trundling toward us. It was gigantic, one of the biggest trucks I had ever seen. It parked next to the ornamental fountain and a black woman dressed in black climbed down from the driver's seat. One of the sheriff's deputies waddled over to speak to her.

'I think I've got it,' said Amelia, with her eyes still closed.

'You think you've got what?'

'I can feel it now. I can feel it so clearly. I can *hear* it, too, it's like singing. Like a church choir, almost.'

'What is it?'

'It's the *key*, Harry. It's the answer.'

'The answer? I don't even know what the question is.'

She opened her eyes, and looked around at all of us, and she was smiling. 'It's the *spirit*. It's the *faith*. It's why the pioneers kept going when they were exhausted and they were starving and the winters were freezing them to death. It's an unshakeable belief in a better world.'

Ranger Edison shook his head. 'I'm sure I don't understand one word of what you're saying to us, ma'am.'

'Let me try and explain it to you. The Native

360

Americans have their magic, and it's Native American magic that blinded you. Those things that look like boxes on legs, they're sun-devils – Eye-Killers, the Pueblo Indians call them – with all of the brightness of the sun in their eyes.

'But when the pioneers came west, they brought their own magic with them. I'm not talking about spells, or incantations, or potions, or charms. For sure, they had deep religious faith, but more than anything else they came with a vision. They had an unshakeable belief that they could make this country blossom, like the Garden of Eden.'

'Hmm,' said Ranger Edison. 'My family came from the west side of Baltimore originally. I sure wouldn't call the west side of Baltimore the Garden of Eden. Not by a long stretch.'

'That isn't the point,' said Amelia. 'Some of the pioneers were greedy. Some of them were murderous. Some of them deliberately wiped out Native American tribes by giving them blankets infected with cholera. But they still had that vision, whether it was right or wrong, and it's the power of that vision that's giving you your sight back. It's the spirit of the pioneers. It's still here. It's all around us. It's in the air, it's in the wind, just like Native American spirits. It's *everywhere*.'

There was a bellow of thunder right over our heads. Lightning crackled on the far side of the main square, and set fire to a poplar, so that it blazed like a candle.

'It's coming,' said Amelia. 'I can feel it. The beginning of the end. What did Dr. Snow say about Memory Valley? It was the last battle of the Indian Wars. The last night of Native American independence, after thousands of years. Now they're fighting back.'

'But what can we do about it?' I asked her. 'We might have the jolly old spirit of the jolly old pioneers, but that hasn't stopped Misquamacus from blinding half the population, has it? And it looks like he's going to blind the rest of us, given half a chance.'

'Erm – we've *seen* something,' Mickey put in. 'I don't really know if it's real, or what it means. Maybe it was a mirage. But it was *soldiers*. Like cavalry, you know? Soldiers from the olden days.'

Haltingly – prompted now and again by Remo and Charlie – Mickey told us what had happened when Infernal John had first blinded them, and tied them all together, and forced them to climb up the promontory and throw themselves off. He told us how they had been rescued, but how their rescuers had vanished by the following morning – although they had briefly reappeared when they had held hands together and their sight had returned.

Amelia listened very solemnly, still holding hands in the spiritual circle. 'This could be good news,' she said, at last.

'What, *more* spirits?' I asked her. 'There are so many goddamned dead people around, there's hardly any room left for us living folks.'

'You heard what Singing Rock told us in Portland,' Amelia reminded me. 'Misquamacus has borrowed the spirits of hundreds of long-dead medicine men, so that he can appear all over the country and blind as many people as possible. But to do that, he will have had to open up the portal that connects the spirit world to the real world.'

'The *portal*?' asked Ranger Edison.

'It's hard to describe it, but it's like a sliding door, and if you slide it open, then one time temporarily overlaps another, just like a sliding door overlaps the wall. You get two times existing side by side, in parallel with each other.'

'Now you really *have* lost me.'

'It doesn't matter if you understand it or not. The most important thing is that if Mickey and Remo have really seen nineteenth-century cavalry soldiers, then *they've* come through, too. And who knows who else. Misquamacus has opened up a connection between two different times, and he's brought through it the spirits of all the medicine men he needs to help him. But he wouldn't have been able to prevent any other spirits from following them. Or maybe – if they're soldiers – they were actively *pursuing* them.'

'So how is this such good news?' I asked her.

'They're *soldiers*, Harry. They're experienced Indian-fighters. And they saved these guys, didn't they, when they were forced to jump off the top of that rock? Is there anybody else you'd rather have on our side?'

I sat back. 'I guess not. Let's hope we can find them when we need them. And let's hope we can find out how to deal with these walking tool-boxes. And Misquamacus, and his less-than-merry medicine men.'

'That's why we're holding a seance at Dr. Snow's this evening.'

There was another burst of thunder that set the coffee mugs rattling. It had started to rain now – that hard, relentless rain that fills up the gutters in just a few minutes, and bounces on the sidewalk. I saw four figures running toward the cafe, their coats and sweaters pulled up over their heads, and then the door burst open and they came inside, shaking their arms because they were so wet.

One of them was the black girl I had seen climbing down from the truck. Close behind her came an emaciated black woman with an extraordinary red silk scarf tied around her head, like an oversized flower from *The Land That Time Forgot*. Then, behind her, a Nordic-looking blonde woman in a black polo-neck sweater, and a tall, well-built guy in a denim jacket which probably had *Surfer Dude* written on the back in metal studs. Inside his half-buttoned-up jacket, the guy was carrying a sleeping baby. There was no question about it, when the world was coming to an end, it sure brought out a motley collection of refugees.

The guy in the denim jacket went up to the girl on the counter and said, 'Pardon me – do you have any baby formula? Or do you know where I can find some? We ran out of it, and this little fella is going to wake up in a minute, and bawl for his supper.'

There was yet another rumble of thunder, and the baby jolted. He half-opened his eyes but then his eyelids drooped again, and he carried on sleeping.

'I saw a drugstore across the street,' said Amelia. 'Harry – can you go buy some formula? These poor people are soaked.'

'Oh – so you want *me* to get soaked, too?'

'Harry, you know what a knight in shining armor you always are.'

She stood up, and so did I, and both of us eased our hands free from Remo and Ranger Edison – gently but very firmly. For a moment they all looked a little panicky – Remo and Cayley and Charlie and Mickey, and Ranger Jim Edison, too – but as soon as they realized that they could still see, even though the circle was broken, they relaxed. 'Here, take a load off, why don't you?' said Ranger Edison, and used his free left hand to turn one of the chairs around. The woman with the giant prehistoric flower on her head said, 'Thank you kin'ly,' and sat down.

Outside it was still hammering with rain. I waited under the cafe's awning for a while, and then I took a deep breath and bounded across the street like Gene Kelly on speed, trying not to jump in any puddles. Because the sky was so black the drugstore was in darkness, except for a row of night-lights on the counter, but at least it was still open. It smelled of dog biscuits and soap. A podgy white-bearded pharmacist in a tight white lab coat used a flashlight to find me a can of Good Start baby formula, and then I bounded my way back to the Aspen Cafe. More lightning crackled, so that for a split second it looked as if the rain had been frozen in mid-air.

When I got back inside the cafe I found that everybody had already made each other's acquaintance. Prehistoric-flower woman was called Ammy, or 'Auntie Ammy' by her family and friends. The truck-driving girl was Jasmine, or 'Jazz.' The blonde Valkyrie was Tina Freely, a reporter for the *LA Times*; and Surfer Dude wasn't a Surfer Dude at all, but Tyler Jones, a stunt person for the movies, or any other occasion when they needed somebody to fall off a building or ride a motorcycle through a fiery hoop or dive seventy-five feet head first into a bucket of water.

'So whose baby is this?' I asked. The red-haired girl behind the counter had been warming up a bottle of formula for him, and brought it over.

'We don't know,' said Tyler. 'Jazz rescued him from a massive auto wreck. His mom – well, his mom didn't survive it, so far as Jazz knows.'

'Does he have a name?'

'Peter,' said Tyler. 'Don't try to call him "Petey," though. It makes him cry.'

Auntie Ammy turned to Amelia. 'Peter is like you,' she said. 'He has eyes that see both sides of the lookin'-mirror. He showed us that Indian shaman you was talkin' about.'

'You *saw* him?'

'He showed us clear as I can see you now. A tall fella, with horns and dangly things perched up on his head, and cockroach-beetles droppin' off of him like he was infestated.'

I looked at Amelia and raised my eyebrows. Auntie Ammy had given us an exact description

366

of Misquamacus.

'So Peter really *does* have the power,' said Amelia.

'But it's very rare for little kids to have it, isn't it?' I asked her. 'You told me that *you* didn't start seeing spirits until you were twelve or thirteen, when obnoxious little girls turn into obnoxious *big* girls. This little guy can't be more than six months old.'

Amelia reached across and gently touched Peter's forehead. He was gulping his formula now, and he irritably waved her away. 'The power most likely comes from his mother. When a parent dies prematurely and leaves a very small child unprotected, their spirit enters into them, and takes care of them. That's how many very young psychics become psychic. They have a deceased parent to introduce them to the spirit world. It works both ways, of course. The parent's spirit can see the child, equally clearly, and watch him grow.'

There was even more thunder, right above our heads. It sounded like cannon, and it echoed from one side of Memory Valley to the other.

'This is no nat'ral storm,' said Auntie Ammy. 'You mark my word, all hell is goin' to break loose tonight.'

Amelia told me, 'They've *all* seen Eye-Killers. Jazz and Auntie Ammy saw at least two of them in Maywood. Tina and Tyler saw some in Hollywood. And both times they had wonder-workers with them.'

'Well, whatever the hell they are, they've been busy here in Memory Valley, too,' said Tyler.

'Before the phones went out, I had a call that my father and mother and sister had gone blind. That's why I came here. I've been to their house but there's nobody there and nobody seems to have any idea where I can find them. Soon as this storm dies down, I'm going to go out looking for them.'

But the storm didn't die down. We sat in the Aspen Cafe for over two hours, and with every passing minute the thunder grew louder and the rain lashed down harder against the windows, and the lightning flickered almost non-stop. Even though the cafe was so crowded, hardly anybody spoke, and from the way they stared out of the windows at the main square, you could tell that they felt that something catastrophic was going to happen, even if they didn't know what it was.

At a quarter of seven, Amelia looked at her wristwatch and said, 'Let's go back to Dr. Snow's. Auntie Ammy's right. This isn't a natural storm. This is Misquamacus summoning the spirits of his ancestors. He could attack us at any time now, and we need to find out how to protect ourselves.'

Ranger Edison, 'You two – you seem to know all about this Indian magic stuff. What's he going to do to us, this Misquamacus?'

I laid my hand on his shoulder. 'Imagine the worst thing that could possibly happen to you. The most pain that you could suffer. The most excruciating emotional loss. Then imagine it going on for ever. And when I say for ever, I mean for ever and ever and *ever*, and no "amen" at the end.'

Ranger Edison looked up at me. 'You're serious, aren't you?'

'I'm always serious, Jim, except when I'm joking. But believe me, I'm not joking now.'

'So what are you planning to do?'

'Me and Amelia, we're going to Dr. Snow's house and we're going to hold ourselves a seance, to see if we can't glean some handy tips from the spirit world on saving all of our skins.'

'You want any of us to come with you?' asked Tyler.

'No, thanks,' said Amelia. 'You all wait here. But I promise you, whatever happens, we'll be back.'

We left them in the cafe and went out into the storm. The wind was so strong that as soon as we stepped out of the cafe door we had a struggle to stay on our feet, and it took all of my strength to pull the door closed behind us. The thunder half-deafened us, and the lightning made the buildings in the main square look strangely two-dimensional, as if they were a stage-set for *The Tempest*.

We turned the corner and then the wind was blowing against our backs, so that we almost had to run. I turned up my collar but all the same the rain ran down the back of my neck and soaked my shirt. Apart from being wet and windy, it was growing cold, too. I took hold of Amelia's hand and she was freezing.

When we arrived at Dr. Snow's house I knocked frantically on the door. Meredith opened it immediately and we lurched into the hallway, accompanied by a whirl of wet leaves and a ghost-train whistle of wind.

'What a storm!' said Meredith. 'I've never known anything like it! The whole house is creaking!'

She took us through to the dining room. There was still no power, and so Meredith had lit three tall candelabra with ten candles in each, with flames that curtsied and dipped like dancers in the intermittent draft. Dr. Snow was already seated at the head of the dining table, wearing a dark brown sweater, with a glass of red wine in front of him. His reflection appeared in the dark polished surface, the white-haired king on a playing card.

'Ah, here you are!' he said. 'Merry, would you bring two more glasses for our guests?'

We sat down on either side of him. Behind him, the heavy red velvet drapes were stirring as if somebody were hiding behind them.

'It's started,' he said. He lifted one finger and there was a drum-roll of thunder, as if he had timed it specially to emphasize what he was saying.

'You're right,' said Amelia. 'He's calling all his wonder-workers together, and he means what he says. There's going to be a massacre, and he's going to turn back time.'

Dr. Snow said, 'Since you came here earlier, I've been doing some more research into the possession of spirits by other spirits – in particular, the spirits of medicine men.'

'What did you find out?' I asked him. 'Anything that's going to help us to sic Misquamacus?'

'Possibly, Harry. Possibly. It appears that the great Iroquois wonder-worker Pakuna was murdered by a jealous rival, Faces The Moon, who suspected him of carrying on with his wife. After he had slit Pakuna's throat, Faces The Moon employed the services of another wonder-worker, Silver Wolf, who trapped Pakuna's spirit in a limestone rock. He dropped the rock into a river, so that it would gradually dissolve and his spirit would be washed away to the ocean, never able to come back to life.

'But while Pakuna was unable to return to the world of touching flesh as *himself,* he was still remembered and honored by his tribespeople and his name was still spoken – much like Misquamacus. When Silver Wolf died, Pakuna was able to possess *his* spirit, and return to the world of touching flesh in that way. He cast a powerful spell which imprisoned Faces The Moon inside the trunk of a tree, and then he forced the spirit of Silver Wolf to blind himself and cut off his own genitalia, so that when Silver Wolf returned to the spirit world, he would be regarded as a worthless woman, and shunned by all the other spirits.

'There is supposed to be giant oak somewhere in the Adirondacks from which terrible screams can be heard whenever anyone comes near. Legend says that is the tree in which Faces The Moon was imprisoned, alive – and still is, and always will be.'

'This backs up what John Singing Rock told

us. He said that Misquamacus had taken over the spirits of other wonder-workers, and come back to the real world as *them*.'

'Yes,' said Dr. Snow. 'And that means that we have to regard these threats of his as extremely grave. He *will* blind us all, with his Eye-Killers, and he *will* kill us all. It is probably beyond even *his* magic to tear down our cities and rip up our highways and our railroads, but the United States will undoubtedly become one of the greatest scenes of devastation on Earth.'

Amelia said, 'In that case, the sooner we try to find out how to stop him, the better.'

Meredith brought us two crystal glasses, and Dr. Snow poured us each a glass of wine. He lifted his own glass in a toast, and said, 'Here's to the confounding of our enemies.'

Amelia had brought a silver dish with her, and she placed one of her berry-scented candles on it, and lit it. She brought out her hazel twig, too, and held it up in both hands, with the point lightly touching her forehead.

'I am seeking a wise man,' she said. 'I am seeking a Hupa who knows the ways of magic.'

Dr. Snow and I waited patiently. Amelia repeated herself. 'I am seeking a wise man. I am seeking a Hupa who is knowledgeable in the ways of demons and spirits.'

She said it again, and then again, with some minor variations. Myself, I couldn't feel the presence of anything, except a chilly draft that was giving me a stiff neck.

Nearly ten minutes went by. 'I am asking for any spirit's help in finding a wise man. I wish to talk to a wise man from the Hupa people. I command you to help me. I command you to find him. I command him to speak to me.'

Without any warning at all, Dr. Snow flung his right arm crosswise and knocked over his glass of wine.

'I do not speak to the monsters who murdered my tribe!' he blurted out. But his voice wasn't Dr. Snow's voice at all. Instead of the meticulous, lip-sipping way in which Dr. Snow usually spoke, this was rough and guttural, like a pit bull barking, with a strong and almost incomprehensible accent.

'Holy shit,' I said to Amelia. 'Who the hell is *this*?'

Amelia ignored me. Instead she leaned forward across the table with her fists clenched and said, 'You must speak to me. I have brought your spirit here and I command it.'

'You murdered my tribe!' said Dr. Snow. 'You raped my women! You cut open my children as if they were animals!'

'You still have to speak to me,' Amelia told him. 'You have no choice. Otherwise I will keep your spirit imprisoned here for ever, and you will never see your tribe again, even as spirits.'

'Why have you summoned me here?' Dr. Snow asked her. 'Have you not done enough to us, without disturbing us in death?'

'Who are you?' Amelia asked him. 'I asked for a wise man who knows the ways of magic, and of demons.'

'I am Nihltak. I know the ways of magic, and of demons. I also know the ways of the white

373

men, who are devils.'

'Listen, Nihltak, I need to know about those spirits which have no substance of their own. I am talking about those spirits who visit the world of touching flesh inside the substance of other spirits. I need to know how to dismiss them.'

'Why would you wish to know such a thing?'

'Just tell me. You must.'

Dr. Snow turned and stared at me. His eyes gave me the creeps. They were totally *black*, as if the sockets were empty. Then he turned back to Amelia and said, 'A spirit who has lost his substance can walk through to the world of touching flesh but he can only appear in the shape of other spirits which *do* have substance. There is a way, though, in which he can take on his own shape.'

'Oh, yes? And what's that?'

'He can summon together all of the spirits which he has possessed, and they can climb together into a Thunder Giant. It will *look* like the spirit who has no substance, but it will stand as tall as many trees, and it will possess all the strength of every spirit which the spirit who has no substance has brought together, and it will crush everything that stands in its path.'

Amelia was frowning. 'The Thunder Giant ... that's only a story, surely?'

'Is that what you think? The Thunder Giants walked the earth many times, in the days before the white people came, when the spirits of one tribe were warring against the spirits of another. So much blood was shed that the rivers ran red for days on end, and it was agreed by the wise men of all tribes that it should never be allowed to rise again.'

'Is there any way to destroy it? Any way to bring it down?'

Dr. Snow was silent for a moment. Then he said, 'An offering will appease it.'

'What kind of an offering?'

'An orphan, who has recently lost both parents. Such an offering will bring it two spirits – the child's father and mother, male and female, and it can use these spirits to recreate its spiritual substance. Once it has substance, it will be able to visit the world of touching flesh again, in its own shape.'

Dr. Snow paused, and then he added, 'It will be obliged to accept such a sacrifice.'

'We have to give him some kid?' I demanded.

Dr. Snow didn't hear me, or else he pretended not to.

'Hey!' I said. 'We can't kill some kid! It's out of the question! Who does he think we are? Incas?'

Amelia raised her hand to shush me. Then she said, 'What about the Eye-Killers, the sun-devils? How can we stop them from blinding us?'

'I will tell you no more,' said Dr. Snow. 'You slew so many of us, why should I care if we slay *you*, in return?'

'You *must* tell me. You have no choice. If you don't, I will trap your spirit inside this table for ever – or as long as this table lasts. Your reflection is in it already, Nihltak, so it won't be

375

difficult!'

There was a very long silence. Dr. Snow's fingers fidgeted on the tabletop as if he were trying to remember some long-forgotten piano piece. Then he said, 'The sun-devils – they themselves will give you everything you need to destroy them. Their weapon is your weapon.'

'What the hell does *that* mean?' I demanded. 'Come on, you have to be more specific than that!'

But almost as soon as I had said it, Dr. Snow stared at me and gave me a quizzical little shake of his head.

'I'm sorry, Harry. More specific about *what*?'

'"Their weapon is your weapon." That's what you just said.'

'Did I? *Really?* Hm, I wonder what I meant by that.' Then he looked around and said, 'Oh dear! How clumsy of me! I seem to have spilled my wine.'

I looked across at Amelia. 'Nihltak's gone,' she said.

'Can't you get him back?'

'Harry – he didn't want to tell us anything at all. If I hadn't threatened to keep him here, trapped in this table—'

'Then why didn't you? At least we would have found out how to fight those goddamn Eye-Killers.'

'Because I couldn't. Because I don't know how. I was only bluffing.'

'Oh, great.'

Dr. Snow was reaching across the table to pick up his tipped-over glass. As he did so, I noticed

376

something moving on the back of his hand. At first I thought it was only an effect of the candle-light, flickering in the draft. But then I looked closer and saw that his veins were wriggling, almost as if they were long blue worms.

'Dr. Snow—' I said, and took hold of his wrist. He, too, looked down at his hand, and his veins *had* turned into worms.

'Oh, my good God!' he choked out, and even as he did so, his entire hand collapsed into a mass of writhing worms, and through his shirt-sleeve and his sweater I could feel his wrist collapsing, too.

'Amelia – !' I shouted. 'His hand!'

Dr. Snow lifted his arm, and the worms that had replaced his hand fell onto the tabletop and lay there, curling and uncurling as if they were in agony. He jerked his arm down, and out of his sleeve poured hundreds more worms, white and glistening in the candlelight, which rolled and twisted on the carpet in a heap.

Amelia shouted out, *'Nihltak! Nihltak! Let him go!'*

But whatever she was trying to do, it was too late. Dr. Snow turned to stare at me in silent panic, and he opened his mouth as if he were going to cry for help. But as he did so, worms fell out of his lips, and then his entire face became a twisted mass of worms. Within seconds, his head dropped into his shirt collar and disappeared, leaving only a few worms scattered on the front of his sweater.

Both Amelia and I stood up, and backed away. I don't know about Amelia, but I was shaking as

377

if I had the flu. Inside his clothes, Dr. Snow's whole body had turned into worms, which slowly crawled down the legs of his chair, and then made their laborious way across the carpet in all directions.

'*Jesus*,' I said. 'What happened to him?'

Amelia's eyes were wide with shock. 'Nihltak took his spirit back with him, to the other side. It was his way of punishing me, for making him help us. He took his spirit, and all that was left was grave-worms.'

Meredith called out, 'Dad? Are you all right in there? Would you like me to bring you something to eat?'

'What are we going to tell her?' I hissed.

'*Dad?*'

But at that moment there was a devastating rumble of thunder, so loud that we could feel the entire house shake. This was immediately followed by another, and another.

Amelia said, 'We'll have to explain this to Meredith later. Right now, we have something a whole lot worse to worry about. He's here. Misquamacus. This is the moment he's been waiting for, ever since he first reappeared.'

'But how are we going to stop him? We can't give him some orphan, can we? Do we even *have* an orphan?'

'There's Peter, that little guy that Jasmine brought with her.'

'And you're going to hand him over to Misquamacus? Only over my dead body. Besides, you really think that Misquamacus is going to be satisfied with one measly baby? He wants to kill all of us, and he probably can.'

'Not if I can help it. Come on.'

Meredith opened the dining-room door. 'Dad?' she said. 'Is everything OK?'

Amelia stepped forward, put her arm around Meredith's shoulders, and practically forced her out of the room.

'What's going on?' Meredith asked her. 'Has something happened to my father?'

Amelia said, 'Please, Meredith. You mustn't go in there.'

'Why? What's happened?'

'Just don't go in there. Your father's dead. Lock the door and keep it locked. Harry and I have to go out now, urgently. You heard that thunder. But we'll be back.'

'He's *dead*? What's happened? Was it his heart? Amelia – please let me past. I need to see him.'

But I stood in the doorway and I wouldn't let her go back in. I didn't have to say anything. I think she could tell by the expression on my face that if she insisted on seeing her father, she would have nightmares about it for the rest of her life. Not that the rest of her life would be very long, if Misquamacus had anything to do with it.

TWENTY-SIX

We battled our way back along the street to the main square. The wind was gusting so strongly that several times we had to stop, and hold onto a picket fence, or a tree, or a lamp post, just to get our breath back. It was raining even harder, and the lightning and thunder were almost continuous.

'This Thunder Giant!' I shouted. 'What the heck is that?'

'I always thought it was nothing but a legend!' Amelia shouted back. 'Back in the days when many of the Plains Indians were fighting each other, some tribes were supposed to have called on the spirits of their dead wonder-workers to help them defeat their enemies!'

We crossed the litter-strewn street. We had nearly reached the main square now and we could see the Aspen Cafe. Its crowded interior was lit by dozens of candles, almost like a church.

Amelia shouted, 'The wonder-workers would all join together in a human pyramid – you know, like acrobats in a circus! They would make themselves into one giant man, maybe seventy or eighty feet high! The stories say that it could cross the prairies faster than a horse could run, and it could tear up tepees and wicki-ups as if they were toys!'

'And Misquamacus is going to do that now?'

Amelia looked up at the sky. 'Nihltak seemed to think so! And all of this thunder and lightning – that's a pretty good indication! The Thunder Giants used to have so much magical power that they were followed by thunderstorms wherever they went!'

We reached the cafe and tumbled in through the door, soaking wet and panting. Tyler came up to us and said, 'You made it back! We were starting to think you'd gone for good!'

Auntie Ammy was rocking baby Peter in her arms. 'Did you talk to the spirits?' she said.

The red-haired girl behind the counter handed Amelia a bar towel, and she roughly rubbed her hair dry. 'Yes, Auntie Ammy. We talked to the spirits. A medicine man from the Hupa tribe, one of the Indians who was massacred here by General Lawrence and his men.'

'I see grief in your eyes,' said Auntie Ammy.

'Yes,' said Amelia. 'During the seance, we lost a very dear old friend.'

'Somebody *died*?' asked Ranger Edison.

I nodded. 'This is very heavy-duty magic, Jim. Life-and-death-stuff.'

'I'm real sorry to hear that. Did you find out how to stop this Misquamacus?'

'I don't know. We're really not sure. There's supposed to be one option: give him an orphan, as a sacrifice. Not that we would. But at least we have a better idea of what we're up against.'

Outside the cafe windows, the main square

381

was lit up by a sheet of lightning so dazzling that it left a green after-image in our eyes. But it didn't only illuminate the buildings, and the trees, and the parked cars. It illuminated a long straggling line of figures, more than a hundred of them, walking steadily toward us. They were still too far away to be seen clearly, but most of them appeared to be wearing hats or headdresses of some kind. Some of them were dressed in coats and suits, but many of them had blankets draped around them.

'*It's the wonder-workers,*' said Amelia.

Auntie Ammy handed Peter to Jasmine, and stood up. She stared into the darkness with her nostrils flared. 'Bad spirits,' she said. 'May Changó protect us.'

More lightning flashed, and now we could see the wonder-workers much more clearly. A few of them wore wide-brimmed hats; others wore beaver-pelt caps or antlers or elaborate woven headdresses that made them look like pirates. Behind them, as the lightning flickered yet again, more figures appeared, at least another hundred, with dead white faces.

One second these figures appeared to be quite far away, on the opposite side of the square. The next they looked as if they had almost reached us. They had box-like bodies and stiffly jointed arms and legs, and they lurched as they walked like marionettes – an extraordinary combination of marching and dancing.

'Eye-Killers,' said Amelia. 'If their eyes start to flash, whatever you do, don't look at them.'

The crowd of people in the cafe started to back
382

away from the windows. Most of them stayed apprehensively silent, but two or three of the children started to whimper with fear, and one woman shouted out, 'Do something! Somebody *do* something! Doesn't anybody have a gun?'

Amelia turned around and said, 'Guns won't help! These things are Native American spirits! They're all dead already!'

'What are you talking about, lady?' said the woman's husband. 'They're not dead! Look at them! They're all walking toward us and it don't look like they're going to stop, neither!'

But Auntie Ammy raised her hand and said, 'It is true. The ones who look like humans, they are spirits who have been brought here from the other side. The ones who look like coffins, they are demons. They have come here to take away our eyes, and to make us their slaves, or to kill us if we try to resist them.

'My ancestors were in West Africa when other devils with white faces came and made us their slaves, or killed us if we tried to resist. I know how angry these spirits feel, how vengeful. And tonight, it is *their* turn to bring fear and destruction and death to you! Tonight it is their turn to tear down your whole civilization.'

One young man said, 'You're talking crap, lady! Indian spirits? Demons? What the hell is that all about? Somebody give me a gun, I'll show you "dead already"!'

Now the lightning was flashing so rapidly that the main square was lit up as brightly as if it were day. The wonder-workers had crowded in the middle of the square, with the Eye-Killers surrounding them. Half a dozen of them gathered close together, facing each other, with their arms on each other's shoulders. Another half-dozen did the same, only twenty feet away.

'What are they up to?' asked Ranger Edison. 'Having some kind of powwow or something?'

'They're making a Thunder Giant,' said Amelia. 'We're probably the first white people who have ever seen one.'

'They're making a *what*?'

Once the two groups of wonder-workers were firmly braced together, more wonder-workers began to climb onto their shoulders, and then more climbed onto their shoulders. With frightening speed, they formed two legs, and then a body, and then two arms. At last, five of them swarmed up the torso and entwined themselves together to give the giant figure a head. They raised their arms so that it looked as if it were wearing a headpiece made of horns.

The Thunder Giant was nearly a hundred feet high. I could see the individual faces of each of the wonder-workers that made up its body and its head, but at the same time it had its own distinctive face, and there was no mistaking who it was. *Misquamacus.* He had returned at last. I couldn't mistake those angular cheeks, and that slab of a forehead, and that lipless slit of a mouth. Most of all, though, I recognized his eyes. They had been recreated by the faces of two wonder-workers, but somehow they were still filled with all the black fury that Misquamacus could muster.

Lightning crackled around the Thunder

Giant's horns, and it started to walk toward us. Its first steps were ponderous, but gradually it began to develop a fluid, human-like stride. My eyes saw it but my brain couldn't take it in. Even when I had fought with Misquamacus before, I had never been numb with fright, but I have to admit that I stood there watching this apparition coming nearer and nearer and I just stood there with my mouth open and I couldn't even work out how to run.

The Eye-Killers surrounded the Thunder Giant on all sides, walking toward us with an unnerving up-and-down motion like scores of sewing-machine bobbins. Their eyes began to glitter with blue-and-white light, and Amelia said, *'Don't look at them! Don't look at them! If you don't want to be blinded, look away!'*

But looking away from the Eye-Killers and the Thunder Giant was almost impossible. Especially when Tyler suddenly shouted, *'Look!* Look over there!'

He was pointing toward the right-hand corner of the square. When the lightning flashed again, I saw five people running diagonally across the square toward us, only a few yards in front of the advancing Eye-Killers. For some reason they were holding hands.

'It's my dad!' said Tyler. 'It's my dad and my mom and my sister!'

He wrenched open the cafe door and ran outside. I heard him screaming out, *'Mom! Dad! Maggie! It's Tyler!'*

One of the five people stumbled, but the others pulled him to his feet and they kept on running.

Tyler started to run toward them. The Eye-Killers were less than fifty yards away now, and coming jerkily closer.

Tyler had almost reached his parents when the Thunder Giant took a long stride forward and bent down over the heads of the Eye-Killers. With a huge hand that was made up of interlocking wonder-workers, it seized the five running people and hurled them upward, high into the windy sky. I heard them screaming as they were thrown over the tops of the trees that surrounded the square. They landed on the roadway close to Jasmine's truck, and lay there broken and unmoving.

Tyler dodged to one side. He was obviously trying to outmanoeuvre the Thunder Giant, so that he could run across the square and help them. But the Thunder Giant bent down again, and tried to scoop him up. Tyler double-somersaulted across the sidewalk, and dived back in through the cafe door. His eyes were wild and he was gasping with shock and exertion.

'It killed them!' he panted. 'It *killed* them!'

He leaned up against the counter, his head bowed. Tina came up to him and put her arm around him.

'It killed them,' he repeated. He turned around and stared at me. 'It's going to kill all of us, isn't it?'

I looked across at Amelia. Then I looked down at Peter, in Jasmine's arms.

'We can't,' said Amelia.

'I know. But what about all of these people – and all of the people that Misquamacus has killed already?'

I looked out of the cafe window. The Eye-Killers were standing right outside, staring in at us with those expressionless white clay faces. Their eyes weren't flashing yet, but I knew they would. It was my guess that Misquamacus wanted to frighten us as much as he could before he blinded us. He wanted to terrify us, and taste our terror on his tongue.

'I wish I could work out what Nihltak meant by using the Eye-Killer's weapons against them,' said Amelia.

'They don't *have* any weapons,' I told her. 'Only their eyes. How do you use somebody's eyes against them?'

For almost a minute it seemed to be a stand-off. We looked out of the windows and the Eye-Killers looked back in at us, and behind the Eye-Killers the Thunder Giant stood motionless, as tall as a tree, with lightning dancing around its head. Little Peter suddenly woke up and looked blearily out of the window and started to cry.

As he did so, we heard a sharp rattling sound, from outside in the square somewhere. One of the Eye-Killers staggered, and I saw that a large hole had been punched in the middle of its wooden body. Then another Eye-Killer rocked backward, with a large semicircular chip blown away from its cheek. The rattling sound grew louder, and more ferocious, and the Eye-Killers were thrown into confusion.

'That's rifle-fire,' said Tyler. He stepped up to the window and looked across to the left-hand side of the square. 'What the heck? Somebody's *shooting* at them.'

Bullets flew into the Eye-Killers like a swarm of hornets. None of the Eye-Killers fell. They were demons, and you can't kill demons with bullets. But the impact knocked them off balance, and for a few moments they were milling around as if they were drunk, clattering against each other and disjointedly waving their arms.

'There,' said Remo. 'Look over there, by the trees.'

We looked. Underneath the trees, kneeling in a long ragged line, were more than seventy soldiers in slouch hats, with long-barreled rifles. Behind them was a contingent of cavalry, maybe twenty of them, their horses pacing impatiently from one end of the line to the other. The soldiers fired, and reloaded, and fired again, and fragments of wood and clay flew from the Eye-Killer's bodies and faces and were scattered across the sidewalk.

'It's the army,' I said. 'But *which* army? It sure doesn't look like the National Guard to me.'

'The same army that fought the Battle of Memory Valley the last time,' said Amelia.

'What?'

'General Lawrence's men, from eighteen ninety-one. It's just like I said. Misquamacus opened the portal, so that all of his wonder-workers could come through. But General Lawrence and his men have followed them.'

I watched with a growing feeling of unreality as the soldiers climbed to their feet. They fixed bayonets and then they advanced toward the main square, with the cavalry trotting up close

388

behind them. All of the Eye-Killers were still on their feet, and as the soldiers came closer they started to flicker their eyes on them, faster and faster, until it looked as if the soldiers were being photographed by scores of paparazzi. The lights were so dazzling that I had to cup my hand over my eyes.

'They're not being blinded!' I said. 'Look at them – they're not being affected at all!'

Auntie Ammy was standing close beside me. 'They walk, they fire guns, they fight, but they are long dead,' she said. 'There ain't nothin' that can blind a man who is long dead.'

But as the soldiers came closer, the Thunder Giant stepped in. He walked toward them, and reached them with only five long strides. The soldiers stopped, but they held their line, and fired volley after volley at the Thunder Giant until the main square was whirling with wind-blown smoke. Behind the riflemen, the cavalry-men had brought up a packhorse with some kind of primitive-looking machine-gun strapped onto its back, and two of them were desperately struggling to unload it.

The Thunder Giant raised both arms upward. As he did so, lightning forked out of the clouds above him and into his fingertips, so that thick showers of sparks fell to the ground below. The soldiers were firing so furiously now that pieces of the wonder-workers' clothing were being blown like a blizzard into the air – blanket, fur, buffalo-hide. But then I heard a noise that was so loud that it was almost beyond all hearing: a clap of thunder that made the earth shake and cracked all the cafe windows from side to side.

The Thunder Giant lowered his arms and pointed at the soldiers, and the lightning that he had drawn from the sky jagged out of his fingertips and blew them apart. They might have been spirits, but they still had substance, and that substance was blasted into skulls and ribs and bloody rags of ectoplasmic flesh. Even the horses' legs were blown off, and they lay smoking and disemboweled on their backs, like burned-out canoes.

Now the Thunder Giant turned back toward us, and I knew that he was coming to finish what he had started. As pockmarked and bullet-ridden as they were, the Eye-Killers reassembled outside the cafe windows. I took hold of Amelia's hand and said, 'This'll teach us not to meddle with spirits, won't it?'

She looked at me. Her hair was sticking up, and her eye make-up was blotchy, but I had never seen her look so beautiful.

'I love you, Harry Erskine,' she said.

'And I love you, Amelia Carlsson.'

I looked around at all the people in the cafe. They all knew that they were going to be blinded – those who hadn't been blinded already. But they stood facing the Eye-Killers with their backs straight and their eyes open, holding hands together in the spirit of the pioneers. I felt proud of them. Even little Peter had stopped crying, and was staring out at the Eye-Killers and the Thunder Giant.

'A *gah*!' he said.

'Yes, honey,' Auntie Ammy told him. 'A *gah*.'

As I looked from face to face, I saw myself in the mirrors on the back wall of the cafe. I could see the Eye-Killers, too, outside on the sidewalk.

Their weapon is your weapon. That's what Nihltak had said. And what was their weapon? *Their eyes.*

I turned back. The Eye-Killers' eyes were starting to glimmer. Blue and white light that no man could look at, like no man could look at the sun.

'Down!' I shouted. 'Everybody get down on the floor! Shut your eyes and lie flat as you can!'

For a moment nobody understood what I meant. But then I screamed it again. *'Down! Do it now!'* and everybody dropped to the floor as if they had all been struck by simultaneous heart attacks.

Even with my eyes tight shut, I could see the intense light that flooded the cafe. It seemed to wax brighter and brighter, as if the Eye-Killers were determined to pry their way into my brain by the power of light alone.

But then I heard a splintering explosion, and a hideous scream. It sounded like a small child being thrown onto a blazing bonfire. Then I heard another explosion, and another scream, just as terrible – then another, and another. The bright light abruptly died away.

I opened my eyes and cautiously lifted my head. Amelia was looking up, too. The interior of the cafe was lit not only by candles but by dancing flames. Gradually, all of us climbed to our feet and looked out of the window. The Eye-Killers were alight, every one of them. Some of them were still standing, but their box-like bodies were engulfed in fire. Most of them were lying on the sidewalk, in pieces, their white masks shattered like broken plates. There were no skeletal babies in the coffins that had become their only means of walking through the world. The Eye-Killers had been nothing more than dazzling light, and now that light had vanished forever.

'What happened to them?' said Mickey.

'*They* did,' I said, and pointed toward the mirrors.

But without warning, the cafe windows imploded, and we were blasted by a hailstorm of shattered glass. Men shouted, women screamed. The mirrors were sprayed with blood. Amelia had a deep cut across her chin, and I felt blood running down my left cheek. There was another deafening burst of thunder, and the interior of the cafe was lashed with wind and rain, as well as a whirl of cinders from the burning Eye-Killers.

Standing in the main square, the Thunder Giant looked down at us, its horns crawling with caterpillars of static electricity.

'You have defied me again, little brother,' he said, and his voice was the combined voices of all the wonder-workers who made up his arms and his legs and his body and his head. It was like listening to a hundred people all chanting at once. 'You have defied me and you have destroyed my demons. For this, I will punish you with more than darkness. I will give you everlasting agony, and I will give your loved ones

392

and your children everlasting agony. I will do to you what you did to us – I will give you the pain that never ends, for all eternity.'

'Oh God,' said Charlie. 'It's going to be a massacre, isn't it? He's going to throw us all around, just like Tyler's dad and mom.'

'No such luck,' I told him. 'He's going to do something very much worse than that.'

'Then why are we standing here, man? Let's make a run for it!'

'There's absolutely no point. We couldn't run fast enough.'

Little Peter lifted both hands toward the Thunder Giant. He didn't seem to be afraid of him at all. 'A *gah*!' he shouted. 'A *mm-mm*!'

Again I looked at Amelia, but both of us shook our heads. Whatever Misquamacus was threatening to do to us, however much we were all going to suffer, little Peter's life was sacrosanct.

The Thunder Giant lifted his arms again, and again lightning leaped from the clouds and into his fingertips. But even above the spitting of the lightning and the rumbling of the thunder and the shrieking of the wind, I heard the harsh, buzzsaw sound of a motorcycle engine.

I looked around. At first I couldn't see where the sound was coming from. But I heard the motorcycle rev, and rev, and rev again, and then it appeared from the parking lot beside the cafe – a big black Kawasaki with Tyler sitting astride it.

He came burbling up to us and stopped.

'What are you doing?' I shouted at him. 'How the hell did you get that started?'

'I was taught by the best motorcycle booster in the business!' Tyler yelled back. 'He was a great stuntman, too!'

'Look – if you're making a break for it, how about taking Amelia with you, and baby Peter?'

'I'm not making a break for it!' He pointed up to the Thunder Giant. 'I'm going to stop him!'

'What?'

'You said we could stop him if we gave him an orphan!'

'What?'

'An orphan, that's what you said! Well, *I'm* an orphan now!'

'I don't understand!'

'Just watch me!'

He didn't give me the chance to say anything else. He revved up the Kawasaki again and rip-ped away, circling around the main square faster and faster, as if he were riding the wall of death. In the center of the square, the Thunder Giant was slowly bringing down his arms. I put my arm around Amelia and held her tight but I couldn't think of anything to say to her – not even goodbye.

The Thunder Giant took a step toward us. We could feel the ground shake, but we all lifted our heads and looked back at him defiantly.

'Misquamacus!' I screamed at him. *'Whatever hell you believe in, you bastard, may you rot in it for ever!'*

At that moment Tyler came tearing across the main square, with the Kawasaki's dazzling quartz headlight on full beam. He was standing up in the saddle, and he was shouting something, although I couldn't hear what it was. He roared straight toward the Thunder Giant, and he must have been touching seventy by the time he reached him. Then he suddenly braked, and the motorcycle's rear wheel kicked up like a bucking bronco. Tyler let go of the handlebars, and he flew upward, with his arms held out in front of him, like some superhero.

'Take *me*!' I heard him shouting. 'Take *me*!'

For a split second, I thought that he was going to tumble back down to the ground, and that the Thunder Giant would toss him bodily across the square like his parents and his sister. But he grabbed two of the wonder-workers who were linked together to make up the Thunder Giant's torso – catching hold of their blankets and their buckskin jerkins to stop himself from falling backward, and as he hung there, he found himself a precarious foothold on the shoulders of the wonder-workers in the next tier below. All of the wonder-workers had their arms intertwined, like the dancers in *Zorba the Greek*, so there was nothing they could do to stop Tyler forcing his way in between them. He disappeared inside the Thunder Giant's chest like a man plunging into a cave. It was the most incredible display of gymnastics I had ever seen.

There was a long pause – ten seconds, twenty. The Thunder Giant stood very still, and then he swayed slightly. He stared down at us with those eyes which were actually human faces, as if he were confused. Then very slowly he raised his arms again.

With a coarse spitting noise, all of the lightning that he had drawn down from the clouds came pouring out of his fingertips, and back up into the sky. At the same time, he let out a deep, frustrated roar. A hundred voices, all roaring at once.

A single wonder-worker began to disengage himself from the Thunder Giant's right shoulder, and spread his arms wide. At first I thought he was going to climb back down to the ground. But he hesitated for only a moment, and then he stepped off into the air.

'Oh my God,' said Amelia. From the Thunder Giant's shoulder to the sidewalk, it was at least an eighty foot drop.

Instead of falling, however, the wonder-worker rose up vertically into the low-hanging clouds, and disappeared. Another wonder-worker freed himself from the Thunder Giant's arm, and he rose upward, too. Then another, and another. We stood and watched in silence as the entire Thunder Giant disassembled itself. His head gradually broke apart, and then his shoulders, and the rest of his arms, and the wonder-workers floated up into the sky as silently as balloons.

We crossed the street and looked up at the Thunder Giant in awe.

'They is all spirits,' said Auntie Ammy, shaking her head. 'They is all spirits, an' they is returnin' to the world of the spirits, which is where they belongs.'

As the Thunder Giant's torso started to break up, however, we heard the beginnings of a deep, soft rumbling sound. It grew louder and more vibrant as the last of the wonder-workers rose up into the clouds. Within seconds the ground beneath our feet was quaking, as if a monstrous locomotive were approaching, a hundred times larger than life, and we were almost deafened. More lightning flickered all around us, and on the other side of the main square an oak tree abruptly burst into flames. I felt drizzle in the wind, but it was *warm* drizzle.

'Holy shit,' said Remo, right behind me.

I looked up. At first I couldn't understand what I was looking at. But then a crackling fork of lightning lit up the sky and in a thousandth of a second I saw where the drizzle was coming from. Where the Thunder Giant's chest had been, a huge mass of bloody debris was suspended high above us. It was like some grisly airship, made up of a tangled mass of human and animal body parts, as well as twisted metal and saplings and pieces of fencing. Even in that thousandth of a second, I could see decapitated men and women, and cattle carcasses, and disemboweled dogs. They were all parceled together by criss-cross lengths of barbed wire and telephone cable, and skewered with iron railings.

The warm drizzle that was sifting across the main square was *blood*, which was falling from this floating abattoir and drenching the grass all around us. It even began to drift across the road, until the sidewalks were glistening red, and it spattered the windshields of the cars parked all around the main square and slid along the gutters.

'What *is* that thing?' I yelled at Amelia. 'Look at it, it's *beating*, like somebody's heart!'

'That's exactly what that is!' Amelia shouted back at me. 'It's the Thunder Giant's! His body has gone, but his heart is still here! All of the cruel deeds that Misquamacus has ever done, in all of his lifetimes, all wrapped up into one! Dead, but still living and still beating, and still pumping blood, like a *real* heart!'

We looked at each other in horror and disgust. All of us were soaked in blood now: our hair, our faces, our clothes. It looked rusty-colored, and it *smelled* rusty, too.

'Let's get the hell out of here!' I yelled, and reached out for Amelia's hand. But then Amelia said, *'Look!'*

I turned around. Walking through the steady torrent of blood toward us was Misquamacus. He was much taller than I remembered him, and he was wearing his buffalo-horn headdress, decorated with beads and feathers and birds' skulls, all of which were dripping with blood. Around his neck hung six or seven necklaces, as well as the silver medallion which symbolized the tentacles which grew from the face of the greatest of the Great Old Ones. He wore bracelets, too, and anklets, and he was carrying his silver-skull medicine stick. Apart from these ornaments, he was completely naked, although when he came closer I saw that a mummified rat dangled from his penis, its teeth embedded in his glans. His skin gleamed like polished copper.

He came within twenty feet of us, and then stopped. More lightning danced across the square, and three or four times it struck the huge slowly beating heart which hung above our heads, obviously attracted by the barbed wire which was wrapped around it. Sparks came spraying down on top of us, so that we were all standing in a shower of blood and fireworks. There was a strong smell of charred wood in the air, as well as burned, bad meat.

Misquamacus stood there for a long time, saying nothing. Amelia tugged at my hand, trying to pull me away, but I knew that Misquamacus couldn't hurt me, not any more. At least I *hoped* that he couldn't.

'*You!*' he called out, pointing his medicine stick at me. 'You think that you have defeated us, little brother!' His voice was deep and echoing, as if he were shouting at me down a long tunnel.

Lightning spat and sizzled around the heart yet again, following the tic-tac-toe pattern of the barbed wire that held it all together. This time the sparks fell down on us so thickly that it was like standing under a cutting torch. One of the wires snapped, and four or five heavy pieces of timber and fencing dropped to the ground only a few yards away from us. They were followed by two mangled bodies – a headless, armless man, and a torn-open goat's carcass.

'Harry, come *on*!' Amelia insisted, and pulled at my sleeve.

'Don't worry about it!' I shouted back at her. 'He can't touch us!'

I might have sounded confident, but I was praying that Dr. Snow had been one hundred

percent sure about his Native American mythology, and that if Misquamacus had accepted
Tyler's self-sacrifice, he would have to back off
and return to the Happy Hunting Ground and
stop trying to wreak his revenge on us.

Misquamacus came even closer. The blood
was coursing down his angular cheeks and it
made him look as if he were weeping with rage.
'I will destroy you one day!' he said. 'Now that
I can return to the world of touching flesh, I can
promise you that!'

'Oh, really?' I yelled back at him. 'I'd like to
see you try!' I was exhausted, and seriously
pissed. 'The only reason you can stand here and
threaten me is because we gave you the soul of
a white man, and you took it! A friend of ours,
somebody we respected and cared for! Without
us, you'd be nothing but a cold draft, blowing up
some old Wampanaug woman's nightgown!'

Misquamacus was breathing deeply. Above
our heads, there was yet another lightning display, and this time even more debris came
thumping onto the bloody grass all around us.

Misquamacus shouted, 'How many times did
your people make promises to my people, and
how many times did they break their promises?
This is my people's land! These are my people's
mountains, and lakes, and hunting grounds! But
where are my people now?'

He paused, and then he said, so quietly that I
could hardly hear him, 'I will say one thing to
you. You think you are a false shaman. You do
not believe in yourself. You think you have no
power but the power of trickery. But I will say to

400

you that you are a true wonder-worker, as I once was.'

I didn't know what to say to that. But I wasn't going to stay around to ask Misquamacus what he meant, because now the lightning had burned through most of the wires that held the floating heart together, and the blood was pouring down in a warm red blizzard, and all kinds of hideous remains were bouncing onto the ground. A woman with only one leg and no face at all. The forequarters of a black-and-white cow. A garden bench. A tangled-up slew of dead cats.

Misquamacus raised his voice again, and waved his medicine stick from side to side. 'I make you this promise! Now that I can return to the world of touching flesh, I will return! And I will burn this land from one ocean to the other!'

Amelia screamed, *'Harry! Leave him! Come on!'*

Auntie Ammy and Remo and Charlie and the rest of them had already left us, and were hurrying away down the side street. But I couldn't turn away. Not now, not again. Not after all these years. I was no goddamned hero but I had lost too many friends and witnessed too much pain and too much death and too much goddamned destruction.

A long cast-iron fence pole had fallen onto the grass only a few feet away from me. It had a spike on the end, like a medieval spear. I side-stepped my way toward it, keeping my eyes on Misquamacus all the time.

Misquamacus began some kind of chant. I don't know what it meant. I don't even know what language it was in. But I guessed that it was a curse, or a promise, or maybe a bit of both. There was no way that Misquamacus was ever going to accept what the white men had done to his people, whether he was alive or dead or half-dead.

He was still chanting and waving his medicine stick when I bent down and picked up that fence pole. It was much heavier than I had thought it was going to be. In fact I could hardly lift it. But I hefted it up in both hands and without any hesitation at all I swung around and ran at him. I think I shouted, *'Geronimo!'*

I saw Misquamacus stretch his mouth wide open in a silent scream. He probably *did* scream, out loud, but I didn't hear him. I saw his eyes, too. They were utterly black, and empty, as if there was nothing inside his head but infinite space. It's hard to describe, but it was a hair-raisingly intimate moment. We had never come so physically close to each other before, but now here we were, like two lovers rushing into each other's arms.

The point of the fence pole penetrated his chest with only the faintest *plock!* and I felt barely any resistance as I pushed it right through him. He wasn't flesh and blood and bone, after all. He was ectoplasm, the cloudy substance of spirits: visible and audible, but as insubstantial as gauze. When I let go of the fence pole, however, and stepped away from him, he remained impaled. He gripped the pole in both hands, trying to tug it out of his chest, and all the time he stared at me with an expression of cold and absolute rage.

Above us, lightning struck the floating heart again – or what bloody bits and pieces were left of it – and it suddenly collapsed. A last cascade of body parts and timber and broken concrete dropped down on top of us, and I was struck on the shoulder by a severed arm. All the barbed wire unraveled, too, and fell on us. A twisted length of wire caught in my hair, but I managed to disentangle myself, although I cut open the ball of my right thumb while I was doing it. Still – I was already plastered in blood, so it didn't make too much difference.

Misquamacus staggered around and around, wrenching the fence pole from side to side. He started to roar with frustration and pain, but I suddenly realized that he didn't have the strength or the substance to drag it out of himself.

'You!' he bellowed at me. *'You! I curse you for ever!'*

But at that instant, a blinding bolt of lightning struck the point of the pole protruding from his back. Misquamacus exploded, so violently that I was thrown almost ten feet backward. There was a deafening bang of thunder, so loud that I couldn't even think.

A thousand sparkling fragments burst into the air above us. But this was more than an explosion. The earth felt as if it were *twisting*, underneath me, and even the sky seemed to be distorted. There was an echo, and then another echo, and then I heard a high shrieking sound coming toward us. For a few seconds, we were buffeted by a screaming wind, and it was then that I saw how powerful Misquamacus had been, and how much he had nearly changed the course of history.

I felt as if time itself had collapsed, and I heard drumming and shouting and a thousand voices chanting. I saw buffalo, thousands of them. I saw fires and dust and snow and men dressed as demons. I saw the sun rise and immediately go down again. I saw the moon, circling the sky. I saw what might have been, if Misquamacus had been able to take us all back to the days when America belonged to *his* people, and the Great Old Ones still ruled the world.

There was another shattering bang, as if a huge door had been slammed shut, and then the main square was quiet again. I lay on my side, stunned. Then I felt a hand on my shoulder, and I raised my head and saw Amelia hunkering down next to me. I couldn't hear what she was saying at first, but she was nodding, and smiling, and then she kissed me on the forehead, even though both of us were sticky with drying blood.

I managed to sit up. There was no sign of Misquamacus, only a few remaining sparks that drifted down on us, and then winked out. The fence pole was lying on the grass, bent double like a giant bobby pin.

'He's gone,' said Amelia, in a voice as tiny as a fairy in a bottle.

I stood up, with Amelia's help, and walked over to the spot where Misquamacus had been standing. The grass was scorched, and some beads and birds' skulls were scattered about, as well as the black-charred body of the mummified rat, but nothing more.

We looked around. The main square was littered with terrible remains, as if a bomb had exploded, and I could hear people sobbing. But the smoke and the clouds were beginning to clear, and the stars were coming out.

Amelia bent down and picked something out of the grass. She held it up and looked at it, and then she handed it over to me.

'Souvenir,' she told me.

'What?' I shouted at her, cupping my hand around my ear.

'*Keepsake!*' she said. '*I think you deserve it!*'

I looked down at it. It was the silver medallion that Misquamacus had worn around his neck, embossed with the writhing tentacles of the greatest of the Great Old Ones. I was tempted to throw it away as far as I could, but then I thought: *No, this is for Singing Rock. I'm going to keep this in his memory. He deserves it much more than I do.*

Not far away, among the carnage, we found Tyler, lying on his side, next to the Kawasaki that he had commandeered. His arms and legs were at awkward, impossible angles, but his eyes were open and he looked unexpectedly peaceful and calm.

Tina knelt down beside him. 'He's gone,' she said. 'Looks like his neck's broken.'

'Guy was a fucking hero,' said Remo.

I turned around. The crowd from the cafe were gradually returning to the main square. Some of

405

them were looking up at the stars, but many of them were still blind, and were holding tight to their friends and asking what had happened.

'Yes,' I said. 'He was a hero. And so was everybody else who was here tonight.'

We were still gathered around Tyler's body when a black Cadillac Escalade appeared from the south side of the main square, with red and blue lights flashing. It was followed by two more. The motorcade drove right up to the side of the cafe, and immediately the doors opened and at least eight guys in dark suits and white shirts and sunglasses climbed out. They formed a circle around the Escalades, and one of them called, 'Clear!'

I went up to him and said, 'What's going on?'

'Please step back, sir,' he told me, but the 'please' didn't sound at all like a polite request and the 'sir' was very much less than respectful.

But then the rear door of the second Escalade opened up, and President David Perry stepped out. I stepped back, like I was told. I hadn't voted for David Perry but he was still the President, after all.

He approached us, with his Secret Service detail staying in close. He was wearing a black overcoat but no hat.

'Jesus,' he said. 'What happened to you? You're all covered in blood. Are you hurt?'

'No, sir, Mr. President,' I told him. 'We were in kind of a fight, that's all. You should have seen the other guy.'

The President looked slowly around Memory

406

Valley's main square, and then at the Aspen Cafe, with its smashed windows, and the smoking remains of the Eye-Killers lying strewn on the sidewalk in front of it. Then he looked up at the stars.

'Never seen a storm blow itself out so quick,' he said. 'They wouldn't let me fly up here from SFX, on account of the weather. Now look at it.'

'Name's Erskine,' I told him. 'Harry Erskine. And this is Mrs. Amelia Carlsson.'

The President held out his hand. I showed him my own hand, which was covered in drying blood, but he said, 'I'm not squeamish, Mr. Erskine,' and shook hands with both of us. 'What exactly happened here?' he asked me.

I said, 'You didn't come up here by accident, Mr. President, did you?'

'No, Mr. Erskine, I didn't. I was warned that something pretty damn catastrophic was going to happen.'

'It nearly did. But you can breathe easy now. We found a way to stop it.'

The President started to walk toward the smoldering coffin-bodies of the Eye-Killers. I followed him.

He stopped, and then without looking at me he said, 'Does the name "Misquamacus" mean anything to you, Mr. Erskine?'

'Yes, sir.' I realized then that the President already had a rough idea of what had happened in Memory Valley that evening. Not the details, of course. He wouldn't have known anything about the Thunder Giant, or the sacrifice that Tyler Jones had made to save us; or about the

407

ghostly reappearance of General Lawrence and his men. But if he knew the name of Misquamacus, The One Who Went And Came Back, then he must have guessed what kind of a battle we had fought here.

'Someplace we can go and talk?' he asked me. 'Maybe you can fill me in.'

'Sure,' I nodded. 'Mrs. Carlsson and me, we're staying at a bed-and-breakfast, just along the street there. But there's one or two things I need to do first. We lost an old friend tonight, and a new one, too.'

The President turned to the people from the Aspen Cafe, who were gathered around us in bewildered but respectful silence.

'Whatever you folks did this evening, your country thanks you,' he said. He went across to Mickey and held out his hand. Mickey hesitated. He was holding Cayley's left hand with his right hand, and if he let go of her, he would lose his sight again.

'Mr. President, sir—' I said, but Mickey took the plunge, released his grip on Cayley, and blindly held out his hand.

The President shook it, and said, 'What's your name, son?'

Mickey stared at him. 'I can see,' he said.

'Excuse me?'

'I'm not holding on to Cayley's hand any more, and I can see.'

'You were blinded?' asked the President.

'All of us were, me and my friends here. We found out that we could see if we held each other's hands, but now I've shaken your hand–'

he held up both of his hands in front of his face – 'I can see!'

The President said, 'Is there anybody here who is still blind? Could they come forward, please?'

A gray-haired man in a plaid shirt was led forward by his grandson. The President took hold of his hand, and squeezed it. Almost immediately, the man blinked, and looked around, and said, 'I can see! I can see everything!'

The President turned back to me and said, 'I don't have any idea how this works, but I was blinded, too. Not that it was ever announced.'

'But you can see now,' said Amelia. 'How did you get your sight back?'

'Misquamacus,' he told her. 'He didn't want me to miss the sight of our society being turned back to the days of buffalo-hunting and bows-and-arrows. He was like a murderer who kills a man's family in front of him.'

Amelia said, 'He probably used a very simple spell to open up your eyes again. White witches used to use a spell like that in Romania, if a village was hit by uveitis or trachoma. First of all, the witch would restore the sight of the most senior sufferer in the village, and then he or she would pass on the cure to every other sufferer – either by clasping their hands or kissing them. In fact it's not even a spell, in the strictest sense of the word. It's the same as laying on of hands, which is common to almost all faith healers.'

The President said, 'Wow. You know your stuff, Mrs. Carlsson.'

'She's the best there is,' I told him. 'If anybody deserves medals for what happened here this

409

evening, it's Tyler and Amelia.'

'But what does this mean? Do I have to go around the country, shaking the hands of every blinded person there is? There must be hundreds of thousands of them!'

Amelia shook her head. 'The cure passes from one person to another. It's what we call a chain spell. All you have to do is announce that every blinded person in the country shakes the hand of another blinded person.'

The President nodded. 'So we can heal ourselves?'

'Yes, sir, Mr. President. We can heal ourselves.'

TWENTY-SEVEN

We spent most of the night telling President Perry about Misquamacus and his repeated attempts to destroy the invaders who had taken away his land and obliterated his culture. A little before dawn, he stood up and shook our hands and said, 'Thank you for everything. I believe this country owes you. It's going to take a hell of a lot of time and a hell of a lot of money for us to get back to business as usual, but we will. Then I think I have some Russians to talk to.'

It was raining again when his motorcade drove off, but only lightly, and the red-and-blue flashing lights of his Escalades were reflected in the asphalt.

Amelia and I sat down at the kitchen table with Belinda Froggatt and had a breakfast of smoked ham and apples from the orchard. Afterward, we went outside, and stood by the orchard gate. The rain had stopped, but the grass and the trees were still sparkling.

'Back to your Miami matrons, then, Harry?' Amelia asked me. She had washed and brushed her hair and it was shining in the morning light.

'I don't know. That kind of depends.'

'On what? I thought you loved it down there. I thought you were Don Johnson, with a pack of Tarot cards and a pocketful of mystic mottoes.'

'It kind of depends on *you*, Mrs. Carlsson.'

'Meaning?'

'Meaning, do you want to go on being Mrs. Carlsson, or do you want to find out what your fortune would be with me?'

She leaned her head against my shoulder. 'Sometimes, Harry, when you've made a choice in life, you have to stick with it. Where would we be, if we didn't?'

'At the Delano Hotel, on Miami Beach, sucking on a Nagayama Sunset?'

She smiled wistfully. She kissed my cheek.

'Come on,' she said. 'Let's get back to civilization.'